WINDY CITY BRIDES

THREE-IN-ONE COLLECTION

FRANCES DEVINE

BARBOUR
PUBLISHING

Cover Design: Kirk DouPonce, DogEared Design

Published by Barbour Publishing, Inc., P.O. Box 719, Uhrichsville, Ohio 44683, www.barbourbooks.com

Our mission is to publish and distribute inspirational products offering exceptional value and biblical encouragement to the masses.

ecpa Member of the
Evangelical Christian
Publishers Association

Printed in the United States of America.

Dear Readers,

I've always been fascinated with turn-of-the-century Chicago, so when I decided to write historical romance, I naturally turned to that locale and time period first.

Once a Thief, Blake and Danielle's story, was the first idea that came to my mind. A longtime Dickens fan, I thought it would be fun to do a type of *Oliver Twist* story with a girl as the heroine. Once I got into the actual writing, though, Blake's parents, Sam and Katie, and Katie's father, Michael O'Shannon, took on a life of their own. I knew I had to go back and write their story, *A Girl Like That*. *A Girl Like That* became book one and *Once a Thief* took its place in the middle of the series.

Danielle's younger brother, Jimmy, also had a story that needed to be told, so he and a young minister's daughter named Cici became the hero and heroine of book three, *Sugar and Spice*.

Recently, I asked God: "How do I draw nearer to You, Lord?" His answer was "Love others and share my grace with them." That answer touched me deeply, but I had no idea until I re-read these three books, that was the theme of *Windy City Brides*. I guess you could call them Good Samaritan stories.

Most of the main characters already have a Christian background, but I've tried to help them grow in character as their stories progressed. I pray that you, my readers, will enjoy and be blessed by these stories of spiritual growth.

God Bless you,
Frances Devine

A GIRL LIKE THAT

Dedication

Dedicated with love to my son Rod Devine and my granddaughter Robyn, who
took care of everything and put up with me while I was writing this book.
To Tracey, who stayed with me at the hospital for several days,
polished this up for me, and sent it to Barbour so I wouldn't miss my deadline.
Love you, sweetheart. Many thanks.
Also to Steve, Sandy, Linda, Jack, and Bill, who helped in other ways.
I love you more than I can say.
And you, too, Angie.
To my precious grandchildren and great-grandchildren. You are my angels.
To the Hughes Center Gang and the prayer warriors at Lebanon Family Church.
Thanks for your prayers.
Special thanks to Carol Maniaci for praying me through it all.

Chapter 1

Chicago, May 1871

Katie O'Shannon stood on the platform and faced the teeming crowd waiting to board the train. The train from which she had just disembarked. She took a wobbly step forward then stopped short as loud shouts and excited greetings assaulted her ears. Sounds she'd longed for after four years on the farm. And yet, a twinge of fear in her stomach made her wonder if she'd been away from the city for too long. *Turn around, Katie. Smile at the friendly conductor and return to your nice, safe seat.*

Before she could take her own advice, the conductor cleared his gravelly throat. "Move along, miss. Others are waiting to disembark."

Katie's face turned feverish with embarrassment as she glanced over her shoulder into the frowning face of a tall man with bushy gray eyebrows and a curly mustache. "S–Sorry, sir." She gulped a deep, determined breath, clutched her reticule tightly, thankful she'd sent her trunk on ahead, and stepped forward.

To her surprise and relief, the crowd parted. She cleared the throng and glanced around for her father as she walked toward the depot.

Her Irish temper flared as she realized he was nowhere to be seen in one direction. She whipped about on her booted heel. Before she could begin her search, she slammed into a rock-hard wall. No, not a wall. In a beat of confusion, she felt a pair of strong hands grasping her arms, steadying her. Gasping, she stared at dark brown eyes, shadowed with annoyance, looking down at her from a strong, handsome face. "Saints preserve us, I've got to learn to watch where I'm going."

For a second, his eyes seemed to soften. But he gave an abrupt nod, followed by a hasty departure as he shoved past her.

Katie's face flamed. Not five minutes in Chicago and she'd already behaved like a country bumpkin. Still, he needn't have been so rude. She glanced around, relieved to see that no one seemed to have noticed the incident.

"Katie. Katie O'Shannon!"

The next moment, she found herself enveloped in Michael O'Shannon's sturdy, comforting arms.

"Pa, I thought you forgot all about me!" She snuggled into the tobacco and peppermint smell of him and looked into his beaming face.

"What are you talking about? How could I forget my little girl? But for the life of me, I can't understand why you'd want to leave your grandfather Mason's nice, quiet farm and come to this crowded, filthy city."

Katie laughed. "That's just it. The farm is too quiet. Besides, I missed you, Pa." She squeezed his arm and threw him a saucy grin.

He winked and tweaked her nose as though she were still a child. "Now don't you go telling me lies, Katherine O'Shannon. It's the excitement of show business you've been missing. But don't you be getting any ideas about acting onstage, because I'll not have it. Just because you're eighteen now doesn't mean you can do as you please." The twinkle in his eyes belied the gruff voice, but Katie knew he meant his words.

She was spared the problem of replying as they reached a three-seated conveyance with HARRIGAN's written on the side. An ancient horse snorted and pawed the dirt.

"Sorry about this monstrosity, my girl. The regular carriage wasn't available."

Katie scrunched up her nose as she climbed in and sat on the cracked leather seat. "What's that awful smell?"

"Ah, we've been having an outbreak of fires for going on a month now. It's been dry for spring." Michael took the reins, and they moved down the street amid the *clip-clop* of horses' hooves on the wooden street.

Katie glanced nervously at the wood structures lined on each side of the street.

"Don't you be worrying now, Katie girl." Michael puffed his lips. "It's a fine fire department we have these days."

"Oh, I'm not worried. I'm much too happy to worry. How far is it to the theater? Can we go there first?" Katie restrained herself from craning her neck to take in all the sights. After all, she was a grown woman. And regardless of her foolish moment of doubt as she disembarked, she was thrilled to be in Chicago, noise and all.

Michael gave her a sideways glance, and a smile puckered his lips. "Well, I guess we can, since I have a show in thirty minutes."

They pulled up in front of a two-story green and white wooden structure. Across the top hung a sign bearing the title, HARRIGAN'S MUSIC HALL AND THEATER, in bold letters.

Katie's stomach lurched with excitement. This was the moment she'd waited for since she was fourteen, when her father, newly widowed, had taken her from the exciting vaudeville scene of New York City and dropped her at her grandparents' farm in southern Illinois. She'd watched, lonely and feeling abandoned, as he snapped the reins and drove away to find work. Pulling herself from the unwelcome thoughts, Katie took her father's hand and stepped down onto the board sidewalk.

Immediately, a boy appeared at her father's elbow and took the reins. Vendors, pushing carts down the street, hawked their wares while dodging hansom cabs and other traffic.

Katie followed her father around to the side and entered the building.

A green-vested man looked up from his newspaper and grinned. "So this is the lovely Katie O'Shannon we've all been hearing about." He stood and gave Katie an elegant bow.

"It is, Thomas Harrigan, and you'll be keeping your distance." Michael gave the man a good-natured glare, which was returned with laughter.

"Katie, this rogue you see standing here is the theater owner and manager of the troupe. And he's really not a bad sort."

"It's very nice to meet you, sir." Katie offered her hand, which he took gently.

"And it's nice to meet you, my dear." He smiled then turned to Michael. "You didn't tell me she was a beauty and had a voice like an angel."

"No, and you can forget it. My daughter won't be performing in this show or any other."

Thomas twisted his mustache, looking her up and down in a way that made Katie feel like a thoroughbred filly. He took in a deep breath and shook his head with regret. "It's a crying shame, my friend."

Michael set his jaw. "That's a matter of opinion, and yours doesn't count where my girl's concerned. Come, daughter. I'll take you to a seat where you can watch the show. I have to get into costume." Michael took her hand and led her through a door into a large auditorium, already filled with people.

Ten minutes later, Katie sat mesmerized as house lights lowered and the curtain came up. The smell of grease paint tickled her nostrils, and the bright, shiny costumes filled her eyes with stars, bringing back sweet memories. But soon her nostalgia became lost in the excitement of the moment, as Katie laughed with the other afternoon theater patrons at the hilarious musical comedy.

As a young man with dark brown eyes sang a love song, the eyes of the man at the train station intruded upon Katie's thoughts. Her eyes drifted shut as suddenly she became the female lead and the handsome stranger sang to her in perfect baritone. Lost in the ebb and flow of the scene playing in her head, she started as applause flooded the packed theater. Her eyes flew open, but in her heart, the applause was for her.

Her heart thudded to the rhythm of the boisterous clapping. If only her pa wasn't so stubborn. No matter. "Soon, it will be me up there," she promised herself. "I was born for this."

Cʒ

Sam Nelson stormed through the door of the Nelson Law Firm and tossed his hat onto the rack in the corner.

Several desks were scattered around the room, all but his own occupied by harried-looking young men. Some were bright, overworked attorneys just grateful for a job in the illustrious firm founded by Sam's father. Others, like Charlie Jenkins, held lesser positions, but important nonetheless.

The secretary looked up from his desk in the corner. "Your father is waiting for you, sir."

"Thanks, Charlie. I'm sure he is. I'm an hour late."

But I wouldn't have been, he thought. Not if Harvey Simons had arrived on time. Harvey, a witness in one of the elder Mr. Nelson's cases, had taken a later train than he'd promised, throwing off Sam's schedule for the day. By the time Harvey's train arrived, Sam's temper was sharp enough to cut leather.

Sam thought of the lovely, golden-haired young woman he had brushed aside at the train station. Judging from her clothing and the uncertain smile of apology, she was fresh off the farm. He'd regretted his abruptness immediately and had gone back to apologize, but she'd already disappeared, lost in the crowd. He would have liked to have made amends to her, but it couldn't be helped. And he had no time to dwell on an unfortunate situation over which he had no control.

When he walked into his father's office, Eugene Nelson looked up from a sheaf of papers he was riffling through. "I'm pleased you could finally join me."

"Sorry, Father, but—"

"Never mind. You're here now." He bit the end off a cigar and puffed loudly as the flame from the match flared. "I have a case for you."

"What is it this time?" Probably another squabble over property lines or something just as trivial. Even after five years of working for his father, the elder Mr. Nelson treated Sam's efforts as though he were still a boy learning his ABCs.

"Jeremiah Howard has retained us for an injury case involving an Irish immigrant. I'd intended to give it to Bob, but he has a family emergency and won't be back for several weeks." He looked at his son through narrowed eyes. "This could be important for you. Do the job right, and it could push you up the ladder. You know what I mean."

Sam knew what he meant, all right. There was one position open for junior partner. Three young lawyers, including Sam, were gunning for it. And his father wasn't one to play favorites. If anything, Sam was expected to work harder and be smarter than anyone else. Sam had started at the bottom like everyone else, and it was up to his own efforts and abilities to rise to the top.

Sam flopped into the leather armchair in front of his father's desk. "Details?"

His father shoved a file folder toward him. "It's all here. Howard wants to get it settled before the end of the year."

Sam took the folder, left his father's office, and went to his desk. He leaned back for a moment, inhaling the smells of leather, old books, and cigar smoke. Smells he loved, familiar to him from his childhood.

He skimmed through the papers then returned to the first page and began to peruse the information.

One Chauncey Flannigan, an Irish immigrant employed at Howard's Warehouse and Lumberyard, had been involved in an accident while performing his duties. A large stack of lumber had slipped and tumbled down on the employee, knocking him to the floor.

According to Mr. Howard, who had been on the premises at the time, Flannigan had suffered nothing but a few scratches and scrapes. He'd been sent home for the rest of the day. When the man failed to return to work the following morning, Mr. Howard had naturally hired a man to replace him.

Two weeks later, bandaged and on crutches, Flannigan had shown up at Mr. Howard's office. He had just been released from the hospital, where he had undergone surgery for a head injury. He had also been treated for several broken bones. He claimed the injuries were a result of the incident at work and demanded restitution. Mr. Howard, the firm's long-standing client, denied the claim.

Within the file were two signed affidavits from witnesses claiming to have seen Flannigan at a tavern the night of the accident. The witnesses claimed there had been a fight. There was also a letter, signed by the foreman and several employees of the lumberyard, stating that Flannigan's injuries from the accident were minor and he'd left on his own two feet with no evidence of a head injury or broken bones.

Sam straightened the papers and leaned back. The case seemed open-and-shut to him. A ne'er-do-well attempting to profit at someone else's expense. Of course, he'd visit the lumberyard and talk to the witnesses. He'd also pay a visit to Chauncey Flannigan. That way he wouldn't be surprised by something detrimental to his client on court day.

"Hey, Sam." Jack Myers, one of the junior partners and Sam's friend, stood in front of Sam's desk.

"Hi. What's going on, Jack?"

"Just wanted to see you working on the case that's going to win you a promotion."

Sam glanced around the room, but no one seemed to have overheard. "It's not mine yet."

Jack laughed. "Okay. Actually, I wanted to see if you were busy tonight. Sally's cousin Janet is in town, and we need you to make it a foursome for dinner."

"Sure. Where do I pick her up and what time?"

"I thought we'd go together to pick up the girls. Meet me at my place around seven."

Sam nodded and watched with a twinge of envy as his friend went, whistling, back to his office. A small office, true. But at least it was Jack's alone.

Sam glanced down at the stack of papers on his desk. Maybe he shouldn't have accepted the invitation to dinner. He should probably be spending every minute on this case. But, after all, he needed to eat. And a little relaxation with a young woman wouldn't hurt either. Maybe it would help him forget the pair of brilliant blue eyes staring up at him from a face momentarily washed over with embarrassment. Embarrassment he was responsible for.

Sam shook his head. There was nothing he could do about that. And since it was unlikely he'd ever see the girl again, why did the memory keep intruding into his thoughts?

He leaned forward and started once more at the beginning of the first page. Yes. Cut-and-dried.

One corner of Sam's mouth turned up in a smile of satisfaction. The position of junior partner was right around the corner.

Chapter 2

Ma Casey's dining room rang with laughter.

"Yes, it canna' be denied. Bobby Brown is a fine young lad, and he most definitely has taken a shine to our Katie girl."

Katie laughed at the good-natured bantering and turned her attention to the teasing Pat Devine. Old enough to be her grandfather, he'd taken it upon himself to tease her unmercifully and almost continuously for the entire month she'd been in Chicago.

She loved everything about this city. The theater. The boisterous troupe. Celebration parties at the boardinghouse after a successful night. And the bantering. But most of all, she loved the familiar feel of show business and show people. If only her mother were here, everything would be perfect again.

With a toss of her head, she shoved the pain away and planted her hands on her hips. She tossed Pat a fake scowl. "And what business is it of yours, mister, if he has? And what business would it be of yours if I returned his affection? Which I don't."

The room exploded with another round of laughter. It was no secret that Bobby Brown, one of the stagehands, was sweet on her, but she'd told him in no uncertain terms she wasn't interested. And it had nothing to do with the handsome face of the man from the station that continued to invade her thoughts and had even slid its way into her dreams once or twice.

"All right now. That's enough harping on my daughter." Michael's booming voice got their attention. "Come on now, it's almost noon. We need to get to the theater."

Father coming to her rescue, as always. Although, Katie was plenty able to hold her own with this rowdy crew. She'd been embarrassed and confused the first few days among the Irish troupe but had quickly come to realize their teasing was all in fun. The entire troupe had taken her under their wing, so she might as well get used to it.

Katie picked up her dishes and took them into the kitchen.

Ma Casey took them from her with a gentle smile. "They don't mean any harm. Don't you be paying them any mind now."

"I won't, Ma. Thanks for the wonderful meal. The oatcakes were the best I've ever eaten."

"Ah, go on with you." The tall, robust woman, who took care of them all, gave Katie a swat on the backside with her dish towel.

One by one, the members of the Irish troupe got up and cleared their dishes from the table. Gathering their things together, they headed out the door.

Katie always found this moment exciting. This was when her day really began.

Turning a deaf ear to Katie's own pleading, Father still thwarted the manager's attempts to add Katie to the cast of the show. But he'd reluctantly agreed she could work backstage until she found other means of employment.

Katie was happy to at least be working at the theater, but she had in no way given up her dream.

As she walked the five short blocks to the theater, she noticed the smell of smoke seemed stronger today. "Father, do you think there was another fire last night? My throat burns, and the smell is awful."

"It wouldn't surprise me, sweetheart. But look at the sky. Rain clouds are coming in. That'll put an end to the fires."

Hardly a day passed that at least one fire didn't break out somewhere in the rain-deprived city or surrounding area. The last letter from Katie's grandmother had revealed that rain had been almost as scarce in southern Illinois, and Gramps was getting a little worried about the crops.

As they neared the theater, a disturbance across the street drew Katie's attention. A young man struggled to free himself from the tight grip of a patrolman. "Get your hands off me. I didn't do anything." The young man squirmed loose and took off running with the officer close behind.

The troupe had stopped, and Katie noticed the dark clouds upon their faces as they watched the incident.

"Another Irishman persecuted," Pa grumbled.

"Now, Michael, we don't know that. It looked to me like the man had stolen something." Rosie Riley's voice was soft as she patted Michael's arm.

"And why, do you suppose, would that be? They're starving down there in Conley's Patch. Yes, and in all the other immigrant shacks across the city."

Katie followed the others into the theater. She caught her father's arm before he could step into the men's dressing room. "Father, what did you mean? Who is starving?"

"Never you mind, daughter. There's not a blessed thing we can do about it except be charitable whenever we're able." A shadow crossed her father's face as he looked absently at Katie. "Be getting to your work now."

Puzzled, Katie stood, hands on hips, as her father walked away. She stomped toward the women's dressing area, where she had been assigned to work. She knew who would tell her what she wanted to know. And she'd find out before the day was over.

Katie spent most of the day with needle in hand, mending costumes. After the afternoon show, she took a break and found Bobby Brown behind the stage repairing ropes. "Bobby, I have a question for you." She put on her sweetest smile for the young man. A twinge of guilt afflicted her, but she quickly pushed it aside. She couldn't help it if he liked her more than she liked him.

Staring at her with near adoration, Bobby jumped up. He was a nice-looking young man, with blond curls and honest eyes.

Katie told him about the incident outside the theater. "Who is starving, and what is Conley's Patch?" she questioned.

"Irish immigrants," Bobby stated, his expression somber.

"What do you mean?" Katie stared at him. "Most of the folks in this troupe are immigrants, including my father. I don't understand."

Bobby scratched his ear. "These immigrants are different, Katie. They came in throngs after the potato famine. They weren't received very well. It was hard for them to find jobs in the beginning. Things are better now, employment-wise. But they're shamefully underpaid, and most live in shacks in communities that are called shantytowns."

Katie tapped her foot impatiently. "So, what about that Patch place?"

He took a deep breath. "Conley's Patch is the worst of them all. The crime rate is high, and poverty and sickness affect near about every family. Some resort to stealing just to keep their families from starving."

"But isn't there some sort of aid for them?" Katie's heart picked up rhythm at the very thought of those poor people. "Surely they aren't just ignored."

"Of course. There are a number of societies that provide food and medical attention. But most of the folks who live there are too proud to take charity except in dire circumstances."

Sleep evaded Katie that night as she tossed and turned on the soft feather bed. How could a whole group of people be treated so badly? Especially right here in America. What if she could do something to help?

ભ

"So. You're mooning over a girl you saw once for thirty seconds." Jack shook his head and grinned across the table at Sam. "That must have been some meeting."

"I wouldn't exactly call it mooning," Sam retorted, stirring sugar into his coffee. "Of course I noticed her. She was beautiful. And it's only natural I'd think of her now and then, because of my conscience at the way I treated her."

"Oh, I see," Jack said with a chuckle. "It's your conscience that's preventing you from pursuing the lovely Janet, who has made it fairly plain she wouldn't find said pursuit distasteful."

Sam tossed his friend a sheepish look. "I know. You're right. So. . .you think Janet's interested?"

"Good. You're coming to your senses," Jack said. "Of course she's interested. Want me to set up another double date?"

Sam couldn't honestly say he was all that interested in the pretty young woman, but she was a nice diversion from his hectic life. "I guess. But don't make her any promises on my behalf."

"Would I do anything like that?"

"Yes, so don't. I don't mind taking her to dinner or the theater, but marriage to a stuffy socialite is out of the question."

"Isn't that sort of reverse snobbery?"

Sam shrugged. "Call it what you wish." He wasn't sure exactly why the young women in his parents' circle of friends had never appealed to him.

Jack grinned again. "All right, I'll leave out the proposal of matrimony when I send her the invitation to dinner and a show."

Sam turned his attention back to work. He had to finish some research for one of his father's senior partners before he could turn his attention to his own case. By early afternoon, he had completed his task and headed out to the hospital where Chauncey Flannigan had been treated.

Despite Sam's power of persuasion, the doctor who had performed Mr. Flannigan's surgery refused to speak with Sam without permission from Flannigan, so Sam left and went to the courthouse. After a few minutes with Judge Cohen, a friend of Sam's father, he returned to the hospital with a court order to release information to the Nelson Law Firm.

Dr. Voss sat, his eyes stormy, the lines of his face deep and forbidding as he stared across his desk. Without offering Sam a seat, he gave a detailed report on Flannigan's injuries. According to the doctor, the head injury had been serious and, without surgery, could have been fatal. The other injuries involved a broken leg and wrist.

Sam gave him a grudging nod and turned toward the door to leave.

The sound of the doctor's voice stopped him short. "The conditions at the warehouses and lumberyards are appalling. And the mills are even worse. Why the owners won't do something about it is beyond my understanding. The cost would be nothing compared to the bodily harm inflicted."

Sam eyed the doctor who, it seemed, was hostile to Jeremiah Howard. "There are those who say Mr. Flannigan's injuries have nothing to do with the lumberyard."

The look of surprise on the doctor's face couldn't have been fabricated. "What else could have caused it?"

"There are witnesses who have stated there were only minor injuries from the accident at the lumberyard. There are also witnesses who claim the major injuries were the result of a tavern brawl."

He stared at Sam. "That's ridiculous. Mr. Flannigan came to me unconscious. And not from any tavern."

"Are you sure about that?"

"His neighbor carried him across his back for miles. Neither was drunk nor appeared to have been in a fight. His injuries are consistent with an accident."

"Then are you prepared to swear on oath that Flannigan's injuries could only have been inflicted by the incident at work?"

"Well. . ." The doctor hesitated. "Of course, I didn't actually see the accident."

"When did Flannigan arrive at the hospital, Dr. Voss?"

"The morning after the accident. His wife had been trying to get him to come since the night before, but he wouldn't hear of it. No money. When Mrs. Flannigan couldn't wake him the next morning, she banged on the neighbor's door."

Sam couldn't deny the doctor sounded convincing. But the doctor didn't deal with liars and cheats every day the way an attorney did. Sam's evidence came from witnesses. The doctor was only guessing. "I see." Sam wrote in his notebook. "Then you can't be certain the injuries didn't occur at the tavern the night of the accident, as the witnesses have stated."

"Well, no, but. . ."

"Thank you, doctor. You've been very helpful." Sam tucked the pencil into his breast pocket.

The doctor stepped forward as Sam started to walk out the door. With a pained look on his face, he spoke. "Maybe I can't swear to what happened. But I believe with everything in me that Flannigan is speaking the truth. This isn't the first time I've had to treat injuries that occurred at one of Howard's places of business."

"I'm sure it isn't," Sam said. "Injuries happen every day. I wouldn't want your job."

"And I wouldn't want yours, young man."

Sam, his confidence a little shaken, stared in surprise as the doctor turned away. Why was the man so sure of Flannigan's innocence? He shrugged and left the hospital. The injured man must be a good actor. But then, most con men were.

He returned to the office and looked over the witness affidavits. They were definitely legal. And what reason would the men have to lie?

He finished up his work for the day and went home to get ready for a visit to Sally Reynolds's house to see Janet. As he dressed, he tried to remember what the young woman looked like. He remembered her auburn hair and a rather annoying laugh, but when he tried to remember her eyes, all he could see were the brilliant blue eyes of the girl at the crowded depot.

Shaking himself free from the memory, Sam walked out the door. He would get to know Janet better. Who knew? Maybe she wasn't like other girls in their social set.

Four hours later, he stood in his bedroom once more, changing into pajamas and robe. His evening with Janet had been pleasant. She was a nice girl and very entertaining. But she chattered incessantly. He sighed, wishing he had stayed home and done some more reviewing of the Flannigan case.

He went to open his window and noticed a pink sky in the distance. Another fire. This time in the direction of the river. He hoped some family hadn't lost their home tonight. The sky had been cloudy that morning, promising rain, but hopes were dashed when the sun had come out before noon.

He extinguished the overhead gaslight and climbed into bed. His mind began to go over plans for the following day. He yawned and closed his eyes. The sound of Dr. Voss's angry voice seemed to shout into his brain. Sam knew it was time he met the man who'd instilled such loyalty into the doctor. Very soon, he intended to pay a visit to Chauncey Flannigan.

Chapter 3

The clatter of dishes and the aroma of cabbage and onions assailed Katie as she ladled out bowl after bowl of hot soup.

The kitchen had opened at noon, and two hours later, the line still coiled through the door and down the wooden sidewalk outside. Mrs. Carter, the director and, as it seemed to Katie, the most untiring worker, handed out thick slices of bread and words of encouragement to the downtrodden throng who passed through. Katie had learned that the Irish had no monopoly on poverty. The people who came here for food were of every race and nationality.

Katie had inquired about and found the location of this food kitchen three days ago, right after Bobby had told her of the existence of the charitable organizations. Mrs. Carter, happy to have another pair of hands, had put her to work on the spot. Katie could only work her days off at the theater, so this was her first day on the job.

A tall man with enormous arms and not a tooth in his mouth carried a full pot of soup from the kitchen. He grunted when Katie thanked him. He grabbed the empty pot and disappeared behind the door without a word.

Katie hoped there was plenty more soup back there. She didn't think she could stand to turn anyone away hungry.

A girl, who appeared to be around Katie's age or perhaps a little older, stepped up in front of Katie. Red curls escaped from the pulled-back bun and fell across an oval face. She lifted hazel eyes to Katie. "Miss, would it be at all possible for me to take a wee bit of food home to Ma and my little sister?" The girl's voice wasn't much more than a whisper and sounded weak.

"Why. . .I don't know. I suppose it would be all right." Katie glanced at Mrs. Carter, who shook her head.

"But. . ."

The director sighed and spoke directly to the girl. "I'm sorry, dear. It's against the rules for us to send food off the premises. But, if you'll bring your family here, we'll be happy to give them something to eat."

An imploring, almost desperate look washed over the girl's face. "But you see, my sister is ill, and my ma would never be able to walk this far."

Regret crossed Mrs. Carter's countenance, and sympathy filled her eyes as she looked at the girl. "As I said, I'm not allowed to do that. Nothing can leave the premises."

A choked sound emitted from the girl's lips as she turned and walked away. As she reached the door, she stumbled then caught herself and stepped out on the sidewalk.

Katie swallowed around the knot in her throat and, without a word, handed her ladle to Mrs. Carter. Tearing off her apron, she tossed it onto a stool. "Sorry, I have to go after her. I'll return when I can." She threw the words over her shoulder as she hurried toward the door.

The girl was halfway down the street. Just as Katie started after her, she saw her sway and fall to the sidewalk. Pedestrians hurried past her, hardly slowing to even glance at the fallen girl.

With a cry of indignation, Katie pushed her way through the crowd and knelt beside the unconscious girl. Frightened, she rubbed the chapped hands and patted the pale face. "Come on now, wake up. Please." She felt the girl's pulse, relieved to find it strong.

"Wha...? What happened?" The girl struggled to get up, and Katie took a firm grip on her arm and helped her to her feet.

"You fainted," Katie said, still holding on. "Have you been ill?"

"Oh. No, I'm just—" She stopped, a red flush washing over her face.

"When did you eat last?" Katie's no-nonsense tone seemed to calm the girl.

"I'm not sure. A couple of days ago, I think."

"Oh my goodness!" Katie, who had never skipped a meal in her life, couldn't imagine such a thing. "Come on, we'll fix that right now."

"No, no. I couldn't possibly eat anything when Ma and Betty are hungry. Betty had the last of the soup last night." She stopped and blushed again, apparently realizing she'd just shared personal information with a stranger. "I've been trying to find work, but no one wants to hire me."

"Well, you wouldn't be able to work if you did find employment. You're much too weak." Katie threw a quick prayer for wisdom up to heaven. How could she get some food into this girl without touching her pride? Noticing a small park bench at the end of the street, she guided the girl toward it and sat beside her. "I'm Katie O'Shannon," she said. "What is your name, if you don't mind my asking?"

"Bridget. Bridget Thornton."

"Listen, Bridget. The best thing you can do for your mother and sister is to get some nourishment into your body so that you'll have the strength to help them."

The girl sighed but said nothing.

"I'll tell you what. While you sit here and rest, I'll get you something to eat. Then we'll take some food to your home."

Katie's heart ached as she saw hunger and pride battle for predominance on the girl's face.

"All right," Bridget whispered. "I don't know what Ma will say, but I can't let them starve to death."

A half hour later, Katie and Bridget stepped out of a cab in front of a tiny, weathered shack—one among rows of the same lined up on either side of the narrow dirt street. Curious neighbors stared as Katie reached up and paid the carriage driver. Then they went inside.

The Thornton home was clean in spite of the evident poverty. As the grateful mother and little sister ate, Katie learned from Bridget that the family had arrived from Ireland a year earlier.

"Things were na' so bad at first. Hard, but Da always made sure we had food on the table. Then, two months ago. . ." Bridget's eyes filled with tears as she continued. "A fire broke out in a house down by the river. Da went to help. He saved a woman and her three children. But he didn't make it out of the house." A sob caught her throat, and she stopped.

Katie knew the Thorntons weren't the only family in dire straits. She could see poverty and grief in every inch of Conley's Patch. She didn't know what she could do. But she knew she would do something.

∽

The shacks were lined up so close they were almost touching on each side of the road. Between the rows, a canal running down the middle of the street carried waste of all kinds.

Sam looked on in disbelief, touching his fingers to his nose to ward off the stench of waste and garbage.

Chickens and children ran here and there. Raucous laughter rang out from somewhere up the street, and sounds of an argument proceeded from a house across the street from Chauncey Flannigan's.

Sam stepped up onto the ramshackle porch and knocked on the door. The sound of a chair scraping the floor assured Sam his knock had been heard.

The door swung open, and a woman just past her first youth stared at him. Her warm brown eyes held a questioning look.

Sam removed his hat. "Mrs. Flannigan?"

"Yes?"

"My name is Sam Nelson. Is your husband at home?"

"Who is it, Sarah?" The booming voice came from across the room.

Sarah turned. "A fellow by the name of Sam Nelson. He's wanting to see you."

"Well, what does he want?" The voice sounded impatient.

Mrs. Flannigan turned inquiring eyes to Sam. "And what would you be wanting, sir?"

Amused, Sam answered, "Please tell your husband I'm an attorney and wish to speak with him about his injuries."

"He says—"

"I heard him. Let him in."

The tiny woman stood aside and allowed Sam to pass into the room.

Whereas the outside of the home had been little more than a shack, Mrs. Flannigan had apparently tried to turn the inside into something resembling a cozy home. Clean, crisp curtains hung on the lone window looking out at the filthy street. The worn, broken plank floor was brushed clean, and the walls shone as though they had been freshly scrubbed. It was obvious the Flannigans had seen better times, for a cuckoo clock hung upon the wall over the fireplace and several porcelain knickknacks held places of importance on the mantle.

Chauncey Flannigan was rugged, or he would have been had the color not been drained from his sunken cheeks and his eyes not circled with dark rings that marked nights of worry. His thin body bespoke more than a few missed meals. His dark brown eyes squinted with suspicion from the sofa on which he sat. A crutch leaned against the wall beside him, and something steamed from the mug he held.

He motioned for Sam to sit on a nearby chair. "What can I do for you, Mr. Nelson? I can't afford a lawyer, so if it's me business you're after, I'm afraid you're wasting your time." He raised his eyebrows, questioning.

"As a matter of fact, Mr. Flannigan, I'm not here to solicit you as a client. Our firm has been retained by Jeremiah Howard."

For a fraction of a moment, a scowl appeared on Flannigan's face. "I see. Howard is still determined not to pay my hospital bills. I'd hoped he might be having a conscience in there somewhere and just maybe he'd be changing his mind."

"Ungrateful wretch of a man," Flannigan's wife said as she stood over a pot at the stove. She seemed not to be speaking to the men at all. "After Chauncey never missed a day of work. Not even when he had pneumonia."

"Please, Sarah, let me speak with Mr. Nelson."

She turned innocent eyes on her husband. "And who's stopping you? I was just stating my opinion."

Sam hid his grin beneath a cough. He opened his briefcase and pulled out a copy of the witnesses' statements, having left out the names for the sake of privacy. He handed the papers to Flannigan.

The injured man glanced through the papers, and confusion filled his eyes. "But why would anyone be saying such things about me?" He looked at Sam and shook his head. "I can't imagine, sir. But I wouldn't darken the door of a tavern. My Sarah would have my hide."

"And ain't that the truth of it?" the woman said, stirring her pot. "What are they sayin' about you, Chauncey?"

"That I left the lumberyard with only a few scrapes and bruises."

She gasped, turning, the ladle in her hand like a scepter. "Chauncey Flannigan leaving his job over a few scrapes and bruises? Losing wages? Taking food out of his children's mouths over a few scrapes and bruises? Never. It's a pack of lies."

"Well, Mrs. Flannigan, my client doesn't think they are lies. And I haven't found any evidence that they're anything but the truth."

"So that's the way the land lies." Flannigan's voice took on a hard note. "I'll be saying good-bye to you now, sir. But let me tell you this. I'm an honest man. And I'll not sit by and let a bunch of greedy liars, paid off by Howard, ruin my good name." He thrust the papers back at Sam. "You can be showing yourself to the door."

Sam slipped the papers back into his briefcase and left. He stood on the porch for a moment, glancing around at the neighborhood. A wave of nausea arose in his throat. How could people live like this? His breath caught as he glanced at the house next to the Flannigans'.

The young woman from the train station stood knocking on the rickety door, a cloth-covered basket on her arm. She turned and absently glanced in his direction, and a startled look of recognition crossed her face.

A sudden puff of wind caught at the napkin, and it flew off the basket and down the steps.

As if instinct took over, Sam ran to the napkin, which had stopped just before reaching the filthy canal. He picked it up and walked to the side of the porch where she stood, her eyes wide. He grinned as he handed her the cloth. "I doubt you'll want this now, but here it is."

"Thank you, sir," she said, taking the napkin by one corner. "It will wash."

Sam cleared his throat. "I don't know if you remember me. We ran into each other at the train station a couple of months ago."

"I remember," she murmured, lowering her eyes.

"Well. . ." *Get it out, Sam. Since when were you ever tongue-tied in the presence of a beautiful woman?* "I'd like to apologize for my manners. I was in a terrible hurry, but that's no excuse to be rude. Especially to a lady."

As Sam stood with bated breath, the girl raised her beautiful eyes to him and flashed him a smile that seemed to light up everything in Sam's line of vision. "I forgive you, sir."

The door jerked open. "Katie, I knew you'd come today!" A laughing little girl grabbed the young woman's hand, dragged her inside, and slammed the door.

Sam took one impulsive step forward, tempted to climb the steps and knock. Then he stopped. Of course he couldn't do any such thing.

He walked to his buggy and untied the horse. So the girl of his dreams was an Irish immigrant from shantytown. That rather surprised him. But at least now he could put a name to the face that haunted his every waking moment. *Katie. Katie.*

He drove away from Conley's Point, musing. *Now I know where to find you, Katie girl. So don't be surprised if you see me again very soon.*

Chapter 4

No, no, and a thousand times no."

Katie bit her lip as her pa's voice boomed across the stage and through the empty theater. He stood nose to nose with Thomas Harrigan, and for a moment, Katie thought he might strike the manager.

"Michael, would you be seeing my point of view for one little moment?" Harrigan's voice of reason hadn't gotten through to Katie's irate pa so far. "I'm not asking for her to be part of the show. Just one song before the first act."

"One song? Not even one line. I've been telling you my daughter won't be part of the troupe. And that's the end of the matter."

Katie's heart sank at the finality of his words. From experience, she knew he meant what he said. Still, she couldn't let this opportunity pass without at least trying to change his stubborn mind. "Father, would you just listen?" Katie tugged on his hand until he glared at her.

"Don't be wheedling at me, Katie O'Shannon. I've said my piece, and I'll not be changing my mind." His features wrinkled in anger. "No daughter of mine is going to kill herself performing day after day and night after night."

Surprised, Katie stared as her pa's eyes flooded with moisture. Angrily, he rubbed a fist across his eyes and stomped off the stage.

So that was it? He believed the stage had caused her mother's illness and death? But. . .she died of pneumonia.

Katie squared her shoulders. She'd talk to him later. This wasn't the end of it.

"Well, as he said, I guess that's that." Mr. Harrigan threw her a regretful glance and then walked toward the wings.

"Don't be too sure about that," Katie called after him. "I'm not giving up yet."

The tenor who usually performed before the first act had received a better offer, packed up his things, and left with about an hour's notice. Mr. Harrigan had hoped Katie's father would let her fill in until he could find a replacement.

Determined to reason with Pa, Katie hurried backstage. She glanced around and saw him near the dressing rooms talking to Rosie. Their backs to her, she stopped as she heard her father speak her name.

"I'm not going to let her get mixed up in it, Rosie. Not my Katie. Her mother, bless her soul, wanted something better for her. And so do I."

"Now, Michael, I understand your wantin' a better life for Katie, although show business isn't so bad, as far as I can tell. But you're only going to push her into it if you don't stop being so stubborn. Let the girl sing for a couple of weeks until Thomas finds someone. Maybe that'll be enough to get the theater out of her system."

Katie held her breath, waiting for her pa's response. Her heart jumped when she heard him heave a deep sigh.

"Ah, Rosie. It's a hard thing, it is, raisin' a girl without her mother." He sighed again. "I'd hoped she'd meet some young man and be pleased to wed by now."

Rosie's lips stretched into a grin. "I'm sure there's a young man or two here in Chicago who'd be happy to oblige. And the girl will more than likely be a wife soon enough. But, in the meantime, let her sing, Michael. What's the harm in it?"

"Do you really think so?"

Excitement clutched Katie's stomach. At last. A small sign of her pa's mind opening to reason.

"Yes, I really do."

Katie could have grabbed Rosie and hugged her. She bit her lip to keep from shouting.

"Well then, maybe I'll think about it." Without another word, he went into the men's dressing room.

Katie burst forward. "Rosie! Thank you."

The buxom redhead turned in surprise. "Katie O'Shannon, it's eavesdropping you are now?"

"Couldn't help myself. And it was well worth it." She sent the older woman a saucy grin.

"Don't be countin' your chicks before they're hatched, missy. He hasn't said yes."

"Yet." Katie kissed Rosie on the cheek. "And don't you be trying to marry me off. I heard what you told Pa."

"Ah, I was only calmin' the man down. I'm still trying to get myself married off."

Katie was pretty sure she knew who Rosie wanted to marry but decided she'd best keep her lips buttoned. Her pa would have to realize Rosie's worth on his own.

"Thanks for reasoning with him. I want to be on that stage. I want it so badly."

"I know you do. But remember one thing—the new wears off, Katie. And youth wears off, too. Don't wait as long as I did to discover show business isn't enough to fill a person's heart forever."

The image of a handsome young man, running after a wayward napkin, flashed across Katie's mind. Her heart raced for a moment as she remembered the look on his face as he apologized for the incident at the train station.

Closing her mind to the memory, she sent Rosie a saucy grin. "I don't need any young man to make me happy. The theater is quite enough for me." But as a pair of dark brown eyes invaded her mind once more, a twinge of doubt bit at her heart.

She spent the rest of the morning mending costumes and arranging the unruly wigs that the dancers wore. The actresses, with their friendly banter, kept her laughing. She reveled in the backstage atmosphere and wanted nothing more than to be a real part of it all. If only Pa would change his mind. One thing she was pretty sure of: The stage hadn't killed her mother. She'd been the picture of health and happiness until she came down with pneumonia.

At lunchtime, Mr. Harrigan called Katie to his office. His eyes danced as he ushered her in. Katie's stomach did a flip-flop when she saw her pa standing across the room. This was it. She knew it was.

"Katie, your father has generously decided to let you fill in until I find another singer to replace Roger." Before Katie could respond, the manager added, "He has a few conditions. So I'll let him take over from here."

"Yes, Pa?" Katie's voice shook with excitement as her father cleared his throat and stood frowning at them both.

"Here's the way of it," he said. "There'll be no revealing of the ankles nor of. . . anything else that would be indecent."

Katie's face heated from hairline to neckline. "Pa!"

Frowning, he raised his hand for silence. "I'll approve all costumes to make sure they are fittin' and proper for my daughter to wear. And I'll approve the songs you'll be singing to make sure they are decent and moral."

Indignation sparked. "As though I'd wear anything improper or sing an immoral song. Grandma would—" At her pa's scowl, Katie snapped her lips together.

He shook his finger at her. "Don't be interrupting me, young lady. I'm not finished." He turned a stern eye on her. "You're not to be accepting dinner invitations from any of the young bucks that're sure to be asking, and you don't go anywhere with anyone without my approval."

"Where would I go?" She scowled back.

His eyebrows rose, and she mentally stepped back. "Yes, Pa," she said with unaccustomed meekness.

Harrigan's eyes twinkled, and he winked at Katie. "All right then, Michael, is that it?"

"For now. If anything else comes to mind, I'll be letting you know."

℃

"Sam, stop pacing and get down to whatever is bothering you." The older Mr. Nelson's impatient tone revealed his tiredness as he leaned back in his favorite leather chair in the library. Sam figured his father was stuffed from dinner and probably wanted nothing more than to close his eyes and doze off for a few minutes.

"Sorry, Father." Sam dropped into a chair across from his father, considering how to broach the subject. After all, several of their influential clients had business interests in or around Conley's Patch. "I met with Chauncey Flannigan today."

His father paused with a match halfway to his pipe. "You went to the Patch?" He struck the match to his pipe and then tossed it onto the clean hearth of the fireplace.

"Yes." Sam frowned as he watched the match burn down to ash.

"Well?"

"Have you been down there lately, Dad?"

"To shantytown?" He frowned at his son. "Why would I?"

Why would he indeed? Father's contributions to the poor were more in the manner of a few pennies in the offering plate variety. "Conditions are terrible. I saw children playing near an open ditch, containing garbage and human refuse, that ran down the middle of the street. The smell was horrible." Sam jumped up and began to pace again. "And that's not all. The housing is unspeakable. Hardly more than shacks for the people to live in."

Sam's father frowned. "What exactly are you trying to say, son?"

"Well, shouldn't something be done to help these people?"

"Sit down," his father commanded. "I refuse to speak with you while you are pacing the floor."

Once again, Sam dropped into the chair.

Mr. Nelson peered over the top of his steepled hands. "Sam, your compassion for your fellow man is commendable, but I don't believe you understand this particular condition."

"What do you mean?"

He raised his palms and sighed. "These shanty Irish are a shiftless bunch. Lazy and slothful, not to mention deceitful and dishonest. Just look at this Flannigan character."

His father's voice stopped as though that settled the matter, but that far from satisfied Sam's concerns about an entire community living in such deplorable conditions. "Please continue."

"There really isn't much more to say about it. These people will take everything they can get and come back for more. You could put them in a mansion, and a year later, it would be in shambles. They have no pride and no gumption." He leaned forward and peered at Sam. "Trust me, son. There's nothing you can do for these people."

Sam knew better than to try to argue with his father. The man was a seasoned attorney, after all. He never lost an argument. There was no point in telling him about Sarah Flannigan's attempt at making a shack into a cozy home. There was no point in mentioning Chauncey Flannigan's outrage at being called anything less than a man of honor. He dropped the subject and excused himself.

Going out onto the veranda, he leaned against a pillar and gazed out into the night. A haze from recent fires hovered in the air. Most of them had taken place across the river, although a few had broken out in the city. And there was no getting away from the haze and smell of smoke in any part of Chicago.

Sam had overheard some of the employees at the office talking about their concerns. They feared if it didn't rain soon, conditions could only get worse.

Sam felt they were worrying unnecessarily. After all, Chicago now had a real fire department. The volunteers had been scattered all over town, and too often, homes and businesses had burned to the ground before they arrived. Yes, surely with the new fire department, Chicagoans could rest assured that they were in good hands.

Sam walked back inside and found his mother about to go upstairs. She lifted her cheek for his goodnight kiss. Reaching up, she brushed her hand across his forehead.

"Son, is anything bothering you?" She peered closer. "Or are you ill?"

Sam took her hand in his and smiled. "Nothing's wrong, Mother. You worry too much."

"A mother's duty." She gave a small sigh. "You do know I'm always willing to listen if you need to talk about anything."

"Of course, I know, Mother. Nothing's wrong. I promise." But as he watched her climb the stairs, he knew something was—if not wrong—different.

Grabbing his briefcase from the hall table, he went upstairs. He'd glance through the papers on the Flannigan case before he went to bed. But he had no reason to doubt his father's assurance that Flannigan was simply another Irish ne'er-do-well out to get something for nothing.

And yet, a twinge of doubt intruded into Sam's mind. Flannigan had been angry, but who wouldn't be under the circumstances? After all, Sam was a hostile attorney out to win the case for the other side. And he'd shown up at the Flannigans' home uninvited. The Flannigans had appeared to be poor but decent people.

What if his father was wrong? He'd admitted he hadn't even been to the Patch recently. So what did he base his judgment on? Was he so involved with his wealthy clients he couldn't see the other side at all? Or didn't want to? Sam brushed the idea away. He knew his father was an honest man. Still, a man could be honest and shortsighted at the same time, couldn't he? Even a man as great as his father.

The questions plagued him as his mind replayed the scene in the Flannigans' home, the living conditions in Conley's Patch. He was a facts man and tried not to be ruled by emotions, so the letters of testimony by witnesses at the lumberyard should be all the evidence he needed. But something tugged at him. Something he couldn't quite put his finger on.

His heart picked up rhythm as an image flashed across his mind. Would he see her again if he went back to shantytown? Regardless of the outcome of this case, there was one thing Sam knew: The lovely young Irish girl with the golden curls and shining blue eyes couldn't possibly be lazy or shiftless. He'd bet his boots on that.

Uncertainty stabbed him sharply. *Lord, what should I do?*

Silence was his only answer. He couldn't really expect anything else. He hadn't spent time with God in a long time. And it had been months since he'd attended church.

A sudden wave of loneliness washed over Sam. He pushed it down and turned to his work.

ও

"Ladies and gentlemen, welcome to Harrigan's, where our one desire is to entertain to your delight and satisfaction. Our production of *The Golden Pipes* is nearing an end. We've only two more weeks, but never fear. There'll be another great production coming up before you know it." Thomas Harrigan's voice seemed to fade, and his frame became a blur.

Katie's legs felt like rubber as she stood in the wings awaiting her cue. *Oh God, please don't let me faint.*

"And now, ladies and gentlemen, I'm pleased to introduce a young lass with eyes as blue as the skies of Erin. But don't any of you fellows be getting any ideas. Because she has a proper Irish father with fists like mountains."

The roar of the laughing crowd startled Katie, and she stood up straight.

"So let's give a true Chicago welcome to Miss Katherine O'Shannon."

Katie walked onto the stage, propelled by sheer emotion.

Thomas gave her a smile and walked off, leaving her alone on the suddenly unfamiliar stage.

As she faced the applauding audience, she could feel the brush of the curtains against her hair and she envisioned herself falling backward in a faint, ripping the curtain from the rope. *Stop it. Think of Mother and Father. Make them proud.*

Her lips curved in a faint smile, and she heard murmurs of approval from the people in front of her. The opening bars of her music floated to her ears. A surge of strength encouraged her, and she opened her lips and began to sing.

The next thing she knew, the last line of "A Little Bit of Heaven" trilled from her throat, and the audience was on its feet, applauding and cheering. Katie blushed, gave a little curtsy, and then hurried off the stage.

She fell into her father's arms. A wide grin split his face. "Go back, Katie girl. Sure and they're wanting more." He turned her and gave her a little shove.

Rejuvenated, she almost danced onto the stage and sang the last few lines of her song again. She floated off the stage and in a daze heard her friends congratulating her.

Katie watched the show from the wings, too excited to sit and too jittery to do any sewing. Over and over, she relived the performance and the wonderful reception the audience had given her.

That night, she repeated her number and was received with the same enthusiasm as she had before. By the time she and the troupe got back to the boardinghouse, she was so emotionally exhausted she practically stumbled through the door to her room. She went to bed convinced she wouldn't sleep a wink, but exhaustion won out and she quickly fell into a deep slumber.

ও

The next two weeks flew by for Katie. She loved performing her songs but secretly hoped her father would allow her to take a small part in the next musical comedy. She'd read it over and over and was mesmerized by the enchanting Maggie Donovan and her crooning suitor, Sean Kelly. All the major roles had been assigned, with Emma Gallagher getting the lead female role. Katie knew she wasn't ready for those anyway, but she had her eye on the one-line part of the housemaid, Rose. When she tried to broach the subject to her father, however, he threatened to pull her from the singing number if she brought up the subject again.

The first official rehearsal day was bittersweet for Katie. It was exciting to see the troupe walking around the stage practicing their parts. Her father had acquired the role of Sean Kelly's Uncle Andrew and had everyone in stitches in the boardinghouse living room as he became the bumbling Irish tavern keeper.

Patsy Brown had gotten the part Katie coveted and let everyone know she wasn't very happy with it. Katie felt like slapping the girl every time she heard the whining complaints. As she watched Patsy's rather insipid characterization of the young housemaid, Katie told herself she could have done a much better job.

They were beginning the second week of rehearsals when Rosie Riley tripped over a rope that had been left on the floor backstage. The doctor's proclamation of a broken foot set the cast astir.

Katie was just coming out of the ladies' dressing room when her father found her.

"Katie girl," he said, "it's against my better judgment, but the show opens next week, and someone has to take over for poor Rosie."

Katie's jaw dropped open. "Me? I get to take Rosie's part?"

"Well, of course not. And you having never played a show in your life? Patsy steps into the role of Maggie's cousin, Sally, and you get the part of the housemaid. But only until Rosie can walk again." He sighed, and worry crossed his face. "It's obvious you've got stars in your eyes and won't have peace until you give the stage a try. But Katie girl, I can't help but hope it'll wear off and someday you'll settle for a more normal life."

"Oh, but Father, I don't understand why it worries you so. You love show business yourself. And I know Mother did, too. I can still remember how her face would glow before she stepped onto the stage."

"Maybe so, but I'll always be blaming myself for taking her away from her parents' farm and into this crazy life. Maybe she wouldn't have gotten sick."

"Father, you don't know that. Why, just last year, little Annie Samson came down with pneumonia. She was only six years old and was gone in no time. People on farms get sick and pass away, too."

He cleared his throat and looked away, clearly finished with the current conversation. "Well now, you better get with Patsy and see if she can give you some tips about your part. You'll be needing a script, too." He kissed her and walked out of the dressing room.

Katie couldn't help the little scream of joy that escaped. She glanced around to make sure no one heard. She wouldn't want anyone to think she was glad Rosie broke her foot, because she certainly wasn't. But, oh, she was in a play! At last!

∽

"I'm not handing out good money to some inexperienced clerk!" The tall, burly man sitting across from Sam's father was red-faced with anger. He leaned forward, and his eyes squinted at the elderly attorney.

"Mr. Howard, I can assure you my son is neither inexperienced nor is he a clerk." Sam could tell from the glint in his father's eyes that he was fast losing patience with Jeremiah Howard. "Sam is a bright young attorney who is being considered for partnership. He is well qualified to represent you."

"That's not good enough. I want a senior partner, and that's all there is to it."

"Yes, well, I'm sorry, but neither I nor the other senior partners are available. So if you do not wish to be represented by Sam, you're welcome to find yourself another attorney."

Sam, seated next to his client, almost laughed at the bevy of emotions crossing the man's beefy face.

Howard started to stand then dropped back into his chair and cleared his throat. "Well, all right. I suppose I can give the boy a chance."

Sam, in spite of his hopes that this case would win the partnership for him, was almost disappointed with Howard's decision. Everything about the man filled Sam with distaste. From the smell of his apparently unwashed body to the spittle that sprayed from his mouth when he talked. And this character was one of the wealthiest men in Chicago.

At a nod from his father, Sam stood. "I'll see you to the front, Mr. Howard. Our secretary will make an appointment for you to see me later this week, and we'll go over the case so you can see where we are in the legal process."

Howard hefted his form out of the chair. "An appointment won't be necessary. Let me know when to appear in court. I expect to win this case, Nelson. See to it."

Sam escorted his client to the front door and said good-bye. He wished he could put his foot on the man's backside and give a push. He neither liked nor trusted Mr. Howard. But liking his clients wasn't part of his job. If the man was innocent of wrongdoing, as evidence seemed to support, he had a right to counsel.

As he was about to leave the office later that day, Jack hailed him. "How about a game of billiards tonight?"

"Billiards? Where?"

"My father just finished renovating two rooms on the third floor." He grinned. "Mother finally rebelled against the cigar smoke and loud voices of Father's cronies. He's calling tonight the grand opening. Nine o'clock?"

"Sure, I'll be there."

Sam wasn't sure what his own father would think of his plans. Isaiah Myers owned one of Chicago's more notorious taverns featuring dancing girls and backroom gambling. But Sam didn't see any harm in a game of billiards, especially since it was at the Myers home. Jack was a decent fellow and wouldn't have invited him if anything wasn't on the up-and-up.

When Sam was ushered into the third-floor room promptly at nine, cigar smoke nearly knocked him over.

Jack waved from across the crowded room and motioned him over.

The sharp crack of the billiard balls assaulted his ears, and by the time he reached his friend, his eyes were watering from the smoke. Maybe this wasn't such a good idea.

Jack introduced him to the men around his table, and they played a couple of games before Sam begged off.

"You should just see the little darling. I tell you she's a beauty and has a voice like an angel."

Sam turned as the voice reached his ears from the table next to them.

Laughter greeted the man's declaration. "Yeah, but I wouldn't be getting any ideas if I were you. They say she's a sweet young lady, but her father guards her with fists of steel."

Sam lifted one eyebrow and sent a puzzled glance at Jack.

"I think they're talking about the new singer at Harrigan's," Jack said. "Have you seen her yet?"

Sam shook his head. "I haven't been to a show in weeks."

"I hear there's a new musical comedy starting next Friday. Maybe the girls would enjoy it, and you could get a glimpse of the gorgeous Katherine O'Shannon." He laughed. "But don't fall for her and break Janet's heart. Sally would blame me."

"Don't worry. I hardly think Janet would care. We're only friends. And I'm not likely to fall for a showgirl. Even if I was so inclined, my folks would kill me."

"And if they didn't, I would. Couldn't stand by and watch you ruin your career." He slapped Sam on the shoulder. "So, shall I invite the girls for opening night?"

"Sure, sounds like fun. I'll stop by Sally's tomorrow after work and invite Janet. Shall we all ride over together?"

"No, let's go separately. I need to talk to Sally privately."

"Fine with me."

"Don't you want to know why?" Jack was grinning. In fact, it seemed like he'd been doing a lot of that tonight.

Jack glanced around, his face red with excitement. "I'm thinking about proposing marriage to Sally tonight."

Sam whistled and held his hand out to his beaming friend. "Congratulations!"

"If she says yes, you mean."

"She will. I'm sure of it."

"Maybe you'll be popping the question yourself soon. Janet's a lovely girl."

"Who just happens to be nothing more than a friend," Sam retorted. "Besides, marriage is the last thing on my mind."

But once more, the young woman from the Patch filled his head. He brushed the thought away and grabbed a billiard stick. "Come on. Maybe I'll let you win this one."

Chapter 5

How can I ever be thanking you for recommending me for this job, Katie? And me being nothing to you but a poor stranger."

Katie frowned at Bridget, who was pushing a moistened strand of thread through the tiny eye of her sewing needle.

"What do you mean 'nothing,' Bridget Thornton? You've become a dear friend to me, as I hope I have to you."

Bridget gasped. "And now I've gone and offended you. The one person, besides me ma, I have the most respect for."

Katie reached over and placed her hand momentarily on Bridget's arm. "Not at all. I just don't like to hear you belittling yourself. It hurts me."

"Then I won't be doing it again. I promise." The girl cast a shy smile at Katie then ducked her head over her work. "And Mr. Harrigan is a mighty good man to be paying for my room and board through the week. It'd be awfully hard to walk all the way here from the Patch and back again every day."

"Yes, it is nice of him to do that for the unmarried women of the cast."

"I thought Ma was going to stay on her knees all night, thanking the Lord for such a blessing. She said I should thank you and Mr. Harrigan for her, too. You can't imagine the difference my wages have made in our lives."

Katie thought she did know. The wonderful smell of stew now wafted through the Thornton home every day, and Mrs. Thornton and Bridget's little sister were both recovering, due to nourishment and the medicine Bridget had been able to provide. Katie and Bridget had become fast friends, and Katie had taken to dropping by to help with the endless mending when she wasn't rehearsing.

"Katie, I'm so excited you got the part. You must be about to burst with happiness."

Katie's heart thumped at the thought of her luck. It must be the Irish in her. Although, Grandmother had always reprimanded her whenever she'd said that. "Katherine, dear," she'd say with a worried little shake of her head, "blessings come from God. Not luck."

Katie shrugged. Whoever or whatever was responsible for her getting the part, she was thankful. If only some of those blessings would flow to the people of the Patch as well. "Bridget, what can we do to make things easier for your neighbors?"

"Why, I don't know, Katie. Most of the men are doing all they can. Wages are just so low. And most of the women have a passel of little ones to care for."

"Well, couldn't some sort of child care be arranged so that the women can bring in extra money?"

A little frown appeared on Bridget's face. "Some of the women do take turns,

31

but it's not really enough to help. And when a woman has worked her own full shift, it's mighty hard to take a turn at running after someone else's brood."

Katie nodded, but wheels began to turn in her head. "What if. . ."

"What if what?"

"Nothing. Let me think on it a bit."

"Okay, but you'd better get onstage. I think it's almost time for you to rehearse."

"Oh my. You're right." Katie jumped up, tossed her mending in a basket, and, throwing a hasty good-bye over her shoulder, headed out the door.

She arrived onstage just as Maggie was saying the opening lines. Her heart still thumped hard every time the moment for her one line drew near. But the rest of the cast assured her she was a natural and doing a wonderful job. Tomorrow was opening night, and Katie looked forward to the dress rehearsal and the party that would be held tonight.

After rehearsal, Katie and Bridget went back to Ma Casey's. The troupe was pretty rowdy with the excitement of the new show, so the two friends found a quiet place to talk out on the wide front porch.

"Okay, I have an idea," Katie said, leaning back in one of the wicker rockers.

"About what?"

"The children at the Patch."

"Hmm. I wouldn't be making decisions about other people's wee children. They won't be liking it."

Katie laughed. "No, no. They'll like this. It's to help the mothers who need to work. And it's only a suggestion."

"Well, in that case. . ."

"There's a society here in town that has established a day care for workers' children."

"We know about that. It's too far from the Patch to do any good. And I don't think the women there would trust outsiders to care for their children anyway."

"I know. But wouldn't it be possible to create something similar at Conley's Patch?"

"How would you be thinking we could bring that about?"

"Okay, first we'd need to find someone with a big enough house. Then several women can care for the children while the others work. The women who work could contribute a share of their earnings to pay the ones who care for the children. This way everyone is earning wages."

An expression of hope and excitement crossed Bridget's face. "It might work. But how do we get it started?"

"We could call a meeting for those who are interested in working. Once we introduce the plan, we can help them get organized. After that, it will be up to them to keep things going."

Excited, the girls discussed the possibility of the day care until Katie's father interrupted them. It was time for a light supper before dress rehearsal. They joined the rest of the troupe, then after supper, they headed for the theater.

Katie loved her costume. She was a little disappointed to find there was no wig with it, such as some of the others had. But Mr. Harrigan, laughing, assured her that her own bouncing golden curls were perfect for the part.

The celebration at Ma Casey's broke up early. Mr. Harrigan insisted. After all, he couldn't have a sleepy bunch of actors stumbling around the stage on opening day.

∞

"Oh, Sam, I'm so excited. I've never been to Harrigan's before."

Sam tried not to wince at the shrill tone of Janet's voice. Had she been this annoying before? And the way she clutched at his arm, digging her fingers into his flesh, made him wonder if she truly understood the nature of their friendship after all. The *clip-clop* of the horses' hooves seemed to be attempting to compete with the young woman's incessant chatter. But perhaps she was nervous. Forcing a smile, he turned to her. "Then I'm delighted to be the one to give you the pleasure."

She flashed a coquettish smile at him, and dropping her lashes, she turned away. "Oh, look! There are Jack and Sally."

The couple stood by the theater entrance, apparently awaiting Sam and Janet's arrival.

Sam pulled to a stop in front of Harrigan's and, after helping Janet from the carriage, threw a coin to a boy who, with obvious experience, grabbed the reins and led the horse and carriage away.

Janet joined Jack and Sally while Sam went to purchase their tickets.

Animated voices greeted them as they walked into the auditorium. They found their seats, very near the front, and Jack and Sally scooted in first.

As Sam seated himself on the aisle seat, the lights dimmed and the auditorium quieted.

The boisterous emcee greeted the audience and told a couple of jokes. Then he announced Katherine O'Shannon.

Sam glanced with curiosity toward the wings as a small figure walked out onstage. His breath caught, and he blinked. Surely it was his imagination. After all, the light was dim.

Then she stepped into the spotlight, and there was no doubt. That lovely smile. The golden curls. The sky blue eyes. Oh yes. It was her.

Sam sat mesmerized as she sang a pretty Irish ballad, turning it into a masterpiece, then stood to his feet and applauded loudly as she left the stage.

"Sam, you idiot, sit down."

Jack's whisper brought Sam back to his senses, and he realized he was the only one standing. He dropped back onto his chair but continued to applaud. After all, everyone else was clapping, too.

The girl walked back onto the stage and did a short encore, then she hurried off the stage.

As the emcee returned to the stage to announce the first act, Sam leaned back, suddenly conscience of the girl seated next to him. He glanced at her and was met with a look of fury and stony silence.

The curtain rose and the play began.

In the middle of the first act, Sam was delighted to see Katherine O'Shannon step onto the stage in a housemaid's uniform. After that, although she only appeared once more and spoke only one line, he had no idea what the rest of the play was about.

During intermission, Sam followed the other three to the lobby.

After the girls excused themselves, Jack turned to Sam with a look of unbelief. "Are you crazy? Why were you gaping at that actress? You'll be lucky if Janet ever speaks to you again, much less agrees to see you."

"It's her, Jack." Sam almost whispered the words.

"What? Who?"

"It's the girl from the train station," Sam said.

Suddenly, understanding appeared on Jack's face, and he frowned. "The one who lives at the Patch?"

"The very same."

Jack groaned. "Don't do something stupid, Sam. You'll regret it when you come to your senses."

Sam was saved from answering by the return of the girls.

Janet gave him a cold smile but took his arm as they returned to their seats to await the next act. "What do you think of actresses, Sally?" Janet turned to her cousin, but her words reached Sam clearly.

"Why, what do you mean?" Sally asked.

"Well, I've always heard their morals are atrocious. Haven't you heard that?" Without waiting for Sally to reply, Janet's malicious words continued. "Take that singer, for instance. She looks so demure, and her voice is so, so sweet. But of course, that's only an act. I wouldn't want to even think what sort of life she lives after the curtain goes down."

Jack and Sally stared at her in surprise, but Sam, attempting to hold back his anger, knew her words were spoken for his benefit. "Perhaps you should reserve your judgment. Especially about a girl you don't know." Sam heard the words almost before he realized he'd spoken.

Janet's mouth flew open in disbelief. "Well! If that's the sort of girl who interests you, I'm certainly glad I found out now." Her face was red, and she spoke loudly enough that people around them were taking notice.

Sam groaned inwardly. His parents would have been mortified if they'd heard him. "Janet, I apologize. I shouldn't have spoken to you as I did. It was ungentlemanly of me. But I do think you spoke those unkind words without thinking."

At her angry gasp, he realized he'd done it again. Well, he'd tried. At first.

"Well, the very idea! I refuse to stay in your presence any longer. I'm leaving." The girl jumped up and, with Sam, Sally, and Jack trailing after, rushed to the lobby.

"I'll take you home then." He didn't want to miss another possible glimpse of Katherine, but he obviously couldn't let Janet leave unescorted.

"No, you most certainly will not take me home! I wouldn't go anywhere with you if I had to walk every step of the way home." She frowned at him and then turned her back. "But I'm sure Jack will see that I don't have to do that. After all, he is a gentleman."

"Sally and I will see you home, Janet, of course." He shook his head at Sam. "To be honest, I don't care for the show that much, and Sally and I have plans for the rest of the evening."

After they'd left, Sam headed back to his seat, feeling guilty. . .at first. He should probably have tried harder to reason with Janet. He couldn't really blame her for being angry. But then, he'd only been defending the honor of another young woman. Janet's words had been downright mean.

After a while, he managed to convince himself he'd done all he could and admitted he was relieved she'd left. Because he had no intention of leaving the theater without an attempt to speak to Katherine O'Shannon.

Chapter 6

Katie bit her upper lip and squinted her eyes in an attempt to hold back the tears. She ran into the ladies' dressing room and flung herself onto a stool, her head leaning on the dressing table. The memory of the young man's shocked expression as he stared at her from the audience stabbed her, and humiliation tore at her in relentless frenzy.

"Katie! Whatever is the matter?" Fear sharpened Bridget's voice. "Did something go wrong onstage?"

Katie looked up. "No, no. It's nothing. Nothing at all. Just nerves, I guess." She stiffened and swiped at the moisture in her eyes. What right did he have to be shocked that she was an actress? He was probably some rich man's son who'd never worked a day in his life. The snob.

The other actresses spilled into the room, their sudden entrance catching Katie by surprise.

"What a great first night. I don't think we've had this good an opening since last holiday season." Caitlyn Brown threw her wig on a table and slipped off her shoes. "And Katie, honey, you did a wonderful job. Congratulations."

"Thank you." Furtively, Katie dabbed at her eyes.

A tap sounded on the door, and Caitlyn walked over and flung it open.

Katie gasped at the sight of her tormenter, holding a bouquet of flowers he must have bought from the street vendor outside the theater.

He cleared his throat, his clean-shaven face red with embarrassment. "Uh, could I speak with Miss O'Shannon?"

Caitlyn eyed him then glanced sideways at Katie, who shook her head. "Sorry. Miss O'Shannon is indisposed at the moment."

"Oh." He glanced across at Katie then looked away.

"But perhaps if you come back in ten minutes, she will see you."

His face brightened. "Good. Will you give her these?"

Caitlyn took the bouquet and shut the door. With a teasing look, she handed the flowers to Katie. "Your first performance and already an admirer at the door."

"Why did you tell him to come back?"

"Because he's a bonnie handsome lad and I couldn't resist the pleading in his eyes."

Katie removed her makeup and changed into her street clothes. Maybe she had misunderstood the look on his face. Perhaps it wasn't revulsion, after all.

Ten minutes later, right on schedule, another tap sounded on the door. She threw a reproachful look at Caitlyn and went to answer. She supposed she mustn't be rude.

He stood, hat in hand, and in spite of herself, she nearly melted at his smile. "Miss O'Shannon?"

"Yes." She stepped out into the hall and closed the door. "Is there something I can do for you, sir?"

"You do remember me, don't you?"

"Of course. You're the gentleman who returned the napkin that fell off my basket." She paused then continued. "The man at the station."

He grinned and gave a little laugh. "Good. I was afraid you'd forgotten me."

"Sir, you know my name, but I have no idea of yours." She crossed her arms and waited, determined not to be at that sort of disadvantage another moment.

"Oh, I'm so sorry. I'm Sam Nelson."

She held out her hand for a shake, and to her surprise, he lifted it and brushed his lips softly against her fingers. A bolt went through her, and she jerked her hand away.

"Forgive me. I don't know what I was thinking." He smiled.

She shook her head and laughed. "Well, all right. You're forgiven. But don't ever take such liberties again." She tucked her hand into her pocket to make sure. "The flowers are lovely. Thank you."

"You're very welcome." He cleared his throat. "I wonder if you would consent to dine with me."

She drew back in surprise. "Tonight?"

"No, no. Of course not. How stupid of me. I'm sure you have plans. Well, how about tomorrow night?"

Katie blushed. She had no plans except to go home and get a good night's sleep. But she would never accept a dinner invitation on such short notice, especially from a young man she barely knew. Besides, her father had forbidden it. "No, I'm sorry. That won't be possible." She noticed she was picking at a nonexistent thread on her dress. She curled her fingers up and crammed her hand back into her pocket.

"I see. Very well, I'll see you tomorrow night. Thank you for allowing me to speak with you." He bowed, turned, and walked away.

What did he mean he'd see her tomorrow night? Didn't he hear her refuse his dinner invitation?

She turned and went inside, nearly knocking Caitlyn down. "Oh. You were listening!" Katie declared, scandalized.

Caitlyn burst out laughing. "Yes, I admit it. Unfortunately, I didn't hear much. Do tell us."

"There's nothing to tell. He invited me to dinner, and I refused. That's all."

"You refused? Why? He's gorgeous." Caitlyn rolled her eyes.

"Now you be leaving her alone." Bridget glared at the teasing actress. "Pay her no mind, Katie."

"Thanks, I won't." She smiled at her defender and at the playful actress, happy to have friends who cared.

Katie and Bridget walked home. As they trailed behind her father and Rosie, Katie told her friend about the incident at the station and the encounter at Conley's Patch.

A thoughtful expression settled across Bridget's brow. "It seems to me he's setting his cap for you. Be careful. Who knows if his intentions are honorable or not?"

Fear shot through Katie. Could Bridget be right? It was strange that he'd had that shocked look on his face. Then he came with flowers and an invitation so soon.

Katie gasped. Did Sam Nelson think she was a loose woman?

CB

Sam reached inside his vest pocket and pulled out the string of tickets he'd purchased before he'd gone backstage. Row one, center seat. If the show outlasted what he'd bought, he'd buy more.

He placed the tickets in the top drawer of his bedside table and berated himself for being so bold with Miss O'Shannon. Just because he'd been thinking of her for weeks, did he think she would jump into his arms?

Sam's thoughts continued to chastise him as he tossed and turned in his bed, finally falling into a troubled sleep sometime near dawn.

He was front and center the following night. Once more he carried a bouquet to her dressing room and asked her to dine with him the next evening. She declined the invitation.

There was no show the next day, as the theater was closed on Sundays, and Sam spent the afternoon fidgeting until his mother finally turned to him with a frown.

"What in the world is the matter with you, Sam?"

"I'm fine." He sent her a rather sick smile that even he knew was unconvincing.

Suddenly her face brightened. "You're in love, aren't you? That's why you're mooning around."

"Really, Mother. I'm not some young lad with a crush."

"Mmm-hmm." She busied herself with her knitting. "Who is she?"

Sam was silent for a moment as his mind considered opening up to his mother about Katherine O'Shannon. No, not yet. He didn't need a reaction from her just yet. "Mother, when there is actually a young woman in my life, I promise to tell you all about her." There. Not a lie. But maybe not the complete truth either.

The two weeks that followed were a world of contradictions. During the day, Sam was the serious, hardworking attorney, focusing his attention on the Flannigan case.

Evenings were a different matter altogether. Like a lovesick schoolboy, in the middle seat of the first row, he sat mesmerized by Katherine O'Shannon.

Every night, after being turned down again, he told himself he would stay away from Harrigan's from now on. But the following night, there he sat, swimming in the depths of her blue eyes. If his mother had again accused him of being in love, he couldn't have denied it.

Jack was about to lose patience with him. "Sam, my friend, you're going to let that showgirl rob you of your partnership."

"No, I'm not. And don't call her 'that showgirl' in that tone of voice."

His friend sighed. "Sorry, but man, you're losing your mind."

Sam bristled. "I'm doing my work just fine."

The Flannigan folder peeked out from under the stack of books piled on Sam's desk. Something about the case still bothered him. At this point, he was mostly getting paperwork together and checking for any evidence that might have been overlooked.

Making a sudden decision, Sam stood up. "As a matter of fact, I'm heading out to Conley's Patch now to interview Flannigan again. I've got a hunch there's something I'm missing."

"The Patch, huh?" Jack's suspicious tone grated on Sam. "You sure you're not hoping to run into the actress?"

"I hope I do, but that's not my reason for going. I honestly do have business to attend to."

"All right. But I hope you know what you're doing."

Sam considered his friend's words all the way to Conley's Patch.

The heat in the Patch radiated from the stinking street, and the smell from the ditch running down the center was so bad Sam would have covered his nose and mouth with a handkerchief, but he didn't want to offend Flannigan more than he already had.

The meeting with Flannigan did little except confuse Sam. The injured man's attitude and demeanor simply didn't line up with the accusations against him.

Disturbed, he left the house, determined not to let the seeming inconsistencies get him off course. Flannigan should probably be performing at Harrigan's. After all, a con man wouldn't get very far if he wasn't convincing.

He got into his buggy and headed back to the office.

A young woman walked down the dirty street, her golden curls peeking out from beneath her bonnet. The tilt of her head, the set of her shoulders, even from the back he knew it was her. He urged the horse forward and pulled up beside her. "Miss O'Shannon."

Startled, she turned. Her eyes grew wide, and Sam knew he wasn't mistaking the gladness he saw there.

"May I give you a lift somewhere? It's awfully hot to be walking."

Nervously, she glanced around. "I had hoped to hail a cabbie, but there doesn't seem to be one in sight."

He didn't want to say that cabbies didn't usually hang around this area. Strange she didn't know that. He stepped out of the carriage. "I assure you, I only wish to help you if you'll allow it."

Her eyes shifted with uncertainty then looked fully into his own, nearly robbing him of the ability to breathe. "If it's not an inconvenience," she said in a tiny voice. "I could use a ride to the theater." The feel of her tiny gloved hand filled him with awe as he helped her into the carriage.

He urged the horse to a trot and glanced at her with a smile.

A pink blush washed over her face, and she gave him a sweet smile. "Mr. Nelson, I feel I should explain why I haven't accepted any of your invitations when you've been so kind." She gave a slight cough.

"You owe me no explanation, Miss O'Shannon. You have a right to refuse me if you please."

"But you see, I would have accepted if it were up to me." Once more the pretty blush caressed her cheeks.

"What do you mean?" He hoped his eagerness didn't startle her.

"My father has forbidden me to accept invitations from any young man without his approval. And after all, he doesn't even know you."

Sam tried hard to control the grin that started in his heart and worked its way to his lips. But it was a hopeless task. "Well," he said, "we'll just have to do something about that, won't we?"

Chapter 7

Katie jumped out of the carriage before the young man had a chance to assist her. If her father saw her, there was no telling what he'd do. Oh, why hadn't she asked Mr. Nelson to drop her off a block away from the theater?

She heard his startled exclamation as her feet hit the street, and she turned, throwing him an apologetic look. "Thank you so much for the ride. It was very kind of you, but I must be going."

She started off toward the side of the building, hoping to avoid anyone she knew. At the sight of Bobby and Molly standing at the corner, she groaned and stopped.

Bobby shot a glare at Mr. Nelson, who still sat in his carriage, watching her. "Who's that?" Bobby demanded, sending Katie a reproachful look.

"Why, he's an acquaintance of mine, Bobby Brown, if it's any of your business." She frowned at him, and he turned and stalked off.

"Ah, poor, poor Bobby. Now you've gone and broken his heart." Molly grinned and looked pointedly at the carriage and its occupant.

Katie felt heat rise to her face. Why in the world was he still sitting there? "Well, I don't know how his heart could be broken," Katie retorted. "I've never given him reason to think I was interested in anything but friendship." Well, maybe she had flirted a little bit. A pang of conscience stabbed her as she remembered her ploy to get information from him about Conley's Patch.

"If you say so, dear." Molly rounded the corner of the building.

Katie's heart thumped. She didn't need to look back to know he was still there, watching her. But she looked anyway. Land's sake. What was he doing?

He tipped his hat and grinned.

Katie waved and then bolted around the corner, her stomach doing little flips. Stepping through the open door into the theater, she couldn't help the smile that tilted her lips.

"I saw that." Molly was waiting for her just inside the door.

Setting her chin, Katie sent Molly what she hoped was a firm look. "Mr. Nelson is merely an acquaintance. Not even a friend, much less a suitor."

Molly laughed. "Hey, I'm only fooling. Don't get riled up, now."

In the crowded dressing room, Katie made her way past women getting ready for the afternoon performances. She hurried to get into her costume then sat at a dressing table to apply her makeup.

Oh, what had she done? She knew better than to accept a ride from a man who was practically a stranger. When her father found out, and he would, he'd likely put her on the first train back to the farm. Katie cringed at the thought. But there was no getting around it. She had to tell him herself. Right after the show.

For the first time, she didn't enjoy performing. Her heart didn't soar as it usually did when she sang her solo, and she recited her lines without feeling. As soon as she'd made her final exit, she rushed to the dressing room and poured her heart out to Bridget.

"Now, now. Don't be frettin' so. After all, your da would probably rather you took the ride than be walking down the streets of the Patch. What with all the—" The girl stopped and gave Katie a curious look. "What do you think a fine young gentleman would be doing at Conley's Patch?"

"Well, I don't know. Maybe he had business there." She frowned. What was Bridget getting at?

"At the Patch? What sort of business would he be in?"

"I'm sure I don't know. How should I?"

"If he's going to be hanging around you, you'd best be finding out everything you can about him. Including his business." Bridget's eyes widened. "He could be a gambler or even criminal of some sort. They often look like gentlemen."

"Bridget, you're scaring me."

"Well, and I mean to. A girl can't be too careful, after all."

Katie sighed. "Guess I needn't worry about it. If my father doesn't send me away, he'll watch me like a hawk."

"I won't be arguing with you about that." Bridget darted a sympathetic look at her.

Just then, the rest of the women flocked into the room, and Katie took a deep breath. The show was over. There was no putting it off any longer.

She found her father removing the paint from his face.

"Katie, my girl." He sprang from the chair and planted a kiss on her cheek. "It's glad I am you came to see me. You're usually running off someplace before I can hardly say hello and good-bye."

"You're stretching the truth, Pa, and well you know it." Katie smiled, relieved to find him in a good mood. Maybe he wouldn't be so angry after all.

"Pa, there's something I need to tell you." She cleared her throat and swallowed.

"Well, and here I am. What is it?"

"Please don't be angry with me, because I'm very sorry."

He frowned and peered at her. "Have you been spending too much of me hardearned money now? Is that it?"

She shook her head vehemently. "I have my own money now." The very idea.

"That hasn't been stopping you from spending mine, too, now, has it?" He patted her on the arm. "But I don't mind a bit, my Katie girl. So don't be fretting."

Maybe she should let well enough alone. After all, there was no harm done. She gave her father a tremulous smile and turned to go. No, it would be much worse if he found out from someone else. She turned and faced him again. "I accepted a ride to the theater from a young man this afternoon."

"Ah yes. You'll be referring to Mr. Nelson. I thanked him nicely for rescuing my daughter from the streets of shantytown." He pursed his lips and scowled. "And how many times have I told you not to be walking around Conley's Patch by yourself?"

Katie gasped. He told her father? But how was that possible? "When did he tell you?"

"Right after he dropped you off at the door. He wanted me to know why you were in his carriage. A fine upstanding young lawyer, he is. And very concerned that I might get the wrong idea."

Gladness and relief rose up in Katie's heart. An attorney. Good. So he wasn't a criminal, after all. "And you don't mind that I accepted a ride from him?"

"Not after he explained that he was a patron of Harrigan's and recognized you from your performance." He glared at her again. "He was concerned you might be accosted. Otherwise, such a fine young gentleman would have never suggested such a thing."

ଔ

Sam whistled through the grin that wouldn't leave his face as he walked into the office. Michael O'Shannon was a good man and a grateful father.

It had been obvious Katie hadn't wanted to be seen in his carriage. When he saw her talking to a couple of performers outside the theater, he knew he had to avert scandal. And perhaps get on her father's good side at the same time. It had been a streak of genius that led him to reveal to Katie's father that he'd given her a lift. Instead of being angry at his daughter and thinking the worst of Sam, he had slapped Sam on the back and thanked him for taking care of Katie.

Now, if Sam could only be patient and let O'Shannon get to know him better, he thought he had a pretty good chance of winning the protective father over so he could court his daughter.

Charlie Jenkins looked up from his desk and gave him a nod. "Glad to see you in a good mood, sir. Your father wants to see you. He said as soon as you got here."

"Uh-oh. Is it bad?"

Charlie glanced around and lowered his voice. "I wouldn't want to say, Mr. Nelson, but I will say he didn't seem very happy."

"Well, nothing is going to spoil my mood." Sam headed to his father's office, wondering what he'd done. "Charlie said you wanted to see me."

The senior Mr. Nelson turned slowly and peered at Sam through narrowed eyes. "Jeremiah Howard, *your client*, waited for you for some time. Would you mind divulging where you've spent your afternoon?"

Sam looked at his father in surprise. "I don't remember an appointment with Howard."

"That's beside the point. If you'd been in the office, he could have spoken to

43

you instead of railing at me for two hours."

"I went to see Flannigan again. Something just isn't ringing true to me." He picked up a newspaper from his father's desk and riffled through it.

"So, did you get anything out of the man?"

Sam continued to scan the newspaper, wondering what to say. "Father, Chauncey Flannigan doesn't seem like a con man to me."

When his father didn't say anything, Sam looked up and met silence.

Eugene Nelson eyed his son. "Don't forget who our client is, Samuel."

"I won't. I promise."

"Very well. Send a messenger boy to Howard's office with an appointment for tomorrow."

"I will, sir."

Sam dispatched the messenger then sat at his desk, tapping his fingers against the oak desktop. His father was right. Whatever he personally thought about Howard, he was representing the man and needed to give him his best. He'd been meaning to visit the lumberyard and speak to some of the employees and decided that would be the first thing on his agenda in the morning. While he was there, he'd try to meet the foreman who'd been on duty that day.

Sam leaned back and considered what else could be accomplished while he was in the area. The two tavern witnesses who'd given statements needed to be spoken to. It wouldn't do for them to waver in their accounts of the fight.

Taking a legal pad from his desk drawer, Sam made a list of questions for the men he hoped to interview. He also intended to look over conditions at the lumber mill and make sure there was nothing to which an accusing finger could be pointed.

The shuffling of feet and opening and closing of file cabinets announced the office was getting ready to close for the day.

Cramming his pad into his briefcase, Sam stood and made his way to the front, amid friendly good-byes. The thought of seeing Katherine quickened his steps. He was relieved to see that Charlie had sent someone to the livery to bring his horse and carriage around.

As he rode home in the stifling heat, he glanced up, hoping for the sight of a rain cloud. It was the middle of September. But the driest September Sam could remember.

When he arrived at home, he found his mother in the kitchen supervising dinner preparations.

"Sam, dear. We're having guests for dinner. Could you possibly bring the ice cream freezer out? Everything is mixed and ready to go. You have time to crank out a batch before you change, if you wouldn't mind."

"Of course, Mother. Let me go hang up my suit coat." When he came back downstairs, he went to the storage room off the kitchen and took his mother's pride and joy out of its box.

She poured the mixture of cream, sugar, and vanilla into the container and added salt and cracked ice to the freezer.

Sam started cranking. "Who are the guests, Mother?"

"Oh, I think you'll be pleasantly surprised. The Langleys' niece, Martha, is visiting, and Ella wants her to meet young people her own age. I told her I was certain you would be happy to meet Martha and perhaps introduce her to some of your friends."

Sam grinned, amused at another of his mother's attempts to help him find her future daughter-in-law. She'd been hinting for some time that he should be settling down. She'd be quite surprised if she knew he had already chosen his future bride. "Yes, of course, Mother. I'd be happy to show her around, but I have plans for tonight."

She held both hands up to her pretty, plump face. "Oh dear. I should have checked with you first. But I'm sure they'll be leaving by nine. Would that upset your plans? I'll be so embarrassed if you can't be here."

When Sam saw his mother's hopeful expression, he knew he wouldn't be seeing Katherine O'Shannon tonight.

Chapter 8

Katie walked into the stifling room and held her breath, trying not to gag from the smell of cabbage and onions steaming from a pot on top of the small stove in the corner. The one-room, run-down shack contained two beds pushed up against opposite walls. A threadbare, faded quilt lay neatly folded at the end of each bed, and twin rickety chests stood side by side against the front wall. Four chairs, with sagging seats, hugged the uncovered table near the back door.

A colorful painting of an Irish meadow on the wall above the table, the only suggestion of color or beauty in the neat but drab room, caught Katie by surprise. As she followed Bridget and her mother, she noticed the dirt floor was swept clean and smooth. Mrs. Thornton opened the back door, and Katie sighed with relief as they walked out into the small backyard and she inhaled fresh air.

About a dozen women stood in clusters of twos and threes, seeming to ignore the nearby hodgepodge of chairs, stools, and wooden barrels.

A tiny woman, her blue eyes sparkling and black hair pulled back in a bun, turned from two others and hurried over to Mrs. Thornton. "How are ya farin', Margaret? I hope this heat won't be too much for ya."

"I'm feeling much better. Thank ya, Susan." The paleness of her lips and dark circles beneath her warm brown eyes belied the brave words, but her neighbor nodded and smiled.

"It's glad I am to be hearing it." She turned to Bridget and patted her on the shoulder. "And here you are working and helping your ma and the wee little one. A good thing."

"Mrs. Bailey," Bridget said, taking Katie's hand, "I'd like for you to meet my friend Katie O'Shannon."

The woman smiled. "It's pleased I am to meet you, Miss O'Shannon. And happy that you'd be caring about the poor people of Conley's Patch."

Katie blushed. "Please call me Katie, ma'am. And really, it's just an idea for child care that Bridget and I came up with."

"Well, anything to help put food in the mouths of the children is a good idea."

Mrs. Thornton shook her head, a worried look on her face. "I'm not sure everyone is agreein' with you."

"Well, and if they're not, they should be. Now you be sittin' down and resting yourselves."

Katie felt a glow of pride as she sat on a stool next to Bridget. Finally, someone

46

older was taking her seriously.

The other women gathered around and found seats then looked expectantly at Katie. Her hands sweaty and breath coming in gulps, she threw a frantic glance at Bridget. Maybe this wasn't such a good idea after all.

Bridget stood and smiled at her friends and neighbors. "I'd like ya all to meet my friend Katie O'Shannon. She's the one who helped me get my job at Harrigan's."

"And proud we are of you, Bridget, dear." The gray-haired woman smiled sweetly at Bridget.

"Sure and it's a shame on you, Granny Laurie, if you're proud of one of our own lasses a-workin' in a devil's den of iniquity." A woman, just entering the Bailey yard, flashed a hard look at Katie. "And you a-prancin' around here callin' yourself Irish and pretending you want to help us."

Katie gasped. Had she heard the woman right? Surely not. Most of the ladies were frowning at the woman who'd spoken, but she noticed two or three nodding in agreement.

Mrs. Bailey stood. "The shame is on you, Bridie McDermott, for insulting a kind young stranger in our midst, as well as our own Bridget Thornton."

Katie stood. "Maybe we should leave, Bridget," she whispered.

"No." Bridget grabbed Katie's arm and tugged her back to her seat. "We're not going to let that woman and her bitterness keep us from doing what we came to do."

Katie, surprised at Bridget's assertiveness, acquiesced.

"I hope you'll stay and listen to what these young girls have to say, Bridie," Mrs. Bailey continued. "But if you're only here to cause trouble, you can be leaving."

One of the women who'd seemed to agree with Bridie motioned her over to a chair next to her. With a venomous look at Katie, the angry woman walked over and sat down.

Somehow Katie managed to get through the meeting, letting Bridget do most of the talking. Bridie McDermott was right. Who was she to think she could help these women? Just because she saw a need and felt compassion didn't mean she could do anything about the problem.

Shame washed over her. She'd been proud to think they'd listen to her and thank her and tell her how wonderful she was. She saw that now. Humiliation pounded at her temples, and by the time the meeting ended and she and Bridget left, she had a full-blown headache.

"Katie, they loved the idea of the day care. Did you hear the excitement in their voices?"

Katie stared at her friend, who continued to chatter. "Are you sure?"

"Of course I'm sure. And where were you that you didn't see it, too?"

Throwing her friend a sheepish grin, Katie said, "I guess I was thinking about what a failure I was."

"Ah, Katie. But this isn't about you now, is it?" Bridget ducked her head. "I'm sorry. I need to be buttoning my lips."

"No. You're right. This isn't about me. It's about the people of Conley's Patch. Your people, Bridget. And if any credit is due, it's to you, not me."

"Not me, neither. The credit goes to God. Only God."

The girls climbed into Harrigan's carriage, and the driver clicked to the horse. As they rode in silence to Ma Casey's, Katie thought about her friend's words. So much like Grandmother's. She hadn't thought much about God since the day she boarded the train for Chicago. When she did think of Him, it was as though He were some unreachable, powerful Being, watching over His world from afar. Did God really intervene in the daily worries of ordinary people?

She didn't remember Him ever intervening in hers.

CB

Sam stood in the corridor outside Michael O'Shannon's dressing room, his heart thumping, waiting for a reaction from Michael O'Shannon. . .any reaction.

The man merely stood there, a grim expression on his face, peering at Sam. "So you're wanting to court my daughter, are ye?"

"Yes, sir. With your permission, of course." Sam waited again as Katie's father bit his bottom lip and looked up at the ceiling.

"Well," O'Shannon said, "it's like this, Nelson. I'm inclined to like you, and it's true I'm beholden to you for escorting my little girl away from the Patch. But before I'll be letting you court her, I'll be getting to know you better."

"I understand, sir." Inwardly, Sam groaned. How long would it take O'Shannon to think he knew him well enough?

"So, with that in mind, I'll be expecting you for dinner on Sunday." He motioned with his hand, and Sam followed him into the men's dressing room where he wrote on a small card. "Here's the address. We sit down to table at three on Sundays, and Ma Casey frowns on anyone being late."

Sam stuck the card in his inside jacket pocket and held out his hand to O'Shannon. "Thank you, sir. I won't be late."

He checked his pocket watch. Almost time for the evening performance, and he didn't want to miss Katie's solo. He dashed to his seat, unable to help the bounce in his step as he walked down the aisle. He'd half expected O'Shannon to give him a kick in the pants and throw him out of the theater.

Programs rustled all around as Katie walked, smiling, onto the stage. He fought the urge to stand to his feet and shush them all.

Sam caught his breath as she looked straight at him. He smiled, and she blushed and lowered her eyes. Pride arose in Sam as Katie began to sing. Her sweet ballad moved the audience to tears. His girl. His girl, Katie. Well, she would be, if he had a say in it. He'd move the ocean if he had to, because he was in love with the girl. There was no denying it, even to himself.

After the performance, he rushed backstage and tapped on the door. This time, Katie herself opened it. He complimented her on her performance, gave her a wink and a lingering glance, then tipped his hat and left. He didn't want to take a chance on angering her father. He hoped to have a long talk with her after dinner Sunday.

As his horse trudged toward home, Sam leaned back in the buggy and wiped his linen handkerchief across his brow. For so late at night, the temperature didn't seem to have cooled off much, if any at all.

The heat hit him as he walked into the house, although it seemed every window was open. He went into the parlor where his mother sat on the flowered cushions of a Chippendale settee, fanning herself.

"Hello, Mother." He leaned over to kiss her cheek.

"Oh, Sam. I can't believe this weather."

"I know. I'm sure you're uncomfortable." He sat in a wingbacked chair near her.

"Yes, I am." She held up the newspaper she'd been reading. "Did you know we've only had an inch and a half of rain since the Fourth of July?"

Sam nodded. "It's terribly dry."

"Yes. The autumn leaves won't be pretty at all this year."

"I know you'll be disappointed." She looked forward each year to the changing of summer into autumn.

"Yes, but at least we have our home." She breathed a soft sigh. "Thank the Lord for that."

"Harrumph." Sam looked up to see his father standing in the doorway.

"Hello, Father."

"Well, son, how was your evening?"

"Enjoyable. Thank you for asking."

"Hmm, out to dinner with friends, I suppose?"

"Actually, I went to the theater," Sam said briefly. He grinned as his mother perked up.

"Oh, how nice, dear. Did you take a young lady with you?"

"No, as a matter of fact, I went alone."

"Oh. Which theater?"

"Harrigan's." Sam held his breath, afraid of what was coming. He should have been more careful.

His father was the one who responded. "Hmm. Haven't you been going to Harrigan's a lot lately?"

"Well, I don't know if I'd say a lot."

"I believe they've been running the same show for several weeks, haven't they?" His father's knowing glance seemed to bore into Sam.

Sam fixed his gaze on a vase of flowers standing on the rosewood table in the corner. Anything to avoid his father's intense scrutiny.

"I believe so." Once more he avoided his father's stare.

His father turned his gaze on Sam's mother. "Amy, I'm going on the porch to smoke. Why don't you go up and change into something cooler. I'll be up shortly."

"Very well, Eugene." She arose and sauntered from the room.

"This blasted heat is getting to her. I'm not sure how much longer she can stand it."

Sam looked at his father in surprise. "Oh, but surely she'll be fine."

"Yes, yes. I'm sure you're right." He opened the front door and stepped out onto the porch, with Sam close behind.

They stood in silence for a moment, listening to the chorus of crickets and night birds.

"All right, Sam. Out with it. Why are you spending so much time at Harrigan's?"

Sam took a deep breath. How could he answer truthfully without revealing too much? He knew his parents wouldn't approve. After all, they didn't know Katie. They'd assume the worst. "I enjoy the Irish troupe, Father. And the show is hilarious. I've had so much on my mind lately with the Flannigan case that I needed a diversion."

The keen look his father shot at him said he didn't believe a word of it. "And this diversion. . .it wouldn't happen to wear skirts, would it, son?"

Sam could feel the heat in his face. He coughed. "Father, I've had a busy day. I'm going up to bed. Perhaps we can discuss this another time."

"But—"

"Good night, Father."

Sam went up to his room. He removed his coat and flung it across a chair. A tiny white card fell out onto the floor. Katie's address. Sam picked it up and scanned the contents.

Ma Casey's Boardinghouse. Sam peered at the address scratched below. It was near the downtown area. Katie didn't live at the Patch? Relief washed over him. But why in the world was she spending so much time in that dangerous shantytown?

Chapter 9

Katie sat beside Sam on the porch steps, with the door open for propriety. A haze blanketed the moonlight, and even the gaslight on the corner was almost useless, veiled as it was by the smoke that hung over the city. Her father had given tentative permission last week for Sam to court her. He'd even allowed them to go for walks without a chaperone but only in the daytime.

"A penny for your thoughts, Miss O'Shannon."

Katie knew it was respect that kept him from using her first name. But to be honest, she was getting a bit impatient with his continued use of "Miss." How awkward would it be to be kissed by someone who addressed her so formally? She blushed at the direction of her thoughts. The very idea. As if she'd allow him to kiss her.

Katie cleared her throat. "I was thinking about the terrible fires across the river." Well, she couldn't very well tell him what she'd really been thinking.

"Yes, terrible. I hope they get them under control before the wind changes."

Katie tensed, wishing she'd thought up a different lie. The possibility of the warehouses along the river catching fire was too frightening to talk about.

"Miss O'Shannon. . ."

"Oh, for heaven's sake, call me Katie." At his silence, she turned her head to look at him. When her eyes met his, her stomach sank. His usual smile and that crinkle in his eyes were gone. Had she offended him? Oh, when would she learn to button her lip? "I'm so sorry," she whispered. "I don't know what you must think of me."

The muscles in his face relaxed, and relief shot through Katie as he smiled. "I think you're perfectly wonderful. And if you're certain you won't think I'm being disrespectful, I'd be delighted to call you Katie."

"Of course I won't. After all, it is my name."

"Very well then, Katie it is. And it would be my pleasure if you'd call me Sam."

Katie had been calling him Sam in her mind since she'd heard his name, but of course he didn't know that. "All right. Sam." There. A little bubble rose up in her stomach. Almost like a giggle, only inside. She pressed her lips together and tried unsuccessfully to prevent the smile that tilted her lips. And then she said it again, "Sam."

He grinned, and the crinkle returned to his eyes. "Thank you."

The screen door opened behind them, and Katie's father stepped out on the porch. "Well now, daughter, it's about time you were coming inside. Morning comes early."

While Katie's father stood with lips pursed in a silent whistle, Sam said good night.

Katie watched him drive away then followed her father inside.

Bridget, who had spent the day at her mother's, sat in the parlor talking to Rosie. When she saw Katie, she stood. "I'm going to bed. Good night, everyone."

Katie stared after her friend. How strange. Bridget didn't even speak to her. Was she upset about something or perhaps coming down with a sickness?

Determined to get to the bottom of her friend's off behavior, Katie followed Bridget upstairs, catching her as she opened the door to her bedroom. "Bridget, wait."

The girl turned, a look of near panic on her face. Her attempt at a smile wouldn't have fooled a tot. "Yes, Katie?"

"What's wrong with you? You pushed right by me without so much as a glance."

"I'm sorry. I'm tired, and I guess I didn't see you."

"Of course you saw me," Katie retorted. "You can't pretend you didn't. Please tell me what's wrong. Have I somehow offended you?"

Bridget's face crumpled. "Won't ya come inside? There's something I need to be telling you."

Curious and a little uneasy, Katie stepped inside Bridget's tiny room.

"Here. You take the chair, and I'll sit on the end of the bed," Bridget said, still not looking at her.

Katie sat in the small cushioned rocking chair. "Now what is it?"

"I hate to be the one tellin' ya this. I know how much ya like the man, and I don't want to be losing your friendship."

"Bridget!" Katie stomped her foot against the hardwood floor. "Just get on with it. Nothing could break up our friendship."

Bridget continued to stare at her silently, and Katie began to fidget. Could it be that Bridget had feelings for Sam? Heat washed over her entire body.

"Has Mr. Nelson told you what his business is at Conley's Patch?"

Oh, a business matter. Relief welled up in her. "Well, no, the subject never came up. I suppose he has a client there. He's a lawyer, you know."

"A client?" A short, humorless laugh exploded from Bridget's mouth. "And who at the Patch do you think would have the money for a lawyer?"

"Perhaps he's doing volunteer work."

Bridget bit her lip and twisted her plain white handkerchief. "Have ya met my next-door neighbors, the Flannigans?"

"No, I don't think so."

"Chauncey Flannigan was severely injured while doing his job at a warehouse awhile back. He's been unable to work, plus he has doctor and hospital bills he can't afford to pay. His employer refused to give him any compensation at all, even denying that Chauncey was hurt there."

"Oh, I remember seeing Sam come from that house one day." Excitement raised Katie's voice. "So that explains it. Sam must be representing Mr. Flannigan without charge."

Bridget shook her head, and a vise seemed to clamp on to Katie's heart and squeeze. She wanted to put her hands over her ears. Shout at her friend to stop talking. Sam was a good man. She knew he was.

"I'm sorry, Katie. It's true Mr. Nelson is working on the case, but it's not Chauncey he's tryin' to help. He's working for Jeremiah Howard, the man who owns the warehouse."

Anger like fire shot through Katie. How could he? Here she was, trying to find a way to help the people at the Patch, and he was trying to push them down further. Didn't he believe in justice? He seemed so kind.

His arrogant look that day at the train station flashed through her mind. He hadn't been kind then. Of course, he'd apologized for his rudeness and explained the reason without trying to excuse his behavior. But perhaps that was because he was attracted to her. "I'm sure there must be a mistake, Bridget. I'll talk to him. But if he is indeed representing a cruel employer and refuses to listen to reason, I can assure you he won't be coming around here anymore."

☙

"Katie, you don't understand. The shanty Irish are a lazy bunch who'd rather lie, steal, and cheat than work." Sam had arrived a half hour ago, expecting a warm welcome from Katie. Her father had finally agreed to allow him to escort her to dinner unaccompanied. He'd been looking forward to it all day.

Her face had paled. "The Irish are lazy? And have you forgotten my father is Irish and I'm half Irish? Are you saying I'm lazy? That my pa is lazy? Why, he could outwork a soft-handed evil lawyer any time of the day."

Sam felt the blood leave his face. "No. Of course not. I didn't say all Irish are lazy. I'm talking about the shanty Irish."

"So you're only referring to folks like my best friend, Bridget." She blew a lock of golden hair from her eyes. Eyes that glared like a pair of torches.

"Katie, please be reasonable."

"Reasonable? And is it reasonable to peg a whole community of people as lazy thieves and liars? I'd like to know where you get your information, Sam Nelson. How dare you assume that all the men in Conley's Patch are lazy and shiftless. Aren't there shiftless, lazy men in your neighborhood? Well? Aren't there?"

Sam drew back. Oscar Willows who lived down the street from the Nelsons— as far as Sam knew, he'd never worked a day in his life. Lived off his mother's family inheritance and spent his days and nights gambling and drinking whiskey. But that had nothing to do with this. "I have witnesses who say Flannigan walked away from the warehouse on his own two feet with only minor injuries. I also have signed affidavits from two men who claim to have witnessed a tavern fight in which Flannigan was injured."

Katie placed her hands on her hips. "How very convenient for Jeremiah Howard. I wonder how much he's paying these so-called witnesses. Perhaps you'd better go find out, Mr. Nelson." Katie turned on her heel and walked inside, slamming the screen door behind her.

Sam slapped his hat against his leg and plopped it back on his head. With tight lips, he stalked off the porch and climbed into his buggy. Lost in his thoughts, he gave the horse its head and soon found himself near his own neighborhood. Not wishing to converse with anyone, he urged the horse around a corner, with a vague idea of finding someplace quiet to have dinner.

How could she be so unreasonable? She seemed to have tunnel vision where the people of the Patch were concerned. Why was she so certain?

Once more, doubt wormed its way into his thoughts. Should he consider again the possibility that his father was wrong about the shanty Irish, and Flannigan in particular? Katie had been so angry and so sure of herself. Doubtless she knew something about the people of Conley's Patch. Sam was now aware of the charitable work she did there, as well as her desire to help the people, especially the children.

Deep in thought, he rode past the downtown district toward the river and soon found himself near Flannigan's neighborhood. As he drove aimlessly through the Patch, raucous curses and bawdy laughter assailed him from the darkness. After just coming off Michigan Avenue with its gaslights and brightly lit stores, an uneasiness shot through him. Perhaps this hadn't been the wisest course of action. The only lights, dim and flickering, came from the taverns lining the main street of Conley's Patch. He slapped his reins, wishing he'd had the forethought of switching the buggy for his horse, Jude.

As he rounded a corner onto a pitch-black, narrow street, he heard scuffling and a sharp cry. Pulling his buggy to a halt, he peered into the darkness.

A pair of shadows hunched over a kneeling figure, pounding him with their fists. Sam jumped from the buggy and ran toward them. "Hey, you! What do you think you're doing?"

Before he could reach them, the two took off running toward the river.

The victim struggled to his feet and took the hand that Sam offered. "Thank ya."

"Are you injured?"

"Naw," the man panted, "just me pride, I guess."

"Were you robbed? Or did they just have a grudge against you?"

He stretched his back. "Oh, I was robbed, I was. Just comin' home with me pay. They took every cent. Took the bread from me children's mouths, they did."

"I have my buggy. I'll be glad to take you to find an officer of the law to report this."

A short laugh emitted from between the man's teeth. "Ain't no officers around here. Wouldn't be no use if there was. Me money's long gone now. Thanks for coming to my rescue. Name's Jack O'Hooley."

"Sam Nelson. I'm glad I was passing by." Sam reached into his coat pocket and pulled out some bills. "Here, buy some food for your family."

O'Hooley drew back with a scowl. "What do ye think I am? I ain't takin' no charity. A man takes care of his own." He turned and stalked off.

Sam stood staring at the money still in his hand. The fellow couldn't have much left, and he still refused the money.

O'Hooley stopped in front of a shack midway down the street and looked back. "I thank you again for your help and your good intentions. Don't worry none. We'll manage. We always do."

Stunned, Sam returned to his carriage. How could this happen to a peaceful family man walking home from work? It was almost as though the attackers had been waiting to accost their victim. Sam drove around the neighborhood, searching for a patrolman. He could at least report the incident.

Thirty minutes later, he pulled on the reins, bringing the carriage to a halt in front of a small café. Not one police officer in the whole neighborhood. Where in the world were they?

He tethered his horse and went inside. As he sat drinking a cup of coffee, he asked the man wiping the counter about the absence of patrolmen in the area.

With a laugh, the man continued wiping. "Are you nuts? They won't come down here at night. Can't say as I blame 'em. They're overworked and underpaid as it is. Why risk their lives in a place like this?"

Later, in the safety of his home, Sam couldn't fall asleep. Every time he shut his eyes, the face of the proud, hardworking O'Hooley, who'd been robbed of everything, hovered in his thoughts. That man was not shiftless or lazy. He was just a poorly paid, hardworking laborer. How many more like him lived in the Patch and other shantytowns throughout the city, barely surviving? Was Flannigan one of them?

Chapter 10

He hadn't been there when she sang her solo before the show. Why had she thought he would be?

The image in the mirror distorted, and Katie reached up and swiped her eyes. The tears seemed to come out of nowhere when she least expected them. She was getting altogether too much well-intended sympathy from the other members of the troupe, and she wasn't sure she could take any more of it just now.

The thing to do was pretend she didn't care a bit that Sam Nelson had turned out to be an intolerant, unfeeling cad. Only, she did care. Way too much. Worse than that, she wasn't sure he really was all those things. Maybe he was just ignorant and misled about the true conditions of the Patch. And she'd sent him away.

She jumped up before the tears could well up again. Her makeup would just have to do. Grabbing her maid costume from the rack, she lifted it high.

"Here, let me help you with that." Bridget took the costume and dropped it over Katie's head and shoulders. Katie felt a tug at her waist as her friend cinched the frilly white apron over the black dress.

Katie peered into the mirror and pinned the mobcap to her curls, the final touch to her maid ensemble.

She caught Bridget's frowning image in the mirror and turned.

"What's wrong? It's straight, isn't it?" Katie took a closer look in the mirror. The cap was perfect as far as she could tell.

"I'm sorry, Katie," Bridget choked out.

Katie's stomach tightened. "What? Is something wrong?"

"I wish I'd never told you about Mr. Nelson and Chauncey Flannigan. It's hurting you. And it's all my fault."

Katie began shaking her head even before her friend finished her sentence. "You've done nothing wrong. I needed to know."

"I'd give anything to take it back. I'd eat my words, I would."

"Bridget, you only told me the facts. And you were right to do so." Katie took her friend's hands and peered into her eyes. "Now stop worrying about it. I'm all right. Really, I am."

But was she? She left the dressing room and walked down the hall to the stage wing. At her cue, she took a deep breath and, smiling, walked on the stage. Would he be there? As though of their own accord, her eyes went once more to Sam's special seat. Empty. Disappointment washed over her. She swallowed deeply and focused on breathing normally. Of course he wasn't there. It was silly to think he might be. Determined to take control of her thoughts, she threw herself into the performance. If only she had more lines or more action during the performance. Anything to fill up the moments.

As soon as the show was over, Katie rushed through the wings and headed down the hallway.

"Hold on there a minute, Katie girl." She turned and forced a smile as her pa walked up to her. "You've been avoiding me all week, you have."

"Why, Father. Between here and the boardinghouse, we're together day and night." She threw him an innocent glance, hoping he'd buy it.

"Don't be blinkin' those eyes at me, Katherine Marie O'Shannon. You're knowing exactly what I mean. It's time we're having a bit of a talk."

Katie sighed. "All right, Pa."

"I thought we'd go for a walk after we get home tonight. How does that strike you?"

Katie nodded and headed for the dressing room. Going for a walk with her father didn't strike her that well, but she knew their little talk was inevitable, so she might as well get it over with.

At least it had cooled a little by the time Katie and her father set out from the boardinghouse.

"Ah, nothing like the night air to fill a man's lungs before bedtime."

Katie watched, startled as her father took a deep breath. "Pa, do you think that's—"

Her warning was interrupted by her father's fit of coughing. She pounded him on the back as he wheezed and coughed in an attempt to breathe.

Finally, the spasms lessened, and he sucked air in between gasps.

"Are you all right?"

He nodded and waved his arm in her direction.

She waited until he was breathing normally again.

"It could be this night air isn't quite so good for the lungs as it used to be." He laughed, and Katie joined in with relief.

"Let's sit on that bench for a few minutes, Father, till you get your breath back." She guided him toward the small wrought-iron bench that sat beneath the lamp at the corner.

"A good idea." He stretched and sighed as he leaned back on the bench.

They sat in silence for a moment. Katie waited, knowing he'd speak as soon as he collected his thoughts. The space between her shoulder blades tightened as she anticipated his scolding.

"Now then, daughter. It breaks my heart to see you moonin' over that young fellow."

"That's not what I'm—"

"Yes, it's mooning you've been doing. No doubt about it."

His tender smile warmed her heart, even while she dreaded this discussion. "I suppose."

"It's probably all for the best, you know."

Katie frowned. "I thought you liked Sam."

" 'Tis true, I did. Everyone knew I liked him. But lately something's been weighing on my mind." He paused and squinted up at the lighted gas lamp.

"I don't understand."

"Katie, dear, all the weeks he was coming to call, did Sam ever ask you to his home? Did he ever mention wanting you to meet his family?"

Pain, as from a knife, sliced through her heart. She'd thought of it. The possibility that Sam was trifling with her. Having some fun with the showgirl. But every time the ugly thought had pierced her heart, she'd pushed it away. She'd told herself there was a reason he hadn't asked her to his home. The time simply wasn't right yet. But deep inside, she'd felt fear. And now, her father had put her fear into words.

Unable to bear the thoughts bombarding her, Katie jumped up and ran toward home.

◌ৈ

As he drove through the streets of the Patch, Sam was struck again by the abject poverty. How could there be hope in such a dismal place? The encounter with O'Hooley had brought a drastic change in Sam's outlook. While still holding reservations about Flannigan's honesty, he nevertheless looked at Conley's Patch with new eyes.

A little girl stood near the filthy canal in front of the house next to Flannigan's. Two other children, one about her size and the other one bigger and a head taller, stood by her.

Sam pulled up in front of Flannigan's and watched as the two girls crowded the little redhead closer and closer to the edge. Sam jumped from his carriage and ran toward the children. But he was too late. He watched in horror as the little girl tottered on the edge of a board for a few seconds then fell with a splash into the sewer.

When the two children noticed Sam charging toward them, they took off down the street. Sam jumped into the filthy water and grabbed the sputtering child by the shoulders. Tossing her to safety, he pulled himself out, dripping with slime.

The little girl stared at him, unmoving. He looked around helplessly. Where was everyone? Didn't anyone see what happened? Stooping down beside her, he gave her a gentle smile. "Where do you live, sweetheart?"

Her eyes widened at the sound of his voice, and tears poured out over her grimy cheeks. She raised a small finger and pointed to the house next to Flannigan's. He gave her a puzzled look. She seemed to be glued to the spot. Would she scream if he picked her up?

"Is it all right if I carry you home?"

She stared silently for what seemed to Sam like forever then nodded her head and raised her little arms toward him. He lifted her and stood. As he walked toward the house, warmth ran from his arms straight into his heart. Who could have known it would feel like this to hold a child in his arms?

Before he could step up to the porch of the shanty, he felt a tug on his collar.

"Ma's over there." She pointed toward the house next door.

"Your mother is at the Flannigans'?"

She nodded, so Sam turned and walked across the hard earth and sprigs of weeds that passed as a yard. When he stepped onto the Flannigans' porch, he could hear voices through the closed door. At his loud knock, the voices stopped, and almost immediately, the door swung open.

Mrs. Flannigan stood and stared, glancing from Sam to the child, her eyes wide.

"Oh! What in the world? Margaret, you'd best come here." She stood back and motioned for Sam to enter.

"Betty!" The woman rushed forward to take the child from his arms. "What happened to her?"

"I'm afraid she fell into the sewer."

She examined the child from head to toe and then looked at Sam. When she spoke, her voice was a hushed whisper. "You jumped into that nasty muck to save her. How can I ever thank ya?"

"I'm sure anyone would do the same. And I don't think she was in any real danger."

"Betty, where are the Morgan girls? Beth was supposed to be a-watching you."

Sam watched in admiration as Betty ducked her head and closed her lips. She wasn't going to tattle. Sam, however, had no compunction at all. "If you mean the pigtailed tyrant who crowded her over the edge, she and another little girl ran off down the street when they saw me."

The woman's voice rose with anger. "You mean Beth pushed her?"

"Not exactly. But she might as well have. The little monster kept crowding her toward the edge until she fell in. I saw the whole thing."

The little girl's voice shook. "B–B–Beth said I had to walk the plank."

Sam's heart wrenched with sympathy, and he hoped the would-be pirate would get what she deserved.

"Mr. Nelson, thank you so much. I'm beholden to you. Now I need to get my child home and get her cleaned up."

How did she know his name? Then it hit him. "You're Mrs. Thornton, aren't you? Bridget's mother."

"That I am. Now I must be getting home."

"Sarah, dear, don't be leavin' Mr. Nelson to stand there in those filthy clothes." Sam looked in surprise at Chauncey Flannigan. He sounded almost friendly. "Get him some water to wash up, and he can borrow my Sunday suit."

"Thank you, Mr. Flannigan. I'm not going to argue with you about that. I'd hate to drive home in this mess. But your Sunday suit won't be necessary. Anything will be fine."

Fifteen minutes later, somewhat cleaner and wearing the Sunday suit in spite of his protests, Sam sat at the Flannigan table and shared a pot of tea and tried his first bowl of Irish stew.

"Mr. Nelson, we've been so caught up in little Betty's adventure that I haven't asked your reason for being in the neighborhood."

Sam hesitated. Why exactly was he here? He wasn't sure. He only knew that after his experience with O'Hooley, he had to hear Flannigan's account of the accident again. Because when he'd come before, he had already judged this man guilty. This time he came with an open mind. "Mr. Flannigan, you don't owe me a second chance, but I would like to hear your side of the story again. I can't say if I'll change my mind about this case or not, but I promise to listen this time without a preconceived idea of the truth."

"Ah well, I may have misjudged you, too. Anyone who would jump into the sewer to save a child can't be all bad."

Chapter 11

Runnin' late, are ye?" a toothless old man teased, setting off laughter among the folks around them, as Katie made her way past the crowd. The ragtag line of hungry-eyed people ran all the way around the corner and up the sidewalk to the door of the soup kitchen.

Katie grinned and continued to smile and joke with those she recognized as she worked her way forward. How some of these poverty-ridden people could find a laugh or a smile in the midst of their drab lives constantly amazed her.

She squeezed through the front door, hoping she hadn't thrown off everyone's schedule by being so late. Morning rehearsal had gone over by nearly a half hour, and she'd had to scurry to get here at all before the lunch rush was over. By the looks of the crowd, there was still plenty of time to help.

She pressed her way across the room and into the kitchen.

Mrs. Carter stood by the stove, spooning chili from the huge cauldron into a large serving pot. "Oh, thank goodness. Grab that container on the table, please, and take it out front."

Katie got the pot of soup out just as two more emptied. She slipped it into one of the empty places, ladled hot mixture into a bowl, and handed it to a young boy who stood licking his lips.

"Thankee, ma'am." The boy took the soup and moved to stand before Mrs. Gilrich, another volunteer, who handed him a hunk of bread.

A bent, white-haired woman stepped up to the counter. She accepted the dish with a shaking hand and started to walk away, passing up the bread as she balanced the bowl of soup in one hand and leaned on her cane with the other.

Katie's heart lurched. She hung the ladle onto the rim of the pot and stepped around the end of the counter. Grabbing a piece of bread, she hurried to the elderly lady. "May I please help you, ma'am?"

The woman relinquished the bowl and followed Katie to an empty place at a table in the center of the room. Katie placed the food on the table and smiled. "Promise you'll call to me if you need anything."

A twinkle appeared in the faded blue eyes. "Thank ya, lass. You're verra kind."

Shaking inside, Katie rushed back to the food line. *Dear God, how many of these old people are homeless and starving?*

By the time things slowed down and Katie glanced over to check on the woman, she had already left. Sadness washed over Katie. Did the poor old woman have a home? Or was she sleeping in an alley somewhere?

When Katie arrived back at the theater for the afternoon performance, she felt a familiar squeeze in her chest. Sam hadn't been to the show since she sent him away, but a day didn't pass without her wondering if he'd show up. Strange that her thoughts hadn't turned to him even once while she was helping at the soup kitchen.

Perhaps if she threw herself into her charitable work and her performances, she wouldn't spend so much time grieving. And why should she be distressed over a man whose only interest in her had been that of a trivial flirtation? She'd been naive and foolish to think he really cared for her. A twinge of uncertainty wiggled its way to the forefront of her thoughts, right along with a vision of Sam's deep brown eyes. Eyes that had glanced at her with what she thought was love.

That night, Katie played the part of Rose the maid with an intensity that drew curious glances from her friends. She didn't look at Sam's empty seat a single time.

She left the stage and headed down the hall. If she changed quickly and left the theater before the others, she wouldn't get trapped into a conversation with anyone.

"Hold on a minute, Katie." Mr. Harrigan touched her arm as she rushed past him. "I noticed you really got into your role just now." His smile was kind, so perhaps she wouldn't have to deal with anything but a few words of friendly camaraderie.

"Thank you, sir."

"It's okay to put yourself into the part, but try to keep it as close to the way it's written as possible." His eyes twinkled as he patted her shoulder and walked off.

Katie put her hands to her burning cheeks. Oh dear. If Mr. Harrigan noticed, everyone else surely did, too. They'd surely know the reason for overplaying her role.

She walked into the ladies' dressing room and found it full. So much for getting out ahead of everyone.

Giving up on her idea to avoid company, she walked back to Ma Casey's surrounded by friends. Friends who, to her relief, didn't mention her performance.

A few minutes before time to return to Harrigan's for the evening show, Katie and several other members of the troupe were relaxing in the parlor when a knock sounded on the front door. A moment later, Rosie Riley stood in the doorway. "Katie, it's Mr. Nelson. He's asking for you."

Feverish heat shot from Katie's head all the way down to her toes. She cast about for the right words. "Tell Mr. Nelson I've no wish to see him." Katie almost choked on the words. Did she really mean it?

Rosie threw her a worried look. "Are you sure?"

"Yes, I'm sure." Her whispered answer rang like a knell of death in Katie's ears.

Rosie turned and left the room, and Katie rushed to the window. So what if everyone was watching? She didn't care.

She peered through the lacy curtain and watched as Sam turned and walked away. Her stomach tightened. The dejected look on his face reflected the ache in her heart.

ᦂ

Sam nudged his horse, urging him toward the river. He'd spent most of the morning at Conley's Patch talking to Flannigan's friends and neighbors. Story after story of the man's kindness and helpfulness to others were repeated as Sam went from house to house. The main two qualities that emerged were that Chauncey Flannigan was as honest as the day was long and that he was a hardworking man who provided for his wife. Sam also learned that the Flannigans' only child, Patrick, had died on the boat coming over from Ireland four years ago.

The Chicago River wove its way through the city, cutting it in two. So far, most of the fires had broken out on the other side. This side of the river was a hodgepodge of warehouses, stores, and other businesses, with a line of small frame houses where children played. Farther down, in the other direction, lay the docks where riverboats loaded and unloaded both passengers and goods to be hauled downriver. But on this stretch, Howard's Warehouse and Lumberyard took up an entire block.

Sam hitched his horse in front of the lumberyard and made his way through stacks of wood and piles of sawdust. The sounds of dozens of saws rang throughout the huge open-air shed.

Two men, bending over a sawhorse, looked up as Sam approached then returned to their work. Sam cleared his throat, and they both looked up again. One middle-aged man with a beard that reached almost to his collarbone frowned. He spat and a wad of something landed by Sam's foot. "Can I do somethin' for you, mister?"

Sam took a step away from the disgusting glob and shot a look at the speaker. "Maybe. If you were a witness to Chauncey Flannigan's accident."

The man's companion sent a startled look in the direction of the main warehouse.

"Well, now," the bearded worker drawled, "it depends. Who wants to know?"

Sam wasn't sure how to answer, but he decided to be forthright. "I'm representing Mr. Howard, but my main concern is to find out the truth about what happened."

The other worker turned and walked over to another group of men, speaking to them in hushed tones.

The bearded man stared at Sam, working his jaw. He turned and spat. At least this time not in Sam's direction. "I don't reckon we saw anything." He turned his back and headed over to the huddle of men.

Sam stared after the old-timer. That didn't go very well. If the men knew anything, they weren't talking. If Sam was reading them right, they appeared more nervous than antagonistic.

Stacks of lumber, some reaching nearly to the ceiling, stood around the shed. He eyed them as he passed through on his way to the warehouse door. There didn't appear to be any sort of restraints on them, and although Sam had no prior experience as reference, the whole area seemed unsafe to him.

A wide gaping door with a gate hanging in the air above served as passage for smaller stacks of lumber being carted through from the lumber shed. Sam veered to the left and went through the smaller door and into the warehouse.

A man in a business suit looked up from a ledger he held in his hand. "Can I help you, sir? I'm Jonas Cooper, the manager."

Sam walked over and held out his hand, which the man took. "I'm Sam Nelson, the attorney representing Mr. Howard in the Flannigan case. I wonder if I could speak to the workers and get a clearer picture of the accident."

Lines appeared between the man's eyes as he frowned. "You say you're Howard's attorney?"

"That's right." Sam nodded.

The man stood. "Well then, I believe you have the testimony of the witnesses here and at the tavern where Flannigan got hurt in a brawl. That's all you need. Our men don't have time to talk. Anyway, no one saw anything except the ones you have on record." He rocked back on his heels and gave Sam a determined look. "I think you'd best go back to your fancy office and get to work on the case."

Sam gave the man a wry smile, thanked him for his time, and left through the door to the lumber shed. Mr. Howard's foreman bore a startling resemblance to his employer. In personality at least.

But Sam wasn't going to be put off that easily. Turning his steps toward the lumberyard, he squared his shoulders. He had a job to do, and he was determined to get to the bottom of this situation before he was forced to accept the sworn statements of men whom he increasingly suspected of lying for the establishment.

When he stepped into the lumber shed, he darted a look around, hoping one of the workers would change his mind and talk to him. But of one accord, they averted their gazes. Disappointed, Sam left, got into his carriage, and clicked to his horse.

He skirted the Patch, choosing instead to go in the direction of the docks and cross the Clark Street Bridge to get to his office. He'd had enough of Conley's Patch for today. He left his carriage at the livery and walked around to the Nelson building.

Charlie looked up and appeared relieved to see him. He handed Sam a stack of papers six inches thick. "Your father wants you to take care of these documents. They're in relation to a custody case he'd like for you to do some research on." Charlie grinned. "In your spare time, of course."

Sam took the papers and locked them in his file cabinet then headed for his father's office. The custody case could wait until later.

It was time he and his father had another talk. Something wasn't right at Howard's warehouse. And he had a hunch it involved Chauncey Flannigan's accident. Sam wouldn't make a decision without facts, but his intuition told him Howard and his witnesses were lying about the accident.

And after their talk, Sam intended to make another attempt to see Katie.

Chapter 12

Katie almost gasped when she came out onstage for her solo and saw Sam, first row, center seat, as though he hadn't missed a single show. She felt her heart pounding, and from the way his eyes brightened, he'd noticed the effect his presence had on her, too. The grin he tried to hide sent her pulse racing. And her number tonight was a love ballad. How in the world was she going to get through it?

The first note was a little shaky, but Katie managed to relax her throat and sing without choking. However, no matter how hard she tried, she couldn't keep her eyes from drifting his way before she left the stage. Warmth washed over her at the expression in his brown eyes. So convincing. If he wasn't in love with her, he should have been on the stage himself.

She hurried to change into the maid costume. Every time a noise sounded by the door, she started. She hurried into her costume and headed back to the stage wings, dragging Bridget with her. "Look and see if he's still there." The panic in her voice matched what she felt.

Bridget tiptoed out onstage and peeked through a crack in the curtain then drew back and walked softly across to Katie, who had twisted her handkerchief so tightly it left marks on her hands. "He's there all right. And starin' right at the stage as though he can see straight through the curtains."

Katie leaned toward Bridget, and the girl grabbed her shoulders to steady her. "Here now, don't you go a-faintin'."

"I won't." Katie took a deep breath and steadied herself. She knew if she messed up during the performance, Mr. Harrigan wouldn't trust her with a bigger part later. Not that she cared very much at the moment. She simply wanted to get through the show and back to the dressing room. Would he come? And if he did, should she see him?

Katie played her part, saying her one line without a mistake. But by the time the play was over, her curls were plastered to her forehead.

After the show, she hurried back to the dressing room, got into her street clothes, and removed her makeup, listening all the while for a knock at the door.

Thirty minutes later, everyone had cleared out except for Katie and Bridget, who refused to look her in the eye.

Katie stood. "Well, that's that."

"We could wait a little longer, if you're wantin' to."

"No, if he was coming, he'd have been here long ago. Let's go home." Katie trudged down the hallway, beside Bridget, to the performers' entrance. She pushed open the door and stopped in her tracks.

A tall form leaned against the building. Even in the darkness she recognized him.

Stepping through the door, she waited for Bridget to follow her. Her friend's sharp intake of breath revealed that she'd seen him, too.

He removed his top hat and stepped in front of the girls. "Miss O'Shannon, Miss Thornton."

"Good evening, Mr. Nelson," Bridget stammered and curtsied.

Katie remained silent, her eyes lowered. She was pretty sure she couldn't have spoken if her life depended on it.

"Miss Thornton, I had the honor of meeting your mother and sister yesterday."

"Oh, did me mum seem well to ya?" The eagerness in Bridget's voice revealed her concern at being away from her family.

"They both seemed quite well. I met them at the Flannigans' when I was visiting there."

Katie jerked her head up. "You went to see Mr. Flannigan again?"

"Yes. If you'll permit me to see the two of you home, I'd like to talk to you about it." He smiled. "As well as other things."

Katie bit her lip then lifted her eyes and looked into his. "I'm not sure that would be wise."

"I promise to leave without protest whenever you ask." His sincere gaze set her heart to pounding again.

"Oh, Katie, what can it hurt?" Bridget piped up. "I for one would rather ride than walk. My feet are killing me."

Katie threw Bridget a sideways glance. Her friend wasn't fooling her a bit. Grateful to her for making it easier to accept Sam's offer, she nodded.

"Very well, Mr. Nelson. I don't suppose there's any harm in accepting a ride." She blushed as he offered one arm to her and the other to Bridget.

The ride to Ma Casey's was a little uncomfortable as Sam had put both girls in front and she was squeezed close to his side. The very idea. He did that on purpose. She pressed her lips together as she felt a smile coming on.

They pulled up in front of the boardinghouse, and as soon as Sam had helped Bridget down, she yawned and said she was going to bed. Before Katie's shoes hit the pavement, the front door had closed behind her friend.

Katie and Sam sat on the wicker chairs on the porch, and she listened, mesmerized, as he related the incident with O'Hooley and then his talk with Flannigan. She could see that although he said he hadn't totally decided on his course of action, his heart knew the truth.

"I've spoken to my father about conditions in the Patch. I think he believes I'm exaggerating, but at least he's agreed to ride over with me tomorrow and take a look for himself. I don't know how much good he could do, but he does have some influence in the city."

"What about Mr. Flannigan? Are you still going to represent his employer?"

She held her breath as she waited.

"Father is adamant that he won't drop the case without proof that Howard and his witnesses are lying."

"Well, can't you take Mr. Flannigan's case yourself?"

He shook his head. "I can't go against my father. But I promise I'll do everything in my power to uncover the truth."

It wasn't until Katie was lying in her soft feather bed that she realized the matter of his not inviting her to meet his family was still unresolved. She flopped over onto her side. Next time she saw him, she'd ask him right out. She had to know if Sam was ashamed of her for being on the stage. Or even for being half Irish.

C∞

The carriage dipped and swayed over the dry, rutted streets of the Patch. Neither Sam nor his father had spoken since they'd entered the filthy shantytown. Stealing a glance at his father, Sam noticed his mouth was tight and the creases at the corners of his eyes were deeper than usual. Sure signs that he was disturbed.

They turned onto Flannigan's street. As they neared his house, Sam turned to his father. "The last time I was here, a little girl fell into that sewer." Sam paused then added for effect, "I jumped in after her."

"What?" The astonishment on his father's face spurred Sam on. "Yes, Flannigan gave me clean water to wash with and his Sunday suit to wear home. His wife gave me Irish stew."

"You ate with these people?" Sam thought he may have revealed too much. His father's face had reddened, and a vein protruded at his temple.

"Calm down, Father. Their home is spotless." As an afterthought, he added, "And the soup was very good."

"Do you realize you're not supposed to fraternize with the enemy?"

"The Flannigans are hardly the enemy, Father, and I was merely attempting to discover the truth. If you want the truth, I am sure Howard is lying. And so are his so-called witnesses."

"Sam, you do realize if you continue down this route, I'll have to remove you from this case." He glared. "Promise me you'll stay away from Flannigan."

"Father, you're an honest man. I can't believe you don't want me to search for the truth."

"I've told you before. If you can bring me proof Howard's lying, I'll send him packing. But as long as he remains our client, we're honor bound to do what we can to win this case for him."

"Very well, Father. I'll find you that proof."

"I've seen enough. Turn around and let's get back to the office. This place is a disgrace, no doubt about that. But I don't see what I can do about it. And we've both got work to do."

Sam complied, and they drove back to the Nelson building in silence. He knew his father wouldn't take him off the case. But he didn't like being at odds with him over anything.

He pulled up in front of the office to drop his father off before driving the carriage to the livery. As he watched his father step onto the sidewalk, he noticed for the first time the older man moved more slowly than before. He'd never thought of his father getting old.

Eugene stepped out onto the sidewalk, put his hand on the side of the carriage to steady himself, and peered up at Sam. "Put Davis on it. I'll give you two weeks."

Elated, Sam leaned over and grabbed his hand. "Thanks, Father. If I don't find anything by then, I promise I'll drop the subject and represent Howard to the best of my ability."

Eddy Davis had done work for the Nelson firm before. When they needed investigative work done behind the scenes, so to speak. Sam drove to a livery down near the Clark Street Bridge, left his horse and carriage, and then set out on foot to a small dive down by the docks.

Even on this sunny afternoon, Sam had to stop just inside the door of Gert's Club until his eyes could adjust to the dark. The smoky cabaret was almost half full even this early. Sam crossed the small dance floor and rounded the corner by the counter. A door in back led to a line of offices. He tapped on the door of the last one and entered a tiny, cluttered room.

Eddy Davis sat with his feet propped up on a mammoth desk. "Hey, Sam. Haven't seen you in years." He swung his feet off the desk and stood, reaching his arm out.

Sam shook his hand and grinned. "It's only been two months, Eddy."

"Oh yeah. That divorce case. Some old bird's young wife cheatin' on him." He slammed his hand on the desk. "So, what can I do for you?"

Sam picked a piece of paper and a pencil from Eddy's desk and wrote Howard's name. He slipped the paper across to Eddy.

In spite of the shady accommodations and Eddy's less-than-respectable appearance, Sam knew he was professional and thorough on the job. And one of the best-kept secrets in Chicago. You had to know someone who knew someone to obtain Eddy's services.

The man glanced at the name and whistled. Placing both hands on his desk, he leaned over and raised both eyebrows. "This ain't no cheatin' wife case."

Sam shook his head. "I need everything you can find on him. Past and present. And I need it fast."

Eddy whistled again. "This is heavy stuff, Sammy boy."

"You'll be well paid."

"Yeah. If I'm around to spend it."

Sam laughed. "You're kidding, of course."

Silence fell on the room. Heavy. Ominous. Could there really be danger?

A laugh exploded from Eddy's mouth. "Sure I am. Just kiddin'. I'll get right on this for you."

Relieved, Sam shook his head and grinned. He gave a sizable retainer to the detective and left, with a promise from Eddy to report to the office every day.

Eddy almost had him going this time. The man had a sick sense of humor. But a moment of doubt worked at Sam's mind. For just a moment, Eddy had sounded afraid. Impatient, he clamped down on his imagination. Eddy would be fine. He was the best detective in town.

Chapter 13

Katie pushed the needle into the satin fabric and pulled the thread through. She'd known this day would arrive sooner or later, but she'd hoped it would be a little bit later.

"Rosie, dear, it's grand to see you back. The show wasn't the same without you."

Rosie patted the puff across her face and laughed. "Don't be silly, Faye. I've been here every day, cheering you all on."

"Yes, but that's not the same, and ya know it."

Katie bit her lip to keep back the tears. She was happy that Rosie was fit and ready to take over her role as Sally. And this, of course, put Patsy back in the housemaid role. At least Katie wasn't complaining the way Patsy was. She wasn't about to make that kind of fool of herself.

Rosie stood. As she walked by Patsy, she smiled. "I thank you for filling in for me, Patsy. I've been watchin', and you did a wonderful job."

Katie lifted her eyes and glanced at Patsy. Surely the girl would be gracious.

"I don't know why I couldn't have continued with the part," Patsy snapped. "After all, as you admit, I did a good job."

A ball of anger clutched at Katie's stomach as she saw a pink flush wash over Rosie's face. Oh, how she'd love to grab a handful of Patsy's sleek black hair and yank it from her head. She looked at Rosie and was met with a smile and a shrug. Katie grinned.

"And you, Katie girl. . ." She placed a gentle hand on Katie's shoulder. "You're the talk of the town. Your singing is causing quite a stir."

"Really?"

"Yes indeed."

A flush of pleasure warmed Katie's face at the praise. "I love doing it."

"There'll be other acting roles for you, too. Don't you be worrying about that." With a smile and a pat on Katie's shoulder, Rosie took her leave. The room quickly emptied, leaving Bridget and Katie alone.

"You're not frettin', are you?" Bridget laid her sewing on her lap and peered at Katie.

"I'm fine." Katie smiled at her friend. "You don't need to be worrying over me about every little thing. Besides, this will give me more time for my work at the kitchen. And maybe I'll find other places to volunteer."

"Oh, Katie, I have some news for you. I forgot to tell you." The gladness in her eyes proclaimed her news was happy.

"What is it? Tell me."

"Benny O'Malley stopped by this morning with a note from me mum. They've formed a child care center of sorts. Mamie Todd is running it, with some of the young girls helping. She already has three little ones."

"Oh, that is good news! I wonder if there's anything we can do to help."

"No doubt about that. They'll be needin' blankets for pallets and kitchen stuff, too, I'm sure."

"Good, let's get right on that this afternoon. I'll ask Pa to help, too."

"You know somethin', Katie?"

"What?"

Bridget's lips puckered into a smile. "You have a lot more excitement in your eyes when you're talking about helping people than when you're talking about show business."

Surprised, Katie stared at her friend. Bubbles tickled her stomach as she wrapped her mind around her friend's words. It was true. She felt her eyes crinkle. "Bridget, I believe you're right. But that doesn't mean I'm giving up show business."

Bridget tossed her red curls and laughed. "I never expected ya would."

The girls went shopping as planned during the long afternoon break. Katie's father had been generous, so their arms were piled high with parcels when they climbed into a public carriage and headed to the Thornton home.

"Bridget!" The tiny version of Katie's friend ran pell-mell down the steps and flew into Bridget's arms, sending packages flying.

Laughing, Bridget swung her little sister around then set her down on the ground. "Now look what you've done, you little scamp. Start picking 'em up now."

A few minutes later, Katie and the two sisters dropped the parcels on Betty's little bed.

"Sister, I fell in the sewer, and a nice man jumped in and saved me." Betty was bubbling over with excitement.

"Ma, what's she talking about?"

Bridget's mother had come in from the other room, wiping her hands on a towel. She smiled at Katie and gave her elder daughter a hug. "I wasn't expectin' you until evening. You're still coming for the weekend, aren't you?"

"Of course, Ma. We brought some things over for the child care center. Now what's this about Betty fallin' in the sewer?"

Bridget's mother waved her hand and gave a loud, dramatic sigh. "It was quite a thing, let me tell you. Some other children crowded Betty over the edge of the ditch. Mr. Nelson jumped in and saved her. Carried her to the Flannigans' to find me." She shook her head. "He was a mess, he was."

Katie placed her hands on her cheeks, her eyes wide. "Do you mean to say Sam. . .I mean, Mr. Nelson. . .actually jumped into the sewer?"

"That he did. Plucked our Betty out of the slime and marched over to the Flannigans' with her in his arms." She smiled at her little girl. "He's a hero, he is."

Sam never said a word about it. Why hadn't he told her about saving Bridget's little sister? Had he thought it would sound as though he were tooting his own horn?

Warmth and a tenderness she hadn't felt before filled her heart. He truly was a good man. Even if he should decide to continue representing Howard, she would still know that he was a good man.

Katie watched as Bridget tore open the packages and presented the goods to her mother, who watched with astonished eyes.

"Oh, you darling girls! I can't tell you what this means."

"Mrs. Thornton, if Mrs. Todd and the other ladies won't be offended, I think there are others who would be happy to sponsor this endeavor until you get things going."

"I don't think anyone would be offended. I know I wouldn't. This is to help our people. And I know you won't approach anyone who would try to bring shame on us."

Katie and Bridget got back to the theater just in time for Katie to run through her new song before the performance. When she walked out onto the stage, her eyes found Sam. He winked, and her heart fluttered. Then she began to sing.

ᴄ𝘴

Sam slammed into his father's office and threw the folded newspaper on the massive oak desk. "They killed him."

"What? Who killed whom?" He picked up the paper and scanned it. "I don't see—"

"There. Right by that advertisement. It's Eddy."

"Davis?" He peered at the small print and read aloud: " 'A body found beneath the Clark Street docks on Tuesday night proved to be that of Edward Davis, a private detective. The absence of money or other valuables lead authorities to assume Mr. Davis was the victim of robbery.' "

"It wasn't robbery, Father. You know it wasn't. He got too close to something illegal. It was Howard."

"You're making assumptions, Sam."

"Maybe. I don't think so. Eddy implied the case was dangerous. Then he laughed and pretended to be joking. I should have known he was serious. Looking back, I can see it. But all I could think of was finding something on Howard." Sam tightened his lips and took a deep breath. "If it's murder, I'm going to find out."

"Don't do anything foolish. There's no proof Howard had anything to do with the death. It could have been a simple robbery as the police believe." He sighed. "And if it was murder, you could find yourself in danger. Leave it alone, Sam. Please."

Sam threw a short nod his father's way and left the office. He stopped briefly at his own desk to look over some files and then started toward the door.

"Sam, wait a minute." Jack was just leaving his office. "Where've you been keeping yourself? You're in and out of the office all day, and I haven't been able to catch you in weeks."

"Sorry. I've been really busy. How've you been?"

"Fine, fine." He lowered his voice. "I guess you're still seeing that girl."

"Shh. I haven't told my parents yet."

"What do you mean, yet? Why would you want to tell them and upset them? Unless. . ." He shot a worried look at Sam. "You're not serious about her, are you?"

"Jack, I'd love to stand and talk, but I have things to do. I'll see you later." Sam grinned to soften his words and left the building.

Driving toward the docks, he tried to set a plan of action. He had no idea how to start his investigation. "God, I could use some direction here."

The dock was teeming with activity as workers loaded and unloaded the boats that carried goods up the river and back. Sam tried to question a number of men who were willing to stop and listen to him. But if anyone knew anything about Eddy, he wasn't talking.

Discouraged, Sam walked to Howard's lumberyard and warehouse where he got the same response as before. He spotted the two men he'd spoken with in the shed the last time and walked over to them. "I don't suppose you men have thought of anything since the last time I was here."

The bearded one spat his glob of tobacco out of the side of his mouth. "Listen, fellow. If I were you, I'd get out of here and not come back. There's nothing for you here but trouble."

Realizing he wasn't getting anywhere, Sam turned to leave. He spotted two men by the warehouse gate, whispering. One pointed in his direction. Sam started toward them, but they turned away. Anger like a hot poker stabbed him as he left. They knew something. Some of them did, anyway.

He'd left his carriage in a livery across the bridge, so he headed there. The sound of footsteps caught his attention, and he turned to see a figure dart behind a building. Suspicious, he ambled on down the street, listening intently. This time, when he turned, he saw the man plainly. With long strides, he got to the man before he could duck behind another building. "Okay, why are you tailing me?" He grabbed the man's arm and frowned into his eyes.

"Hey, wait a minute. I'm not meanin' you no harm. I got a message for you." He jerked his arm away.

Sam gave a short laugh. "If you have a message for me, why were you sneaking around? Why not just give me the message?"

"'Cuz I don't know ya. That's why. Didn't want no fist in my face."

"Okay, okay. What's the message?"

The man looked around then leaned in closer to Sam. Lowering his voice, he said, "There's some of us what wants to help you. But we gotta be careful, ya see?"

Excitement shot through Sam like a bolt of lightning. "Yes, I understand."

"Okay then. Here's the deal. There's an old shed in back of Wiley's Feed and

Grain in the Patch. Be there at midnight. And make sure you're by yourself."

Before Sam could answer, the man turned and slipped around the corner. Should he follow him? Sam hurried to the corner and looked down the street, but there was no sign of the messenger.

Deep in thought, eager with a hint of dread running through him, Sam walked to the bridge and crossed over to the livery stable. Was he finally close to an answer to the Flannigan question? Would he discover something tonight about Howard's shady dealings, perhaps even something that would lead to the truth about Eddy's death?

Avoiding the office, he urged the horse toward home. He needed to calm down before facing his father's scrutiny. It wouldn't do for him to find out what Sam planned to do. He'd say it was foolhardy and probably forbid Sam to go. Right now, the one he needed to talk to was his mother. He couldn't tell her what he planned to do tonight, but he could ask her to pray with him.

Suddenly a vision of Katie's face filled his thoughts. Yes, it was time to tell Mother about Katie, too. She'd understand and perhaps help prepare the way for Sam to tell his father.

But not yet. First, Sam needed to get this other situation taken care of. To-night, at midnight, he'd be waiting at a shed in Conley's Patch.

Chapter 14

S o you see, they need to get the child-care center going so the women can work. They need more space. Even one extra room would help. The men can do the building. Once they get all the supplies they need, they can take care of it themselves."

"I think it's a wonderful idea." Rosie's eyes shone. "I get so tired of hearing about how lazy and worthless the immigrants in the Patch are. You can count me in. I'll do what I can."

Katie glanced at Bridget and smiled at the murmurs of agreement coming from the lips of the actresses and seamstresses. Rosie's enthusiasm had stirred up their interest.

By the time the curtain went up for the evening performance, most of the troupe from actors to stage crew had pledged to help with food and supplies to get the child-care center on its feet.

With a light heart, Katie stepped out onto the stage. She glanced toward Sam's seat, expecting to see him smiling up at her. Empty. *Don't be silly. He's a busy man. Something must have come up.*

After the show, she said good-bye to Bridget, who was going home for the weekend. She watched the Harrigan's carriage pull away with Bridget inside. The weekends were long without her friend, even though Katie had her solos the next day.

She walked to the corner where her father waited for her. He held out his arm for her, and they walked down the plank street toward Ma Casey's.

The moonlight was bright tonight. There had been no fires this past week, and gradually the haze was lifting. Hope filled Katie's heart as it did the rest of the city. Perhaps the devastation was over for now. She asked her pa as much.

Scratching at his chin, he gave a shrug. "Well, it's still mighty dry. Just as dry as before. The little bit of sprinkling we had last Sunday isn't going to help much."

Katie sighed.

"But it's the third week in September. The rains are sure to come soon." He nodded. "Yes, no doubt about it. It always rains in September."

They walked in silence for a few minutes. Katie hoped her father was right. But the constant fires were frightening. How much longer before lives were lost?

Her father cleared his throat, a sure sign he had something to say that he knew she wouldn't like.

Katie's stomach tensed. Something about Sam, most likely.

"Daughter, I've got something I'm wanting to say." He continued to walk, looking straight ahead. "I know you like the lad. And I can't say I don't. It's a good thing you got over the arguing, but I still have the same concern as before." He took a deep breath and let it out loudly. "If he's serious about you, he'll be taking you home to meet his folks. If he doesn't do that soon, then he's just playing around with a pretty Irish lass."

Katie hated to consider the thought, but Pa was right.

"I know what you're saying, Da." A little choking breath emanated from her throat. "And you're right. I've already been thinking about it. And the matter will be settled soon, or I'll not be seeing him. I promise."

He patted her hand, and they stopped in front of Ma Casey's. Reaching over, he pushed back her curls and kissed her forehead. "That's the first time you've called me 'Da' since you were just a wee girl. It did my heart good."

"I love you, Da." She leaned into his big, comforting chest.

"And I love you, Katie girl. I'm praying your young man turns out to be true."

They walked up onto the porch and into the house.

ᚶ

Sam clicked at his horse and sat up straight in the saddle. It wouldn't do to be too relaxed as he rode down the pitch-black streets of the Patch.

He'd looked all along the main business district of the Patch but still hadn't found Wiley's Feed and Grain. It had to be on one of the side streets. He urged his horse around another corner and squinted his eyes to adjust to the difference in the blackness.

A curse sounded from down the street, followed by a scream and then a shout of bawdy laughter. As he drew near, his stomach churned. Apparently, the Patch's version of a prostitution district. Sam flipped the reins, the horse trotted to the next intersection, and they rounded the corner.

He pulled out his pocket watch and peered at the face but was unable to see the hands or the numbers. Spying a tavern at the end of the street, he spurred his horse into a gallop and pulled to a stop in front of the run-down shack. The hitching post was full, with three sorry-looking nags, so Sam tied his mount to a tree branch and went inside.

After the thick darkness of the outside, the tavern's dim interior was enough illumination to see fairly well. Sam made his way through a mass of whiskey-reeking men and, to Sam's dismay, a number of women as well. He stepped up to the scratched counter and started to pull his watch out then thought better of it.

"Name your poison." The man sported a patch over his left eye and squinted the other at Sam.

"I'd like to purchase a block of matches, please." Sam tossed a coin on the counter.

Without a word, the man turned and grabbed the block and laid it in front of Sam.

"Anything else?"

"I wonder if you could tell me where Wiley's Feed and Grain is."

The man pointed his thumb behind his head. "About three blocks back that way to Quincy then turn west. But they ain't open this time of night."

"Thank you." Sam elbowed his way through the crowd, having to steady more than one staggering patron before he got to the door.

Relieved to be out of the place, Sam loosened his horse's reins and mounted. He rode down another block and then stopped. Pulling one of the matches from the block, he used his thumbnail to strike it, holding his head back from the sulphurous fumes. The match head sputtered and flamed up with plenty of light to see his watch. Eleven thirty. Still enough time.

He rode down the street, turning at the corner, and headed in the direction the tavern keeper had indicated. His heart pounded in his chest as he rode the three blocks then turned onto Quincy.

Wiley's, which looked like a ramshackle barn, stood dark and forbidding, one of three buildings on the block. The other two appeared just as deserted.

Sam hesitated then urged his horse around the side of the feed store. About six feet behind the building, a small shed leaned to one side, its door hanging open.

Sam hesitated again. He could be walking into a trap. Something snapped, and he caught his breath. Careful, so his saddle wouldn't squeak, he looked around. Nothing was in sight. Maybe an animal.

He dismounted and stepped forward, leading his horse until he reached a clump of bushes where he tied the reins firmly. With nerves taut and senses heightened, Sam crept toward the shed. The rigid muscles in his throat ached, and he relaxed them, scoffing silently at his fear.

He kicked open the door and paused, ready to jump back at the slightest threat. His chest pounding, he stepped inside.

The first blow glanced off his shoulder, but before he could turn, a fist hit his head sending pain through his skull. A blow to his stomach sent him to his knees. But they kept coming. His strength ebbed. His heart raced then slowed. Dizziness threatened to rob his consciousness. Then he fell forward, his face hitting the rough slab floor. Unable to move, he awaited the next blow and cried out when a foot to his side sent spasms through his ribs and back.

"Okay, that's enough!" A rough voice yelled, but not soon enough to stop one last blow from landing on his head.

"I said that's enough! We're not supposed to kill the guy. Remember?" Sam looked in the direction of the voice, but his eyes refused to open. He heard a grunt then the sound of something hitting the wall. Someone cursed. At least he wasn't the one who'd been thrown.

"Ouch. What'd you do that far? I wuz just havin' some fun."

"We ain't here to have fun. Come on."

Sam heard the door being flung open. Good. Maybe they were leaving.

He tried to push himself up, but his arm refused to move. He lay still as the voices of the two men grew fainter. . . .

He woke to an iron fist crushing his body. Pain shot through his head and behind his eyes from a constant jolting. He gasped. His eyes could only open a crack, but that was enough to see he lay in a wagon bed.

The wagon stopped. He lay still, afraid even to breathe. Hands grabbed him, one on his shoulder, the other by his belt, and heaved. Air gushed from between his burning lips as he hit the iron-hard ground. Then darkness came once more.

෴

"Mr. Nelson. Wake up."

Gentle fingers patted Sam's hands and then his face.

He groaned and tried to open his eyes. Through slits of light, he made out a man's shape.

"Sarah, hold the light closer."

Sam willed his eyes to open wider. Flannigan.

"Mr. Nelson, it's Chauncey Flannigan. We found you unconscious in front of the house. Do you know who did this to you?"

He groaned again, but words refused to pass through his dry, cracked lips.

"Never mind. We've sent word to your father. He should be here soon. Try to stay awake."

Sam drifted in and out of consciousness. Senseless words floated around him. Sometimes the straw mattress rustled beneath him. Other times someone gently lifted his head and poured cold water between his throbbing lips then laid his head down again.

"I need to let Katie know."

Sam started. He knew that voice. Even whispered. Bridget?

"You'll do nothing of the kind, young lady. There's not a thing she could do tonight. In the morning will be soon enough to be taking word to her." The voice, although quiet, was firm.

"Sam. Sam, wake up."

Sam opened his eyes.

His father towered over him. "I've brought Dr. Tyler."

Firm hands probed and prodded until Sam yearned for darkness to take him once more.

"A concussion's almost certain. Four broken ribs. Left ankle may be broken." The man paused. "If this gash had been a half inch to the left, he'd have lost his sight in that eye."

Relief washed through Sam. Dr. Tyler had treated him all his life. He was in good hands. With that thought, he closed his eyes, and the next thing he knew, someone had lifted him. Fear washed over him. "What?"

"It's all right, Sam. Mr. Flannigan is taking you to the coach. We're going home."

"But Katie. . ."

"Katie? Who is Katie?"

"Never mind."

The jostling ride home was agony as bolt after bolt of pain stabbed through Sam's body, and he yearned even for Flannigan's straw mattress.

Finally they stopped. Sam winced as Fred, the coachman, lifted him. Every inch of his body screamed as he was carried inside.

"Oh, Sam." The distressed voice of his mother cut through the pain. "Be careful, Fred. Eugene, are you sure he should be carried up the stairs? I could have a bed made up in the back sitting room."

"Amy, he'll be fine. Stop fidgeting, and let us get him to bed."

Sam's back touched his mattress, and he sank into the downy softness. He sighed. Nothing compared to a body's own bed.

"Come in, Nancy. Put the basin on the table. I'll take care of him." His mother's gentle fingers touched his forehead, smoothing back his hair. The *swish* of the maid's skirt filled the air before the door clicked shut.

Sam's eyes closed, and he surrendered to the comforting warmth of the wet cloth on his face.

"Was he able to tell you who did this?" his mother whispered. She must think him asleep.

"No." His father sounded grim. "But I have a pretty good idea who is behind it. And if I'm right. . ."

Sam struggled to push through the fog. He had to get out of bed and stop his father from going after Howard.

Chapter 15

Katie buried her head in her fluffy pillow to try to drown out the pounding. There, that was better. Oh no. There it was again. Arrgghh. What was that awful banging?

"Katie, wake up."

Bridget? What on earth?

"Katie!" Bridget's insistent voice was followed by more loud knocking.

Katie grabbed a wrapper and stumbled over to the door. She yanked it open, and Bridget tumbled in, almost losing her balance.

The girl gasped and fell onto the bed where she sat breathing hard. "Mr. Nelson's been hurt."

"What?" Katie blinked and tried to make sense of Bridget's words through her sleep-induced fog. "What did you say?"

Bridget took a deep breath and grabbed Katie's hand. "Mr. Nelson was attacked last night. Someone beat him up real bad and dumped him in front of Mr. Flannigan's house."

"Oh. . ." Fear shot through Katie. "He isn't. . ."

"Oh no. No." Bridget shook her head. "He's alive, and the doctor says he'll be all right."

"Where is he?" Katie grabbed her dress from the closet and threw her robe across the bed. "I must go to him."

"His father took him home." Awe crossed Bridget's face. "You should have seen it, Katie. Old Mr. Nelson drove into the Patch in this big black coach. Just like a fairy tale. Then he came marchin' in like a king, bringin' this fancy doctor with him."

"Oh." Despair crashed over her at this giant wall that rose before her. A wall that separated her from Sam. She dropped down onto the bed, the dress on her lap. "I can't go to his house."

"Why not?"

"Because I've not met his folks yet. That's why not." She bit her lip and blinked at the tears that welled in her eyes. "I don't know if they're even aware of my existence."

"Oh, Katie," Bridget murmured. "I'm so sorry. I forgot."

"Oh well." Katie forced a smile. "I'm sure he'll get word to me. . .somehow."

"Of course he will," Bridget said, patting Katie on the shoulder.

Rosie stuck her head in the door and gave Katie a scrutinizing look. "Are you all right?"

"Sure I am. I'm just fine." But the forced smile on her face wouldn't have fooled anyone.

"Ma sent me up to get you girls. Breakfast is on the table." She wheeled and headed for the stairs, the bottom of her skirt twirling around her ankles.

Katie stood. "Why don't you go on down and get your breakfast while it's hot? I'll be down as soon as I'm dressed."

"Oh, I have to get back to Ma's. I promised to go to church with her." She darted a glance at Katie. "Wouldn't you like to go with us?"

Katie sighed. Bridget knew she liked to rest on Sundays. "Not this time."

"All right." Her voice was soft with disappointment. "I'll be seeing you tonight then."

Katie watched her friend leave and sank back onto the bed. Nausea rose in her stomach at the thought of food.

The day dragged by as Katie dawdled around the parlor and out on the porch and waited for word about Sam. Perhaps Bridget would have news for her tonight. Although, she wasn't sure just how she thought Bridget would hear anything.

"Daughter."

As her father stepped out onto the porch, Katie looked up from the embroidery she'd been stabbing at aimlessly.

"You haven't eaten a bite all day." His forehead wrinkled with worry.

"I had some soup awhile ago, Pa. Remember?"

"Well now, I do recall you twirlin' a spoon around in your bowl. But I don't remember you putting anything in your mouth."

Katie swallowed past the knot in her throat. "I'm sorry."

He sat beside her on the wicker sofa and put his arm around her shoulders. "Now, now. And it's sorry I am to be fretting you. I know you're worried about young Sam."

Katie laid her head on her father's sturdy shoulder and let the tears flow. "If only I knew he was all right."

ᛢ

The aroma of coffee and ham drifted to Sam's nostrils. He stirred and opened his eyes. He moaned and raised his hand to shield them from the bright light streaming into the room, stabbing at his eyes like a thousand knives.

"Sorry, son. Let me close the curtains." His father stood up from the wingbacked chair pulled up next to Sam's bed. Stepping to the window, he yanked the heavy curtains shut, blocking out the light.

"Thanks." The pain was milder now. Bearable. Sam took a deep breath. At least he could open his eyes a little more than a slit this morning.

"Well, you're a sight, son."

"I'll bet." He tried to grin, but his cracked lips protested. He ran his tongue over them and immediately regretted it as fire blazed across them.

"Could I have some water, please?"

His father held a glass to his lips, and he gulped the cool liquid.

"Here, your mother brought some salve for your lips."

He held out a flat jar, and Sam dipped a finger in the aromatic gel and rubbed it onto his sore lips. Ah. The soothing balm felt cool and soft.

His father replaced the lid and put the jar on the table.

Sam felt around his face, his hand touching several bandages. "Maybe I'd better see a mirror."

"Hmm. Let me save you the trouble." His father eyed him and shook his head. "Both eyes are black. You have a gash running from your mouth to the bottom of your chin and another from the left side of your forehead almost to your right eye. That was a close one. You also have numerous visible bruises, as well as many that aren't."

"Thanks. I appreciate your candor."

His father's hearty laugh landed like a sledgehammer against Sam's temples.

"Sorry, I forgot you have a headache. Probably will for a while."

"Probably. Father, you haven't tried to see Howard, have you?" Sam held his breath while he waited for his father's answer.

"I'm smarter than that, son." He sat on the edge of Sam's bed and nodded. "Much smarter. But it seems fairly obvious to me he was involved in this and maybe with Eddy's death. But knowing it and proving it are two different things. I have some people on it. In the meantime, I plan to have a talk with Howard. In my office."

"Be careful, Father. I don't know what sort of racket he has going, but if he'll kill for it and take a chance on having me ambushed when he surely should have known we'd suspect him, well, he's not playing games."

"And neither am I." The steel that Sam saw in his father's eyes confirmed the statement. "But I'm not sure he knows we're on to him or that Eddy was working for us. I think he just decided Eddy was getting too close. And the same about you. And now, that's enough unpleasantness for now." He slapped his hand on the bed. "What can I do for you while you're recovering? You must have unfinished business at the office I can help you with."

Sam looked thoughtfully at his father. Was this the right time? Well, if not, it would have to be. Bridget was sure to have told Katie about the attack. She'd be worried sick. He had to let her know that he was alive and doing well.

"Actually, I'm caught up at the office. But I do need to speak to you about something."

"Anything. What do you need?"

Sam's head pounded, and his neck hurt. He forced himself to relax. How hard could this be? His father was a reasonable man.

"I've fallen in love with someone." He paused, weighing what his next words should be.

His father's mouth flew open, and he beamed. "Why, that's wonderful, son. Your mother will be ecstatic. She's wanted a daughter for years."

Sam smiled. "Yes, I know. I hope she'll be happy. I hope you both will."

"And why wouldn't we be? Who is this young woman you've been keeping from—" He stopped, and a wary look crossed his face. "Who is the young lady? Please don't tell me it's that actress at Harrigan's."

Sam stiffened. "If by 'that actress' you're referring to Miss Katherine O'Shannon, then yes, Father."

The bed rocked as Sam's father jumped up, his face red and twisted. "No. I won't see you ruin your life and career for a shanty Irish showgirl."

Sam clenched his teeth, ignoring the pain. He knew if he spoke now he'd say something he'd regret. He watched as his father paced the floor, ranting about showgirls in general and Irish ones in particular. He'd calm down in a minute.

Finally, the older man flung himself into the wingbacked chair and mopped his face with a handkerchief. "Sam," he said, his voice quieter than before, "surely you aren't thinking clearly."

Picking up the glass from the bedside table, Sam took a long drink. "Father, contrary to what you think, Katie isn't from shantytown, but even if she were, it wouldn't change anything. She's a wonderful girl. Kind, gentle, and a lady in both manner and action."

"Yes, yes, I'm sure she is. I'm sorry if I was hasty. I know you wouldn't fall in love with someone trashy. But there is also a question of social station. And whether we like it or not, that does matter."

"Not to me it doesn't. If our friends and acquaintances don't respect my choice for a wife, they aren't my friends."

"You say that now. But you may have cause to change your mind later."

"Won't you at least meet her?" A last ditch appeal, but maybe, just maybe, he'd agree.

"Not a good idea. It would only encourage her. That's not really fair to the girl."

He'd hoped his father would understand. But of course, it wouldn't be that easy.

"I won't give her up, Father. As much as it will hurt me to go against your wishes, I intend to marry Katie O'Shannon." He watched, with a tight chest, as his father stood and stalked from the room, letting the door slam.

Now what? He tried to sit up, but the pain in his ribs and head took his breath away. He had to find a way to send word to Katie.

Struggling, he stretched his arm toward the bell cord hanging by the bed. Agony pierced his entire body, but he finally grabbed it and pulled.

Within a minute, the door opened and Nancy stood there. She curtsied. "Yes, sir? What can I do for you?"

"Nancy, would you write a letter for me and have it delivered?"

"Of course, sir."

"You'll find writing material in the top drawer of my desk." He gasped as pain stabbed his ankle. How many more injuries did he have?

Nancy wrote as he dictated, and then with a promise to send the letter by one of the house servants right away, she left.

He leaned back on the bed and tried to sleep, but thoughts of Katie ran through his mind. Her soft curls, her wide blue eyes, the dimple on her cheek that dipped when she smiled. He didn't want to be estranged from the parents he loved. He had to somehow make them understand.

An hour passed. She should have his letter by now. He pictured her opening it. Saw the relief on her sweet face as she read that he was safe.

Sam sank back against the pillows and surrendered to sleep.

⁓

The clock in the parlor seemed to tick louder and louder.

Katie listened, her dry eyes wide, staring at nothing. The others, including Bridget, had gone to bed an hour ago. She should, too. It was foolish of her to stay awake so late. After all, she had to go to the theater tomorrow morning. And anyway, of course he wouldn't send word this late. It was after midnight.

Chapter 16

Sam tossed the newspaper on the floor and leaned his head back against the high back of the chair. A slight breeze drifted through the open window, cooling his damp face. He closed his eyes and drifted.

A crow cawed loudly, bringing him back from a near doze. He twisted, trying to find a comfortable position. His pain had diminished, although his ribs were still sore and he could only hobble on his ankle. But the inactivity was driving him crazy.

He turned, leaned forward, and peered out the window. He'd lost count of how many times he'd looked, hopeful, out that window in the week since he'd sent the message to Katie. Why hadn't she come or at least inquired about him? Had he only imagined she returned his affection? No, he was sure she felt the same way he did.

Frustrated, Sam picked up the small bell on the side table and gave it a furious shake.

A moment later, Nancy tapped and opened the door. "You rang, Mr. Nelson?"

"Yes, come here, please."

The girl stepped lightly across the floor and stood in front of Sam. "What do you need, sir?"

"I know I've asked you before, but are you absolutely certain you sent the message I gave you last week?"

Consternation filled the girl's eyes. "Yes, sir, I'm sure. Just like I said before."

Sam sighed. He shouldn't be badgering the poor maid, but he couldn't believe Katie could be so unconcerned. "All right. Let's run through this step-by-step. You left the room with the letter."

She nodded, her curls bobbing below her mop cap.

"You called the messenger boy?"

Another emphatic nod.

"You placed it in his hands and watched him carry it away."

A flicker of something crossed her face, and she hesitated before answering. "Well, sir, not exactly."

At her worried look, Sam groaned. Something had gone wrong.

"Tell me exactly what happened, please."

"I took the letter downstairs and sent for a messenger boy, just like you said. Then, you see, Cook called me to take a fresh pitcher of lemonade to Mrs. Nelson and her friends, so I gave the letter to Franklin and asked him to give it to the messenger."

Sam frowned. Okay, this detailed account was a little bit different. Still. . . "Thank you, Nancy. Will you tell Franklin I'd like to see him at his convenience?"

"Yes, sir. Right away." She curtsied and walked away, turning at the door. "Did I do something wrong, sir?"

"No, no. Not a thing."

Sam leaned back in his chair. Franklin had been the Nelsons' butler since Sam was ten. He was extremely loyal to the family and very efficient. He'd have made sure the message was delivered.

The door opened. Sam turned, expecting to see Franklin, but his father walked toward him instead.

"Well, well. And how are you feeling this afternoon, son?" His father, always uncomfortable around convalescents, said the exact same words every time he entered Sam's room.

"Much better, thank you. Any news for me?"

The older man lowered himself into a chair across from Sam and shook his head. "Nothing yet. These things take time."

"Did you meet with Flannigan?" After meeting Chauncey and his family the night of Sam's attack, his father had decided he might have been wrong about the Irishman.

"No, I thought you might like to be in on that. After all, he is your friend."

Funny he'd say that. In spite of the fact that he'd only spoken with Flannigan a few times, Sam had found himself thinking of the man as a friend. He nodded. "Perhaps you could send someone to inquire when it would be convenient for us to go there."

"Yes, I'll do that."

"Father, I'd like to talk to you about Katie."

A guarded look shaded his father's eyes. "Not now, please, son. I've things that require my attention this afternoon. Perhaps later."

Disappointment surged in Sam's chest. He'd hoped to change his father's mind about meeting Katie. Sam suspected he was deliberately avoiding the subject.

"Wait," Sam called as his father walked to the door. "Will you see if you can find a crutch for me? I have to get out of this room and at least walk around the house."

"Yes, I'll get one from Dr. Tyler. But if you'd like, I can help you downstairs now. Perhaps you'd like to sit on the porch for a while. Get some fresh air."

"At this moment, there's not much I'd like better."

Leaning on his father's arm, Sam hobbled down the stairs.

"Eugene. What are you doing? Be careful with him." Sam's mother stood at the bottom of the stairs, her hands on her cheeks and distress in her voice. "Where are you taking him?"

"I'm fine, Mother." Sam struggled to speak after the difficult walk downstairs. "I simply need to get out of my room for a while. I'm going to sit on the veranda."

"Well, I don't suppose that will do any harm." She followed them out on the porch.

Sam sighed with relief as his father helped him settle onto one of the cushioned chairs on the wraparound porch.

The slight breeze that had drifted through his window earlier had disappeared. But though the air was still, the foliage of tall oaks and sugar maples, assisted by a curlicue overhang, shaded the porch.

"There. You should be comfortable enough here." Sam's father took his gold watch out and looked at the time. "I need to get back to the office. I'll send word to Flannigan, as you suggested." He kissed his wife and, with obvious relief, walked to the curb where Fred and his carriage waited.

"Would you like for me to read to you?"

Sam smiled at his mother as she patted him on the shoulder. "Thank you, Mother, but I believe I'll just sit here and watch the people go by." Although no one seemed to be braving the hot sun this afternoon. "However, if you'd send Nancy with a cold glass of lemonade, I'd be in your debt forever."

As Sam sat on the veranda drinking his lemonade, thoughts of Katie bombarded him. Had something happened to her? Or had her father forbidden her to contact him?

Franklin stepped out the door. "You wanted to see me, sir?"

"Yes, thanks. I wonder if you can straighten a matter out for me."

"I'll try, sir." Franklin's face was stiff. Sam could count on his fingers the times he'd seen the stately butler smile.

"Do you recall Nancy giving you a letter last week to pass on to a messenger boy?"

Something flickered for an instant in the butler's eyes, a muscle next to his mouth jumped, then his face straightened as though he'd suddenly donned a mask. "I'm sorry, sir. I can't recall. We have so many messages going to and fro."

Surprised, Sam stared. He had never known an incident involving the family in any way to have slipped the ever-efficient butler's memory. He nodded, and Franklin turned and went back into the house.

Sam, puzzled, sat and stared across the lawn. What was this all about? Why would Franklin lie? Sam hated his suspicion of the elderly servant. Could it be that he truly had forgotten the incident? After all, he wasn't getting any younger.

☃

Why hadn't he contacted her? Katie peered out into the darkened theater. She'd hoped against hope he'd be in his seat as good as new with that quirky smile and a sparkle in his eyes. It had been nearly a week since Bridget had stumbled into her room with the terrible news of the assault.

Katie took a deep breath and sang her ballad for the second time that day. After her encore bow, she changed into her street clothes and slipped out the door. If she hurried, she could be back before the show was over. Father would never know she'd gone out on her own this time of night.

She stood outside the theater, considering the best way to get to Sam's house.

If she used Harrigan's carriage, Father would find out. The trolley didn't go that far, and there might not be a cab available at the end of the line.

She bit her lip and eyed the carriage for hire standing nearby. She hated to spend the money, but with resolution, she hurried down the sidewalk, her heels tapping against the planks. Nodding to the driver, she gave him the address and got inside.

The carriage lurched, and Katie grabbed the side of the seat. Leaving the theater district, they passed the business district, bounced past cafés and board-inghouses then small, modest, private homes. They started up a slight incline, and the lighted windows of the larger homes revealed a more affluent lifestyle. Finally, they turned down a tree-lined street, with stone roads and sidewalks. How in the world did the residents keep their grass so green?

At the end of the street, a huge three-story brick house stood in royal splendor. The carriage turned into a circular drive and stopped in front of a wraparound porch. Light streamed out from nearly all of the windows, welcoming, inviting.

"Here ye be, miss. Do ye want me to wait for ye?"

Katie sat, unable to speak. Sam lived here? In this mansion? Her throat seemed to close up, and she swallowed with difficulty. What was she thinking? How could she believe a prince who lived in a house like this could be serious about her?

"Miss, I say we're here. And do ye want me to wait for ye?"

Perspiration popped out along the entire surface of Katie's face. She took a deep breath and stiffened her back. She'd come this far. She might as well complete her mission.

She stepped from the carriage. "Yes, please wait. I won't be long." *Unless of course, Sam opens the door and brings me in to meet his parents.*

She walked up the broad steps and across the porch to the heavy oak door. Lifting the knocker, she tapped it once and then once more against the smooth, rich wood.

The door swung open. A tall, well-dressed elderly man stood stiff and regal against the light of the hallway.

"Yes, miss, may I help you?"

Katie lifted her chin. "Is Mr. Sam Nelson at home? I heard he was injured."

The man looked at her in some surprise. Then an amused look crossed his face. "Young Mr. Nelson has been ill. He's much better now but is not receiving callers. However, if you'd like, you may leave a message."

Katie licked her lips. Her fingers tingled, and her legs felt as though they'd fold up any minute. "Yes, please tell him Miss O'Shannon inquired about his health."

She heard the door shut before she got to the carriage.

ભ

"Katie, you've got to stop your mopin' around like this." Rosie, hands on hips, stood in the open doorway of Katie's bedroom.

"I can't help it. Why doesn't he contact me? Doesn't he know I'm worried?" A sob caught in Katie's throat. "Or maybe he's deathly sick and can't send word."

Rosie walked in and stood by the chair where Katie sat with tears streaming from her eyes. "Now, stop it. All this frettin' isn't helpin' a bit. And your father is beside himself with worrying about you."

"You don't understand. I can't help it, Rosie. What can I do?"

Rosie stood, a tender look on her face. She reached over and smoothed a curl back from Katie's eyes. "Sweet girl, have ya thought of talking to the Lord about it?"

Surprised, Katie stared at the older woman. Rosie went to church every chance she got. But Katie had never heard her talking about God before.

"You mean pray?"

"That's it. God loves you, whether you know it or not. And He cares about that young man of yours as well. Talk to Him, Katie girl." With another tender glance, she left the room, her steps light on the wooden floor.

Talk to Him? Was it really that simple? Just as Grandma used to say?

Katie slipped off the bed and knelt. "God? Are You there?"

Chapter 17

Katie's heels clacked on the boardwalk as she rushed down the street to the soup kitchen. The line seemed longer than usual, if that was possible. Gasping, she attempted to get a clear lungful of air. She wheezed and then coughed as she breathed in the acrid air. The short reprieve had ended, and fire after fire had thickened the air once more.

"Miss O'Shannon, thank the good Lord you're here. We have our hands full today. More families have lost everything."

Grabbing an apron and tying it over her dress, Katie took her place between Mrs. Carter and Sally Sloan, another volunteer, and started ladling soup into bowls. "Do we have enough to go around?"

"Yes, thankfully, I got word in time to cook extra." The director handed a chunk of bread to a little boy who walked away balancing a bowl in one hand and the bread in another.

Katie's heart lurched. The children broke her heart. She needed to do more to help them. But what? Her hours were already full, and she was pouring nearly every extra cent into the child care house at the Patch.

At least her busy schedule kept her from thinking about Sam. A deep peace about him descended on her after she'd knelt before God last Sunday, enveloping her like a warm blanket. She'd never felt like this before. As though God Himself walked with her all through the day. And although she didn't totally understand, she gratefully accepted His presence in her life.

"Eighteen of 'em so far this week." The old man's voice carried up the line, and Katie started.

"Yeah, I heard that, too. The fire department can't hardly keep up with 'em." His statement was interrupted by coughing, and it was a moment before he continued. "The whole city's liable to burn down if we don't get some rain soon."

A little girl, her brown eyes filled with fear, glanced up at Katie as she waited for her food. "Are we gonna burn up?"

Katie winced at the panic in the child's voice. Why couldn't people keep their mouths shut around the little ones? She summoned her most reassuring smile. "Of course not, sweetheart. They're just being silly because they have nothing better to talk about."

The little girl giggled and followed her mother and another child to an empty place at one of the long tables.

God, please let what I just said be true. Send us rain. Please send us rain. She'd read this morning about the prophet, Elijah, praying for rain six or seven times before he saw a cloud in the sky. A shiver ran through her body. Had anyone in Chicago been praying for rain?

By the time the long line had been served and Katie had helped with cleanup, she had to rush to get back in time for her afternoon solo. Almost faint from the heat and the pain that now clutched at her side, she stumbled the last few steps to Harrigan's. Maybe she should drop out of the show. After all, there was so much work to be done at the kitchen, and there were other organizations that could use her help.

She walked through the back door of the theater, and her heart clenched. Another good reason to quit. As long as she was busy, she hardly had more than a passing thought of Sam. But the moment she walked through the theater door, a vision of his beloved face arose before her. The peace that she'd relied on for days suddenly lifted, and pain shot through her heart.

Oh, Sam, where are you?

ᆭ

The familiar odor of sewer and cabbage assaulted Sam when he and his father stepped from the carriage in front of Flannigan's. He didn't like the idea of his father being at the Patch after dark, but it couldn't be helped if the workingmen were to be present. Slowly, he walked to the house where Flannigan stood in the open doorway.

"You're lookin' much better than the last time I saw ya. Glad to see ya on your feet. Come in. Come in." The Irishman shook their hands then stood aside.

At least two dozen men stood in the crowded room.

"Make way, so these gentlemen can sit down. Sarah, bring cold water. I'm thinking Mr. Nelson's needing it."

With effort, Sam smiled. Just the short walk to and from the carriage had sapped his strength. "I'll admit I've felt better, but I'm getting stronger every day."

The crowd parted so that Sam and his father could get to the chairs against the wall. Gratefully, Sam sank down onto the cane-bottom chair.

Flannigan handed glasses of water to Sam and his father. "I know ya got hurt because ya were seekin' the truth about my injuries. And I thank ya for that."

"Is anyone else coming?" Sam's father asked.

"No, sir. I think all are here who want to be."

The men dragged chairs in from the backyard. Apparently, they'd brought their own and stashed them outside while they were waiting.

When everyone was seated, Sam's father stood. "My name is Eugene Nelson. Some of you know my son, Sam. I believe most of you are aware of the fact that our firm has been retained to represent Jeremiah Howard in the matter concerning compensation for Mr. Flannigan's injuries."

He paused as a murmur passed through the crowd then continued. "Several incidents have recently occurred that cause me to question Howard's words as well as his business practices. Especially concerning safety in his warehouse and lumberyard. I understand a number of you work for him at one place or another."

Again murmurs. Relief washed over Sam that this time they were murmurs of agreement, and the expressions on the men's faces, while not especially friendly, were at least not hostile.

His father continued. "I've asked Flannigan to relate what happened to him. When he's finished, if anyone has anything to contribute, I'd be more than happy to listen."

The room quieted as Flannigan stood and looked around the room. He told about the day of his injury and how he'd come straight home and fallen into bed, the pain in his head so intense he couldn't feel his other injuries. He told about his trip to the hospital and his treatment there, sharing the details of his injuries. Then he sat down.

One by one, others stood and told of their experiences as Howard's employees. Some had been injured on the job, although none as severely as Flannigan, but not one had received any sort of compensation. Several spoke of being cheated out of wages.

Sam's father nodded at him, and he stood. "If I can get enough evidence against Howard, my father has agreed to drop him as a client. In such a case, legally I won't be able to represent Mr. Flannigan. However, I will do what I can to bring the truth to light. I know an attorney who will take the case. It may not be possible to gain evidence for your past mistreatment, but testimony from witnesses such as yourselves could make a difference in the question of justice for your neighbor, although I've warned him there is no guarantee. But if enough of these incidents are presented before the court, it will almost force Howard to change his unjust and illegal practices in the future."

"So you want us to go to court and tell about our own experiences?"

Sam looked at the man in the back of the room who'd spoken. "If you will, it could help. We also need those of you who are willing to stand up for Mr. Flannigan's character."

"What if we lose our jobs? We've got families to support," a big man with a red beard and tight red curls called out.

Sam looked at his father. How could he answer a cry like this? What was it like to be trapped in a low-paying job with no way out? What did it feel like to know your small paycheck was all that stood between your children and hunger?

He listened as his father told the men he didn't expect anyone to do what he felt he couldn't do. Each would have to follow his own conscience. And no one would think less of those who refused to testify.

Sam and his father left and headed home. Home where Sam had enjoyed wealth and safety all his life. Where wonderful aromas of good food drifted from the kitchen and the smell of spices and perfumes wafted through the house. Where light shone into every corner and beauty filled every room.

"How do we help them, Father?"

"One case at a time. One step at a time. That's all we can do."

"That's what Katie said."

His father gave him a startled look, and some other expression crossed his face. But Sam was too tired to question him about it.

Sam leaned back into the soft, velvety cushions of the carriage seat. Now he understood why Katie worked tirelessly, trying to help the poor. Once she'd said, "We can't help them all, Sam. But we can help the ones before our eyes. The ones we know about. Little by little, we can make life better for some."

He had to see her. He was stronger now. Tomorrow he'd go to Ma Casey's. He'd find out why she hadn't answered his letter. He'd know, once and for all, if she still cared for him.

☙

Katie walked out of the theater with Bridget, and they trailed after the others so they could talk on the way to Ma Casey's.

"Tell me again why Sam and his father were coming to the Patch tonight?"

Bridget had gone home during the afternoon break to take some things to her mother for the child care house. She'd bounced into the theater bubbling over with her news about Sam. "Like I told you before, Mr. Nelson and his father were supposed to go to Flannigan's tonight to talk to some of the men about Howard. I think they must have seen the light. I can't wait to talk to my mother and find out all about it."

"That's wonderful, Bridget." And it was. She'd longed for Sam to see the people of the Patch as they really were. But her heart ached, just the same. Sam was up and around, and he hadn't been to see her. The only explanation had to be that he didn't care for her anymore. If he ever truly had.

As they walked on, she listened to Bridget's excited and hopeful chatter about how the Nelsons could help the employment condition. Irritated, Katie bit her lip. To listen to Bridget, one would think Sam and his father were miracle workers.

Bitterness bit at her, and anger rose in her heart. All this time, she'd been picturing Sam at death's door, lying in bed, calling her name, only to discover he'd been at a meeting. How dare he trifle with her?

As soon as they arrived at Ma Casey's, she pleaded a headache and went to her room, her body stiff and tight. Flinging herself across her bed, she burst into tears. When the barrage ended, she sat up and rubbed her hand across her eyes. Shame flooded over her. *I'm just selfish. I never knew I was selfish. Oh, but Sam, I thought you loved me.*

She had to stop thinking of him. It was over.

A beam of moonlight caught her attention, and her eyes rested on the small white Bible on the table by her bed. She'd dug it out from her trunk the day after she'd turned her heart over to God. She'd carried it to church during the four years at Grandma and Grandpa's. But she couldn't remember ever opening it outside the church walls until last Monday.

Katie lit the lamp by her bed and picked up the Bible. Opening it to Psalm 1, her eyes scanned the words. She turned the page and devoured psalm after psalm. At the end, she started through Proverbs and read until her eyes were heavy and would no longer focus on the small letters. Yawning, she returned the book to the table and changed into her nightgown. As she sank into the feather bed, the words she'd just read flowed through her.

"Trust in the Lord with all thine heart; and lean not unto thine own understanding. In all thy ways acknowledge him, and he shall direct thy paths."

All right, heavenly Father, I'll trust You to lead me in the way You want me to go.

Her eyes closed, and she drifted off into sweet, peaceful sleep.

Chapter 18

W here are you, Katie? Not here, I think. You've sung the wrong lines again." Donald Jones whirled around on the piano stool and frowned. "It's Saturday. You've got to hurry and learn this piece."

"I'm sorry, Donald. I guess my mind is wandering." Katie leaned forward, peering over her accompanist's shoulder at the sheet of music, and found her place. She wouldn't be singing the new song until Monday, so why was he in such a dither? She should probably be going through today's solo anyway.

Donald tapped his fingers against the piano and frowned. "You know I'll be away tomorrow for my little sister's wedding."

She'd forgotten about that. "Well, Rosie can play for me if I need to practice." Rosie often played for the troupe at night as they sat around singing old ballads.

"Oh, can she? Little girl, Rosie can't read a note. She plays the old songs by ear, which isn't going to help you." He turned back around and placed his fingers on the keys. "Let's try it one more time."

This time, Katie ran through the entire song without a mistake, and Donald turned and grinned. "I knew you could do it. Now, one more time."

They started from the beginning, and once more, Katie remembered her words and sang with no problems.

"Katie, I've called you twice." Bridget's voice rang out above the music.

Donald hit the piano keys, turned, and glared at Bridget. "Can't you see we're busy here, girl?"

Hands on hips, Bridget glared back. "Katie has a visitor, for your information."

"What? Who?" Katie's stomach lurched, and she started toward the hall.

"It's Mr. Nelson, that's who. I left him standin' on the porch. Shall I ask him in?" She cast a worried glance at Katie. "To tell you the truth, he's not looking so good."

Not looking so good? "Mercy, Bridget." Brushing past her friend, Katie rushed to the front door, her pulse racing. "Please come in. I can't imagine why Bridget left you standing out in the heat." Her voice sounded breathless even to her. Maybe he hadn't noticed.

Sam removed his hat and stepped inside, leaning heavily on a cane. Bridget was right. He was pale, and little beads of perspiration stood out on his face.

"Please come into the parlor. There's a little bit of a breeze coming through the window there." She ushered him in, sending Donald a pointed look.

"Don't forget, we need to run through the song again later." Donald left, and with a bit of triumph, Bridget followed, pulling the parlor door shut behind her.

Katie hoped Ma Casey didn't notice she and Sam were alone in a room with the door closed. She stood, tongue-tied, not knowing what to say, then realized Sam was still standing.

"Oh, please sit down. I'm so glad to see you are well enough to be up and around." *And finally here.* She pushed the thought aside. She shouldn't judge him until she heard what he had to say.

He sat on the end of the sofa, and she sat on a wingbacked chair facing him, her fingers twisting her handkerchief. He leaned back and took a deep breath, relief crossing his face.

Katie bit her lip. He must still be in pain. And she'd been blaming him for not coming. But why hadn't he at least sent word?

"I wasn't sure you'd want to see me," he said. Uncertainty crossed his face as he looked at her.

"Not want to see you? Why would you think that? Just because you didn't acknowledge my visit or send word that you were all right?" She knew her voice sounded on edge, and although she truly didn't want to yell at him when he appeared so frail, he was the one who brought the whole thing up, wasn't he?

A puzzled look crossed his face. "What visit? And for that matter, I sent a letter that you chose to ignore. I assumed you had lost interest or were angry with me for some reason."

Katie gasped. *What letter?* "Chose to ignore? Why, I did no such thing. I never received one single, solitary letter from you. Not one."

"But. . .I dictated a letter to one of the housemaids, and she. . ." Confusion, followed by a flash of anger washed over his face. "And you mean all this time, you thought I hadn't tried to contact you?"

"What else was I to think?"

"Katie, I'm so sorry. I promise I did write and was assured my letter was sent."

Katie ducked her head to hide the tears that filled her eyes. He had written. She had no idea why she didn't receive the letter, but that was unimportant now. He did care about her. That was all that mattered.

Joy flooded her heart and radiated from the smile that wouldn't be held back. And needn't be. Sam's face told her all she needed to know.

She held out her hands, and he clasped them in his, holding on tight. "Katie." His voice broke over the one word. "I thought I'd lost you. And didn't know why."

Just then, the door opened, and Ma stood there with a wooden spoon in her hand, twisting her lips in an unsuccessful attempt to hide her grin. "All right, you two. I understand you've been apart for a while, but the door stays open." She frowned, albeit unconvincingly.

"Sorry, Ma. It won't happen again." Katie smiled as Ma left the door open. It seemed as though a smile was permanently fixed to her lips.

"Should you be up and about? Perhaps you need to go home and go back to bed."

"I'm fine. And wild horses couldn't drag me away from you now. I'll need to take things slowly for a while, and Father won't hear of my going to the office yet, but I'm getting plenty of rest. I promise."

Her heart soared. "All right. In that case, please tell me all about what happened and how you're doing." She listened in fascinated horror as he told her of the ambush but clapped her hands together when he spoke with admiration and respect of Chauncey Flannigan.

"I do have one request to make of you, Katie. Please don't be angry. But I feel it's unsafe for you to continue your work in the Patch."

She took a quick breath, and he held up his hand. "I know how important the work is to you, and I respect that. But isn't there some way you could help in the background without actually going into the neighborhood?"

"I don't see how. Or why I should. The people there need all the help they can get, and no one has harmed me."

Sam closed his eyes for a moment. When he opened them, she saw the worry they held.

"Crime is high in the Patch. There are very few police officers even in the daylight hours and none at all at night. It isn't safe for you there." He gave her a pleading look. "Please, Katie, I couldn't bear it if anything happened to you."

Silent for a moment, Katie considered his words. Of course she'd never give up her work. But perhaps she did need to be more careful. "I'll agree to this much. I won't go there after dark. And I'll take someone with me in the daytime."

He breathed deeply then nodded. "All right. That relieves my mind some. But please remain cautious at all times."

"I will, Sam. I promise." She looked deeply into his eyes and smiled.

☞

Sam drove home, his eyes shooting flames. He stormed into the house, his cane thumping loudly on the hardwood floor of the foyer.

"Franklin! Nancy!" he shouted. "Come here!"

"Sam, what's wrong?" His mother ran from the parlor, fear in her eyes. "Are you in pain?"

"No, Mother. I have a matter to settle with Nancy and Franklin."

"But, Sam, that's no way to call the servants. What's gotten into you, son?" She pressed her lips together in disapproval.

"I apologize, Mother." He kissed her on the forehead, and she reached up and patted his cheek.

"You called for me, sir?" Franklin stepped into the hall, and Nancy came scurrying in from the kitchen.

"I'd like to see you both in my bedroom as soon as possible. I have some questions." He turned to his mother, and when he spoke, his voice was gentle. "Mother, I'll be down for lunch. You don't need to send a tray."

He made his way slowly up the stairs, followed by Franklin and Nancy. When they reached the landing, Franklin stepped around him and went to open the door to Sam's bedroom.

When Sam was seated by the window, he looked up at Nancy first. "Please tell me again what you did with the letter you wrote for me last week. The one addressed to Miss O'Shannon at Ma Casey's Boardinghouse."

"Very well, sir. Like I told you, I sent for a messenger boy. But before he arrived, Cook needed me, so I gave the letter to Franklin and asked him to see that the boy got it." Fright filled her eyes. "Is anything wrong, sir? I wouldn't want to lose my position."

"If what you've told me is the truth, you have nothing to worry about, Nancy. You may go now. And thank you."

Sam watched her scurry from the room. Then he turned his gaze upon Franklin, who stood ramrod-straight, his eyes veiled.

"I'd like to know what's going on, Franklin. Why wasn't the letter delivered to Miss O'Shannon? If you misplaced it or forgot to give it to the messenger, that's quite understandable. You've been a loyal and trusted servant for many years. But I want to know the truth."

Sam watched as uncertainty followed by an expression almost like regret crossed the butler's face. When he spoke, it was respectful but firm. "I'm sorry, sir. I can't say."

Surprised, Sam looked at Franklin. "You can't or you won't?"

The elderly man hesitated then opened his mouth as if to speak but shut it again.

"Very well, Franklin. You may go."

Perplexed, Sam decided to send for a tray after all. He hadn't, however, counted on his mother bringing it up. "Mother, you didn't need to do that."

"And why not? I've brought you many a tray when you were a child. You're still my boy, you know." A twinkle in her eyes proved she wasn't upset with him anymore.

"How well I remember. Chicken soup was the meal of the day when I was sick. And also when I pretended to be sick to get out of the classroom."

She laughed. "And those times, it was followed by castor oil. A fitting punishment, I thought."

Sam grinned. "I don't think chicken soup or castor oil can fix what ails me now, Mother."

"I'm sure you're right. Affairs of the heart are not so easily cured."

He looked at her in surprise. "What do you mean?"

"You can't fool me, Sam. I know love when I see it. And perhaps unreturned love from the way you've been moping around."

Sam hesitated. Would she react the same way his father had? And suddenly, a chill went down his spine. His father had intercepted the letter. That's why Franklin was so secretive. Because his first loyalty was always to Sam's father.

"Sam, what's wrong?" His mother's startled voice brought him back from his thoughts.

He attempted a laugh. "I think I've just been overdoing it the last couple of days, Mother. I'm not really hungry. If you don't mind, I think I'll go to sleep."

"Of course."

After she left, Sam crawled between his sheets. Suddenly he really was tired. He leaned back on the soft pillows and closed his eyes.

The sound of footsteps woke him. He opened his eyes to see his father standing beside his bed.

"Are you awake?"

"Yes, what time is it?"

"Nearly six. Your mother said you've been sleeping for hours. Guess you needed it."

Carefully, aware of the ribs that were still not completely healed, Sam sat up, adjusting his pillows behind his back.

"I'm sorry, Sam."

Sam tensed. "Sorry about what?"

"I saw Nancy give the letter to Franklin and heard her tell him it was a letter for your 'young lady,' as she said." His father sighed, and Sam saw sorrow wash over his face. "What can I say except I'm sorry? I thought I was doing the right thing when I took it."

"You read it?"

"Of course not. I disposed of it." Shame filled his eyes. "I was wrong. I'm very sorry, Sam. I thought I was protecting you. Now that I've gotten to know so many of the Irish people, I've come to respect most of them. I asked around about Miss O'Shannon and heard about the good work she's been doing in the Patch."

Sam's chest tightened. He knew his father had thought he was doing the right thing, but could he forgive this outrage?

"Sam, all I can say is I'm so sorry and I'd love to meet the young lady. I just pray you can somehow forgive me."

With awe, Sam saw tears spring up in his father's eyes. Eugene Nelson, tough businessman, was crying.

He reached over and pressed his father's hand. "I do forgive you, Father. And I'm sure my Katie will be thrilled to meet you and Mother."

Chapter 19

Katie put on her best dress and then, peering into the mirror, arranged part of her hair on top of her head. She smoothed the ringlets hanging down on each side then picked up her hat and eyed it critically.

She'd purchased the plum-colored head covering from a catalog shortly before she came to the city. The lace and fake flowers were still as good as new. But the small black bird, which had so fascinated her at the time of purchase, now wanted to lean over onto the brim. She'd have to repair or remove it. But not today. After tugging the bird back into place, she arranged the hat on her head. It would simply have to do.

She'd been excited about church before, but this joy bubbling up inside her wasn't about sitting in the back pew, giggling with her girlfriends. She practically skipped downstairs and was surprised to see her pa, standing beside a smiling Rosie, wearing his best suit and smelling like pomade.

"It's about time you got down here, Katherine O'Shannon. And here we've been waiting for you fifteen minutes or more." He pulled out his pocket watch, gave it a quick glance, then replaced it in his vest pocket.

"Five is more like it, Michael. Don't pay him any mind, Katie. You're very pretty this morning. Isn't she?"

Katie grinned as her father took a closer look at her.

"Isn't that waist a little snug, daughter?" Creases appeared between his eyes.

"No, Pa, it's not snug in the least." She grabbed his arm. "Shall we go? I wouldn't want to be late."

They stepped out into the already scorching hot morning.

"My lands," Rosie said, holding a handkerchief to her face. "Were there more fires last night?"

"Hmm. It wouldn't surprise me any," Pa declared. "The count was at twenty for the week the last I heard."

Katie latched onto one of her father's arms while Rosie grabbed the other, and they headed down the street, turning when they reached the corner. By the time they reached the church, she noticed her father wheezed a little, and her own breathing was difficult as well.

A group of men stood on the steps outside the church, their conversation reaching to the sidewalk.

One man flung his arm upward. "That's right. The whole street's gone. Houses, stores, everything."

"What are they talking about, Father?" *Dear God, please don't let it be what it sounds like.*

Her father patted her hand. "Go inside, Katie. You, too, Rosie. I'll join you shortly."

She followed Rosie into the church, and they found seats in a pew about halfway up the aisle.

A smattering of women and children sat around the sanctuary, and an occasional whisper reached her ears.

Finally, the men drifted in.

Katie scooted over so her father could slide into the pew next to Rosie. "Father, what's going on?" She leaned over and peered around Rosie.

"Shhh." The sound came from the seat behind Katie.

A tall man had stepped onto the platform and made his way to the podium. He stood for a moment with his eyes closed. Was he praying?

"Brothers and sisters, neighbors," the deep voice sounded throughout the room, "some of you have heard about last night's fires. For those who haven't, I'm sorry to be the bearer of sad news."

A sob sounded from the other side of the room, and Katie heard a moan from farther back in the church.

"Four entire blocks were destroyed last night on the southwest side of town. I don't know the exact location, and I'm sorry I don't have more information. If you have family or friends in that area and would like to leave, we will be praying."

Katie averted her eyes as several people got up from their seats and hurried out. *Dear God. Help them. Let them find their loved ones safe.*

"If you'll bow your heads, I'll say a few words of prayer for those who may have lost homes or, worse still, family members." He paused a moment then sighed. "I'm afraid it's also time to pray for the safety of our entire city."

Katie closed her eyes and silently prayed, blinking back tears. Oh, why didn't it rain? *Lord, please send rain.*

"And now, if you'll open your hymnals, we'll continue our service with our brothers and sisters still in our hearts."

As Katie sang the familiar hymns, peace flowed into her spirit. She listened intently to the sermon that followed, almost awestruck. Grandma and Grandpa's church wasn't like this. Was it? If so, where was she at the time? In another world? Perhaps it was the tragedy and common-felt sorrow among the congregation that made it feel different. No, the feeling came from inside. Butterflies tickled her stomach. *God is really real.*

She had to cover her mouth and nose with her handkerchief during the walk home, as did her father and Rosie. She followed them into the house and went up to change into something fresh and lighter before dinner.

Why hadn't she invited Sam to dinner? Perhaps he'd drop by later. If not, the afternoon would drag. If only Bridget were here. But she wouldn't be home until sundown at least.

What could she do to make the time go faster? And get her mind off those poor people? As she walked into the hallway, the aroma of Ma's fried chicken wafted up the staircase. Her favorite meal. Her stomach churned. Who could eat?

ↂ

Sam scanned the front page of the *Chicago Tribune*. His eyes rested on an article covering last night's fire. According to the reporter, the absence of rain had left everything so dry it would only take a spark to ignite the whole city. He shook his head. The southwest wind blowing off the prairie could make that prediction come true.

His mother came in from the kitchen and stopped in the middle of the room. "All anyone at church could talk about this morning was the fire and the possibility of more."

At the sight of her worried face, Sam got up and took her hands in his. "Now, Mother, don't be worrying yourself sick."

"I won't. I'm trying to lift it up to God." She offered a rueful smile. "Most of the time, I remember."

A twinge of guilt bit at Sam. How long had it been since he'd gone to church or even opened his Bible? He could remember a time when he was so close to God he could actually feel His presence. What had happened?

His mother placed her hand on his sleeve. "I'd like to talk to you before dinner."

She sat on the sofa, and Sam returned to his chair. "All right, Mother. What about?"

"Your father told me about Miss O'Shannon."

Sam's stomach tightened. "Yes? You know Father hasn't actually met her yet, and besides, he's given his permission for me to bring Katie to meet him."

"You don't need to sound so defensive, Sam. I'm not planning an attack." A dimple appeared and then hid again at her brief smile.

"You'll have to forgive me, Mother. I've been defending Katie to Father for some time."

"But I am not your father."

He darted a look at her. "Do you mean you approve? Even though she isn't one of your friends' daughters?"

"What do they have to do with anything? I want my son happy, whomever he chooses to love. But as to whether I approve of your choice, I can't say. You haven't given me the opportunity to approve or disapprove."

Sam's jaw dropped open, and he burst out laughing. "You've a point there. I haven't, have I?"

She patted the seat next her. "So, come over here and tell me all about this girl who has managed to capture my son's elusive heart. Goodness knows I've thrown plenty of lovely young women your way with no success at all."

Sam sat where she directed and leaned back. How good it felt to relax when he spoke of Katie. "Mother, you will love her. I know you will. She's not only lovely to look at; she's sweet and kind."

102

Sam paused, wondering how to continue. How to show her the Katie he knew and loved. "Her parents were in vaudeville and lived in New York City. When she was fourteen, her mother died, and her maternal grandparents raised her after that. They have a little farm somewhere in southern Illinois. She turned eighteen a few months ago and came to live with her father."

"Tell me about him."

Sam smiled. "Michael O'Shannon is bigger than life with a stubborn streak and a heart of gold. He came here from Ireland when he was a small boy and is very much American. He's very protective of his Katie, and it took me quite awhile to win his trust so that I could call on her."

"What sort of acting does Katie do?"

"She won her first role after one of the other performers broke her foot. The actress is back now, so Katie only sings a solo before the show. Usually a ballad. She also helps out backstage."

"I always thought it would be exciting to be onstage." Her eyes sparkled.

Sam couldn't help the little choke of laughter at her words. "You, Mother?"

She flashed a smile at him. "I was a young girl myself once, you know. Of course, I'd have been locked up forever if I'd tried to follow that short-lived dream."

Franklin appeared in the doorway. "Dinner is served, Mrs. Nelson."

"Thank you, Franklin."

Sam fidgeted. Had he said enough? Too much?

Mother rose and waited for him then took his arm. "Ask Miss O'Shannon when it would be convenient for her to come to dinner."

A weight lifted off Sam, and he took a deep breath. "Thank you, Mother," he whispered.

"I've always wanted a daughter, you know."

Sam smiled at the dimple that appeared in her cheek.

 こ

Katie couldn't join in the festive mood with the rest of the troupe as Pat Devine entertained them with his fiddle. Why hadn't Sam come to see her? All right. So he didn't say he would be here today. But still. . .

She glanced at the mantel clock again. Seven. Bridget should have been here by now. Katie went to the window and peeked around the lace curtains and through the open window. With a huff, she sat on the wingbacked chair. Bridget wasn't coming either. She turned her attention to Pat, who had everyone in the room but her tapping their toes.

Rosie sat beside her. "Bridget's not here yet?"

"No. She must have decided to stay home tonight," Katie sighed.

"I know it's lonely for you with just us older folks for company." Rosie gave her an understanding smile.

"Oh no, Rosie. I love being with you." The older woman had been a wonderful friend to Katie. Almost like a mother.

"Mmm-hmm." Rosie gave her hand a squeeze. "We love you, too. But it's not the same as having someone your own age to talk to."

A shout of laughter drew their attention back to their boisterous friends.

Katie smiled at her father, who stood in the center of the room, surrounded by the others. "Rosie, they're insulting me."

"Now, you fellows, leave my man alone." Rosie gave a playful frown and went to stand by Michael, looping her arm through his.

Her man? Did Rosie call Pa "her man"? Katie put her hands to her cheeks. She'd known that Rosie had a crush on her pa, but when did he decide to return her affection?

Deciding she needed to collect her thoughts, she went outside and sat on one of the rocking chairs on the porch. The smoke from the night before seemed even stronger than it had earlier, probably carried by the wind blowing from the south. Like Pa said, the fire department was well equipped to take care of any more fires that broke out. Katie shivered. But then why did four city blocks burn to the ground?

Suddenly part of a verse from the minister's sermon came to her. *"When thou walkest through the fire, thou shalt not be burned; neither shall the flame kindle upon thee."* What did that mean? People did get burned sometimes. Just last week, one of Harrigan's business associates had died in a fire.

Another shiver went through her body. She jumped up and hurried back to the parlor. Back to the noisy laughter. Back to where she was safe.

Chapter 20

K atie, wake up." Her father's voice broke through the sleep-filled fog. He shook her shoulder. "Katie."

"What's wrong?" She bolted upright, her eyes landing on her fully dressed father.

"More fires. Get dressed and come downstairs. We'll talk then." He rushed out. The door closed, and his running footsteps receded down the stairs.

Katie flung the covers aside, jumped out of bed, and grabbed the first dress her hands touched. She jerked it from the closet and threw it on over her shift and pantalettes. No time for a corset. Pa's voice sounded frightened.

Five minutes later, curls flying unconfined around her shoulders, she hurried downstairs. Voices sounded in the dining room. She hurried inside, finding the entire troupe there. "What's wrong?" She stopped and took a deep breath. "Is there fire heading this way?"

"Come sit down, daughter." Her father took her arm and led her to one of the straight-backed chairs by the table.

She looked at the small clock on the mantel. Ten thirty. No wonder she was so disoriented. She'd only slept a few minutes.

"Daughter, fire is out of control across the river. They're sayin' it started in someone's barn on DeKoven Street. The southern branch should stop it, but with all the oil floating on the surface, that's not certain."

She gasped. If the fire jumped that part of the river. . . "But the gasworks are near there. And, and. . ." *Conley's Patch and Bridget and. . .*

"I know, child." He patted her shoulder.

"What can we do?" Her knees weakened, and dizziness clouded her thoughts.

"A group is forming to help evacuate. Most of us men are going to join them. We'll be needin' your prayers."

"I'm going with you. I can't stay here when Bridget and her mother and Betty are in danger. And the children." She gasped. "They'll need all the help they can get over there, Father. Surely you can see that."

"She's right. I'm going, too."

Katie could have hugged Rosie. She sent her a grateful look.

"Now listen here, Katherine. I know you're worried about your friends, but you'll not be going, and that's that."

"Pa, please. Am I more important than those babies across the river?"

A look of anguish crossed his face. "No, but. . .you'll not be goin'."

"You have to let me go, Pa. God is able to protect me."

He stared at her as though memorizing every inch of her face. "All right, there's no time to be arguin'. But ya have to be careful. If ya see any sign of the fire getting close, get out of there."

Katie flinched at the panic in his voice. Was she doing the right thing? But she was supposed to go. She felt it deep inside.

"I'll take care of her, Michael." Rosie laid her hand on his arm. "I promise I won't leave her side."

Katie watched in awe as her pa stroked Rosie's cheek.

"And who will be takin' care of you, I'd like to know?" His voice broke.

"I will." Katie put her arm around Rosie's shoulder. "We'll watch out for each other."

"Here," Ma Casey's booming voice rang out as she walked into the room, her arms piled high with blankets. "Take these. If the fire gets bad, you can wet them down and wrap them around your heads and shoulders."

Dubious, Katie took one of the blankets.

She filed out of the door with Rosie and the rest of the troupe. They hurried to the theater and squeezed into Harrigan's three-seater carriage.

To Katie, the conveyance seemed to crawl down the board streets toward the river. Katie's stomach and chest were tight. The longer it took to get to the fire, the less time they had to help those in danger.

Rosie's hand moved under hers, and the older woman flinched.

Katie glanced down, realizing she was squeezing the life out of the poor woman's hand. "I'm sorry," she muttered, dropping the hand.

What if the fire had already jumped the river? They might run right into it. Could they outrun it?

Blocks away from the river, screams and the pounding of feet rose above the crunch and squeak of wagon wheels on the wooden street. Mr. Harrigan shook the reins. The horses sped up, the links on the harness and single trees jingling. They turned onto Clark Street. Terror filled the air. Mothers grabbed the arms of screaming children, pulling them onward. Men pushed carts filled with household goods. Barking dogs dashed among the human wave.

Katie peered forward to see if the fire was nearby. She could see flames in the distance, but they were still on the other side of the south branch.

"We'll never get the horse and carriage across the bridge," Pat yelled. "We'll have to go on foot."

Her heart pounding, Katie jumped from the carriage, still clutching the blanket Ma had pressed in her arms.

Harrigan unhitched the horse and slapped him on the rump. Startled, it whirled then took off.

"But. . .what about the carriage?" Katie whispered.

"Let's go." Rosie grabbed her arm and pushed her toward the bridge.

Katie forced her way through the crowd, her eyes glued to Rosie's back. Suddenly, a burly man pushed by and knocked her to the side. She stumbled, struggling not to fall. Disoriented, she looked around. A wall of bodies met her sight. Where was Rosie? And Father?

She shoved her way between elbowing, shouting people. *Oh God. Oh God.* Fear rose in her, and her heart raced. Finally, she found herself on the other side of the bridge.

"Miss O'Shannon!"

Even distorted with fear, the voice was familiar to Katie. Molly Sawyer. She looked around, but people blocked her view. Coughing and gasping, she pushed in the direction the voice came from. The crowd parted, and she saw Molly and her family. They stood by the dock, bundles tied to their backs about to step onto the bridge. "Molly, have you seen the Thorntons?" she yelled. She pushed her way through and grabbed Molly's shirt to stop her.

"They were still at home when I left. Out on their porch. Mrs. Thornton seemed in a daze. She wouldn't budge. Bridget was shakin' her and shakin', her, but it didn't seem to do no good."

"Molly, what are you standin' there for? Come on!" Her husband grabbed her hand, and Molly turned and followed him onto the bridge. Instantly they were lost from sight in the crowd.

Frantic, Katie looked around. Flames roared just blocks away with only the south branch of the river containing it.

"Katie, over here!"

"Pa!" she cried out with relief as he grabbed her arm and pulled her to him. She held on as he led her to Rosie and the rest of the group who stood behind a small shed.

He turned and gazed at her. "We're crossing over the south branch to try to help those on the other side. You go with Rosie and look for your friends. Don't wait for us. God willing, the fire won't cross the main branch of the river, but I don't want you waiting to find out. Do you hear me, Katie girl? Help those you can to get out of here and then head north."

She grabbed for her father. "No! Please! Don't go over there. It's not safe."

He gripped her hand. "Daughter! Pull yourself together. Trust God." Then he dropped her hands and was gone toward the flames.

She shuddered and took a deep breath. He was right. She swallowed to ease her smoke-sore throat. "God go with you," she whispered.

∞

Sam stood by his father on the porch and watched the flames in the distance. "I can't tell exactly where it is, can you?"

"Not for sure, but it looks like it's near the river." He furrowed his brow and squinted.

Sam fidgeted. "Which side?"

"If you can't tell, how could I? Your eyesight's a lot better than mine." He continued to gaze eastward in the direction of the fire. "If it's on the east side of the south branch, the gasworks could go."

A knot formed in Sam's throat, and he swallowed. *If the gasworks blow, the Patch will be next.* "I think I'll ride down there. Check things out."

His father gave him a startled look. "Let me send Fred. You don't want to worry your mother."

Irritation shot through Sam. If he went himself, he could check on the Thorntons and the Flannigans. But his father was probably right.

A few minutes later, the coachman, lantern in hand, rode off on Fritzie, one of the bay mares that his father prized so.

Sam paced to the end of the porch. He stared eastward but could see no better than he had from his former position.

"Stop fidgeting. What are you so nervous about?"

"I have friends in Conley's Patch, remember?"

His father's face stiffened. "I'd forgotten. Well, chances are the fire won't reach them. I'd think the fire department should have it under control soon."

Sam gave a short laugh. "Like they did last night? The fire department has a scarcity of supplies, and such as they have are of inferior quality."

His father nodded. "I know, I know. I intend to address that at the next city council meeting."

Sam pulled out his watch and peered at the numbers. Ten minutes till twelve. Fred had been gone twenty minutes and should be back soon.

Katie. He dropped to the top step. Could she possibly be in any danger? The boardinghouse was north of the downtown district and should be fine as long as the fire didn't cross the main branch of the river. Still, a thread of concern planted itself firmly in Sam's mind.

The sound of hooves came from down the street. His head jerked in that direction.

Fritzie galloped up the street with Fred leaning forward, almost touching her flying mane. He yanked on the reins, bringing Fritzie to a stop in front of Sam, then swung from the saddle. "The fire's jumped the south fork! Oil on top of the water ignited. There was no stopping it."

Boom!

Sam grabbed his ears to protect them from the deafening explosion. The street and house lights flickered then died.

"What on earth?" his father bellowed from behind him.

Sam jumped to his feet. "That was the gasworks! I have to go." He ran down the steps and snatched the reins from Fred then swung painfully into the saddle. "Father, stay here, please. If the fire jumps the main branch, I'll check on the office. You stay with Mother."

Swinging Fritzie around, he headed east. Before he'd gone a quarter of a mile, he realized his mistake. Why had he thought he could get to the Patch this way with the fire converging on the area? He'd have to go around. He yanked on the reins, turned Fritzie, and then headed north.

Veering back east in the direction of the Patch, he galloped head-on into a mob. The panic shocked him. Shouts and screams rent the night. Men, women, and children, pushing carts and leading goats and cows, milled toward him. Time and again, he turned east, only to be turned back by a human mass that plunged forward into the night, with the fire a red backdrop in the distance.

"Ye half-wit! Why ye headed toward the fire?"

Two shadowy forms stood beside his horse. Sam peered at them in the darkness. The toothless old man gasped for breath and tightened his arm around his wife. The woman looked up, terror bright in her eyes.

"I have friends in the Patch. Has the fire reached there?"

"If it ain't yet, it soon will. The flames are a solid wall. It's gonta jump the main river soon. Bound to."

"God, help me. Show me what to do." Sam pressed his heels into Fritzie's side, and she quickened her step. What if the man was right and the main branch was breached? He had to get to Katie.

He steered Fritzie north again toward the business district. Smoke filled the air, biting his throat. He coughed. Fritzie tossed her head, snorting. Her ears turned back, and she reared up, her front feet pawing the air.

"Easy, girl." Sam patted her neck.

She relaxed a little, lowering her feet to the ground, but her ears remained back.

"It's okay." Sam patted her neck again. "We have to reach Katie." He swallowed and squeezed his legs tighter around Fritzie's sides to encourage her onward.

As he neared the business district, pandemonium filled the area. People stood in the streets in their nightclothes, hollering to each other. Demanding to know what happened to the lights. Had the fires reached them? Others ran from their homes clutching bundles.

Dear God, this whole city is a firetrap. There aren't more than two or three so-called fireproof buildings in all of Chicago. Tension tightened the muscles in his neck and stabbed at his chest.

Policemen strode up and down the street, shouting through cupped hands. "Everyone go back to your homes. There's no danger. The fire can't cross the main branch of the river."

A few people drifted back to their homes, but most ignored the police officers.

Sam urged Fritzie on, skirting the business district and finally arriving at Ma Casey's. He swung from the saddle, tore up the front steps, and banged on the door. Peering through the diamond-shaped window, he searched for Katie.

Ma Casey opened the door, holding a lamp high. Seeing Sam, she flung the door open.

He pushed past her. "Ma, where is everyone? Where's Katie?" He looked around. Surely they weren't sleeping through all the excitement.

"They've gone to help evacuate."

"What? Katie, too?" Fear surged through him. Surely Michael wouldn't have allowed her to go.

"There was no stopping her. Bridget didn't come home last night."

Dear God, please no. Katie at the Patch?

Leaping onto Fritzie's back, he whipped the reins and kneed her sides. She snorted but leaped forward. Through the business section. Onto Clark Street. The air heated as he went. Toward the bridge. He yanked the reins.

Horror hit him. A solid mass of screaming people flowed toward him. Behind them, a raging monster of flames, smoke, and debris licked at the banks of the river, swallowing up buildings, boats, everything flammable in its path.

"God, have mercy."

Chapter 21

A red-hot ember flew over Katie's head and landed two feet in front of her. Sparks spewed up. Searing pain shot up her arm. She screamed and jumped to one side, tightening her hold on the tiny, squirming, crying child in her arms. The boards beneath the still-burning embers began to smolder.

"No!" The cry burst from her throat. Ashes rained down on them, coating the wet blanket she'd wrapped around the little girl.

"Katie, watch out!" Bridget's shout came from behind her.

She turned to see a bay horse, eyes rolling and hooves thrashing the air. She stumbled forward just as the horse's hooves crashed down on the spot where she'd stood.

"God, help us!" Mrs. Thornton's anguished cry was almost lost in the greater, almost solid, sound of people, animals, and the roaring fire. Always the fire.

Katie clung tighter to her charge and ran with the fear-driven mob of people. Betty, running hand in hand with Bridget, screamed a continuous scream.

Katie sobbed. *Sam.*

Lord, I trust You. Don't let me look back. The fire must be close behind.

Sam. Katie's neck and ears burned from the raging heat borne along with the wind. Her chest was so tight. She slowed her pace. If only she could stop but for a moment. *No. Don't think that.*

Sam.

God, help me. Help me run faster.

Glass shattered somewhere near, the sound assaulting her ears. She turned to see a figure hurl itself from a third floor window. *Oh God.* She averted her eyes and ran on. The child was still, and no sound issued from the blanket. *Oh please, don't let her be dead. What if I've smothered her? Should I stop? No, I dare not.*

Sam.

Oh God, please don't let him search for me. Keep him safe.

No, I mustn't think of him. Concentrate on the child. Is she breathing? Don't think of anything but getting her to safety.

From somewhere came a burst of energy, and she quickened her pace.

Rosie. Where is Rosie? She was by my side when we crossed the bridge. I promised Father.

She took a deep breath and gasped. The air was getting hotter against her blistered skin and in her throat.

Shouts from behind. She threw a quick glance over her left shoulder. A building less than a block behind her was burning, its flames already licking hungrily toward the one next to it.

Oh God. Her legs and feet seemed to move of their own volition. Buildings at her side were aflame now.

The courthouse loomed before her. Then the lapping flames caught the dry, wood frame, and it began to burn. Men squirmed through windows on the lower floor and some jumped from the second floor. Suddenly a mass of humanity shoved through the doors, tripping over each other, trampling one another in their terror. They'd freed the prisoners. Thank God. They had a chance. Katie ran on.

More embers sailed through the air, falling all around. Screams of agony told Katie that some had landed on people.

Oh God, she prayed, unable to form any other words.

The crowd in front of her veered to the right. What were they doing?

"To the lakeshore," someone shouted. "It's our only chance."

Hope rose in Katie as she ran after the crowd. Of course. They'd be safe on the shore of the lake. She ran faster.

Suddenly she couldn't feel her legs. A wave of dizziness hit her, and nausea rose in her throat. Her head began to bow. *God, I can't.* The blanket in her arms squirmed, and a hard kick landed on her side. She gasped and jerked upright. *Oh, thank You, God. She's not dead.*

Katie stared forward as she ran. Just a few feet more and she could rest. Her shoes hit sand, and she stumbled onto the edge of the water. Shouts and cries of relief pierced her ears, and she watched listlessly as people plunged into the lake, splashing water over blistered faces and necks. Katie's knees buckled, and she sank to the sand.

☙

Fritzie screamed in terror and reared, her hooves lashing out.

Sam hung on, berating himself for bringing her into this. If he could get her to calm down enough, he could dismount. If he covered her head with something so she couldn't see the flying sparks or hear the roar of the fire that got closer every minute, he could lead her. Her hooves crashed down, and she sidestepped and reared again, her legs flying as she whirled in midair.

Sam hit the ground. Pain seared through his neck and shoulder. A braying, bucking donkey ran past him, followed by a large barking dog. He stayed still until a wave of dizziness passed.

Bounding to his feet, he looked around for Fritzie.

"She took off." A young man with a cap perched sideways on his head yelled above the shouting people and mixed clamor of animal sounds. "I tried to grab her, but she was too wild. You shoulda seen the crowd make way for her. Scared 'em nigh to death."

"Thanks. Did you see which direction she went?"

"Nope. Crowd closed in behind her." The boy took off running.

Sam rubbed his shoulder and stood on tiptoe, hoping to catch a glimpse of her. Nowhere in sight. Doubling his fist, he hit his other hand hard. What now? He had to find Katie. Had to keep her safe. According to a policeman, everyone had escaped the Patch before the fire got to it. Where would the troupe have gone?

A young woman stumbled and fell against him. A mewling sound came from the bundle she held in one arm. He caught her and steadied her, placing his hand against her back. She threw a look of hopeless fear his way and stumbled on, leaning heavily on a stick, her other arm holding tightly to the infant. Were they alone? A lame woman with an infant? She'd never outrun this fire.

He took one quick step and reached her. "Ma'am, would you allow me to help?"

She turned grateful eyes up to him. More than grateful. Maybe a little less than adoration. Now that he had a closer look, he realized she was younger than he'd thought. Probably not much older than Katie.

She stopped and the crowd rushed against them, almost knocking them apart. With a pleading look, she held the wrapped bundle toward him. Did she think he'd take the baby and leave her? His heart wrenched.

"No. You hold your baby." He reached down and picked her up in his arms, and the stick fell from her hands. He kicked it aside and took off running with the crowd. Embers flew over his head, and some landed near him.

Through the cacophony of sound, he heard a loud cry up ahead and looked that way. A body hurtled to the ground from a third-floor window. His stomach churned, and he clamped his teeth together.

He was near the rear of the crowd. The flames roared like a train. Fiery heat burned his neck. The fire wasn't far behind. Screams sounded just behind him. He glanced back, and his heart lurched with fear. A building just a few yards behind him was engulfed in flames that reached out, threatening adjacent buildings.

He sped up with the crowd, and flames that reached out to the buildings beside him, consuming them. The shrieking mob ahead turned toward the lake.

Shifting the woman in his arms, he ran after them. Pain stabbed his ribs. He gasped for breath as the smoky air filled his lungs.

The woman tugged on his shirt. "Please," she shouted. "I'm slowing you down. Take my babe and let me make my own way."

Ignoring her plea, he ran, stumbling as his weak ankle almost gave way. Gasping for air, he reached the edge of the lapping waves. The crowd pressed close around him.

"Make way," he yelled, wobbling where he stood. "I have a lame woman and her baby here."

People scattered to clear a small section of beach.

He set her gently on the sand and held on to her until she was seated with the baby in her arms. Then he fell to his knees, bending over, panting for air. He glanced over at his charges. The woman's head had fallen forward. Was she ill?

The mewling sound began again. Groaning, Sam pushed himself to his feet. He had to check on them. The mother's head jerked up, and she pulled the blanket from the baby's face. Sam inhaled sharply. A newborn. Very newborn.

He stooped down beside the woman and leaned close so she could hear his shouts above the crowd and the roar of the fire. "My name is Sam. Are you all right?"

She nodded and shouted, tears running down her ash-smeared cheeks. "Lucy Owens. God bless you, sir. You saved our lives."

"How old is your infant?"

Her face crumpled and tears filled her eyes. "He was born less than an hour before you found me."

"Do you have family?" He leaned closer to hear her better.

She shook her head. "My man died of the fever just three months ago. There's no one but me. And him." She nodded at the baby.

"Are you lame or just weak?"

She blushed and ducked her head. "I'll be fit as a fiddle when I get my strength back."

Sam looked around, frustrated. He had to look for Katie. But he didn't feel right leaving Lucy alone. Heat and ash from the mile-wide fire fell on them as it raged past, less than a block away. *Dear Lord, please don't let it spread closer to the shore.*

"Sam Nelson, is that you?" The cry was followed by arms flung around his neck. She pulled away, and his eyes rested on the exhausted face of Rosie Riley.

᪥

The child slept on the sand, one hand under her soot-coated cheek, oblivious to the terror and bedlam around her. Betty had fallen exhausted on the shore and lay motionless, covered by the damp blanket Bridget had thrown over her.

Katie leaned against a trunk and shut her burning eyes. The roar of the fire filled her ears. She forced them open. Why did it seem louder with them closed?

"Katie! Daughter!" She jumped up at the sound of her father's voice. His wonderful face was glowing, a smile stretching across his face as he ran toward her, followed by several members of the troupe, almost unrecognizable from the soot and ash. When he reached her, she fell into his arms, leaning against his strong, safe chest.

Now she could close her eyes. But immediately they flew open. "Pa, I'm so sorry. I got separated from Rosie. I don't know where she is." She hid her face in her hands.

She felt his hand gently remove hers from her face.

"Daughter, it's not your fault. The city is a madhouse. We'll trust God to keep Rosie safe."

"We'd just crossed the bridge when someone pushed this little girl into my arms. I looked around to see who it was, and when I looked back, Rosie was gone." She wiped at the tears that rolled down her cheeks. "Should I have searched for her, Pa? I had to get the child to safety, didn't I?"

He pulled her head back to his chest and patted her. "Of course, Katie girl. You did the right thing. Don't fret yourself now."

"Do you think Sam's all right? What if he's trying to find me? What if he got caught by the fire?" Panic clawed at her, like something wild attacking, draining her strength.

"Katie, stop it. You're imaginin' all sorts of things that aren't so. Sam can take care of himself. They're both in God's hands."

Katie swallowed and took a deep breath.

Of course, they were in God's hands. She had to stop falling apart like this. She stood straight. "I'm sorry. I'll be all right now."

Emma Gallagher knelt beside the sleeping child. "You don't know who she belongs to?"

Katie shook her head.

"Katie. Look."

At her father's excited voice, she glanced his way. Sam was running down the sandy beach, his face and clothing gray with ash, just as hers were.

Then she was in his arms, and he was holding her tightly.

"I couldn't find you. I searched everywhere and couldn't find you. I was so afraid." He held her at arm's length and stared into her eyes then pulled her to him again.

Her father cleared his throat, and Katie pulled away from Sam. She looked into his eyes and smiled.

Sam turned to her father. "Sir, Rosie Riley is down the beach. She's helping someone there. I told her if I found you, I'd let you know."

Katie watched joy brighten her father's face. He started off running down the beach, heedless of the wall of fire that had stretched closer to the shore, consuming building after building.

Tiny pieces of ash and debris floated on the wind. How close could the fire get to the lake? Would they be safe here?

Emma reached down and picked up the sleeping child. She trudged off across the sand.

Katie tugged at Bridget's arm. "Come. We have to go with Pa."

Bridget lifted Betty, and she and Mrs. Thornton dragged themselves after the others.

Sam took Katie's hand, and they tripped and stumbled across the sand through a red glow as Chicago burned.

Chapter 22

Katie snuggled into the downy soft bed. She closed her eyes, and a satisfied sigh escaped from her throat. Wonderful.

The hot, sudsy bath had relaxed her tight muscles, and drowsiness washed over her. Could Bridget and Mrs. Thornton and that poor young mother be in as much heaven as she was? The kind housemaid who'd drawn her bath had laid a soft nightgown on the bed and told her she'd be back to help her out of the tub. Katie had almost laughed but didn't want to seem rude. She'd been taking her own baths since she was three and was quite capable of getting herself out of a bathtub.

Someone tapped on the door, but she was too tired to call out. She heard it open.

"Dear, do you mind if I come in?" The door closed.

Katie started and jerked from her reverie. Wide awake now, she glanced across at the white-haired woman standing by the door, her gentle smile resting on Katie's face. Katie drew in her breath sharply. She'd know those eyes anywhere. "Yes, of course." Her voice shook a little, and she cleared her throat.

Sam's mother stepped across the carpeted floor. "I hope you found your bath and bed to your liking." Her voice rippled like water over stones, gentle and singing.

"Oh yes, ma'am. Everything is wonderful. Thank you so much." She swallowed. "Please, would you like to sit down?"

The lady stepped to the wingbacked chair beside the bed and seated herself, smiling brightly at Katie. "I'm Mrs. Nelson. Sam's mother. And you are the lovely Miss O'Shannon."

Katie blushed. "Please call me Katie."

"Thank you. I believe I will." Wrinkles formed between her eyes. "I know you've been through a dreadful ordeal. Sam thought you might be concerned about your friends, so I came to tell you they are being cared for."

Relief washed over Katie. "Thank you. It's very kind of you to take strangers into your home."

"Nonsense. Any Christian soul would do the same." She gave a little nod. "The servants brought Sam's old cradle down from the attic, and our doctor has been here to care for the young mother. Lucy? I think that's her name. He says she needs bed rest but otherwise seems fine. Your friend Bridget and her little sister are sharing a room. Their mother is across the hall from them. They're all well but exhausted, with a few minor burns."

Katie felt the worry that had been nibbling at the back of her mind fade. "That's wonderful. I was a little worried. And the little girl I carried from the Patch?"

Mrs. Nelson lowered her eyes. "The doctor says she needs food and rest. She seems to have suffered neglect for quite some time." She sighed and looked into Katie's eyes again. "We've requested a nurse to care for her until she's well again. In the meantime, my husband and Sam will attempt to locate the parents. Then we shall see."

"The poor child. How old do you think she is?"

"The doctor says not more than two. Don't you worry. She'll be taken care of. And now you'd probably like to know your father has had his supper and is on the front porch with my husband, drinking lemonade. I think they might become fast friends."

"What about Rosie?" Katie had lost count of the times she'd thanked God for keeping her friend safe.

"Miss Riley has accepted the invitation of a member of the troupe whose home was out of the fire's path."

"Sam?"

A dimple appeared in Mrs. Nelson's cheek as she smiled. "My son has cleaned up and eaten an enormous dinner. He plans to join the men on the front porch after a while, as his father requested. But only after I assured him I would guard you with my life."

Katie gasped and blushed.

Laughing, Sam's mother stood. "My dear, you're just as precious as Sam told me you were. And now that I've made you blush, I'll get out of your way. Nancy will be here shortly with your tray. And you may sleep as long as you like." She stood and looked down at Katie, mist forming in her eyes. "It's quite easy to see why my son has fallen in love with you, my dear. And I must say I couldn't be more pleased."

"Thank you, Mrs. Nelson," Katie whispered, barely able to make any sound at all.

Mrs. Nelson gave her one last smile. "Good night, my dear. Tomorrow, we shall get to know each other." She walked softly to the door and left the room.

Sam had spoken of her to his mother. Not only that, Mrs. Nelson said he loved her. A thrill washed over her, and a spontaneous giggle sprang from her throat. Then another thought crossed her mind, and she sobered. What would his father think of her?

ଔ

"Everything was black. The buildings. The ground. Ash falling all around." Sam's voice cracked. How could anyone convey the reality in words? He sat in a chair by his father on the front porch and watched the rain almost with disbelief. If it had only come earlier.

He gathered his thoughts and continued. "Father, you can't imagine what it was like. In moments, buildings, trees, everything incinerated."

117

He paused, reliving the horror. "We could feel the heat by the lake and had to dodge flaming debris as we watched Michigan Avenue demolished block by block."

He stopped and took a deep breath. Pain tore at his singed throat. "I'm sorry. Our building was reduced to rubble along with the others." Most of the factories along the river, including those belonging to Jeremiah Howard, had burned to the ground. No one had heard from him since the fire, not even his wife, so he was assumed dead.

"A lifetime of work for us and so many of our friends—gone in an instant." His father sighed loudly. "However, we have other things to attend to for now. We'll talk about rebuilding in the days ahead."

"I wasn't sure how you'd feel about my bringing my friends home with me."

"I'm not totally heartless, Sam." He frowned. "Did you see any sign of the Flannigans?"

"None. Katie said they left their home at the same time as she and the Thorntons. They got separated somewhere along the way. I can only hope they made it to safety."

"We'll find them."

Sam relaxed. They'd find them.

"I'm pleased that Miss O'Shannon is safe."

Sam darted a look at his father.

"Harrumph." His father cleared his throat loudly. "She's welcome here. As your friend. As your bride."

A heavy weight lifted off Sam. *Thank You, Lord.*

"I can't tell you how happy you've made me, Father. I plan to speak with her father. With his blessing, I'll ask her to marry me at the earliest opportunity."

"I suspected as much. Let me be the first to congratulate you."

Sam laughed. "She hasn't accepted me yet."

Hooves pounded up Prairie Avenue. A horse and rider galloped up the driveway and stopped in front of Sam and his father. The horse's wet sides heaved.

"Mr. Nelson, I've a letter for you, sir." He reached into a saddlebag and produced a long, thin envelope.

"Thank you." Sam took the letter and handed it to his father. "Can you give us any information about the damage?"

"Reports are starting to come in. Just about everything on the southeast side of town is gone. Then a mile-wide path from the river all the way to the far north. Seventy-three streets, that's what I'm hearing. Many of the bridges are gone. The business district is all but gone. Post office, Palmer House Hotel, just about everything." He shook his head, and his eyes looked dazed. "Don't know what's gonna happen."

"We'll rebuild, of course."

Admiration for his father rose up in Sam. He just hoped when he saw the devastation with his own eyes he'd remain optimistic. "Do you know how they finally stopped the fire?"

"Some buildings had to be blown up. After that, there wasn't anything left but a little prairie grass. The fire still tried to keep going. But when the rain started, it kind of burned itself out in the old graveyard." He sat up straight in the saddle and stretched. "I have to go. More of these to deliver."

Sam watched his father rip open the envelope and scan the letter. "They've already started making plans to help the homeless. The mayor has called for a meeting in the morning to discuss the situation. Homeless are our priority. Of course, the city waterworks is gone. It'll take awhile to get it operating again. Those of us with wells should consider ourselves very fortunate."

⊗

Katie looked over her shoulder at Bridget as she pinned a sheet to the clothesline. "Would you bring me that basket? This one's empty."

Three weeks after the fire, the Nelsons were now hosting over a dozen people, including the babies. Which made for a lot of meals, dirty dishes, and of course, dirty laundry. The servants couldn't keep up with it all, so all the women except for Lucy, who was still weak after months of nearly starving while trying to keep her unborn child alive, insisted on helping.

Sam had initially protested when he saw Katie bending over a washtub, but when his mother walked up and plunged her manicured hands into the rinse water, cheerfully singing at the top of her lungs, he threw his hands in the air and walked away.

Katie finished hanging the sheets and went inside. Sarah Flannigan was coming out of the door with rugs slung over her arm. She smiled and ducked her head as she passed Katie.

Fred, the coachman, had found the Flannigans three days after the fire, living in a tent among rows of others. Mr. Nelson insisted the man who'd cared for Sam the night of the attack wasn't living in a tent and they must accept his hospitality until a proper house could be constructed for them.

The gesture solidified Katie's love for the man who raised Sam. It was easy to see the man she loved came by his kindness naturally.

That evening, she headed for the kitchen to help with dinner when Sam walked in the front door. A lock of hair had fallen onto his forehead. His eyes lit up as they met hers. He smiled that smile that made her knees go weak. Her heart pounded. Why did it have to do that every time he was near? Hastily she reached up to rescue the curls that had slipped from the long braid that hung down her back.

"How's the building coming along?" A nice safe subject. She hoped her father wasn't working too hard on the construction that had provided jobs for all who wanted to work. He wasn't getting any younger and wasn't used to that kind of work. But what was he to do? The troupe had disbanded until the theater could be rebuilt, and as he'd told her sternly, he wasn't about to be anyone's charity case.

"I can't believe how much has been accomplished in less than a month." He smiled. "Maybe Chicago will thrive again."

Mrs. Nelson came into the hall. Her eyes sparkled as she glanced from Sam to Katie. "How would you two like to share a pot of tea with me on the porch?"

Katie nodded as Sam threw a questioning glance her way. She went to get the tea then joined Sam and his mother on the porch. She set the tray on a small wrought-iron table. Sam motioned her over to the swing where he sat. His mother rested on a wicker chair across from them.

"Doesn't the air feel lovely?" Excitement trilled in Mrs. Nelson's voice.

"Yes, ma'am." In spite of everything, the autumn air was now crisp and fresh. Katie smiled. "Sam told me how much you love autumn."

Mrs. Nelson nodded and smiled. "It's my favorite time of the year. You know, I've been thinking we should have a party."

"A party? With the city in shambles?" Sam lifted an eyebrow. "Who would come?"

"Don't be foolish. Everyone will come. We'll do a benefit auction with a ball to follow. It will do wonders for the citizens of this city." Mrs. Nelson picked up her cup and stood. "Well, I think I'll have my tea inside after all. It's getting a little cold for me. You two stay."

Katie stared in astonishment as Sam's mother went inside and closed the door, leaving them in the dark. Katie glanced at Sam.

He gave her a tender smile and took her hand, rubbing his thumb across it. She shivered.

"Sweetheart, don't mind her. She's always wanted a daughter."

Warmth washed over her. He'd called her "sweetheart." And "daughter"? What was he saying? Did he mean. . .

"Katie, I'd planned to do this differently, in a more romantic setting, but. . ."

Her heart raced, and she looked into his warm brown eyes. Eyes filled with love for her.

"I spoke to your father last night and received his blessing." He swallowed, slid off the swing, and knelt down on one knee in front of her.

"You must know how I feel about you. From the first moment you lifted those big blue eyes in the train station, I've been unable to think of anything but you. I love you, sweetheart. And it would give me the greatest joy if you'll agree to be my wife." He reached into his pocket and removed a small velvet box. The lid sprang open, and she gasped.

"Katie, this ring belonged to my maternal grandmother. I hope with all my heart you'll wear it. Will you marry me?"

"Oh, Sam," she whispered, "I love you, too. And to be your wife would be the most wonderful thing I can imagine. It will be an honor to wear your grandmother's ring."

Her hand tingled as he slid the ring on her finger. She held up her hand and looked at the sparkling gems as he sat beside her. "It's the most beautiful ring in the world."

"When I told Mother of my intentions, she insisted that you must have it."

"Oh, I must go and thank her!" Katie shifted but found herself locked in a warm embrace as Sam's arms encircled her, pulling her close.

"There'll be plenty of time for that," he whispered, lowering his head.

Katie's stomach dipped, and she raised her head willingly for his kiss.

ONCE A THIEF

Dedication

For my granddaughter, Cat, who loves to act. I'm so happy you've dedicated your dreams to Jesus. I hope you like Danielle's story.

Prologue

Chicago, 1899

Ten-year-old Danielle shivered and crouched down lower as the cold November wind from off the Chicago River whipped around the huge crate. She wrapped one end of her mother's tattered shawl around Jimmy's painfully thin shoulders and drew him closer. They had watched, their stomachs growling, as the dockworkers sat down to eat their lunch. Now only one of the burly men remained, and Danielle's gaze followed his hand as it carried a hunk of sausage to his mouth.

"What kind of ship is that, Danni?" Jimmy whispered.

Danielle's gaze followed her brother's pointing finger to a schooner just entering the harbor from Lake Michigan. Her breath caught in her throat as the sailors on board began to lower the sails. "I don't know, Jimmy. It's pretty, isn't it?"

"Yeah, but why's it full of trees?" A fit of coughing stopped the boy's questions and Danielle patted him gently on the back.

A yell from the remaining dockworker caught her attention, and she watched as he jumped up and ran to help two other men lift a fallen beam from the deck of one of the schooners.

Danielle's glance darted to the bread and sausage left on the upturned barrel. She turned her brother loose and jumped up. "Wait here."

The little boy looked up at her with wide, brown eyes. "Danni, Mama wouldn't want you to steal."

Heat rushed to her cheeks and she hesitated. Jimmy was right. Mama would have been mortified if she'd thought one of her children would even consider stealing. But the hollow look of hunger in her brother's eyes settled the matter. Mama was gone now and she had to take care of Jimmy.

She darted quickly around the crate and over wet boards to the wooden barrel. Grabbing the food, she whirled and ran back, yanked Jimmy up, and took off down the street at a dead run, half dragging, half carrying her little brother, with his crutch bumping along behind.

A shout from behind them warned Danielle they were discovered. Too late, she realized she should have crossed the Clark Street Bridge. There, she and Jimmy would have been lost in the crowded sidewalks of the downtown district.

"Faster, Danni, faster!"

The terror in Jimmy's voice gave Danielle an extra burst of energy and she shot past an alley, only to be jerked to a stop as a hand reached out and grabbed her arm, yanking her around. She screamed and brought her arm up in front of her face, expecting blows to rain down upon her.

"Come on. I'll show you where to hide!"

Surprised and shocked, she stumbled down the dark alley, following the strange boy around a corner, down another street and into a second alley, where he stopped at a doorway and inserted a key. Danielle pulled Jimmy through the door, and as the boy slammed it shut and bolted it, she fell against the wall, gulping air.

As soon as she could breathe freely, she looked at their rescuer, who was pounding his knees and laughing.

"What an adventure! You should've seen the bloke's face when he saw his food was gone."

"Well, Cobb. And who are your friends?"

Danielle's head jerked up at the sound of the deep voice.

A man, dressed in gentleman's clothes, stood in an arched doorway peering at them. He smiled and walked over. Reaching down, he lifted Danielle's hand. "Welcome to our home, young lady. How may I be of service?"

Danielle pulled her hand away and shivered. Mother had warned her about strange men. Maybe they'd better get out of here. But just then, Jimmy bent over in a fit of coughing. She couldn't take him back out into the cold. And after all, the man had sounded kind.

A boot caught him on the chin. Be still."
"Ouch! You little hoodlum. Be still."
"I...said...let me go! I didn't...do...any
Blake dodged another kick aimed towa
"Blake Nelson! You get off that poor
Girl? Jumping up, he blinked har
of auburn curls where a boy's ca
eyes flashed up at him from t
bed of leaves on which sh
A hand pushed him
fixing him with a g
Wait until your
patted her o
Blake s
robbed

B lake Nels
it was an
were danc
But who cared?
of all, his music. J
was a sale. Mothe
Blake could always

He walked quick
that scattered abou   , he pursed his
lips and whistled th   ... from his new show, *Peg in Dreamland*. His new show. Laughter exploded from his throat.

A lady walking by drew her little girl closer and frowned pointedly at him then turned away. Blake winked at the child, and she flashed him an impish grin from beneath her mother's arm. Chuckling, he turned the corner and headed down the street toward the bank. If he forgot Father's deposit, he wouldn't be laughing for long.

"What. . . ?" Jerked from his reverie, Blake swerved to one side, barely avoiding a young man who had rushed past him.

Blake stopped and stared, blinking in confusion. Another boy, younger than the first, headed toward him at a dead run. Blake and the boy each tried to dodge the other, and in doing so, both moved the same way. Blake hit the sidewalk with a jolt.

The boy, who'd landed beside him, yanked his arm from beneath Blake's leg then scrambled to his feet and bolted around the corner.

"Stop them! They just robbed the bank!" The shout came from farther down the street.

Before Blake could pull himself up, he saw a set of boot-clad feet running pell-mell toward him. He swung his umbrella toward the fugitive, catching him around the ankle with the handle. Blake was on top of the culprit before he could scramble up.

"Get off me, you. . . !"

"*Oomph*," Blake grunted and grabbed at the foot that had landed on his stomach. "Not a chance, you rascal."

hing!"

rd his midsection.

girl this instant! What are you thinking?"

d, trying to make sense of the tumbling mass

p had sat a moment before. Gold-flecked brown

he loveliest face he had ever seen. The red and gold

e lay only made the picture more captivating.

aside, and his neighbor, Amelia Kramer, stormed past,

are. "I would never have believed you could be such a bully.

mother hears about this." Kneeling by the squirming girl, she

the arm. "Are you all right?"

ook himself out of his hypnotic state. "But. . .Mrs. Kramer, she just

the bank."

onsense!" She whirled around and leveled him with a fierce scowl. "Does his tiny thing look like she could rob a bank?" She turned her attention back to the girl who sat up, rubbing her arm, and smiled tremulously.

Curious faces peered from the gathering crowd of employees and customers from businesses along the street. Benjamin Kramer, vice president of the bank, rushed toward them. Seeing his wife on the sidewalk, he reached down and helped her to her feet. "Amelia, are you all right, dear? Did you fall?"

"I'm fine, Ben. I was just trying to help this poor girl Blake knocked down and manhandled." She glared at Blake again, and blood rushed to his face.

"I didn't knock her down, and I certainly wasn't manhandling her. I was simply trying. . ." Blake shrugged and released a frustrated breath.

"What's going on?" Benjamin interrupted. "Someone said one of the robbers had been caught." He looked around questioningly at the people who stood around gaping.

A tall, well-dressed man pushed his way through the crowd, his face red and beaded with perspiration. "Well, I certainly hope so. Someone lifted my wallet and managed to get my watch. It's solid gold." The man shifted from one foot to the other, breathing heavily. He showed a cut watch fob, hanging from his vest pocket.

"I thought the bank had been robbed." Blake rubbed his hand across his head in an attempt to smooth his black locks that were more than likely standing straight up.

"No, no." Mr. Kramer said. "Thankfully, not the bank. But Mr. Fowler appears to have been the victim of pickpockets. Did anyone see the culprits?"

Blake stepped forward and said uncertainly, "Actually, I did. Two got away, but I think I've apprehended one of them, sir. This girl was running after the others."

Mr. Kramer glanced down in surprise at the small figure who opened her eyes wide and shook her head.

"Sir, I'm not a robber." Her voice trembled. "I was trying to get to the corner before they got away so I could see which direction they ran. I was only trying to help."

"There, a perfectly logical explanation, Ben. Does she look like a robber to you?" Mrs. Kramer placed a hand on her husband's arm and frowned at Blake.

By this time, Blake was ready to let the matter drop and slink away, but then he glanced down at the girl.

She stared back at him, her full lips tipped ever so slightly in a triumphant smirk.

He tightened his lips and scowled at her. The little thief was going to get away with it unless he insisted. He squinted and spoke with grim determination. "Surely someone saw her in the bank. That should settle this matter." He threw his own "take that" smirk back at the girl.

Mr. Kramer nodded. "Let's go into the bank and wait for the police. They should be able to get to the bottom of this."

Blake heard a sharp intake of breath and glanced at the girl.

She quickly lowered her gaze.

Grim satisfaction swelled in his chest. "Good idea. I'll escort the young lady myself." He snatched the cap from the sidewalk and then took her by the arm, none too gently, and helped her up. When she winced, he felt a stab of guilt and loosened his grip. They trooped down the street and into the bank, with the girl casting scathing looks at Blake. He would feel like an idiot if she turned out to be innocent. But she *had* been running after the other robbers, and besides, what was a young girl doing gallivanting around town dressed like a boy? She was guilty, all right.

"What's the trouble here?" Officer Brady's booming voice preceded his solid frame that shoved through the bank door.

"Mr. Fowler's been robbed!" one of the salesclerks blurted out.

"Well, I know Mr. Fowler's been robbed." The officer turned a scathing look on the young man. "I'm here to get particulars of the crime."

Mr. Kramer stepped forward. "It seems this gentleman was robbed of his wallet and watch. Mr. Nelson here believes he has apprehended a suspect—"

"Mr. Nelson is quite mistaken," Mrs. Kramer interrupted. She motioned to the girl who stood silently. "This poor girl is obviously not a crook."

"And I say, at least find out if anyone saw her in the bank during the robbery," Blake insisted.

Officer Brady squinted blue eyes at the girl.

"All right, then. If anyone saw this wee young thing thieving with a gang of hoodlums, step forward and identify her."

When no one moved, he nodded and turned back to the girl. "What's your name, lass?" He gave her the once-over, and one corner of his mouth pulled up. "And what's a bonny young thing like you doing running around in a lad's suit of clothing?"

Blake stared in disbelief. The officer spoke to the girl like a kindly old grandfather. And with a twinkle in his eye at that.

"Danielle Grays—s—s—s, sir." She stumbled over the words and spoke so softly, Blake could barely hear her.

"And what about the boy's clothes?" Blake demanded, raising an eyebrow in her direction. Was he the only one who thought that was more than a little suspicious?

Panic crossed her face for a moment. She swallowed and suddenly her face crumpled. "They were my brother's." She lifted imploring eyes to Officer Brady and continued. "He died in the orphanage, you see, and when I left, I took his clothing with me." She covered her face with her hands and began to sob. "Because they were all I had left of him." She took the handkerchief Officer Brady offered, wiped her nose daintily, and sniffled. "Then my dress wore out, and I had nothing else to wear."

Blake looked on in astonishment. Officer Brady had fallen for it. Blake couldn't help but feel just a touch of admiration for the performance.

"Now, now, don't you cry, my dear." The officer's lined face seemed about to crumple, too. "And I'll warrant you've been sleeping on park benches now, haven't ye?"

The girl looked startled for a moment, then biting her lip, she nodded.

"Well now, young man," the officer said with a stern look at Blake. "I think your question is answered. And not one person saw her in the bank anyway."

Blake snorted. "Of course they didn't! She had her hair hidden under this cap."

Officer Brady pursed his lips and exhaled loudly, then after throwing a disgusted glance at Blake, he smiled at the girl.

"Little lady, I hate to be troubling you, but if you please, put the cap on and stuff your hair up under it."

ɞ

A bolt of panic shot through Danielle. She looked from the kind face of the patrolman to the challenging expression of the annoying young man who held the cap out to her.

She didn't think anyone would recognize her since she'd only been inside the bank for a few seconds. She had stepped into the doorway to block anyone who might be following Hank and Cobb. That was the plan. Cobb said anyone seeing her would think she was a messenger boy who just happened to step through the door at the wrong time. That would give him and Hank a few more minutes to get away.

Up to that point she had followed instructions. If only she had turned and walked slowly away in the other direction as planned. But she'd panicked. And it didn't help any that she'd almost given them her real name, just now.

She reached for the cap and placed it onto her head, trying to place it in a feminine position. Holding her breath, she waited while every person scrutinized her then breathed a soft sigh as, one by one, each failed to recognize her.

"There. That should be that." The lady who had championed her stepped forward with determination. "If you have no further questions for Miss Gray, Officer Brady, we'll be leaving now." At the officer's nod, the lady took her arm and began guiding her gently toward the door.

Suddenly Danielle gasped. What was she thinking, letting someone lead her off like a puppy with no questions asked? She pulled back and planted her feet firmly. "Where do you think you're taking me?"

"Why, home with me, of course. You look like you could use a good night's sleep. Park bench, indeed." She turned and smiled sweetly at her husband. "You don't mind, do you, dear?"

Ah. Here it comes. My way out.

Mr. Kramer hesitated and then gave his wife an indulgent smile. "I think it would be all right for now. We can discuss things later."

Danielle stared at the man, unable to hold back the surprised lift of her brow. *Mister, you're being mighty stupid. The stuff I could lift in a rich man's house would buy my freedom.*

A bolt of fear shot through her. What would Sutton do if she didn't show up? He'd more than likely think she'd run out on him. Maybe she'd better try to get away now. But on the other hand, if she could pilfer enough valuables, maybe he would let her and Jimmy go, like he'd promised.

She glanced at the gentle face of the woman called Amelia and felt a twinge of uncertainty. But with sudden resolve, she pressed her lips tightly together and followed the lady out the door. After all, a body had to do whatever was necessary to survive.

ভ

Danielle's mouth watered. The smell of freshly baked bread and something chocolate tantalized her nostrils, a solid reminder that she hadn't eaten since early that morning. And only a bun at that. Sutton had rushed them out the door so he could meet with some bigwig friend of his.

Mrs. Kramer had settled her into a small room off the main hall, promising to return momentarily. Danielle ran her hand over the settee's velvety soft fabric. There was nothing like this at Sutton's. And there certainly hadn't been at Aunt Mary's.

A shiver ran through her body. Standing quickly, she went to the bay window and pulled the curtains aside. A squirrel wiggled through a hole beneath the wrought-iron fence and scurried up the oak tree in the yard.

She shivered again, rubbing her arms. It was autumn then, too. Late autumn. Danielle had been ten and Jimmy just four. Papa's ship had gone down the month before with no survivors. Mama had gone to work at Aunt Mary's boardinghouse in order to feed them and keep a roof over their heads. But Mother had died giving birth to a stillborn son. The very next day, Aunt Mary handed Danielle a bundle containing their meager belongings. She wasn't raising two kids, she'd said. Especially a boy with a gimpy leg. After all, they weren't really her kin. They'd have to make their own way.

Danielle's stomach lurched. Again she relived the fear and confusion she'd felt as she took her little brother's hand in hers and walked down the grimy street. That was the day they'd met Sutton.

Sutton had remained a mystery to Danielle for a long time. He was gone most nights by six or seven and didn't return until the next morning. Finally one day, she'd asked Cobb.

"Him? Why, he's from a rich family here in the city. Lives in a posh house with servants and everything." Cobb had snickered. "Guess the business didn't do so good after Sutton's old man died, so he has to supplement his income, you see."

Danielle didn't see, but she did in time.

Hearing a soft laugh, she whirled around.

Mrs. Kramer entered the room with an elderly lady with snow-white hair and sparkling eyes. "Mother, I'd like for you to meet Danielle Gray. Danielle, this is my mother, Mrs. Parker."

"My dear child, I'm so very happy to meet you." The elderly lady stepped forward and took Danielle's hands in hers.

Danielle looked from the smiling face of Mrs. Kramer to the kind, gentle one of the older woman. And suddenly she wasn't sure she could carry out her plan. But she had to. She simply had to. She didn't want to hurt anyone. But she had to free herself and Jimmy from Sutton and his gang of thugs.

Chapter 2

The fireplace crackled and popped, the only sound in the otherwise silent room. Blake's mother's face was a study in emotions. Consternation, pride, and fear. His father, on the other hand, stared with shocked indignation. Blake waited for the explosion.

"Are you insane? Show business! You'd give up a promising law career to write folderol?" Samuel Nelson took a deep breath, and his face turned scarlet. "You can forget this pipe dream, because I forbid it." Stalking over to his son, he glared into his face. "Do you hear me, young man? I forbid it."

Blake stared at his father in frustration. There weren't too many men tall enough to stare eye to eye with him, but his stately father was one of them. Now, standing so close, he noticed the gray hair at his father's temples and deep lines cutting across weathered skin. A knot of anxiety clutched at Blake's stomach. His father was getting old. "Father, if you'll just listen a minute."

"Listen to what? Listen to you try to reason away your future?"

"Now, Samuel. Surely it's not that bad. At least give him a chance."

Blake's heart jumped and he looked at his mother in surprise. She usually stood firmly beside her husband in any and all family disagreements.

"Besides, he can always come back to the firm if this doesn't work out." She reached over and patted her husband's arm.

"Thank you for your vote of confidence, Mother."

"Well, I didn't mean that you would fail, son. I'm sure you are very talented. I only meant, well, you know, if by some chance. . ."

"It's all right, Mother. I know what you meant." He gave her a kiss on the cheek and turned back to the glaring scowl. "Father, I'm sorry you're disappointed. I had hoped you'd be proud I've accomplished something on my own. Show business is becoming quite respectable, you know. It's not vaudeville."

"And just what's wrong with vaudeville, I'd like to know?"

Blake turned with a grin. His grandfather, Michael O'Shannon, filled the room with his presence.

"Now, Papa, shouldn't you be resting? You've been up and around all day." Blake felt one side of his mouth twist up as he watched his mother turn from peacemaking wife and mother to hovering daughter in a split second. She took her father by the arm and attempted to lead him from the room.

"Katie O'Shannon, you'll be getting your hands off my arm. I'm not a doddering old man yet. It's in my prime, I am. And I can surely be taking part in this discussion. After all, my grandson comes by his love of the theater naturally. His talent, too, if I may say so. And don't you be getting high and mighty, my girl, your first bed being a costume trunk."

"All right, Papa. But since you're not, as you say, doddering, you might try to remember my name hasn't been O'Shannon for thirty-five years." Blake grinned as his mother placed her fists on her hips and frowned at her father. He loved it when she forgot for a moment she was the prim and proper Mrs. Samuel Nelson.

Blake seized the moment and patted his grandfather on the shoulder. "Pop, let's go for a walk. I need to clear my head a little before I return to my music. Mother, Father, perhaps we can continue this discussion later." He hurried his grandfather from the room, grabbed a heavy sweater from the coatrack in the hall, and handed it to his grinning pop. They made their escape, laughing as they stepped out onto the broad front porch.

"It's proud of you, I am, my boy. Couldn't have gotten out of the situation better myself."

Blake threw his head back and laughed as they headed off down the sidewalk. "Actually, two situations, Pop. Father was about to let me have it with a vengeance."

"So? And how is *Peg in Dreamland* coming along?"

"Pretty good. I have a couple of more numbers to complete. I'm not too crazy about the actress they've chosen to play the lead, though. She's nothing like the girl in my mind and I'm not sure she can carry the part."

"Well, it's right proud of you, I am. And don't forget it."

"Thanks, Pop. I'm glad someone is."

Blake and Pop crossed the street at the corner and nearly completed the loop around the block when a blaze of black and white fur hurled itself onto Blake's chest.

Laughing, Blake steadied himself and put up his arms to ward off the slurping kisses of a huge sheepdog. "Wooly, old boy! How you doing, buddy?"

ᴄᴈ

Danielle's heart sped up, and fear knifed through her stomach as she watched her accuser from the week before. What was he doing here? She'd hoped she'd seen the last of him.

As he grabbed the Kramers' English sheepdog in a bear hug, Danielle bit her lip. The two looked like old friends. She watched from behind the oak tree as Georgie and David ran through the gate and joined the frolic. She had learned quickly the seven-year-old twins were always ready for any kind of skirmish.

Blake stepped back and laughed as the dog ran circles around him, and the boys cavorted after the dog in what looked like a war dance.

Despite herself, the corners of Danielle's mouth lifted in a smile.

Blake looked up and saw her peek around the tree.

Danielle's heart jumped and heat rushed up, washing over her throat and face. She turned and rushed up the side path and into the kitchen where she leaned against the door, breathing heavily. Why was she behaving so foolishly? There wasn't a man alive who could rile her like this. Well, this one just did. But only because she was worried he might ruin everything for her. It didn't have anything to do with his deep blue eyes that crinkled at the corners when he laughed.

"My dear, whatever is the matter?" Danielle pushed away from the door as Sally, the Kramers' cook, put her knife down by the big bowl of apples and hurried over with a worried frown. "I heard Wooly barking. That rascal dog didn't chase you again, did he?"

Danielle groaned at the memory of her first encounter with the huge animal. She had gone out onto the back porch to get some fresh air when the brute bounded up the steps barking his head off. Instead of taking refuge inside, she was so flustered and frightened she jumped off the back porch and ran lickety-split around the house while the dog barreled after her. When he landed on Danielle's back and knocked her down, she'd thought she was a goner for sure, until the monster licked her face.

"No, I'm fine. The silly dog is playing with the twins and one of the neighbors. Is there anything I can do to help in here?" Danielle asked.

"Lands, no. All the kitchen chores are done and I'm just now getting apples ready for tonight's pies." The older woman turned to look at Danielle. "You run along. You've been working hard all morning."

"If you're sure. . ." Danielle left the kitchen and headed for the room she considered heaven on earth. Leather-bound books lined three walls of the library. A great stone fireplace occupied almost the entire fourth wall. She went to the section that contained the works of Charles Dickens and let her hands run softly over the smooth spines. Ah, there it was. *Oliver Twist*. Danielle slid the book from the shelf and walked to an overstuffed chair by the fireplace, sinking down into the luxurious comfort.

After nearly a week, she still wanted to pinch herself every now and then, to make sure she wasn't dreaming. The day after she'd arrived, she'd jumped out of bed early and tiptoed downstairs, planning to pocket whatever she could and make her escape. But she'd found Mrs. Kramer in the kitchen brewing tea. She insisted Danielle join her. Before their conversation had ended, Danielle found herself employed. The kind woman had talked her husband into allowing her to hire Danielle to help around the house. But the employment had turned out to be as much like an adoption as a job. The Kramers treated her almost like a protégé and allowed her to do no more work than a daughter of the house might have done.

She found the place she'd left off from the night before and was once again mesmerized by the similarity between Oliver's story and her own. Her stomach clenched as she read about Fagin and the orphan children he exploited. She wondered if he'd read the book and got the idea from it. Probably not, though. The evils that occurred to one man could easily occur to another. She couldn't help chuckling as she imagined Cobb in the role of the Artful Dodger. That didn't take too much stretch of the imagination.

Danielle and Jimmy hadn't actually been abused, and until recently they hadn't been forced to take part in any of the criminal activities. Sometimes she thought they were more entertainment for Sutton than anything. For the most part, he had been kind to them, although the rest of the gang got slapped around often.

But of late, Danielle had noticed his looking at her in a different way. Something in his eyes had made her uncomfortable, if not actually afraid. Then came that awful day she could hardly bear to think of. Danielle had been looking at a drawing that Jimmy had done, and Sutton had leaned over her shoulder to take a closer look. Suddenly, she felt his hand on her neck as he smoothed her curls back. She'd turned in surprise just as he leaned toward her, his lips moist, fire in his eyes. Before she could turn her head away, his mouth had greedily covered hers. She shuddered, even now, as she remembered his disgusting advances and the strong smell of garlic on his breath. Pulling herself free, she'd cried out and slapped him. . .hard.

Danielle's stomach tightened as she recalled the look of rage on Sutton's face. With lips clenched tight, he'd gazed at her through narrowed eyes. Without saying a word, he turned and left the house. The next day, he insisted she take part in the "activities of the day" as he called them.

Danielle put down the book. What was she thinking? Here she sat in luxury, doing nothing, when Jimmy might be in trouble. She had to make her move soon. She wouldn't take a lot, just enough to satisfy Sutton. But would he really let them go as he'd promised? Suddenly, Danielle wasn't so sure.

෯

Blake stood on the sidewalk and scowled toward the Kramer house as a flash of auburn curls and blue dress disappeared inside. The fact that the girl had seen it necessary to run had reaffirmed his initial suspicion. He'd been so busy since the incident with the robbers and his accusation of the girl that he hadn't given her more than a passing thought and had no idea she was still at the Kramers'.

He pushed Wooly away. "You boys take him inside and make sure you latch the gate this time. If he runs away, it'll be your own fault."

"Yes, sir," they chorused. Then, with big grins plastered on their faces, they each grabbed Wooly by a side of the collar and dragged him toward the gate.

Blake and Pop walked on toward the Nelson house.

"Who was that pretty young thing?" Blake's grandfather peered sideways at him, his lips puckered in speculation.

Blake's scowl grew deeper. "Pretty young thing? She's a little thief who's wormed her way into the Kramer family. I just hope she doesn't get away with all the silver."

Pop scratched his head and threw Blake a puzzled look. "Well, if she's a thief, shouldn't you be telling them?"

Blake snorted. "Apparently I'm the only one who thinks she's guilty."

Pop nodded. "Ah, I see. Then you didn't really see her do anything."

"Well, no, but. . ." Blake frowned at his grandfather. "Oh, forget it. I'm not going to let that little crook ruin our day."

"Hmm, I see."

"Now, Pop, stop saying that. You don't see anything at all. Don't be overworking your imagination."

"Now don't get all riled up about it."

"I'm not. . .oh, forget it." Blake sped up, and his grandfather's chuckle trailed after him.

Great. Pop trying to fix him up with that feisty little hoodlum was all he needed.

Chapter 3

Blake marked furiously through the notes he'd just written and threw his pencil onto the piano. He had to have this song finished by Friday, but unfortunately, a vision of curly auburn hair played havoc with his concentration. He stood, gave a swift shove to the piano bench with his foot, and walked out onto the side porch. He placed his hands on the top of the white rail, leaned over, and stared at the lawn.

The sugar maple in the front yard released a shower of colorful red leaves, and a picture landed, uninvited, in his mind. Miss Gray, looking up at him with gold-flecked eyes from a bed of red and gold leaves.

He sighed. Why did she keep invading his thoughts? A gray squirrel ran across the yard with nimble, silent feet, not even disturbing the freshly fallen leaves, and headed for the oak tree across the way.

The sound of someone singing drifted over the hedge from the Kramer home. He hadn't realized Amelia had such a lovely voice. Craning his neck, he peered over the hedge, intending to say hello to his neighbor. He inhaled sharply then groaned.

Oh. Her. She sat on the porch swing, swinging gently. The golden tones emitting from her throat were as beautiful and pure as any Blake had heard. How could someone like that little crook have a voice like an angel? From the conversation in this house for the past couple of weeks, it was apparent Mrs. Kramer's little protégé had won the hearts of all the women in their circle, including his own mother.

At least with his work, he had an excuse to avoid the Kramers' party tonight. He had no desire to see that little pickpocket being treated like one of the family. No one seemed to remember that she was a suspect in a robbery. Well, okay, so he was the only one who suspected her. But with good reason. They were just too hypnotized by her to see the truth. Well, he, for one, wouldn't fall under her spell.

Whirling around, he returned to the music room and slammed the French doors behind him. He pulled the bell cord furiously then stomped over to the piano. Enough of this foolishness. He had to get his work done.

The door opened, and June, the new parlor maid, came in. "Yes, Mr. Blake?" The girl's words came out in little more than a squeak.

Blake flinched. He knew he hadn't been in the best of moods lately, but he hadn't been that bad, had he? Composing his face into a more pleasant expression, he cleared his throat. "I'd like some tea, please, June. No, on second thought make that coffee, black coffee."

"Yes, sir." The girl gave a quick curtsy then hurried from the room.

Blake stood by the piano, running his fingers over the keys. He had to get his mind back on his music.

The coffee went down strong and hot, nearly burning his throat. Just what he needed. Blake's mind cleared, and as the song began to take shape, his mood lifted. Maybe this day wouldn't be a total disaster.

The longcase clock in the corner had just chimed, suggesting a break, when the door opened and Blake's mother walked in, heading purposefully toward him.

Uh-oh. He knew that look. And had a pretty good idea why it was there.

"What's this I hear about you not going to the Kramers' party? Have you no manners at all? I accepted for the family last week."

"Mother, I'm sorry, but I have tons of work to do in order to complete my music for the show in time."

"The show! That's another thing. . ."

Disappointment stabbed him. "Please, must we go over this again? I thought only Father disapproved. Not you, too?"

Her face softened and she patted him gently on the cheek. "Of course not. I'm very proud of you. Only I don't want to go against your father's wishes, you know."

"Then what?"

"I only meant you shouldn't take your grandfather down to the theater. He gets too excited. Next thing you know, he'll be trying to do a song and dance number."

Blake grinned. "Don't worry, Mother. I'm keeping a close eye on him. If it makes him happy to feel a part of show business again, what can it hurt?"

Twin furrows appeared between his mother's eyes. "I don't know, son. He's not getting any younger. And he did have that pain in his chest last summer."

Blake's heart softened at the anxious frown on her face. Pop was the only blood kin besides him she had left. The chest pains had turned out to be indigestion, but she had worried about his health ever since.

An idea popped into his head. "I'll make a deal with you. I'll go to the Kramers' party if you'll not give Pop a hard time about the show. And I promise he'll be careful."

"Well. . ." She nibbled on her lower lip then lifted her gaze to Blake. "All right. I suppose, if you promise to watch him closely."

Blake grinned. "I won't take my eyes off him. I promise."

She cast a suspicious glance at him. "You didn't plan the whole thing this way, did you?"

"Now, Mother, would I do that?"

"Hmm. . .just make sure you keep that close eye on him. And be ready to leave at seven. I would like for us to arrive together as a family."

℘

Danielle stood in the middle of her room listening to the hum of voices from the hallway below. Her stomach knotted and she felt herself begin to gag as unwelcome thoughts bombarded her mind.

I can't do this. What if I get caught? Blake Nelson is probably coming and he's sure to watch me. I'll have to be careful. But, I can do it. After all, even if I've never actually picked a pocket, Sutton's been making me practice since I was a child.

She started at a sudden knock on the door, "C—come in."

Mrs. Parker entered the room with a huge smile on her face. "You look absolutely beautiful, Danielle. The amber color of your gown brings out the gold flecks in your eyes."

Danielle ran her hand down the smooth fabric of the new evening gown Mrs. Kramer had purchased for her.

"Thank you, ma'am. You look lovely, too." She could hear the trembling in her voice and then realized she was twisting the lace handkerchief she held in her hand.

"Thank you, dear." She smiled. "Here's a little something I'd like for you to have. It will look lovely on you." A strand of pearls glistened in the palm of the wrinkled hand.

Danielle gasped and blinked against the tears that filled her eyes.

A look of concern crossed the old woman's kind face. "Are you all right, dear?"

"Yes, ma'am." Her reply was almost inaudible. "But I couldn't take that lovely necklace. It is much too valuable." And yet her thoughts battled against her. What was she thinking? Here was something she could give to Sutton that wouldn't even be stolen.

"Nonsense. I want you to have them. Now turn around."

Danielle felt the coolness of the pearls against her throat. She trembled.

"Oh, you poor thing, you're frightened, aren't you?" She walked over and put her arm around Danielle's shoulders. "Now don't you worry about a thing. Most of the people who will be here tonight are old and dear friends. I promise they won't bite, and besides, I'll watch out for you." She gave Danielle a pat and a smile before she left the room.

Danielle shivered and tried to hold back tears. The idea had seemed logical to her at first. There would be a crowd of guests milling about. It would be simple to lift a few items and stash them away. That way, she wouldn't steal from the Kramers but could still manage to buy her freedom from Sutton. As long as she didn't get caught, her friends wouldn't suffer at all.

The only problem was that a wave of conscience having nothing to do with the Kramers had washed through Danielle this morning and hadn't subsided. She wasn't sure where it came from but had a niggling suspicion it might be God.

She had attended church services with the family the past two Sundays, and memories from her childhood had trickled in little by little. A little run-down chapel by the docks and the minister who'd been kind to Danielle and her family.

Mother's sweet voice singing hymns by her bedside and telling stories about Jesus who'd come down from heaven because He loved a little girl named Danielle and a little boy named Jimmy and wanted to save them. Words she still didn't really understand.

Danielle pulled in her breath and straightened her back. She had to gather herself together. Composure was absolutely essential if she were to carry this off.

She inched her way down the stairs to a mercifully empty entranceway. Maybe she could slip into the library for a moment to compose herself. As she reached the bottom of the stairs, the door knocker sounded. Danielle froze and watched as Sally hurried to open the door to the newcomers. Oh no, the Nelsons! And he was with them.

"Why, Danielle, how lovely you look, my dear." With a rustle of skirts, Mrs. Nelson walked over and kissed her on the cheek. "Come meet my husband. I don't believe you know him yet."

Danielle allowed herself to be led over to Mr. Nelson and Blake. She composed her face into a pleasant expression as Mrs. Nelson made the introductions. Glancing at Blake out of the corner of her eye, she winced at the sardonic twist of his lips.

"Come, Mother, let's see who has managed to arrive before us. I'm sure Miss Gray has more interesting things to do than stand in the hallway talking to us." Blake linked an arm with each of his parents and guided them toward the drawing room, leaving Danielle alone in the foyer.

Realizing her mouth hung open, Danielle pressed her lips together and frowned at Blake's departing back. How rude. And he had such a wonderful mother. She hoped Mrs. Nelson would trounce him good. With an angry toss of her head, Danielle turned her back on the safety of the library and headed straight into the drawing room.

In the corner, a trio of musicians sat in formal splendor, their soft music filling the room. Fine crystal sparkled from trays carried by waiters hired for the occasion as they moved deftly among the guests, ladies and gentlemen dressed in finery.

Danielle took satisfaction that her gown was as fine as any of them. Breathing deeply, she stepped farther into the room, her eyes searching for the one who could give her away. He was across the room shaking hands with Mr. Kramer. She would know the back of his arrogant head anywhere. Perhaps it would be amusing to carry off her plan right under his nose.

Danielle glanced casually around the crowded area. She had to choose carefully. The consequence of being caught and facing the Kramers' and Mrs. Parker's accusing, disappointed faces was unthinkable.

A portly gentleman caught her attention as he reached into his coat pocket. The motion caused the corner of his coat to hike up, revealing the sparkle of a gold watch chain.

Danielle's eyes narrowed as she studied the man. The coat had tails, which would make it easier. Winding through the crowded room, Danielle focused on the unsuspecting target.

With a gasp, she froze. Was that a clerical collar? Eyes focused and heart pounding, she slowly took another step. The man turned slightly and Danielle felt faint as the collar seemed to scream out in accusation. She whirled and rushed from the room.

The library door was slightly open and Danielle ran quickly across the hall. She closed the door behind her and stumbled over to the sofa. Dropping down onto the thick cushion, she hid her face in her hands, unable to prevent the tears that flooded and spilled over.

How could she steal when it was the very thing that had her and Jimmy trapped? But what else could she do? Where could she turn? It was hopeless.

⅓

Blake excused himself from the conversation and headed for the empty hallway. He frowned, looking around. Now where did she go? He was sure she was up to no good.

The tick of the stately longcase clock seemed to beat a rhythm to his thoughts. *No good. No good. No good.*

Suddenly he heard muffled sobs coming from the direction of the library, and concern filled his heart. Perhaps one of the children was hurt.

He opened the ornate door and slipped quietly inside, not wanting to frighten the child. The weeping came from the sofa. Tiptoeing around to the other side, he stopped in consternation. Danielle sat huddled against the corner of the sofa, her head buried in a large cushion. He hesitated, wanting nothing more than to turn and bolt, but as he made a move to do so, a heart-wrenching sigh stopped him.

He stood, momentarily, undecided. Then making a sudden decision, Blake knelt down and put his arm around the girl's shoulders. "There now, it's going to be all right."

She started then turned, and without glancing at his face, she nestled her face into his coat lapel and sobbed harder.

He patted her as she wept, and the soft roundness of her shoulder beneath the satiny fabric of her gown sent a thrill through him. Confusion washed over him as his heart sped up. Would a crook have such deep feelings? Had he, perhaps, misjudged her?

Suddenly she stopped crying and became totally still. "I'm so sorry. I don't know what came over me." She looked up and gazed at him through tear-washed eyes. Recognition dawned and a look of horror appeared on her face. Jerking away, she shoved him aside and jumped up from the sofa. "How dare you take such liberties? Now you not only think I'm a thief but a loose woman as well?"

Blake felt his face flame. He stood and gaped at her for a few seconds before he got his bearings. "Well, if the shoe fits." Now why had he said that? "Look, I didn't mean it. I saw you crying and merely wanted to comfort you."

142

"I. . .I. . .I was simply crying over a book I was reading. And you are nothing but a cad and a liar."

"Oh?" Blake looked around. "I'm a cad and a liar, and you've been reading an invisible book." He gave an emphatic nod, as his suspicions came back and then some.

"Well, I had already put it up. Here. See?" She flounced over to the bookcase and grabbed a copy of *Wuthering Heights* from the shelf then sat back down and opened the book. She shot him a pointed look and then commenced to read and ignore him.

Indignant anger flashed through him. And he had almost begun to believe the little crook. He strode to the bookcase and perused the titles. Ah, just the thing. Tossing the book into her lap, he said, "Perhaps this one will be more appropriate."

With a triumphant grin in her direction, he left her staring at the expensive, leather-bound copy of *Oliver Twist*.

Chapter 4

Danielle swung the empty basket from one arm to the other, wishing she didn't have it. However, it was a convenient excuse to get away for a while. She shifted to her other foot and peered around the corner of the building, aware of the passing of time. Sally would be waiting for the vegetables and fruit for dinner. Danielle had been waiting behind the storage shed, near the Clark Street Bridge, for nearly two hours hoping to catch a glimpse of Cobb. She couldn't trust just anyone, but she was pretty sure he wouldn't betray her.

That morning, with worry about Jimmy heavy on her heart, she had paced her bedroom floor. How could she get word to him to let him know his sister was safe and hadn't deserted him? And how could she pass her plan on to Sutton, so he wouldn't take a notion to kick Jimmy out on the street?

One glimmer of hope rested in her heart, the fact that since the day Danielle and her small brother landed in Sutton's parlor the man had always shown compassion for Jimmy. But she couldn't count on that. Not for long, anyway.

Danielle decided she must make a move. She'd fastened her hat on top of her new upswept coiffure and hurried downstairs, not sure what lie to tell about where she was going. It had been a stroke of luck that the very day Danielle decided to somehow get word to Sutton was also marketing day.

A flash of red hair caught her attention, and with relief she saw the stocky, freckled Cobb swaggering down the street in her direction. She stepped out just as he approached her hiding place.

"Whew, Danni, are you ever in trouble. The guys all have their eyes cocked for a sight of you. Sutton offered a dollar to anyone who could find you." He leaned his head back and whistled as he peered at her. "Looks like you're doin' pretty well for yerself."

Danielle grabbed the young man's arm and dragged him behind the storage shed. "Here's your chance to collect that reward. And if you do exactly what I say, you might get an extra quarter from me."

He shook his arm loose and narrowed his eyes. "What's going on? You haven't sold us out, have you?"

"Of course not!" She placed her hands on her hips and glared at Cobb. "What do you take me for?" A pang shot through her chest. Truth be known, Danielle would sell them all out if it would get her and Jimmy out of Sutton's clutches. But she hadn't found a way without incriminating them as well.

"All right. But you better not." He gave her a threatening gaze then shrugged. "So what's going on?"

Danielle grinned. Cobb could never be mean to her. He'd been watching out for her since she was ten. "I got caught."

"What?" His mouth flew open. "So why aren't you in jail?"

"I talked my way out of it." She flashed him a saucy grin. "Not only that, a rich woman who was there that day took my side. I guess she felt sorry for me."

Cobb listened as Danielle relayed the story of how she was caught and accused by Blake Nelson. He howled with laughter as she mimicked Officer Brady.

Guilt shot through her again, but she had to convince Cobb so he'd be on her side when he told Sutton.

"So none of this explains why you're dressed like a rich woman. And where are you staying?"

"That lady in the bank that day took pity on me. She took me to her home and under her wing. That's what I want to talk to you about."

He leaned against the shed. "I'm listening."

Be careful, Danielle. Don't give anything away that will lead to the Kramers or the Nelsons. One little slip and they could be in danger.

"I thought you'd have figured things out by now. The folks I'm staying with are filthy rich. Richer than you can imagine. I plan to rob them and turn everything over to Sutton."

"So, what are you waiting for? You've had plenty of time. I think you're stalling." He raised his eyebrows. "Maybe you like the high life."

"I'm waiting for the opportunity to make a big haul. Sure I could steal a bracelet or something and take off, leaving the real wealth behind." She sent him a challenging glance. "Is that what you'd do?"

"Course not. If there's big stuff at stake, I'd wait."

"Well, that's what I'm doing." She reached into her pocket and pulled out a small velvet bag. She could feel the pearls through the cloth, and for a moment, she wasn't sure she could hand them over. But after all, they were hers. And maybe they would convince Sutton. "Here." She held the bag out to Cobb. "Give these to Sutton. Tell him there's a lot more where these came from. And tell him Jimmy needs some new clothes."

Cobb peeked into the bag and gave a shrill whistle. "Girl, I think you've been tellin' me the truth."

"So you'll tell Sutton?"

"Sure. Leave it to me." He crammed the bag into his pocket and waved as he left.

Danielle inhaled deeply. Jimmy would be safe now. And without that worry, she could plan her next step.

She headed toward the bridge and started across to the downtown area. She'd walk to the market and then get one of the boys there to help her carry packages to the bus stop. She was more relaxed than she'd been in a long time.

∽

Blake pressed his lips together and watched Danielle cross the bridge with a large basket swinging on her arm. He'd walked there from the theater to get some fresh air during the lunch break.

He hated what Rhonda Vale was doing to Peg. For one thing, she was too old for the part. In her hands the innocent young farmer's daughter had become unrecognizable.

When he saw Danielle talking to the tough-looking young man, fear attacked him like a pack of wild dogs. Had she been accosted?

He started to run to her rescue, to tear the ruffian away from her, but something in her relaxed manner stopped him. A twinge of disappointment pinched at his stomach and anger rose up. So his suspicions had been right. They must have been. Or why would she be hanging around the dock in deep conversation with that shady-looking character?

She handed her companion a small bag. When the man turned to go, and Danielle headed toward the dock, Blake walked back to the end of the bridge to wait for her.

She moved lightly, almost with a bounce in her step. Whatever she'd been up to, it must have made her happy.

Jealousy sliced through him like a sword, and he caught his breath, shocked at the intensity of his feelings. Maybe he should leave. He took one step to head back to the theater.

Danielle spotted him. She paused, her eyes widening, then continued the last few steps and stopped in front of Blake. "Good afternoon, Mr. Nelson." Her voice trembled.

"Good afternoon, Miss Gray. Visiting old friends?"

"Yes, that is, I happened to run into an acquaintance."

"Did you just happen to be hanging around the docks, also?"

Danielle took a deep breath and stood straight. Anger replaced the guilty look and she glared at Blake. "For your information, Mr. Nelson, I was on my way to the market for Sally and lost my way. Not that it's any of your business."

Warmth flooded his face. What if she really had lost her way? Reason took over and he gave a short laugh. "So you mistakenly crossed the river on your way to the market?"

She gasped and blushed. "No, I. . .uh. . .I lost my way before that, and when I saw how near I was to my old neighborhood, I decided to visit."

"Your old neighborhood? I didn't know the orphanage was on the other side of the river." *There, get out of that one, you little crook.*

Her face flamed. "I had a life before the orphanage, for your information. Before my mother died."

At the quiver in her voice and the sight of tears threatening to overflow her enormous brown eyes, Blake's heart lurched. Something told him she wasn't faking this time.

"Miss Gray, please forgive me." He reached inside his coat and retrieved a handkerchief. The tears streamed down her cheeks now and he reached over and blotted at them. How could he have been such a brute?

"Well, you don't need to rub my face raw," she sputtered, knocking his hand away.

Indignant at the little waif's ingratitude, he crammed the handkerchief into his pocket. "I wasn't rubbing. I merely dabbed at your tears."

"Well, I don't recall asking you to do that."

Blake took a deep breath. "I was merely trying to help." He flagged down a passing taxi. "Get in. He'll take you to the market and then wait and take you to the Kramers'."

"I don't need—"

Blake twisted his mouth in as sarcastic an expression as he could manage. "I wouldn't want you to get lost and end up on the other side of the river again. I suspect Sally is waiting for her groceries."

He opened the door of the carriage and she flounced in. He paid the driver and gave him instructions. "Good-bye, Miss Gray."

ᘓ

Danielle sat stiffly on the seat and watched Blake walk away. Her heart ached and she wanted to call to him. His tenderness, when she'd begun to cry, had taken her breath away, nearly causing her to lose her focus. She'd wanted to lean her head over on his strong chest and let him comfort her. But she couldn't take the risk of falling in love with this man. She must keep her guard up, or he'd be sure to find her out.

When they arrived at the market, Danielle politely sent the driver on his way. It was only a few blocks from the Kramer home. She hurried through her errand at the market and headed toward home with the full basket on her arm.

Home? Sadness and shame washed over her. How could she consider the Kramer house her home and still plan to rob them?

The Kramer children were playing in the front yard, laughing and kicking at the fallen leaves. Her heart twisted within her. How Jimmy would love such a wonderful place to enjoy. She stiffened her neck and lifted her chin. She would do anything for her little brother. And yet, she couldn't prevent the nausea that stirred in her stomach.

She went around to the kitchen door and entered. "I'm sorry it took so long, Sally. I was detained." There, that much at least was true.

Sally patted Danielle on the shoulder. "I was about to send someone to look for you. I was starting to worry. There are so many ruffians running around Chicago nowadays."

Even Sally cared about her. Impulsively, Danielle reached over and hugged the kind and motherly cook. "I'm fine. Didn't see a single ruffian. Do you need my help?"

"The meat loaf is ready to go into the oven. I'll get the potatoes in, too. Pies are cooling. Salad is in the icebox. You run along. Maybe after dinner, you could set the breakfast table."

"I'll be happy to."

"Make sure to use the napkins in the second drawer."

Danielle smiled. "I will."

She went upstairs to her room. When the door closed behind her, she walked to the window and dropped into the rocking chair with a sigh.

She'd been elated when things had worked out so well with Cobb. Then the shock of seeing Blake and knowing he'd seen her with one of the gang members had weakened her confidence. The emotions she'd experienced in his presence were almost her undoing. She had to be strong and steel herself against Blake Nelson and the Kramers, too, if necessary. But how could she repay their kindness with theft and deceit? How could she when her conscience stabbed her over and over again? Oh, what would her mother think of her?

"Mama, I'm so sorry. I know you must be ashamed of me. Is Jesus ashamed of me, too? Yes, of course He is."

And then a horrible thought crossed her mind. What if she couldn't go to heaven someday? What if she couldn't see her mother again?

Chapter 5

Blake sat in the empty auditorium. His stomach churned and a stabbing pain that had begun at his left temple had now reached his eye. He rubbed his left eyelid and stared at the stage.

A shriek, which should have been a bubble of laughter, emitted from the lead actress's lips and Blake jumped up from his seat. "No! This won't do at all."

Rhonda huffed and tossed an indignant glare his way. "Again? What's wrong this time?"

Bosley, the manager and director, ran his fingers through his unruly hair then threw his arms up. This was the third time since the noon break that Blake had interrupted. He walked down the plush carpeted aisle, grabbed Bosley by one arm, and pulled him aside. "I thought you were going to talk to her about the atrocious way she's playing this part."

Bosley grimaced. "I did talk to her, over lunch. Bought her Chateaubriand with béarnaise sauce. Do you have any idea what that cost me?" He sighed and shook his head. "When I suggested Peg might need to be toned down a bit, she had no idea what I was talking about. Didn't get it at all."

"Then you need to find another actress to play the lead. Rhonda is ruining the play. The woman has turned Peg into a coarse, loud-mouthed wench instead of the soft and innocent serving girl I created. This ruins the whole story."

The stage manager sighed and gave a slight nod. "You're right. But this means shutting down until we find our actress."

Blake bit the inside of his lip. "Sorry. But I want Peg right."

"I know. I suppose the understudy could read her lines until we find the right girl for the part. That way, the schedule won't get so far behind." He frowned. "We have a new potential backer for the show. I'd hate to lose him due to a time delay."

Blake smiled and patted him on the back. "I'm sure you'll find her soon. You know every actress in town."

"Yeah, well, I may know them, but that doesn't mean they're available. I'd better break the news to Rhonda and tell the cast of the change in plans."

Blake nodded and walked out of the theater. He stood for a moment, viewing the bustling activity of afternoon shoppers. He supposed he shouldn't get so upset. It didn't help that he couldn't get Danielle Gray out of his thoughts. If he didn't know better, he'd think he was falling in love. But that was ludicrous. Him? In love with a thief and a trickster?

He stomped off down Randolph Street past several theaters and headed into

149

the cold wind toward State Street and the elevated train. Halfway down the block, he changed his mind and turned down a side street. He'd rather walk home today. Maybe the brisk air would clear his thoughts. Or at least distract him from them.

He picked up his pace. But no matter how fast he walked, he couldn't get Danielle's lovely face from his mind.

☙

Late afternoon shadows lay across the parlor, and the flames in the fireplace crackled. An aura of well-being soothed Danielle as she leaned back against the sofa's cushions. The day had taken more out of her than she'd realized.

For years, Danielle had dreaded the day when Sutton would send her out into the crowded city to pick pockets or take part in a store robbery. Then, year after year, she'd begun to relax. Perhaps he wouldn't ask it of them. Sutton liked her and Jimmy and kept them both busy around the house. When the woman who cooked for them didn't show up one day, Danielle took over those duties. And she and Jimmy kept the old house as clean as possible with twelve boys tumbling around the place. When the dreaded day arrived and Sutton decided to punish her for evading his advances, Danielle had almost thrown up. But Cobb had instructed her to be their lookout, and she'd felt reprieved once more. But now?

Danielle looked around the parlor. Exquisite lace doilies rested on every table and even on the backs of chairs and sofas. A set of gold candelabra graced the mantel above the fireplace, and an expensive painting hung on the wall above. Everything her eyes rested on, including the lace doilies, was obviously top quality and worth more money than Danielle had seen in her lifetime. But they would be impossible to steal. Oh, she could probably stuff one of the lacy cloths in her pocket from time to time, but Sutton would never be satisfied with that.

She knew exactly what he'd tell her. Go for the jewels. But the jewels, diamonds, emeralds, pearls, and more lay on soft satin trays in blue velvet boxes in the bedrooms. And the most valuable were more than likely in a safe somewhere. How would she ever be able to get to them? In the daytime, Mrs. Parker and Mrs. Kramer were in and out, and when they weren't there, Sally was. Occasionally, the family went out at night. Sometimes Danielle went, too, but it would be easy to plead a headache. Yes, that would be the smartest plan.

Her breathing quickened as panic washed over her. Sitting here wasn't such a good idea. She jumped up. Perhaps Sally could use some help in the kitchen, or maybe the clothes on the line were dry. . .anything to get these thoughts out of her head.

At the first step, Danielle realized her skirt was caught. Reaching down, she pulled up on the edge of the cushion and gasped. A gold locket lay bunched up, the broken clasp bright against the red of her skirt.

Heart racing, Danielle reached down and gently removed the fabric from the clasp. Perspiration beaded her upper lip and her heart pounded loudly in her ears. She looked at the locket and chain resting on her palm. Diamonds twinkled around the edges of the gold heart. Her fingers closed around it. Glancing around to be sure no one observed her actions, she opened her hand and let the locket slide smoothly into her pocket.

Sadness flooded over her. For the first time, since she was ten years old and desperate to keep Jimmy from starving, she had stolen.

Holding back tears, Danielle rushed from the room and up the stairs. Her soft bed welcomed her and she closed her eyes and wept.

A soft tapping woke her, and she sat up. "Yes?"

"Dinner is about to be served, my dear. Are you all right?" Mrs. Parker's sweet, musical voice sounded worried.

"Yes, I'm fine. I had a headache, but it's gone now. I must have fallen asleep. I'll be right down."

Hurriedly, she splashed water over her face and dried it with a fluffy towel. The face powder she dabbed beneath her eyes erased all traces of the tears she'd shed. At least she hoped so.

"Ah, there she is." Mrs. Kramer gave a weak smile when Danielle came downstairs. "We waited for you, my dear."

"Thank you, ma'am. I'm sorry I kept you waiting." She noticed Mrs. Kramer seemed agitated. What could be wrong? Could she possibly know Danielle had taken the necklace?

After dinner, Danielle helped Sally with the dishes and set the table for breakfast and then decided to return to her room. As she passed the library door, she heard voices. She peered in and saw Mr. Kramer down on his knees peering under the sofa while his wife stood over him.

"But, Benjamin, I'm sure I wasn't in this room today. I couldn't have lost it here."

Mr. Kramer stood up and sighed loudly. "I'm sure you're right. I've looked in every nook and cranny."

Oh no. They were searching for the locket. Danielle was sure of it. "Is something wrong?" she asked, stepping into the room.

"My wife lost a necklace." Mr. Kramer's hair was tousled and his face red from scooting around furniture. Danielle tried not to stare. She'd never seen Mr. Kramer anything but impeccably groomed before.

"But not just any necklace. Benjamin, you know I wouldn't carry on over any other piece of jewelry." Tears filled Mrs. Kramer's eyes and threatened to spill over as she looked up at her husband. "It's special because you gave it to me on our wedding day."

Cold fingers clamped around Danielle's heart and she felt faint. Oh no. What had she done? "Have you looked all over the house?"

"No, we still need to look in the parlor and dining room," Mr. Kramer said.

"Would you like for me to help you search?" Danielle asked. She knew what she had to do.

Mrs. Kramer reached over and touched her hand. "That would be very kind of you, Danielle."

Danielle followed the Kramers into the parlor and began to pretend to look. While they searched by the window, Danielle stooped down behind the sofa and removed the necklace from her pocket. "Is this it?" she asked breathlessly, standing and holding out her open hand.

With a little cry, Mrs. Kramer rushed across the room and took the locket from Danielle's hand. "Oh, my dear, you've found it."

"It was beneath the sofa." Danielle cringed at the lie.

"Oh. Look, Benjamin, the clasp is broken. It must have fallen off when I was in here earlier." She reached over and hugged Danielle tightly then stood back and beamed. "My dear, how can I thank you?"

Danielle gazed in wonder at the joy on Amelia Kramer's face. What if she had taken the locket to Sutton earlier? Her kind and gentle hostess would have been heartbroken.

03

Blake hurried down the stairs. He was anxious to get to the theater and see how practice went today with the understudy reading Peg.

"Good morning, son," his mother said and smiled as he walked into the breakfast room.

"Good morning, Mother. You're mighty chipper today."

"Yes, it's always nice to hear good news first thing in the morning."

"What good news?"

"Well, when I went outside for a breath of air, Amelia and her mother walked by. They had quite an adventure yesterday." She paused. For effect, Blake was sure.

"Oh?"

"Yes, it seems Amelia lost her gold locket. She said she was totally devastated."

Blake's stomach knotted. Danielle. She'd done it again. "I wouldn't say that was good news, Mother."

She laughed. "Well, of course not, you silly. The good news was that the locket has been found. They were searching in the parlor and Danielle found it underneath the sofa."

Unexplainable relief shot through him. If the girl had found the locket, she'd obviously had the perfect opportunity to slip it into a pocket. Maybe he had been wrong about her all along. "I see. And I agree, that's very good news."

Blake went to the sideboard and filled a plate with bacon, eggs, and toast. He set them on the table and sat down. "Mmm. Good breakfast."

"Hilda's breakfasts are always good. But I'm glad you appreciate her cooking."

"Indeed, I do. Where's Pop?"

"He went for a walk. I hope he doesn't overdo it. He said something about going to the theater after a while to watch the practice."

"Good. He hasn't been down there in some time." Blake was actually glad Pop hadn't seen the way Rhonda had messed up the part of his leading lady.

"How is *Peg in Dreamland* coming along?"

Blake looked at his mother in surprise. He hadn't realized she even knew the name of his musical comedy. "We're having a little bit of a problem finding the right actress to play the part of Peg. Other than that, it's going fine."

"I can't wait until opening night." Her eyes danced with excitement.

"You mean you're coming to see it?" This he hadn't expected, and delight filled him.

"Of course I am. You didn't think I'd miss your play, did you? I'm pretty sure your father will be there, too. Can you reserve a box for us?"

"Father? Are you sure? I most certainly can and will. If everything comes together, we hope to open two weeks before Christmas."

Blake whistled as he walked down the street to the nearest El station. He'd been trying to talk his father into buying a motor car, but so far, he wouldn't consider it. So Blake walked to the parts of town that boasted the elevated trains while his father still rode to work in their horse-drawn carriage. He wondered if his father would ever catch up with modern technology.

When he arrived at the theater, Bosley grinned. "Good news. We won't have to use the understudy after all. I think I've found our star."

Chapter 6

Why, why, why? Danielle stomped across the floor and flopped down on the rocking chair by the window. She must have been out of her mind last night. That locket would have been a substantial deposit against what she owed Sutton. It would have shown him she wasn't ducking out on him.

She had always been strong. Had to be to take care of Jimmy. Even after Sutton had taken them in, Danielle had remained on guard, always. Because she knew she was the only one who really cared what happened to her brother. And Mama would have expected her to take good care of him. What was happening to her? Turning her to mush?

Okay, so the Kramers had been good to her. Was that any reason to melt like she'd done? To forget about Jimmy?

A door slammed and Danielle glanced out the window. Blake Nelson stepped off the porch next door and headed down the sidewalk. Probably on his way to the theater. Envy stabbed at her. If she was wealthy like the Nelsons, she wouldn't be walking anywhere. Why didn't he take his buggy or ride in the family carriage? She flung herself back in the chair, a frown on her face. Why should it matter to her what Blake did? Let him walk his feet off for all she cared.

She jumped up. She might as well go downstairs and see if Sally needed her help. No sense in brooding over yesterday's mistakes. She'd keep her wits about her from now on.

Danielle started down the stairs. The smell of bacon and eggs wafted up from the kitchen, causing Danielle's stomach to rumble.

"Ah, there you are." In the downstairs hall, Mrs. Parker held her hand out to Danielle and they walked into the dining room together.

Breakfast was already laid out on the sideboard, and the coffee urn was steaming. They filled their plates and sat at the table where Mrs. Kramer and her boys sat. The twins were eagerly devouring pancakes dripping with butter and syrup. There was no sign of Mr. Kramer, who often had to be at the bank early.

Mrs. Kramer beamed at Danielle. "My dear, I simply haven't the words to convey my appreciation for your finding my locket."

Danielle felt warmth rush to her face. "It. . .was nothing, really. I merely happened to look in the right place."

"Well, I'm grateful, nevertheless."

Nell, the parlor maid, appeared at the door. "Mrs. Nelson is here, ma'am."

"Thank you, Nell. Please ask her to come in."

A moment later, Blake's mother stepped into the room, a smile on her lips and her eyes sparkling. Danielle bit her lip. The lady had her son's eyes. Or she supposed it was the other way around.

"Would you like some breakfast, Katherine?" Mrs. Kramer asked, rising.

"No, no, sit down. I'll just get a cup of coffee." She brought her coffee cup and saucer and sat next to Danielle. Reaching over, she patted her on the arm. "How are you getting along, dear?"

"I'm doing very well, thank you."

"Wonderful. I have a favor to ask."

"Oh. Of course I'll help you in any way possible."

Mrs. Nelson laughed. "Don't look so fearful, my dear. I've decided to go to the theater and take a look at my son's masterpiece. It would be nice to have some company. There, does that sound terribly frightful?"

Danielle attempted to keep her face composed as excitement poured over her. She'd never been to a theater and had to admit she was curious about Blake's musical comedy. She grinned. He'd probably be furious when he saw her. "Not a bit frightful. I'd be happy to accompany you."

"Good, the carriage will be here to pick you up at ten o'clock."

After Mrs. Nelson left, Danielle rushed upstairs and tried on several outfits before deciding on an emerald green skirt and jacket. She wondered if Blake liked emerald green then blushed at her thoughts. What did she care what Blake liked?

True to her word, Mrs. Nelson arrived at exactly ten. The ancient coachman opened the door for Danielle and she sank into the plush cushioned seat beside her hostess. Guilt pinged at her mind. She should be in her bedroom making plans to free her brother instead of riding in a posh carriage with a fur-draped rich woman. Oh, but it felt so good.

If only she and Jimmy hadn't had such bad breaks. If only their father hadn't died, leaving their mother destitute. If only Mama hadn't died giving birth to a child who never drew a breath. She squeezed her lids shut against the tears that threatened to flood her eyes. She wouldn't give in to tears. She wouldn't.

☙

It wasn't that the new actress was vulgar, like the last one. She tried. Blake had to give her that. But, she wasn't Peg. At least, not the Peg he'd created. The girl was young and willing to give it everything she had. It simply wasn't working. Blake shook his head at Bosley and heard the man groan as he walked over.

"Let's give her another try. I really think she can do it."

Blake sighed and nodded.

"Okay, Hannah, let's try it one more time." Bosley threw the girl a gentle smile. "You almost had it, honey. But try to be gentle without being soppy."

Blake turned at the sound of the doors opening. His mother stood there and someone else was right behind her. His stomach lurched as Danielle stepped into view. And suddenly he knew.

Ever since he'd laid eyes on the girl, it was the vision of her that had transposed itself upon his image of Peg. He felt his eyes widen at the revelation. But that was ridiculous. This girl was as different from his sweet, innocent heroine as night was to day. "Mother, what a surprise."

"A pleasant one, I hope." She smiled. "Do you mind if Danielle and I watch the practice? I promise we won't get in the way."

"I'd be delighted, of course." He looked at her, puzzled. "Does Father know you're here?"

"For your information, I don't have to tell your father my every move...but, yes, I told him my plans for the day."

"Here, let me take your wraps." He removed his mother's fur stole then held his hand out for the coat Danielle had removed. His fingers barely touched hers, but a thrill went through him and he inhaled sharply.

Her face turned pink and she quickly turned and took a seat next to his mother.

Confusion washed over Blake. If she was the type of girl he'd believed her to be, why would she blush over the brush of his fingers against hers? But what about the shady character he'd seen her with down by the docks? A nice girl wouldn't associate with such as that.

"All right, folks. Break is over. Let's get to work."

At the sound of Bosley's voice, Blake shook himself from the disturbing thoughts. The cast drifted back onto the stage and began once more to go through their lines. Everyone was doing great except for Hannah.

After Blake had interrupted her for the third time, he saw tears flooding her eyes. She nodded and started over from the beginning.

He turned and glanced toward his mother and caught a look of total awe on Danielle's face. She seemed enraptured with the simple practice. Like she was watching a first-class performance. Was it possible he was being unreasonable with Hannah? Were his expectations for his Peg, perhaps, too high?

When Bosley broke for lunch, Blake's mother thanked Blake and said good-bye.

"But I was going to take you both to lunch, Mother. There's a wonderful little café nearby I thought you might enjoy."

"Another time, son. I'm rather tired and need to get home. But I love your play, except for the leading lady. She didn't seem quite right for the part."

"Mother, you're amazing. I was beginning to think it was just me being too picky. Thank you, from the bottom of my heart." Blake grinned and somehow his joy must have flowed over onto Danielle, because she smiled so brightly it sent a ray of sunshine into his heart.

Blake watched as the Nelson carriage pulled away. He sighed. He needed to find out once and for all about the mysterious Miss Gray. But how?

He walked to the bridge and leaned against a rail, looking across at block after dingy block of factories and crowded tenements. The dock teemed with laborers, and children played, laughing and sometimes shouting in anger. He hoped to catch a glimpse of the redheaded man Danielle had seemed so chummy with the other day. Maybe he could convince him to tell what he knew about her.

He was about to give up and leave when the sun glinted off a red mop headed down one of the back alleys. From the build and the way the man walked, Blake was almost sure it was the same man. "Hey, there!" Blake started across the bridge at a fast pace, almost running by the time he reached the dockside. He spun around the corner and headed two blocks down to the alley, only to find it empty except for a couple of stray cats snarling at each other.

Frustrated, he straightened his tie and headed back to the theater, feeling a little foolish. Why was it so important for him to find out about the girl? The obvious answer was that he was attracted to her, but he'd been attracted to plenty of girls without getting obsessed like this. But didn't he need to protect his mother and her friends? Of course. Next time, he wouldn't stand on the bridge. He'd walk the streets and alleys in his search.

℣

The swing creaked as Danielle swung slowly beneath the big oak in the backyard. It was pleasantly sunny this afternoon, but she probably wouldn't have known if it was snowing. Her mind and all her emotions were focused on one thing.

The magic of the morning lingered with her. She'd never known anything like it. Ever. As the actors and actresses had read their lines for Blake's enchanting musical, *Peg in Dreamland*, Danielle had been transported into each character. Only one of the musical numbers had been performed, but the atmosphere on the stage seemed to be filled with music anyway. Blake must be the most talented writer and songwriter ever to create something so marvelous. Oh, how she wished she could be there every day, feasting her eyes and ears on such wonder.

She was jerked from her reverie as Wooly came charging at her from across the yard.

"No, no. Bad dog." Too late. His front paws were on her lap, and his rough, wet tongue lapped her face.

Spitting and wiping her mouth, Danielle finally managed to shove the beast away. She didn't know why he seemed to like her so much. She didn't think much of him at all. Her skirt was a wet and filthy mess now. She'd have to change.

She stomped in through the kitchen door, letting it slam behind her.

"Uh-oh. Looks like Wooly got you again." Sally shook her head sympathetically, but Danielle didn't miss the grin the good-natured cook tried to hide.

"I don't know why that dog jumps on me every time he sees me. His slobber kisses are awful."

"I think he just likes you, sweetie." She handed her a towel.

"Well, he can take his affection somewhere else," Danielle complained, wiping at her skirt.

"A dog's affection is nothing to slight, you know."

"Mmm-hmm. Easy enough for you to say. You aren't the one who gets attacked every time you step out the door."

Sally's laugh followed her all the way upstairs.

After Danielle had changed, she sat in the chair by the window and leaned back, lost once more in her thoughts. She wouldn't have to worry here about being trounced on by that monster of a dog.

Danielle closed her eyes. What would it be like to act in a play? As the thought struck her, her eyes flew open and she sat up straight. Would it be possible for her to get a part in a show? She could sing a little. Sutton used to tell her she had a voice like an angel. And she'd never had any trouble mimicking others. Surely acting couldn't be that much different.

Could this be an opportunity for her to pay off Sutton without resorting to crime? Maybe this could be God answering her prayer. She shook her head. Why would He do that for her when she'd been telling lies and making plans to steal from her benefactors?

"I wonder how much money an actress earns." The words, spoken aloud, sent a bolt of excitement coursing through her.

Chapter 7

Where had the excitement gone? Blake walked into the theater and glanced around. His masterpiece had lost its glow. Was it the lead actress's fault or was it the play itself? He wasn't sure.

Bosley stood in the wings talking to someone. None of the cast was in sight.

Blake walked up the stage steps and stopped short at the sight of Rhonda Vale's red face.

Bosley patted Miss Vale's arm, while murmuring something in her ear. She nodded and walked away.

Blake frowned and approached the manager. "What's she doing here? Not trying to get her part back, I hope."

Bosley narrowed his eyes and stuck a cigar in his mouth. "No, she was asking for a part as an extra."

He stared at Bosley. "What? With as much experience as she has?"

"That's right." Bosley struck a match and puffed on his cigar until it lit. "Most of the upcoming shows already have a full cast. And Rhonda can't afford to wait. She takes care of her mother and kid sister."

Blake's stomach tightened. "I didn't know. Do we have anything for her?"

" 'Fraid not. All the parts are filled and everyone seems to be working out, except for Hannah." He heaved a loud sigh. "She can't seem to get Peg's character right, either."

"I know. Maybe she'll do better today."

"Maybe. I hope so. Mr. Vaughan says the prospective backer won't be put off much longer. He wants to see the show soon. But if we can't get Peg right, there's no way he'll invest a dime."

Great. Vaughan was their main backer, but he'd made it clear if no one else came in to help he'd probably drop his support.

Blake sat and cringed throughout the practice. Whether Hannah knew she wasn't playing the part the way Blake and Bosley wanted it or something else was bothering her, she stumbled over the simplest lines. Her frustration threw the whole cast off. But Blake felt so guilty about Rhonda Vale he couldn't bring himself to ask Bosley to fire her.

He chewed on his bottom lip. Without the right actress, maybe he needed to let *Peg in Dreamland* go. But maybe. . . He snapped his fingers and left the theater, whistling Peg's theme song.

☙

Danielle glanced around and darted behind the shed where she and Cobb had agreed to meet. Where was he?

A shadow loomed beside her and she started, clutching her stomach. A large dog trotted on past her with barely a glance.

Relieved, she pressed her hand against her heart and inhaled deeply, letting it out slowly. Peeking around the shed, she peered up toward the bridge, squinting in the early afternoon sun. All she needed was for Blake Nelson to show up. She'd never be able to convince him she was here by accident.

A shock of red hair and a burly set of shoulders sauntered toward her. Cobb. Finally.

She grabbed him by his shirtsleeve and pulled him behind the shed. "What took you so long?"

"Got held up, Danni. Don't be so crabby. I'm only five minutes late."

"Fifteen is more like it." She took a deep breath. "What did Sutton say?"

Cobb grinned. "He said you better be tellin' the truth or you and your brother might end up in the river."

A vivid picture of Jimmy sinking in the filthy Chicago River popped into Danielle's mind, and she shuddered. "You tell Sutton I'm not lying. I took a solid gold chain and locket." There, that was true. He didn't need to know she gave it back.

"So where is it?"

"Somewhere safe. I'm still waiting for an opportunity to get at the wall safe. As soon as I do, I'll take what I can and get out of there."

Cobb narrowed his eyes. "Don't double-cross him, Danni. He wasn't kidding about the river."

"I know. How's Jimmy? Did you give him my letter?"

"Yeah. He sent you this." He pulled a scrap of paper from his coat pocket. Danielle reached for it and he jerked it back, laughing.

"Give it here, Cobb, or I'll clobber you." She doubled her fist and glared.

With his head thrown back, Cobb guffawed. "Like you could. But here you go. I was just teasing."

She took the small scrap he offered her and clutched it tightly.

"Thank you, Cobb," she whispered. She reached into her pocket and retrieved an envelope. "Here, will you take this one to him?"

Not for the first time, Danielle was thankful for the tutor Sutton had provided. Even if the man did show up drunk half the time, he was brilliant, a scholar. He not only taught them to read and write but also to speak correctly and to use social graces. Sutton had laughed and said their skills might be useful someday.

Cobb took the letter. "Sure, Danni. Be careful. I know you learned a lot in the practices, and you were good, but this is the real thing. If you get caught, you'll land in prison, and there won't be any blarnin' your way out of it."

Danielle fought the moisture burning the backs of her eyes. Cobb had been her friend ever since the day he'd rescued her and Jimmy. But could she really trust him? She took his hand. "I'll be careful. I promise. And you'll watch after Jimmy?"

"You know I will. Anyone tries anything with Jimbo, they answer to me."

She took comfort in his words. No one would dare hurt Jimmy with Cobb around. That is, no one but Sutton, if he took the notion. Even Cobb was afraid of him.

On the walk to the El station, snow began to fall. She picked up her speed and breathed a sigh of relief when she stepped into the crowded car. A short ride brought her near the Kramers' home.

A sharp wind slapped her face as she stepped onto the sidewalk. At least it had stopped snowing. A typical October teaser. She pulled her fur-trimmed hood up around her face and crammed gloved hands into the pockets of her warm coat, thankful for the gift from Mrs. Kramer. After a short walk, she burst through the door and headed for the kitchen. Warmth from the cookstove welcomed her.

"Well, look at those rosy cheeks, young lady. Get over here by the stove and thaw out." Sally bustled over and took Danielle's coat and hat.

"Thanks, Sally. It's getting colder and the wind is really strong." She walked across the linoleum-covered floor and rubbed her hands together to warm them. The wonderful aroma of stewing chicken rising from the big soup pot tickled her taste buds. She sighed.

If only Jimmy were here. If only they could both live in a big, safe, warm house like this forever.

ᑕᗩ

The roaring fire in the library drew Blake like a magnet. He hung his coat on the coat tree in the foyer and stepped through the heavy double doors. Finding the room empty, Blake warmed his hands briefly then went in search of his mother.

He found her in the front parlor in her little rocking chair near the corner fireplace, her knitting needles clicking as the dancing flames crackled and popped.

When he entered the room, she glanced up and smiled. "Blake, come by the fire and warm yourself. You look frozen." She raised her cheek to his kiss and motioned to the wingback chair across from her.

"I believe I will, Mother." He sat down and cleared his throat, wondering where to begin.

She gave him a glance and laid her knitting on the small round table beside her. "What's wrong, son?"

"I'm not sure if anything is wrong, except perhaps with me. But I do need to talk to you, if you have the time."

"I always have time for you. You know that." She leaned forward and peered at him then rang the bell on the table.

He strummed his fingers on the arm of the chair and shifted. "Several things are on my mind. I thought perhaps you could help me get them straight."

She nodded but didn't offer any comment, so he continued. "Well, we've run into a problem with the leading lady. We can't seem to find the right actress for the part of Peg."

"You rang, ma'am?" June stood in the doorway.

"Yes, dear. Please bring a cup of strong coffee for my son and a cup of tea for me. Maybe some of those Russian tea cakes as well." She smiled at the girl who curtsied and left the room.

Blake sighed and continued. "I was instrumental in getting the first actress who played the part fired." He looked down at his shoes. "Today, I found out she is the sole support of her mother and a young sister."

"Ah, I see." She lifted her eyebrows. "So what are you going to do?"

Blake felt his lips turn up in a grin. She knew him so well. "What makes you think I'm going to do anything?"

The dimple beside her mouth dipped and seemed to wink at him. "I think I know my son pretty well by now. You have something in mind."

"You're right. I do. You see, she is really a fine actress. So is the actress who replaced her. But they simply aren't right for the part."

June entered with a tray and poured the hot drinks. "Will that be all?"

"Yes, thank you." Blake smiled at the girl and she left the room, closing the door softly behind her. He stirred his coffee and took a sip of the hot liquid.

"So, I'm going to write a part in for them. Something big enough to make them happy but not so big that the backers will complain. Perhaps friends of Peg, or maybe one could be her older sister."

"But that still leaves you without a leading lady."

"Mmm-hmm." Blake picked up his spoon and gave full attention to stirring his coffee again. But the action didn't stop the vision of Danielle's enormous eyes.

"Have you prayed about it?"

Guilt stabbed at him. When was the last time he'd prayed or even picked up his Bible?

"You haven't been to church since Easter."

Blake looked at her in surprise. "Has it really been that long?"

She nodded. "Yes, it really has."

"I'll go with you this Sunday. I promise."

"I think I'm going to hold you to that." She smiled. "But there's more, isn't there?"

Blake leaned back and gave a little laugh. "Yes, but it's crazy."

"Why don't you tell me about it."

"You're not going to believe this, because I hardly believe it myself, but the one person who comes to mind when I think of Peg is Miss Gray." There, he'd said it.

"Danielle?" She frowned and gave him a puzzled look. "Can she act? Or sing?"

Blake laughed. "Trust me, Mother. The girl can act quite well. And yes, I've heard her sing. She has a very good voice."

She stared at him, then her eyes widened. She bit her lip and smiled.

"What?" Now what was she thinking?

"Oh, I was just thinking you should probably talk to Danielle. Find out if she's even interested in acting. She might not be."

Blake thought for a minute. Mother was right. But how could he find out if the girl had any interest in acting? He couldn't just ask her outright, could he? And what would she think if he asked her to try out for the part? This was getting more and more complicated.

"Well, dear. I'm sure you'll know what to do. Now, I'm going to lie down and rest for a while. But you will pray about this, won't you?" She put her cup down and stood.

"Yes, I promise."

He smiled as she leaned over and gave him a tender kiss on his forehead. She closed the door softly behind her.

Blake sat in the silence for a moment then closed his eyes. "Father, I'm sorry I've left You out of my life for so long. Please forgive me and show me what You want me to do. Remind me to keep You first, Father. Guide me in Your ways. Show me how to help Rhonda and Hannah. And let me know if You are the one putting the idea of Danielle in my mind or if it's my own crazy idea. In the name of Jesus, amen."

Chapter 8

The storm that beat against the house, sending sheets of rain against the library windows, seemed but an echo of the storm in Danielle's mind and heart. What was she going to do? She didn't want to be a thief. It had seemed to her that someone, probably her mother's Jesus, had kept her and her brother from such a fate. But that must have been her imagination. Otherwise, she wouldn't be in the predicament she was in now.

Surely there had to be a way. An honest, moral way to earn some money. Of course the fleeting thought she'd had about the theater was ridiculous. The play practices Sutton had insisted they perform didn't count. She loved to sing, but she had no idea if she was any good. Probably not.

Angrily, she swiped the tears from her eyes. Crying wouldn't help. But a sob like a hiccup erupted from somewhere deep in her chest.

"What in the. . . ?" Mrs. Parker had opened the door and stood staring at Danielle for a moment. Then she glided across the room, and Danielle found herself in the elderly woman's comforting arms. "My dear, what has upset you so?"

Danielle drew a sharp breath. "It's. . .it's nothing, ma'am. Nothing to worry yourself about."

"Nonsense. Something has you very distraught. Perhaps I can help."

Danielle's mind grasped at the first thought that came to her mind and she blurted out, "I was thinking about my brother. I'm sorry."

"Oh, my poor girl, there's nothing to be sorry for. Of course you're sad about your brother's death. That's only natural."

Danielle groaned inwardly. She'd told a passel of lies to everyone and had no idea how to get out of them without getting herself and Jimmy thrown into jail. How could she have been so stupid? She'd never get away from Sutton anyway. She probably needed to make her way back there and throw herself on his mercy. But the revolting thought of his wet lips against her neck sent a wave of nausea through her, and she shuddered.

Mrs. Parker's arm tightened around her, and with her other hand, she smoothed back Danielle's hair.

Danielle sighed and closed her eyes. But almost immediately she opened them and sat up straight, gently removing herself from the woman's arms. "You're very kind, ma'am. I'm afraid I don't deserve it."

"But of course you do. Everyone deserves kindness and compassion. And especially a sweet young lady like you." She patted Danielle's hand and rose from the sofa. "I do believe the rain has slowed down some. I'm taking food baskets to poor families in my church. Would you like to come with me?"

"To the church?"

"No, to their homes. Although it would be nice if you'd start attending services with us more often." She peered at Danielle. "I don't know how much you know about the Lord, dear. But I promise He can help you in your grief. There's no problem too big or too small for Him."

"Why would He want to help me? I haven't done anything for Him."

A look almost of pity crossed Mrs. Parker's face, and then she smiled. "He wants to help you because He loves you, dear."

Did God really love her? Like Mama used to say? In spite of everything? If it was really true, then maybe He had led her here for a reason. Perhaps He had a plan all worked out to help Danielle and her brother.

God, if You're there, will You show me a way out of this situation?

A tiny glimmer of hope made its way into her heart. Her curls bounced against her shoulders as she jumped up. "Let's go get those baskets delivered."

A half hour later, the Kramer carriage pulled to a stop in front of a modest home. Danielle followed Mrs. Parker up the narrow dirt path to the front door.

The lady inside invited them in.

As they sat and visited with Mrs. Foster, Danielle glanced around the small room, nostalgia washing over her. The furnishings were old and the curtains and table coverings mended, but everything was spotlessly clean. Just as her home had been when she was small.

A little girl, not more than three or four, came and stood by Danielle's chair.

Danielle smiled at the child.

"Is it okay if I touch your hair?"

"My hair? But why?"

"It's so shiny and I never saw hair that color before."

"Mildred, don't be rude to the lady." Mrs. Foster's voice was filled with consternation.

Mildred drew her little hand back before it made contact with Danielle's curls.

"But I don't mind at all." Danielle bent down.

The little girl touched her locks and then drew her hand back and giggled.

When they returned to the carriage, Mrs. Parker leaned back and sighed. "They have so little. Bob Foster was thrown from a horse last year. His neck was broken. Fanny does laundry and sewing to make a living for her two children. They manage, but it's not easy. Yet she never complains and always gives thanks to the Lord for what He provides."

They visited two more families. Another widow with a child who was very nice then a woman who complained from the moment they stepped through the door.

As they drove home, Mrs. Parker glanced at Danielle. "Don't think too hard of her, dear. We all react differently to hardship."

"Yes, ma'am." But Danielle thought her benefactress was all too kind. *Perhaps I'm lacking in compassion.*

☙

The little stone chapel nestled between two brick tenement buildings that towered over it. Danielle didn't remember the church being so small. But then, she'd only been nine years old the last time Mother had brought her here.

Her hand trembled as she opened the door and stepped inside. Would the same minister be here? He'd seemed fairly old to her all those years ago. But, then again, she'd been only a child.

The little sanctuary was unlighted except for the daylight seeping through the front window. Danielle shivered in the cold and shadows and glanced around the room, taking in the rickety benches. The church seemed to be deserted and she sighed, wondering if her venture would be in vain.

The sound of a door opening at the back of the building drew her attention, and relief washed over her as someone entered. "Forgive me, miss. I didn't know anyone was here. Have you been waiting long?"

Danielle cleared her throat. "No, I came in only a moment ago."

He walked down the aisle, and she saw a young man in everyday workman's clothing. A janitor, perhaps?

He drew near and stopped in front of her. "I'm Brother Paul, the minister here. May I be of assistance?"

"Oh. You're the minister?" Oh dear, she hoped the surprise in her voice hadn't offended him.

Smiling, he nodded. "I don't suppose I look like one, do I?"

Danielle's face heated. "I'm so sorry. I didn't mean to be rude."

"You weren't rude at all. Now, how may I help you?"

"I. . .I. . .wonder if I could have a moment of your time." Flustered, she turned. "Of course, I should have made an appointment. I'll just leave and come another time."

"Appointments aren't necessary here, I assure you. And of course I have time for you. Please don't go. In fact, I'm fairly sure my wife will take me to task if I don't bring you upstairs for a cup of tea."

"Upstairs?" Oh dear. How did she know this man in his dockworker's clothing was a minister at all?

"Yes, we live upstairs in a very modest apartment. It's best that way, so we can be available if we're needed."

"Paul, who is there?" A trilling voice came floating through the door and a young woman stepped through, her eyes laughing. "Oh, I'm sorry. If you're having a meeting with someone, I'll just go back up."

"No, no, my dear. This young lady wishes to speak to me, but we were just in the middle of introductions." He turned, smiling at Danielle. "I believe you were just about to tell me your name?"

Danielle swallowed and forced herself to relax. "I'm Danielle Grayson. My mother used to bring my brother and me here when we were children."

In no time, Danielle found herself being ushered up the stairs and into a cozy sitting room.

The minister's wife brought cups of hot tea and they looked expectantly at Danielle.

"It's just that. . ." Danielle hesitated, wondering how much to reveal. "You see, my mother used to tell me Jesus loved me and died for me. But I don't understand what she meant. And I've done some things that I'm afraid might keep me from seeing my mother again."

Something passed through the minister's eyes and he didn't answer right away.

"Should I tell you what I've done?" *Oh God, help me to know what to say without getting Jimmy and me in trouble.*

"No, no, you don't need to tell me anything you don't wish to tell me. Confessing your sins to me isn't how you get to heaven." He picked up a leather-bound Bible from the side table and opened it. "But I can tell you what your mother meant and how you can be sure to see her again."

Relief hit Danielle like a burst of wind. "Oh, please do."

"Let me read to you from God's Word. John 3:16 and 17 says, 'For God so loved the world, that he gave his only begotten Son, that whosoever believeth in him should not perish, but have everlasting life. For God sent not his Son into the world to condemn the world; but that the world through him might be saved.'"

"Oh. I do believe in Him. I always have. Does that mean I get to go to heaven? Even though I've done wrong things?"

"Well, let's see what else the Bible has to say." He turned a few more pages. "In 1 John 1:8 and 9, we read, 'If we say that we have no sin, we deceive ourselves, and the truth is not in us. If we confess our sins, he is faithful and just to forgive us our sins, and to cleanse us from all unrighteousness.'"

"So I do need to confess?"

"Only to Him. Not to me."

"Oh, He already knows."

A smile tipped Brother Paul's lips. "Yes, but we still have to acknowledge our sins to Him."

"But I've done that."

"Well then, my dear child, you're forgiven."

Joy washed over Danielle, so radiant and strong she felt she would burst from the intensity.

"Then He really did save me." Danielle felt her mouth split into a wide grin.

"Absolutely."

Danielle left a few minutes later, her heart light and her eyes shining. It was all true. Just like Mama said. Danielle couldn't wait to tell Mrs. Parker.

Chapter 9

Blake smiled with satisfaction. It worked. The new parts actually made the play better, so Hannah and Rhonda had no suspicion he'd written them just so they'd have jobs. Bosley had convinced both actresses they'd be doing him a favor if they'd take the parts. They were both doing first-class jobs. Rhonda as the older sister and Hannah as Peg's best friend. He watched them laughing together as they walked off stage and breathed a sigh of relief.

Bosley walked down the aisle and flopped into the chair beside Blake. "I sent out a call for auditions for Peg. Let's just hope someone shows up who can actually pull it off."

Blake cleared his throat. "Actually, I have someone in mind. She seems perfect for Peg. Of course, I realize she'll have to audition and you have the final decision."

"A friend of yours?" Bosley threw a suspicious look in his direction. "Hey, you weren't pulling a fast one on me, were you? Just to get some girl into the show?"

"Of course not. Do you think I'd try to sabotage my own play? I don't even know if Miss Gray will be interested."

"How much acting experience does she have?"

"Er. . .I assure you she can act." Okay, that was evasive, but he wanted to at least give Danielle a chance before Bosley found out she'd never been on a stage.

"Well, okay. Auditions are next Monday. Eight in the morning." He clapped Blake on the shoulder and walked away.

Blake frowned. That gave him less than a week to talk to Danielle and coach her for the part. Maybe he was out of his mind, as Bosley suggested.

And how was he going to even broach the subject to her? She'd probably think he was crazy.

As he rode the elevated train home, he ran scenarios through his mind. Finally, he sighed and ran his hands through his hair. What had he been thinking? The girl probably couldn't carry a tune. The few notes he'd heard her sing were probably an accident. And what if she couldn't act at all? Except to get herself out of trouble.

He moped through dinner, avoiding the glances his parents and Pop threw his way, then slammed out of the house and headed for the Kramers'. He might as well get it over with.

Nell ushered him into the front parlor where he found the Kramers, Mrs. Parker, and Danielle having after-dinner coffee while the twins played on the floor in front of the fire.

Mr. Kramer rose. "Hello, Blake. Come in and join us for coffee." They shook hands.

Blake sat in the only available seat, which happened to be on the sofa next to Danielle. He accepted a cup of coffee and made small talk while trying to decide how to speak to Danielle alone.

Finally, when there was a lull in the conversation, he turned to Danielle. "Actually, Miss Gray, I wonder if I could have a word with you in private." He felt everyone's eyes on him as Danielle stared at him in surprise.

Her face flamed. "Excuse me?"

"I. . .uh. . .I need to speak to you about a business matter." He felt curious looks leveled his way.

"I. . .I suppose so." She stood and gave a nervous glance toward Mrs. Kramer.

"Why don't you two go into the library, Danielle?" The lady smiled at the girl and then at Blake.

He sensed their stares boring into his back as he followed Danielle down the hall and into the library.

As soon as she'd cleared the door, she spun around to face him. "Mr. Nelson, I don't know what game you are playing, but I hardly think you and I have any sort of business to discuss."

Why did she always have to be so cranky? Blake could feel anger rising. Swallowing hard, he pushed it down and smiled. "If you'll sit down and give me a moment, I'll explain."

"Well, all right. For a moment, then." She sat in a wingback chair beside the window and motioned to its twin on the other side. "Please have a seat, Mr. Nelson."

He cleared his throat. "Miss Gray, have you ever done any acting?"

"What?" She jumped up, fury on her face. "If you're going to start your accusations again, you can leave right now."

"No, no, that's not what I meant." He stood and raked his hands through his hair. "Please."

She hesitated then took her seat again. "Will you please just say what you do mean?"

He took a deep breath and sat down. "Very well. But promise you'll hear me out."

She gave a slight nod.

"Miss Gray, this might sound forward, but ever since I met you, I've had you in mind when I think of my main character, Peg."

Interest flickered in her eyes. "You have? Really?"

"Yes. None of the actresses we've tried in the role have worked out. Would you be at all interested in auditioning for the part?"

"Why, I. . .I don't know." Her eyes widened. "Are you serious?"

He let out a slow breath. At least she hadn't told him to leave again. "I'm very serious."

A dreamy look filled her eyes. "But why me?"

Good. She was considering it. "Because you look like Peg. And you have most of her mannerisms." Never mind that before he'd met Danielle, Peg had been blond and blue-eyed. And he had to admit, she might have been a little too sweet.

The corners of her mouth tilted and she pressed her lips together. "What do I need to do?"

"So you'll do it?" He couldn't keep the excitement from his voice.

"I'll consider it. But what if I'm terrible?" The last word came out almost like a sigh.

He grinned. "You won't be. But auditions will be held soon. If you'll permit it, I'd like to coach you."

"Of course. But are you sure about this?"

"Very sure. Could you be free to begin soon? Very soon?"

She nodded and grinned. "I'll be ready."

CB

Moonlight streamed in through Danielle's window. The day that had begun so wild and stormy had ended as calm and beautiful. She sighed and leaned back in her chair, closing her eyes.

Was it really true? Was the dream she'd barely dared to think about actually happening? Or was she dreaming now? If she opened her eyes, would she see the morning sun streaming instead of moonlight? Would she realize it had simply been another beautiful dream?

She opened her eyes slowly and smiled at the moonlight. Silly girl.

Blake's face appeared in her mind. Had she noticed before how handsome he was? Yes, but she'd hardly let herself think about it. After all, he was the only one who didn't believe in her innocence.

Her heart leaped at a sudden thought. Had God, perhaps, been using Blake to convict her of her sin? If he had accepted her story right away, would she have gone on thinking she could get by with lying?

Suddenly Danielle didn't feel quite so good. It was time to tell the Kramers the truth. And Blake had a right to know, too. Maybe he wouldn't use her in the show after all. But worse, what if he looked at her with hatred in his eyes?

She groaned inwardly then took a deep breath. Whatever happened with the show, God would take care of her and Jimmy. For the first time in a long while, she truly believed that God loved her and she could trust Him.

CB

"You're asking me to put a girl with no acting experience in the lead role?" Bosley's eyes widened and he raked his fingers through his hair as he stared at Blake. "Are you out of your mind?"

After a restless night of being bombarded by his conscience, Blake had decided he needed to be honest with Bosley before going any further with his Danielle project. So after breakfast he'd come to Bosley's downtown office. He

170

knew it wouldn't be easy to sell the idea, but he was so convinced that Danielle Gray was right for the part he had no intention of giving up.

"Now hear me out, Bos. Think about Peg. She's young and innocent. And the girl I have in mind can look so innocent she'd convince the angels."

"There's more to the part than looking innocent," the stage manager snapped. "Can she sing? Can she show a change of emotion? Can she follow instructions? Would she even be able to memorize her lines?"

"Yes to everything." He hoped. "Sings like an oriole. And remember, I'll be there to coach her."

Bosley leaned back in his chair and sighed, tapping his fingers against the wooden desktop.

Blake held his breath and waited.

"All right. Bring her to the audition, as planned. But I'm not promising you anything. After all the trouble we've had with the wrong actresses and the new backer, I can't believe you're doing this."

Neither could Blake. What was he doing? He needed to have a serious talk with Miss Gray that very day.

He whistled as he stepped onto the train and headed home. Should he stop at the Kramers' house before he went home? It was still rather early. Maybe he'd go have a talk with Pop, whom he'd been avoiding lately. Mostly because of his grandfather's keen insight into Blake's heart and mind. But Pop could help. Give him tips on coaching Miss Gray.

When he walked in the house, he tossed his hat on the hat rack, hung his coat on the coat tree and immediately went looking for Pop.

Not finding him anywhere in the house, he headed out to the tool shed. Shivering without his coat, Blake walked over to Pop who was leaning over an old, blackened table. "What are you doing out here? It's too cold."

Pop glanced up and grinned. "This old table was a prop in the last show we did before the fire. I found it in the rubble and kept it for sentimental reasons."

"Hmm. Sentimental because your theater burned to the ground?"

"No, sentimental because it was the one show my Katie was in."

"Huh? What are you talking about, Pop? Mother wasn't in vaudeville."

Pop groaned as he straightened his back. "Not vaudeville. That was New York City, before your grandmother died."

"Oh." Confused, Blake stared at his grandfather. "You mean you weren't in vaudeville here in Chicago?"

"I'm sure I've told you before."

"No, all you ever talked about was vaudeville."

"Ah, I see I've neglected your education, lad. I was with an Irish troupe here in Chicago for years. Harrigan's Music Hall and Theater was well known and well occupied day after day, night after night. We did musical comedy, mostly."

"But, I don't understand what you meant about Mother. She wasn't on the stage, was she?"

"Hmm. You'd best be asking her about it. I'll be in enough trouble for me slip of the tongue." Blowing a gust of frosty air, he took a handkerchief from his pocket and wiped his hands. "Now what were you wanting with me, to come out to this dingy shed?"

Realizing he wouldn't be getting anything more about the subject from Pop, he decided to bide his time. But the idea of Mother in a musical comedy both thrilled and disturbed him. "Could we go inside, Pop? I'd like to talk to you about something." He nodded toward the table. "That is, if you're finished out here."

"I am and we can. To be sure, I'm getting a mite cold." He grinned. "But what can one expect? It's almost November."

Blake grinned. "Let's not get ahead of ourselves. That's a week off."

"Guess I've got turkey on my mind." Pop laughed and slapped him on the shoulder.

They settled themselves into the wingback chairs on either side of the library fireplace, and Blake rang for coffee.

"Make mine a wee bit Irish." Pop grinned as June bit her lip and looked worried. "Just kidding, lass. Straight coffee for me, too."

When June had brought their coffee and left, Pop leaned back and peered at Blake. "Now, what's so important you'd pull me away from my memories?" He smiled to soften the words.

"I've decided to coach Miss Gray for the part of Peg. That is, she's supposed to let me know today."

"I see." Pop stirred his coffee for the second time. "And is Bosley in agreement?"

"Well, not exactly, but he's willing to let her audition."

"Hmm. I thought you couldn't stand the sight of the lass."

"Yes, well, I think it's possible I've misjudged her. And I can't get the idea of her playing the part out of my head. So I have to try." He blew on his coffee and took a sip. "I was wondering if you'd give me some advice."

"I see. And what about the other girl? Hannah, I think her name is?"

"She and Rhonda Vale will be taking on a couple of new parts I wrote into the play."

A look of pride crossed Pop's face. "You wrote parts just for them?"

"Well, yes. You see, I found out that Rhonda. . ."

"Was supporting her mother and sister?"

"You knew?" Blake looked at his grandfather in surprise. "Why didn't you say something?"

"Didn't want to interfere. I prayed about it, though."

"You did?"

"Well, yes. Don't sound so surprised. What do you think I am, a heathen?"

"Of course not, Pop. I just didn't realize you knew about it. God really does care about our daily lives, doesn't He?" He took a long sip of coffee.

"I'm sure He does. Now, would you like some coaching tips for your young lady?"

Blake choked on the hot liquid. And felt flames just as hot wash over his face. He should have known Pop would see right through him. He laughed. "I would be very grateful, Pop. Thanks for offering."

∽

"Will you stop overacting?"

"What? Overacting?" Danielle glared at her tormentor and flung the script on the sofa. "I'm not overacting. Why do you have to be so critical?"

"Oh, stop sulking." He stepped closer and shook his finger practically in her face. "If you can't take some simple criticism and follow suggestions, you'll never make it in the theater."

She gasped and knocked his hand away. "How dare you? And I didn't ask to be in your play. If you'll recall, you asked me. Maybe you should find someone else." She swallowed past the sudden lump in her throat, wishing she could take back what she'd just said. What if he thought she was serious? Or what if he decided to get even?

She still hadn't told Blake or the Kramers the truth. After all, she'd convinced herself, she had to find just the right moment and decide exactly how to bring it up. But in her heart, she knew she was simply making excuses. Having it constantly over her head was causing her to be short-tempered.

He backed up and threw a contrite look her way. "Sorry. I didn't mean to shake my finger at you."

Relief washed over her. "Well, all right. I may have spoken a little hastily. I'll try not to 'overact,' as you call it."

Danielle forced a tight smile as Blake breathed a sigh of relief. The practices had been going well, and she knew she'd been doing a good job until today. The audition was tomorrow and her nerves were on edge. Apparently his were, too.

"Shall I try again?"

"Yes, please." He picked up the script and handed it to her.

"Thank you, Blake." She wasn't sure just when they'd switched to first names, but she was glad they had. She had discovered that once he stopped accusing her he wasn't really so bad, after all. It would be nice if she could let her guard down so they could be friends. But of course, that wasn't possible. Not until she found the courage to tell the truth. And after that, well. . .

This time, the read-through went off without a hitch. Blake's smile, as he congratulated her, was radiant, and she basked in it just for a moment.

"Well, I guess I'm as ready as I can be. I'll see you at the theater."

"Nonsense. I'll pick you up in the buggy. No reason for your getting tired out before you get to the theater."

"Well then, thank you. I'll see you in the morning." She held her hand out to shake, but he smiled and bent over her hand. The slightest touch of his lips brushed across her fingers, and a tingling sensation crept from her fingertips all the way up her arm.

With a sharp intake of breath, she watched him walk away.

Chapter 10

Danielle's heart sank as she stood in the wings and watched the pretty blond actress read for the part of Peg. Perfectly. She was wonderful. What chance did Danielle have against someone so beautiful who obviously knew what she was doing?

"Thank you, Miss Jackson. We'll let you know our decision in a day or two."

The actress left the stage, and another girl with the same air of self-confidence took her place. She, too, seemed perfect to Danielle. Maybe she'd better leave before she made a complete fool of herself.

"Miss Danielle Gray."

Danielle started at the sound of her name. She inhaled deeply then stepped onto the stage. She stood for a moment staring out into the shadowy cavern in front of her. She hadn't known it would be like this. But maybe it was better that she didn't see their faces. Perhaps that would be even more frightening.

"Whenever you're ready, Miss Gray."

As the disembodied voice called out, Danielle cleared her throat and stepped closer to the front of the stage. It seemed to her that she went through her lines in a daze, hardly knowing the line she'd just spoken and yet somehow finding the next. As the last word fell from her lips, she bowed and stumbled into the wings.

You were terrible. Terrible. Thoughts bombarded Danielle as she hurried to the coatroom. *Everyone must be laughing that you would dare to try out for a part in this wonderful musical play. Blake must be so ashamed.*

Fighting back tears, she grabbed her coat and hat and hurried from the theater. She barely noticed the strong, biting wind as she rushed to the station.

All the way home, she chided herself. Why had she thought she could do this? Why had she let Blake talk her into it? Pride, maybe? Or a desire for fame? She took a deep breath. No. There may have been a little bit of those, but her reason had been to make a way for Jimmy to have a better life. But why would God allow her this wonderful career when she hadn't even obeyed Him and told the truth?

She stepped from the train and was halfway down the street when she heard the clopping of a horse's hooves against the brick street.

"Danielle, wait, please." She turned and saw Blake's buggy rolling slowly along beside her.

Unable to restrain the tears any longer, she turned her face away and burst into sobs.

She felt strong arms around her, and Blake led her gently to the buggy and helped her in. He handed her a handkerchief and clicked at the horse. A moment later they pulled up in front of the Kramers' house and he turned to her with a wide grin.

"So you think it's funny that I made a fool of myself?" she stammered.

"Danielle, darling, look at me." He took the handkerchief and wiped her eyes. "You got the part."

She gasped. Had he called her darling? Then the rest of his words sank in. "What? What did you say?" Her words were hardly more than a whisper, but it was all she could manage.

"You got the part. You did a wonderful job, and Bosley loves you."

A loud *whoop* came from somewhere, and she realized it came from her own mouth. "I got the part? Really? I'm going to be Peg? Are you sure, Blake?"

He laughed and grabbed her hands, which were pounding his chest. "Unless there is another Danielle Gray around, I'm sure."

"Oh. Come in with me. We have to tell the Kramers and Mrs. Parker and Sally."

Arm in arm, they practically skipped up the walk and went inside.

଼ଃ

Blake hummed Peg's theme song as he drove next door and put the horse and buggy in the carriage house. As he went to find his mother and Pop to give them the news, reality hit him and he bit his lip. While it was true that Bosley had been impressed with Danielle's freshness and her natural approach to Peg, what Blake hadn't told Danielle was that Bosley was still uncertain that she could carry it off with the rest of the cast. They had one week of practices to prove to him that she could. If he had any doubts at that time, he would give the part to Susan Jackson.

଼ଃ

"Sutton wants to see you, Danni." Cobb leaned against the wobbly shed and gave her a sympathetic look. "He said you have to talk to him face-to-face."

Danielle bit her bottom lip and clenched her trembling hands into fists. She absolutely would not show fear. Not to Cobb or Sutton or anyone else.

"I can't imagine why. I said I have a job and will start paying him. Did you tell him that?" They'd been rehearsing for nearly two weeks now, and Danielle calculated she'd be getting her first paycheck in about three days.

"Yeah. He said if you think the pittance you might earn from whatever you're doing is gonna take care of what you owe him, you're wrong, and he wants to know why you haven't emptied out that safe yet."

"Well, I'm not wrong. He's quoted what I owe him many times and I can pay if he'll just be patient." Danielle wasn't exactly sure that was true, but she had to trust God.

"And the safe?"

"If I pay him back out of my wages, I shouldn't have to touch the safe."

175

Cobb narrowed his eyes. "Are you going soft, Danni?"

"No, of course not. I just don't want to get caught and go to jail." Okay, that was true, too. She should tell him about her newfound faith, but he'd just laugh at her. What should she do about Sutton? She'd almost rather face a wolf. However, if she didn't go, he might do something to Jimmy just to spite her.

"Okay, can't blame you there. What about Sutton? You going to see him or not?"

"All right. Let's go now."

It wasn't far. When they turned into the familiar alley, Danielle almost changed her mind. But her brother's trusting face flashed in her mind, and sorrow assaulted her. *Oh, Jimmy.*

Cobb unlocked the door and Danielle stepped through.

"Danni!" Hobbling on his crutch, Jimmy thumped over and stopped short two feet from her. "Hi."

"Hi? Come here, you." She rushed forward and grabbed him in a tight hug until he shoved her away.

"Hey, stop the mush stuff." He growled and blinked hard. But not hard enough to keep one tear from dropping from the corner of his eye. At twelve, Jimmy was small for his age but tried to make up for it in toughness. He had to at Sutton's or the other boys would make life unbearable.

"Okay, little brother. Sorry about that."

"It's okay, I guess." He grinned. "You're just a girl."

"Well, well. And what have we here?" Sutton stood in the doorway to the kitchen, a mocking smile on his face.

A chill swept over Danielle. Déjà vu took her back to the first day she stood in this room.

"Hello, Sutton." She forced a cheerful tone into her voice. She'd fooled him before.

"Hello yourself, Danielle. And to what do we owe this unexpected visit?" His face had a few more wrinkles and there was gray in his hair, but otherwise he was the same as the first time she'd heard him say those words.

"Here at your beck and call, of course." She flashed a grin to make him think she was joking. "Besides, I wanted to see Jimmy."

"As you can see, your brother is doing well. After all, I'm quite fond of the boy and have taken good care of him. Right, Jimmy?"

"Sure." But something in her brother's voice didn't ring true.

She examined him more closely. There were no visible bruises, so he hadn't been beaten. And he didn't appear deprived of food. So what was going on?

Dread hit her. She knew what she had to do. "Maybe I'll stay. I'm tired of living with those people." She almost choked on the lie as she looked around at the squalor of the room. Apparently it had been cleaned very little since she'd been gone.

Sutton threw his head back and laughed. "Oh, I don't think so, my dear."

"Why not? You don't want me to stay?" Surprise cut through her. What was he up to?

"Oh, I'd love for you to stay, dear girl. But not quite yet. First there is a little matter of a safe that needs to be unburdened of its contents." He scrutinized her face. "And I'm very much interested in hearing more about this job you've acquired."

Her heart thumped wildly. What could she tell him? Maybe a short version of the truth would be best.

She put on a bright smile. "You aren't going to believe this, because I hardly believe it myself, but I've acquired a small part in a musical. You know I've always liked to sing."

Amusement crossed his face. "Well, you surprise me. I never thought you'd lower your sweet self to being a chorus girl. And you won't earn much money that way. That is, unless you catch the eye of some rich wolf on the prowl."

Mortified, she felt her face burn, but she breathed an inward sigh of relief. Let him think she was a chorus girl somewhere.

"And now let's talk about the family you're living with and the elusive safe."

"Wh–what do you want to know?"

"Who they are, where they live, and the contents of the safe." The words shot from his lips like bullets.

Danielle swallowed hard. *Please, God.* Breathing deeply, she fired back, "I'm not telling you who or where, but I will tell you about the safe. If that's not enough, then you can tie me up and beat the life out of me. But I still won't tell where I'm living or with whom."

Sutton's eyes blazed with anger for a moment, then he laughed shortly. "Well, still spunky, I see. Very well, then, tell me about the safe and why you haven't done the job yet."

Relaxing a little, Danielle searched her mind for words that would satisfy the man without forcing her to lie.

"I don't know everything that's in there, but I do know there are diamonds and cash." There, that much was true. She'd heard Mr. Kramer ask his wife one day to wait in the carriage while he got some cash from the safe. Another time, Mrs. Kramer had handed a diamond necklace to her husband and asked him to put it back in the safe for her. "I'm trying to discover the numbers for the padlock. Then I'll have to wait until I'm alone in the house."

A greedy look crossed Sutton's face followed almost instantly by suspicion. "You'd better not be lying to me, girl."

೦ಬ

"I told you she'd be good, didn't I?" Blake grinned at Bosley, who slowly took the band off his cigar.

"Yeah. You did. And you were right."

"So you really like her? She's perfect for the part, isn't she?"

"Calm down, Blake. You're acting like a schoolboy with a crush." Bosley cast a half smile at him.

Blake felt his face flame. "That's ridiculous. I'm simply happy to finally have my Peg."

"Well, she really is good at the part. You had that right. Not that she's perfect. She needs to work on her lines. Tell her not to overdramatize every sentence."

"I know, I know. She overdoes the lines a little, but we're working on it. She'll be fine before opening night."

"Well, you seem confident, so I'll take your word on it. Remember, we open two weeks before Christmas." He waved and headed backstage.

Blake walked to the lobby and waited for Danielle. His mother had suggested they come to lunch and do their rehearsing in the library. He suspected she planned to be there.

Grinning, he thought about Pop's revelation. Blake hadn't yet found the opportune moment to ask Mother about her short stint in show business, but he had every intention of doing just that when the right time arose.

Danielle walked into the lobby. One long curl had escaped from the wide sweeping hat she wore, and she lifted a small hand to tuck it back. She glanced around, and when she saw him waiting, her face lit up. Quickly she composed her expression and walked over. She laid one hand on his proffered arm and they stepped out onto the broad sidewalk.

Blake resisted the urge to cover her small hand with his. A sudden need to protect her rose in his chest. Surprised at his own feelings, he laughed inwardly. Like she needed protecting.

As the buggy rolled down the streets toward home, he shoved the feeling aside and turned to her. "Don't be surprised if Mother watches us rehearse. She's very curious about how you're doing."

"Really? Oh, I hope I don't make a lot of mistakes, then."

"If she makes you nervous, I can try to make an excuse to banish her from the room." He laughed and waved his arm dramatically.

"No, I don't think it will bother me to have your mother there. I like her."

Warmth filled Blake's heart, and he smiled. "I'm glad. She likes you, too, you know."

"Does she really? I'm so glad."

They pulled up in front of the wide steps, and a stable boy appeared to take the reins.

03

"My dear, that was wonderful." Mrs. Nelson stood and clapped her dainty hands. "You are just about perfect."

Danielle blushed. "Thank you for your kind words. I know I'm still a long way from perfect."

"Well, you are just as good or better than most of the girls we see on the stage today." She gave an emphatic nod and turned to Blake. "Don't you agree?"

Blake grinned. Here was his opportunity. "Absolutely, Mother. And you should know. After all, you were in the business yourself once, weren't you?"

Danielle cast a surprised glance at Mrs. Nelson, who gasped and blushed. "Well, I. . .that is. . ." She took a deep breath. "Yes, as a matter of fact I was on the stage for a while. That father of mine. He told you, didn't he?"

"I don't think he meant to, Mother. But why be so secretive about it?"

"Oh, I don't know. I was afraid it would hurt your father's career, I guess, or at least his social position." She looked at Blake sternly. "But never for an instant should you think your father felt that way. He didn't care who knew."

"Then why is he so against my show?"

"I think he feels it's different for a man. The law firm will be yours someday. He knew I'd give up the theater in a minute for him. I did, too. But the man is the breadwinner. He wants to make sure you have a reliable means of supporting yourself and the family you will undoubtedly have someday." She cut a glance at Danielle and gave her a smile.

Warmth rushed to Danielle's face, and she stared at Blake's mother. Surely she didn't think. . . Oh no. Danielle cast a glance at Blake, who seemed oblivious to his mother's misunderstanding of their relationship.

"So, Mother, tell us a little about it. What did you do in show business? And how did you get started?"

Mrs. Nelson sat back down on the settee and stared across the room with a faraway look in her eyes. "I was so young. I'd just turned eighteen. I remember arriving in Chicago that day. That's where I saw your father for the first time, Blake dear. I ran right into him. But it was just for an instant. Then he was gone and my father was there holding me close.

"The smell of smoke hung heavily on the air. It was the summer before the Great Fire and already the horrible drought was causing an outbreak of fires throughout the city. But I was so excited to be riding down the street with Pop toward the theater, I hardly noticed.

"Then we drew up in front of a large, colorful building. There was a big sign across the top. HARRIGAN'S MUSIC HALL AND THEATER. I loved it from the moment I stepped inside. At first Pop wouldn't hear of my performing. But then, Mr. Harrigan talked him into allowing me to sing before the opening each day and night. I felt like I was in heaven. Later, one of the actresses was injured, and Pop allowed me to step into the small part of the girl who took her place."

A smile tilted her lips. "Your father reserved the same seat every night. First row, middle seat. Then the fire came. They eventually rebuilt the theater, but by then I was engaged to be married to your father. He would have let me go back. But I no longer had much excitement for the stage. I had only one love. Sam Nelson. And I've never regretted devoting myself to him." She gave Danielle an intent look and smiled.

Oh dear. Danielle bit her lip. She must let Mrs. Nelson know there was nothing between her and Blake.

Chapter 11

Danielle shivered as she waited for Cobb behind the shed, which provided no barrier to the cold wind. Ordinarily on a day like this she would have stayed home from their weekly meeting, but she had to find out why Jimmy had looked frightened when Sutton came into the room. Besides, she hoped the money she'd brought for Sutton would satisfy him for a while.

Cobb came around the corner, his body hunkered against the wind. "It's freezing out here," he scowled. "We need to find another place to meet."

"Well, see if you can think of someplace where everyone's nose wouldn't be stuck in our business."

He grunted and gave a brief nod, obviously not in the best of moods today.

She opened her purse and drew out a wad of bills. "Here. Will you give this to Sutton? Tell him it's most of my first paycheck."

"Sure." He stuffed the bills into his pocket. "He wanted me to tail you, but I won't."

"What?" She shouldn't have been surprised. Could she trust Cobb to go against Sutton?

"He really wants to know where you live. But he won't find out from me. He'll beat the tar out of me if he finds out, but I won't betray you, Danni." He tightened his lips and a grunt of anger emitted from his throat. "But he's almost sure to find out where you're working."

"How?"

"Well now, how many musicals are running at one time? All he has to do is visit one theater every night until he finds you. You shouldn't have told him."

Danielle picked nervously at a tiny loose thread on her sleeve. Cobb was right. Why hadn't she thought of that when she'd bragged about singing in a musical? She would have to keep close watch to make sure she didn't lead Sutton to the Kramers.

Two ragged boys ran down the street, flying toy airplanes. Their laughter fell like screams on Danielle's ears and she started, angry at herself for being so jumpy. Nodding to Cobb, she said, "I guess I'll just have to be careful."

"I dunno, Danni. When Sutton wants something, he usually gets it."

"I don't want to talk about that now. Tell me about Jimmy. Why did he look so frightened when Sutton came in? Is he being hurt in any way?"

"Naw. He ain't been hit or anything. But Sutton has been saying things about you just to rile him up."

"What kinds of things?"

"Oh, how if you didn't come through with the goods soon he'd drag you back here by the hair of your head and how he's going to have you someday, one way or another."

Nausea washed over her. "He said that to Jimmy?"

"Yeah, and other stuff, too. Jimmy got really upset. I thought he was going to tear into Sutton a couple of times."

"Oh, Cobb," she whispered. "I have to get him out of there."

"Don't try it, Danni. I don't know what Sutton would do. But you couldn't pull it off, that's for sure."

"I have to think of something. I can't leave him there much longer, and if Sutton meant what he said, I can't go back. I'd die first."

"Don't talk like that, Danni." Cobb peered at her with something that looked like genuine concern.

Impulsively, she reached over and gave him a hug. "Don't worry. I wouldn't be much help to Jimmy dead, would I?"

ଓ

Pain and anger battled within Blake's heart as he watched Danielle's arms go around the big, hulking redhead. When he'd asked to take her to lunch after morning rehearsal, she'd made an excuse of having errands to run. But something evasive in her eyes had made him suspicious, and he'd followed her. Now, he almost wished he hadn't. But if she was interested in someone else, he needed to know.

Only, why had she given the man money? Was he some sort of scoundrel who lived off women? Or did he, perhaps, have a bigger claim on her? For all Blake knew she could be secretly married. . .or worse. A chill washed over him at the last thought. Then he shook it off. He wouldn't believe such a thing of Danielle. She was too pure for that. He was sure of it.

He started to leave before she came back across the bridge but then stopped himself. He might as well find out the truth now.

He waited at the end of the bridge and watched her walk across, her eyes down as if she were deep in thought. She lifted them just before she reached Blake. A spark of anger appeared in her eyes. "Following me again, Blake? I won't believe it's just a coincidence."

"Yes. I saw the look in your eyes when you said you had errands, so I followed you to see what you were up to."

"Oh." She shot a searing glance at him and walked past.

Stunned, he hurried to catch up with her. "Is that all you have to say? Who was that fellow you were so chummy with?"

He almost ran into her when she stopped in her tracks. Spinning around, she glared at him. "Who I speak to is hardly any of your business, Blake. And what makes you think I have to explain my every move? Just because you got me the part in your show? Because if I'd realized that gave you ownership of me, I'd have refused." She whirled back around and sped toward the theater.

Blake hurried after her, taking her arm. "Wait a minute. It's not like that."

She stopped and looked at him. "Then what is it?"

He sighed. Yes, what was it? "You intrigue me, Danielle. And I'll admit you frustrate me as well. I no longer believe you're a robber, but I also don't believe you knew nothing about it. And I'm almost positive most of the story you told us was concocted on the spur of the moment." There, he'd finally come up with what he really thought about the day they'd run each other down. He wasn't sure until this moment he'd ever figured it out himself.

Surprise and horror stabbed at him as Danielle's eyes filled with tears. "Well, you are correct, Blake. On all points. I'm not a robber. And I do know more than I told about the pickpockets."

"Then why didn't you say so? If you were innocent, you had nothing to fear." He handed her a handkerchief.

She sighed and dabbed at her eyes. "Please, Blake, don't ask me to tell you anything right now. I would if I could, but it's not possible. But soon, I promise."

He took the handkerchief and dabbed at the moisture on one cheek she'd missed. "What would you do if I wasn't around with my handy handkerchiefs when you needed them?"

She laughed. "I don't know. I never used to cry at all."

"All right, Danielle. I believe you and I trust you. I hope that someday soon you'll trust me enough to tell me what's going on. Because something is wrong, and I only want to help you."

"I do trust you. But there are too many things at stake here." She bit her lip. "This much I will tell you. The man I've been meeting is a friend. Nothing more. I've known him since I was a little girl. I'm sorry. That's all I can say for now."

"Then that will have to do. But if, at any time, you wish to confide in me, I'm here for you." He smiled. "And now, I'm starved. We still have time for lunch if we hurry."

The tantalizing aroma of hot dogs drew them to a little stand on the corner. They ate the mustard-and-onion-topped frankfurters on the way to the theater, arriving just as rehearsal was starting.

While Danielle hurried onto the stage, Blake took a seat in the middle of the front row so he wouldn't miss anything. Suddenly he remembered his mother's story about his father buying tickets for front row, center seat, and he grinned. Well, that story had a happy ending, so maybe this wasn't coincidence. One thing he knew: He was in love with Danielle. But under the circumstances, he had no idea what to do about it.

He looked up as Pop scurried down the front aisle and sat in the seat next to him.

"Hi, Pop."

"Hello yourself. How did it go this morning?"

"The whole cast did great. There wasn't a single hitch. And Danielle played Peg to perfection."

"Well, she's a bonny lass and a smart one, too. You could go a long way and not find one like her."

Blake darted a glance at his grandfather. Was he talking about her acting ability or something else?

Pop stared straight ahead and whistled a bar of Peg's theme, then he turned and winked at Blake.

Blake grinned. The old fox. He'd been onto him from the beginning. He thought about the day he'd first found out Danielle was staying with the Kramers. Even before Blake himself realized his feelings for the girl, Pop had picked up on it.

He turned as Danielle stepped out onstage and instantly became Peg. *Peg in Dreamland.*

Am I in some sort of dreamland, as well? Am I fooling myself that Danielle might care for me and trust me enough to reveal her secrets?

○೩

Danielle's eyes found Blake. How she longed to bare her soul to him. To lay her head against his chest and feel comforting arms around her and gentle words telling her everything would be all right.

But what if he didn't respond that way? What if he thought it was his duty to report Sutton and the gang to the authorities? She didn't really think he would turn her in. But Jimmy was at Sutton's. What would happen to him? No. She couldn't risk it. She'd have to wait. God would show her how and when. She had to believe that.

Blake's grandfather, seated beside him, gave her a wink and she shook herself from her thoughts and smiled at the kindly white-haired man.

She dove into the part she was playing, and in spite of her troubles, playing the part of Peg gave her a reprieve from her anxiety.

Afterward, Blake drove her home. She was glad Mr. O'Shannon was with them. Blake wouldn't try to question her with his grandfather right there. They pulled up in front of the Kramers', and he hopped down then helped her out on the driver's side. "I'll walk you to the door."

"That's not necessary. It's still daylight, Blake."

"Nevertheless." He put his hand on her arm, and they walked up to the porch. "I'll be over after dinner to help you run through your lines. If that's all right?"

"Oh, I don't think so, Blake. I'm awfully tired. Can't we skip one night? After all, Mr. Bosley said I was quite good. Did you hear him?"

"Yes, but you do know the new backer will be there tomorrow. We want it to go the best it can."

She sighed. "All right. One run-through. But that's all. I want to wash my hair and go to bed early."

She went inside and, not seeing anyone, went up to her room to rest before she had to change for dinner. She loved acting, but it was tiring. A lot more so than she'd have thought.

She sat at her dressing table and rubbed cold cream onto her face. The motion and the feel of the coolness relaxed her, and she closed her eyes.

Immediately, Blake's face flashed into her mind. Quickly she opened her eyes. She could no longer deny her feelings for him. Danielle had never been in love before, but she knew. She loved Blake Nelson with her whole heart. And she was almost certain he felt the same way. But her secret stood in the way of a true relationship between them. How she wished she had simply refused to allow Mrs. Kramer to take her home with her that day. She would never have fallen in love with Blake and wouldn't be suffering like this now.

Of course, she also wouldn't have had the opportunity to buy hers and Jimmy's freedom from Sutton. Her lips tightened. Somehow she must find a way to get Jimmy away from that house before Sutton carried out his plan, whatever it was. Once Jimmy was safe, then she could tell Blake everything.

Cobb's words screamed in her mind. *"He's saying he's going to have you one way or another."*

Danielle would rather go to jail any day than have Sutton ever lay his hands on her.

Chapter 12

The aroma of biscuits, ham, and eggs tantalized Blake's senses as he walked down the stairs and into the dining room. He planted a kiss on his mother's cheek and walked to the sideboard. Suddenly his stomach churned, and the food that had smelled so good a moment before didn't appear very appetizing. He poured a cup of coffee, speared a slice of toast onto a plate, and sat down.

"Blake," his mother scolded, "you need to eat more than that."

Pop laid the morning paper beside his plate and grinned. "Don't pester the boy, Katie. He's too excited to eat."

"I'm afraid Pop's right, Mother. But I promise to eat a hearty lunch."

"What's so exciting about today?" She lifted her deep blue eyes and smiled.

"Our new backer will be at the theater. Bosley is so nervous he's decided to do a dress rehearsal this afternoon so the man can get into the theme of the play." He shook his head. "I heard one of the members of the cast muttering about it being bad luck to have a dress rehearsal before the eve of opening night, but that, of course, is nonsense."

"I'm glad you're sensible enough to know that, son. You just trust in the Lord to keep things right."

"I will, Mother." He smiled across at her then turned to his grandfather. "You'll be there, won't you, Pop?"

"Wouldn't miss it for anything. The afternoon rehearsal?"

"That's right. We'll take a short lunch break. Then the cast will get into their costumes and be ready to begin when the backer arrives."

"Who is he, by the way?"

"Some wealthy businessman. An acquaintance of one of the other patrons." He shoved his chair back and stood.

"I'll be praying," his mother said, lifting her cheek for his good-bye kiss. "And tell Danielle I'll be praying for her, too."

"I will. Thank you."

"Oh, and Blake, why don't you invite Danielle to Thanksgiving dinner?"

He grinned. "Good idea. Thanks, Mother. She may have plans with the Kramers, but I'll ask."

A stable boy had brought the buggy around and stood holding the reins when Blake walked out of the house.

"Thanks, Tommy. Cookie's looking mighty spruce today. Did you do the grooming?"

"Yes, sir." The boy stood straighter and handed him the reins.

"Here. I think you deserve a bonus."

Tommy caught the coin Blake tossed him and then waved and grinned again as Blake drove away.

Danielle was waiting on the porch as he pulled up in front of the Kramers'. She huddled against her side of the buggy, silent and pale, as they drove to the theater.

Blake reached over and took her trembling hands. Even through the gloves he could feel the cold. "Your hands are like ice. You shouldn't have waited for me outside."

Her teeth chattered as she spoke. "I was too nervous to wait inside."

"There's nothing to be afraid of. Just do what you've been doing. It'll be fine."

"What if it isn't? What if you made a big mistake and I'm not right for this part at all? What if this backer hates me?" Her hands trembled beneath his.

"He won't hate you. He'll love you, just like everyone else does." *Especially me.* He wondered what she'd do if he voiced those words. For a moment he was tempted. Then he shook himself free from the thought.

"Look, you won't even have to see the man while you are performing. This will be as much like an opening night as possible. The theater will be dark except for the stage lights."

"But he'll see me."

Blake laughed. "Well, of course he'll see you. That's the point of having him there."

They arrived at the theater, and he gave her hand a squeeze. "You'll do fine. Try not to worry."

She gave a tremulous smile and headed for the dressing rooms.

He sighed with relief as Rhonda walked into the lobby. "Rhonda, Danielle has a bad case of stage fright today. Will you see what you can do?"

She flashed him a bright smile and patted him on the shoulder. "Go sit down and stop worrying. I'll take care of her."

Knowing he'd done all he could to help her for now, he headed for his seat in the first row and waited for the curtain to rise on the first rehearsal of the day.

Danielle stumbled over some of the words in the last scene, but otherwise the practice went perfectly.

Blake couldn't help but notice the worried little pout on Danielle's face as he escorted her down the sidewalk to the café on the corner. When they were seated, he picked up his menu, determined not to mention her slipup and to get her mind off it as well. "I think John Turner got a little too amorous in the romantic scene." He looked over the top of the menu to see her reaction.

"Don't be silly. He played it exactly the way you wrote it."

He smirked behind the menu. So far so good. "I'm not so sure. He hugged you pretty tightly."

She inhaled deeply. "Blake, John didn't hug me. Alan hugged Peg. Whatever is the matter with you?"

He continued the tactic with a loud huff. "I'm not so sure of that. And was that a real kiss he planted on you? He's not supposed to do that."

She flung her menu on the table, raised her eyes, and frowned. "Blake Nelson, I can't believe you're behaving this way. You know very well it was only acting."

He raised his menu to cover the grin he couldn't prevent, but not fast enough.

"Oh, you." She burst out laughing. "I see what you're up to. And it worked. I almost forgot how awful I was. Blake, I was terrible."

"Nah. Everyone gets the jitters when they know a lot is at stake. You'll do fine this afternoon."

She sighed. "I hope so." She picked up her menu again, but this time she seemed to really see it.

☙

"You'll knock 'em dead, kid. I promise." Rhonda patted Danielle on the arm then scurried to get into her costume.

"But what if you're wrong? What if I freeze and forget my lines or something?" Danielle fumbled with her hair and attempted to work the strands together into one thick braid. The smooth locks kept slipping from her fingers, and she was about to burst out in tears.

"Here, let me do that." Another actress, fully costumed, shoved Danielle's hand away from the strands and began to weave them into a smooth braid.

"Thanks, Mary. I don't know what I'd do without all of you."

Rhonda stepped away from the mirror, giving a last-minute pat to her hair. "Sweetie, we've all had our moments of panic. Still do sometimes. But when you step out on that stage, you'll be fine. You won't even think about the new guy."

Oh, how I pray she's right.

She bit her lip and followed the others to the wings. The starting characters took their places. The music began, and the curtain went up.

When she heard the opening bar of Peg's theme, her cue, she took a deep breath and stepped out onto the stage. She became Peg. Lost in the part, she spoke her lines and moved from one scene to another as though she was born on a dairy farm, among the rolling hills of Missouri. She was loving, teasing, and filled with laughter as she played the part of little sister, friend, and beloved daughter. Then, she became shy when the leading man appeared.

When the curtain came down on the last scene, she heard clapping and a murmur of voices from the small unseen group of watchers.

She stumbled, almost numb, into the dressing room and flopped onto a settee, trying to still the wild pounding of her heart. All around her, laughter and satisfied comments about the show filled the room.

Rhonda leaned over and gave her a hug. "See? I told you you'd knock 'em dead."

Danielle smiled. "If anyone knocked them dead it was you and Hannah. In fact, everyone was wonderful. I forgot about everything except the life of *Peg in Dreamland.*"

"Honey, you did very well," Hannah said with a smile. "I've no doubt the new man will be willing to put up the rest of the money for the show. In fact, I'm so sure I think it calls for a celebration. How about we all go out for a milk shake?"

The door flew open. Martha, a prop girl, pushed her way in among the flurry of actresses changing into their street clothes. Her eyes found Danielle. "Mr. Bosley and Mr. Nelson want you in the office at your convenience. But I think what they really mean is get there lickety-split."

Danielle stared at Martha, her pulse jumping in her throat. "Thanks. I'll be there as soon as I've changed." With a heavy heart, Danielle slipped out of her costume then went to work on removing the makeup. What did they want with her? Did the new backer hate her performance? Did he refuse to back the show? Blake would try to let her down easily, if they had to let her go. She only hoped the show could be salvaged with or without her. Blake was a wonderful writer and composer, and he didn't deserve to fail because of her.

Fifteen minutes later, Danielle stood in front of the office door, gathering her nerves. When she tapped, the door flew open and she was surrounded by Blake, Bosley, and two of the early backers.

"Young lady, you did it." Arlin Greene, beaming from ear to ear, bowed over her hand.

"Great job, Miss Gray." Bosley patted her shoulder and smiled.

She glanced from one to the other, her eyes resting on Blake. "Does this mean. . . ?"

"Yes, it means. . ." Blake laughed, his eyes sparkling. "You did it, Danielle. He's not only willing but very enthusiastic about investing in the show. In fact, he's so enthusiastic he's gone to the bank now. But he specifically asked us to have you here when he returns. He wants very much to meet you."

Bosley laughed. "I don't think I've ever seen anyone so enthralled. He couldn't keep his eyes off you from the moment you stepped onto the stage."

Danielle blushed. "But the others did well, too."

"Of course they did," the manager agreed. "But you are the star, Miss Gray. Without you, this great ship would have been left standing in the harbor."

She looked at Blake, who met her glance with an encouraging smile. "He's right, Danielle. You are the star."

"But. . .it was your wonderful show that impressed him. I'm sure of it."

Bosley cast an amused smile at Blake then turned his attention back to Danielle. "Of course the show is wonderful and to Blake goes the credit for that. But it takes more than words and music on paper to make a great show. Someone has to bring them to life. And you've done just that, my dear."

Someone knocked and Mr. Greene headed for the door. "That must be James now."

He opened the door and a giant shadow fell across the room and rested on Danielle's face and heart.

Mr. Greene bowed. "Miss Gray, allow me to introduce you to our new backer and business partner, Mr. James Sutton. I'm sure you'll be getting to know each other over the next few weeks."

Sutton's tall form stepped forward and took the hand that hung limp by her side. "Delighted, Miss Gray. Imagine my surprise when I arrived today to find such a lovely, talented young woman before my eyes. I'm sure as the days go by we'll get to know each other very well."

The tall form was all too well known to her already, from the amused smile on his rugged face to the eyes that could sear a small child with one sharp look.

She stood frozen, unable to move or even hardly to breathe. This had to be a dream. Or some cruel joke.

God, please. . .let me wake up from this nightmare.

Chapter 13

Danielle stood frozen for a moment. Forcing a smile, she slipped her hand from Sutton's and gave a nod. "How do you do?"

Amusement flickered deep in his eyes. "Very well, thank you. How charming you are, my dear."

Wanting to scratch his eyes out, she continued to smile. "Thank you for deciding to back the show."

Before he could answer, she glanced around the room. "I'm feeling a little tired from all the excitement. If you'll excuse me, I'll go lie down in the dressing room for a while."

With their murmurs of concern trailing after her, Danielle left the room and hurried down the hall to the side door. Slipping through, she fell against the wall of the building. Her breath quickened as anger and panic fought within her. How long had Sutton known? Had he been toying with her emotions all along?

Dear God, please don't let him know where I'm staying. Please don't let him harm the Kramers or Nelsons in any way.

She started as the door opened. Sutton stalked toward her then grabbed her arm. "Well, my little sweet, did you think you'd put one over on me?"

Wincing from the pain, she yanked her arm free. "What do you mean? I told you I was in a show and would pay you each week."

"Ah yes, you did mention a show. But you led me to believe you were a chorus girl." He gave a menacing grin. "This isn't quite the same, is it? How did you manage it, my dear? And don't hold out on me or you'll be very sorry."

Danielle calmed her breathing. Perhaps he didn't know everything after all. "I heard they were auditioning for several parts and thought I'd try out. I never thought I'd get the lead, though."

His eyes narrowed. "You'd better not be lying to me."

"I'm not. Why would I?" She'd simply left out a few facts. Such as Blake's part in getting her the role.

He straightened, and a calculating look crossed his face. "Very well, my dear. I think I do believe you. And there might be grand opportunities here. Let me think about it, and I'll let you know what I want you to do."

Danielle shuddered as Sutton walked away. He had appeared surprised to find she had the lead in the show. Could it be coincidence that he'd happened to be the new patron, or was he manipulating her again?

One thing she knew: No matter what evil deed he thought up for her to do, she'd not steal for him. Nor do anything else to harm others. Not even for her own safety. Tears formed in her eyes. Not even for Jimmy's. Peace washed over her. She knew, somehow, God watched over her and Jimmy. She'd have to trust Him to take care of this new situation.

The door opened and Blake rushed to her. "I've been looking everywhere for you. Are you all right?"

She wiped a remaining tear from the corner of her eye and smiled. "I'm fine. The excitement was a little overwhelming. I needed to be alone for a few moments."

Relief crossed his face. "Let me take you home so you can rest. You've been so tense waiting for this showing for James Sutton, I'm sure your rest has been sporadic at best. Besides, you're shivering from the cold. Why didn't you get your coat before coming outside?"

She realized he was right. Her hands were like ice and the tips of her ears tingled. Gratefully, she allowed him to escort her back to the empty ladies' dressing room, where she retrieved her coat and hat.

They walked outside to where Blake's carriage had already been brought around. Blake took her arm to help her into the buggy, and at the gentleness of his touch, she felt herself relax.

As the horse's hooves clattered on the street, Danielle turned to Blake. "What do you know about this man Sutton?"

"Oh, not much. He's some sort of businessman and filthy rich."

Danielle couldn't help the smile of wry amusement that tipped her lips. Blake's family was surely one of the wealthiest in Chicago. However, she'd noticed he didn't seem to care all that much. Of course, he'd been wealthy all his life and probably thought little about it. He had no idea what it was like to stumble down a cold street shivering in a ragged dress and threadbare sweater, with a little brother clutching tightly to your legs.

She shoved the thought away. That had been long ago. And even though Sutton hadn't bought them fine clothes, they'd had enough for their needs.

They said good-bye at the Kramers' front door. As she was about to go up to her room, Mrs. Parker stepped into the foyer from the direction of the kitchen. She smiled, her eyes bright with anticipation. "Danielle dear, come into the parlor and tell me what happened."

Not knowing how to get out of it without being rude, Danielle handed her coat and hat to the downstairs maid with an apologetic smile then followed the sweet lady into the parlor where a warm fire blazed.

Mrs. Parker seated herself on the settee and patted the space beside her. "Here, sit here by me."

Danielle smiled and did as she was told. "All right. What do you want to hear?"

"Everything." The lady's cheeks were pink with excitement.

"Would you like me to ring for tea?" Danielle asked, stalling for time. She knew she'd need to be careful when speaking of Sutton. Mrs. Parker was very wise and had a sharp eye.

"No, no. I don't want tea. It's almost dinnertime." She waved an impatient hand. "I want to hear about your day. Did the man decide to back the show?"

"Indeed he did." Danielle hoped she'd put the right amount of excitement in her voice.

"Well, tell me all about it."

Danielle related the events of the morning, including Blake's silliness at the café when he attempted to avert her thoughts from the mistake she'd made at morning rehearsal.

The elderly lady giggled. "That Blake. I think he's fond of you."

Danielle blushed. "Nonsense. He's kind. That's all."

"Mmm-hmm." She gave her a knowing look. "Perhaps I'll have my daughter invite him for Thanksgiving. Now tell me what happened next."

Danielle laughed. "All right. When we arrived back at the theater, I was still very nervous, but the other girls talked me through it. Then when I stepped onto the stage I felt like I could drop dead any minute."

She told about the almost euphoric feeling she had during the show. How she'd been exhausted afterward. Then how they'd sent for her.

Mrs. Parker clapped her hands in delight as she heard about the excitement in the office.

Danielle skimmed over the meeting with Sutton, hoping her dear friend wouldn't notice. "I was so overwhelmed with all the excitement I had to go outside for air. After a while, Blake came to find me. I had no idea how cold I was until he mentioned I had no coat on."

"Oh, my dear. You must be chilled to the bone." She stood. "You really must go upstairs and soak in a hot tub. I'll have one of the girls bring you tea."

Relieved to have gotten by so easily, Danielle played along. "Well, the tub sounds good, but I think I'll forego the tea. After all, as you said, it won't be long until dinnertime."

"Perhaps you should have a tray in bed, dear."

"No, thank you. That's not necessary."

Danielle was halfway up the stairs, when Mrs. Parker called out, "When you're feeling better, you must tell me all about this James Sutton."

ദ

Blake wasn't sure what was going on with Danielle, but something was wrong. He stood on the veranda as snow fell softly around him. She'd seemed fine when she came into the office. But then she changed. Her face was pale as she spoke to the new backer. Could it have something to do with this man Sutton? Did she know him? Blake scoffed at his imagination. It seemed as though where Danielle Gray was concerned, his protective side came roaring in. She was probably just exhausted from the excitement, as she'd said.

The snow was coming down harder. Reluctantly, Blake went inside.

His father stood at the bottom of the stairs. "Ah, Blake. How did things go with the new man? Did he decide to invest in the production of your show?"

Blake stared at his father. He'd never so much as mentioned the show to Blake since the day they'd fought about it. That was the day he'd found out Danielle was living with the Kramers.

"Son? Is something wrong?"

"Oh, I'm sorry, Father. Thank you for inquiring. Mr. Sutton did indeed agree to contribute a fairly nice amount to the show."

"Sutton?" A frown appeared on his father's face. "That name sounds familiar. Sutton. Hmm. Can't place it. Ah, well, I must be mistaken. I'm happy for you. I know a lot was depending on him."

Blake felt his face flush with pleasure. "You don't know how happy it makes me to know you're interested."

"I was wrong to be so hard on you, son. Your mother reminded me of a few things and set me straight."

Blake smiled. "I found out recently about Mother's short stint in show business."

"Yes, I was there on opening night and nearly every performance afterward. Until the fire shut everything down. She was quite talented, your mother. And she did love show business." He threw a quick glance at Blake. "I didn't make her give it up."

"I know. She told me."

"So, your mother thinks you are in love with Miss Gray."

Blake started at the sudden turn in the conversation. "Er. . .when did she say that?"

"Just this morning. Any truth in it?" He peered sharply at his son.

Blake hesitated for a moment. Maybe it was time to admit his feelings, not only to himself but also to Danielle. He knew he needed to be honest with his parents. They'd always been there for him and they didn't deserve to be left out now.

"To be honest, Father, I'm a little confused. But I am in love with Danielle. And it's time I let her know."

His father nodded and laid his hand on Blake's shoulder as they walked up the stairs side by side. The warmth Blake felt for his father had been missing for a long time. Gratefully, he welcomed it back.

"Wait a minute. I just remembered where I heard the name Sutton. The family used to be fairly prominent. Owned a button factory and did quite well. They've been deceased for a number of years. Their only son and heir took over the business and pretty much ruined it. His name was James. A scoundrel, if I recall. Hope it's not your man."

Blake felt sick. "I'm afraid it is, Father."

ଔ

Danielle leaned back against the porcelain tub, submerging her tired body in the hot sudsy bath then sighed as her tight muscles began to relax in the hot water.

It had only been a few hours since she'd left for the theater, but it seemed like days.

Her thoughts wandered to the events of the day, starting with the moment she stepped onto the porch to wait for Blake. She remembered how he'd scolded her for waiting outside in the cold morning air. He'd seemed very concerned. Her memories jumped right over the morning rehearsal and to the little café where they'd gone for lunch. How dear he was. Teasing her like that so she wouldn't worry. She felt a smile tilt her lips, and she sank farther into the water.

Suddenly the moment Sutton stepped into the office popped into her mind. *No, no, I won't think of Sutton.* She fought to erase his menacing face from her mind, but the harder she fought, the clearer it became until finally she could even hear his voice laughing, mocking, threatening. *Please, God.*

Something was pounding in her ears. Danielle sat up straight in the tub. Oh, what was that? She shook herself awake. Someone was knocking on her door. That was all. She must have fallen asleep.

"Danielle! Are you all right?" Mrs. Parker's worried voice drifted through the door.

She realized suddenly her face was wet with tears and heaviness pressed against her heart. Should she pretend to be asleep? She'd never be able to hide her distress from Mrs. Parker's knowing eyes.

Maybe it was time to stop trying to hide the truth from this kind friend. She grabbed a towel and hopped out of the tub. "Just a minute," she called. She slipped into her bathrobe and hurried to the door. Flinging it open, she threw herself, sobbing, into Mrs. Parker's arms.

"My dear, what is wrong?" Mrs. Parker pulled Danielle back inside and shut the door behind them.

Chapter 14

Danielle sat at the breakfast table in the kitchen, wan and nervous from the events of the day before as well as her bad dreams last night. Fear sliced through her when she remembered how she'd broken down when she saw Mrs. Parker in her doorway and how close she'd come to revealing everything. Thankfully she'd had the good sense, while sobbing in the woman's arms, to overcome her moment of weakness and insist it was only a case of nerves stemming from the stress of the day.

Although she didn't think for a moment the dear lady believed her, at least she hadn't pressed the issue. Danielle knew when it was time to tell, it shouldn't be to this gentle lady.

Today was Sunday, so she wouldn't have to face Sutton again quite yet. She'd planned to go to church with the family but wasn't ready to face Mrs. Parker, either. So she waited until she heard them leaving then came down to the kitchen, where Sally and Nell were bringing the remains of breakfast from the dining room.

"There you are," Sally said. "You sit right down in the dining room, and I'll get you a hot breakfast. This is all cold."

"I can just eat some toast."

"No, you can't. Mrs. Parker told me to make sure you ate a good breakfast and Mrs. Kramer said make it fresh and hot."

"Then, if you don't mind, I'll sit here in the kitchen." She poured herself a cup of coffee and sat down.

"Now why would I mind?" Sally glanced at Nell, who was getting the dishpan out. "Nell, I'll take care of the dishes in a bit. Why don't you finish up in the dining room and set the table for dinner? After that, you can get ready and go to second service at your church."

After the girl had scurried out of the room, Sally laid slices of bacon in a skillet and broke two eggs into another. When she had everything ready, she set them on the table, poured herself a cup of coffee, and sat across from Danielle. "What's wrong with you, girl? You look like you've seen a ghost."

Danielle gave a short laugh. "Maybe I have. Or something worse."

"Now what would you be meaning by that?"

Danielle stirred her coffee and didn't say anything.

A loud huff caused Danielle to raise her head and look at Sally. The normally cheerful cook's lips were tight and she almost glared at Danielle. "Now you listen here, young lady. I know something is wrong, and I have a feeling you're needing to get it off your chest." She folded her arms and waited.

Could she? Would Sally keep her secret? Danielle knew the kind cook wouldn't intentionally do anything to hurt her, but was she ready to tell? She knew she wasn't. At least not everything.

She sipped her coffee then looked at Sally. "I saw someone yesterday. An evil man. It frightened me to see him. Especially to see him in my present world."

Understanding dawned on Sally's face and she nodded. "Aye. That can be a frightful thing. It's happened to me before."

"I can't say any more, Sally. At least not now."

"Of course you cannot. It's too fresh in your mind." She stood and placed her hand on Danielle's head. "Father in heaven, please be watchin' over this young one. Keep her safe in Your own hands and lead her according to Your paths and purposes for her life. In the name of Your own Son, Jesus, amen."

Danielle took a trembling breath and felt peace wash over her. How blessed she was to have good Christian people to pray for her. "Thank you, Sally."

"You're welcome, and now, you eat that breakfast. You've not touched it."

"I will. I promise. I couldn't before, but I will now." She picked up her fork and before long, she'd eaten every bite. *Prayer really does change things.*

She washed her dishes and hurried up to her room. In a few minutes, she'd changed her clothes and put on her hat. She grabbed her coat and rushed down the stairs. If she hurried, she'd get there before the sermon started.

∽

As the Kramers seated themselves, Blake noticed with dismay that Danielle wasn't among them. She hadn't missed a service of late, and her absence bothered him.

The choir filed in to their places, and he turned his attention to the service. Opening his hymnal, he tried to enter into worship, but he couldn't seem to push away his concern for Danielle.

As the organ music faded away, he heard a rustling of skirts and turned to see Danielle scoot in past Mr. and Mrs. Kramer and the twins and take a seat beside Mrs. Parker. She still looked a little pale but otherwise seemed fine.

At the end of the service, he hurried out as fast as possible and caught up with Danielle just as she was getting ready to step into the Kramers' carriage. "Danielle."

She turned as he spoke her name and smiled. "Hello, Blake."

"Would you allow me to take you home?"

"Well. . ." She looked at Mrs. Kramer, who nodded and smiled.

Mr. Kramer tossed him an understanding glance. "Why don't you come to dinner, Blake?"

"I believe I will, sir." He helped Danielle into his buggy, got in, and flicked the reins.

"So are you ready for another grueling rehearsal tomorrow?" Was that a shiver? "Are you cold?"

"No, I'm quite comfortable." She smiled, and he relaxed. He'd probably imagined the shiver.

After dinner, they spent a few hours rehearsing, then Blake suggested a walk around the block. They bundled up and headed down the sidewalk, her hand tucked into his arm.

He glanced at her face, but it was just dark enough to prevent his seeing her expressions. Maybe this would be a good time. "Danielle, I think I'm falling in love with you."

He heard her gasp as she stopped still. She pulled her hand away and faced him. "What?"

"I said I'm falling in love with you." There, he'd left out the word *think* this time.

"But. . .but you can't." She stared at him with wide eyes.

Blake laughed. "What do you mean, I can't?"

"You just can't, Blake. I. . .I. . .oh, I can't explain." Stunned, he watched as she ran down the sidewalk and into the Kramer home.

He walked back to the house and got his buggy from the stable, wondering what had gone wrong. They'd been so happy lately and the day had been wonderful. He'd been sure Danielle was beginning to feel the same way he did. Had he completely misread the affection he'd thought she had for him?

He flicked the reins. As the *clip-clop* of the horse's hooves beat a rhythm on the brick-paved street, he pondered Danielle's reaction to his declaration of love.

In a few short minutes he arrived at his own house. He greeted his parents who were relaxing in the parlor then went up to his room.

No, he was sure Danielle cared for him. But then. . .why had she reacted the way she had?

Making a sudden decision, he went downstairs and asked to speak privately with his father. They retired to the library and closed the door.

After they'd seated themselves in the deep leather chairs near the fireplace, Blake's father smiled. "You came in at just the right time, son. I was so sleepy I was about to excuse myself and go to bed but dreaded the displeasure that would have surely crossed your mother's face."

"You know Mother could never be displeased with anything you do, Father."

"You know, I believe you're right. She loves me as much as I love her. But I've not spent much time with her lately, due to the workload. Sometimes I feel like I'm being unfaithful with work as my mistress."

Blake raised one eyebrow. "Then maybe you should slow down. . .hire an extra attorney."

"Umm. Maybe." He gave Blake a sideways smile. "Probably won't, though."

Guilt bit at Blake's conscience. He knew why his father wouldn't hire anyone. He was holding the spot in case Blake decided to come back.

"Now"—his father threw him a keen look—"what did you want to discuss with me?"

Blake tried to think how to begin then just blurted it out. "I think I'm in love. No, I know I am."

"Ah. . .with the pretty Miss Gray, I presume?" His father pursed his lips and winked.

"We've spent a lot of time together the past few weeks because of theater rehearsals and our own private sessions. I started to truly respect and admire her and I believed she felt the same. I still believe she does. But when I spoke of my love for her, she ran away. With no explanation. Perhaps I mistook her friendship for something more, but I don't really think so." Blake stopped. When put into words there hadn't been a lot to say. "Maybe I'm being foolish."

His father shook his head slowly. "A man usually knows when a woman cares for him. Perhaps there is some obstacle you aren't aware of."

"Perhaps. I know very little about her past. Just what she's told us all about growing up in an orphanage and that her brother died." He raked his fingers through his hair. "If there is an obstacle, I wish she'd tell me what it is."

೮೩

Danielle paced her bedroom floor. Why had she run off like that? Surely she could have thought of something to say without bolting like a frightened child. What must Blake think of her?

But what could she have done? She couldn't truthfully say she didn't return his feelings, because she'd known for some time she was falling in love with him. Sometimes, she felt it so strong it was almost painful. But it wouldn't be fair to accept his love while hiding her past. Even though she'd never taken part in a theft, until that last one, she'd still been part of the gang.

Even if he loved her enough to overlook her past, the fact remained that Sutton was evil, and she couldn't risk a chance on his taking revenge on Blake or his family. He might even harm Jimmy to get back at her if he knew she was in love with Blake.

Oh, why did Jimmy and I have to end up at Sutton's when we were children? If only they had run another way that day on the docks. Of course, they'd probably have been caught even if they hadn't run into Cobb. And more than likely they'd have been placed in an orphanage. Maybe they would have been better off if they *had* been caught and placed in an orphanage. At least they wouldn't have been raised with thieves and robbers. They wouldn't have received their criminal education at the hands of Sutton. But they would have been separated, perhaps even adopted by separate families, never to have seen each other again. No, in spite of everything, she was glad that hadn't happened.

But what now? She knew Sutton would come up with some scheme involving dishonest acts on her part. He could even find a way to force her back to the gang. She was strong, but she knew she had no power against Sutton. All she could do was try to convince him it was to his benefit to allow her to continue at her present course. If she only had more time, somehow, surely she could find a way to get Jimmy away from him.

If Jimmy weren't there, she would almost be willing to turn Sutton over to the authorities. But of course, she wouldn't want to get Cobb in trouble. And most of the gang there had fallen in with Sutton the same way she and Jimmy had. Homeless, with no one to care for them, they were easy prey.

Dear God, please show me what to do. Protect us all from that wretched man. And, oh Father, please don't let Blake hate me. Even if I can never accept his love, please find a way to let him know I do care for him.

Chapter 15

B lake wasn't sure whether he should pick Danielle up the next morning or not. But after all, they'd been riding to the theater together ever since she'd gotten the part of Peg. He decided to drive to the Kramers' and knock on the door. Act as though nothing had happened. Maybe he could at least salvage their friendship.

He was relieved when she answered his knock, wearing her hat, coat, and gloves. Apparently, she'd expected him.

When he offered his arm, she gave him a timid smile and rested her hand on his forearm.

Blake breathed a sigh of relief. Perhaps she'd thought over his declaration and decided it wasn't so repulsive to her after all.

Don't be an idiot, he thought. *She's simply being polite.*

When they entered the building, they were met with a bedlam of laughter and shouts.

"What in the world?" The words were no more than out of Blake's mouth when Hannah and Rhonda rushed over to Danielle, each grabbing an arm, and dragged her away.

"You're not going to believe it. Everything is brand new." Rhonda's excited voice cut through the noise and into Blake's ears as he watched them head in the direction of the dressing rooms.

He walked into the auditorium and headed to the stage where Bosley stood waving his hands at two men who were bringing backdrops out onto the stage. "Not here. Put them backstage with the rest."

He turned and grinned as Blake ran up the steps to the stage. "Isn't it great?"

"What's going on?"

Bosley took off his cap and wiped his forehead with his shirtsleeve. "Sutton came through, all right. He wants the best of everything. New backdrops, furniture for the sets, brand-new costumes. Won't even let us use the ones we had that are still in good condition."

Blake frowned. "Seems a little extravagant, doesn't it?"

Bosley shrugged. "It's his money. I'm not complaining. You'd better not, either, if you want to see *Peg in Dreamland* in production."

"So he's making the decisions now?"

"Well, of course not. Not about the show itself. But if he wants to spread his wealth around, why not?"

Why not, indeed, Blake thought as he took a seat and waited for the morning rehearsal to start. He knew that once the show opened, there would be a matinee and an evening performance. But for now, the cast and managers had their evenings free to rest and relax.

"Mind if I join you, Mr. Nelson? Or may I call you Blake now that we're business partners?" James Sutton walked down the front aisle and sat in the seat next to Blake.

"Not at all," Blake said, trying to sound as though he meant it. Although he was grateful to the man for contributing needed funds, he wasn't sure he liked him. He seemed a little too suave. A little too well-dressed. Something in his glance seemed almost calculating. And after the information Blake's father had imparted, he didn't trust the man.

Don't be ridiculous, Blake. A man can change. You're imagining things.

The curtain opened, and Blake turned his attention to the stage. He didn't want to miss a moment.

When Danielle stepped onto the stage, Blake heard a sharp intake of breath from Sutton. He darted a look at him and almost struck out at the vile look on the man's face.

"So, Mr. Sutton, when did you become interested in the theater?" Anything to get the man's eyes off Danielle.

Sutton glanced at him, and a look of amusement crossed his face. Almost as though he knew what Blake was doing. "Let's see now. My first interest was strictly a financial one. One of your other backers convinced me the show would be a roaring success." He narrowed his eyes and continued. "But my interest came into full bloom when I saw Miss Gray's performance."

Blake couldn't keep his lips from tightening. "Yes, Miss Gray is a very good actress."

"Rather amazing, isn't it? I understand this is her first part."

"Yes, it is. But she seems to have a natural talent, and of course she was coached."

"Coached by whom, may I ask?"

"By me, as a matter of fact."

"Yes, I rather thought so." He rubbed his finger along his mustache. "And what exactly is your relationship with Miss Gray?"

Blake felt his face grow hot as anger rose up inside him. His chest felt tight, and he had to fight to control his breathing. "I hardly think that's any of your concern, sir. And now, if you don't mind, I'd like to watch the rehearsal."

"I don't mind at all. I find it very delightful myself." The man's tone of voice was offensive. Was he deliberately baiting Blake for some reason?

The rehearsal went fairly smoothly, with only a few minor errors. When the curtain went down, Sutton stood, bowed, and walked away.

CB

Danielle crammed her hat on her head, grabbed her gloves from her coat pocket, and slipped them on. She didn't know if Blake was waiting for her or not, but if he was, she couldn't leave him standing there. She pushed through the door and ran smack into Sutton.

"Ah, the divine and talented leading lady." Sutton smirked and steadied her, laughing when she jerked away. "We need to talk, my dear."

She winced as he grabbed her arm and almost dragged her down the hall to the exit. He gave her a slight push and followed her outside.

"What do you want?" she snapped through gritted teeth.

"Why, I simply want to congratulate you on your fine performance this morning."

"Sure, you do."

He threw his head back and laughed. "You know me too well, Danielle. Very well, I'll admit I have other reasons for wishing to speak with you."

He drew his face close to hers, his eyes narrowed to slits. "I have plans for opening night. Big plans. I expect you to do your part. Is that understood?"

She turned her head in an attempt to avoid his breath. "What exactly is it you expect me to do, Sutton?"

He straightened up. "Not yet, my sweet. I'll let you know in due time. And if you don't do what I say, you'll wish very much you had. You and that little brother of yours."

"You wouldn't hurt Jimmy?" she cried out then bit her lip.

He smiled. "I assure you I wouldn't want to, but sometimes one must do what one must do." He started to turn away then turned back. "By the way, my pretty one, I don't know what's going on between you and the Nelson fellow, but you'd better nip it in the bud."

Danielle felt as though her heart sank, and she swallowed hard. "We're only friends."

"I see. That's good. I want you to be friends with the handsome young writer." He threw her a threatening look. "Just don't let it go any further if you have any concern about his health. I won't let you get involved with another man, Danielle. Someday you will realize where your destiny lies."

He tipped his hat and walked away.

⁂

Blake, his throat dry, rushed out and found a vendor who gave him a cup of water. Blake handed him a coin. He waited in the lobby nearly fifteen minutes, and when Danielle didn't appear, he headed for the dressing room area. He tapped on the ladies' door and Hannah informed him Danielle had left a few minutes earlier.

Concerned, he hurried to the exit and shoved the door open. Sutton was just disappearing around the corner of the building. Danielle stood still as a statue, her lips drawn tight, and her eyes flaming with anger.

If that creature had said or done anything ungentlemanly, he'd—

Danielle turned as she heard his footsteps. Her lids came down, and when she raised them, her eyes appeared guarded.

"What's wrong, Danielle? That was Sutton, wasn't it?"

"Yes." She flashed him a smile. "He was praising the show. He really loves it."

Blake looked at her, uncertain. She sounded sincere. Had he been imagining things about the new patron? Was he, perhaps, allowing jealousy to put ideas into his head?

He took a deep breath and returned her smile. "May I take you to lunch?"

"Well, I think I'd better. . ." she floundered, apparently unable to find an excuse.

"Please, just as friends. I want to talk to you about something."

She only hesitated for a moment. "In that case, of course. I'm actually quite hungry."

℘

Danielle sat across the table from Blake and glanced, unseeing, at the menu. Had she managed to fool Blake about Sutton? She didn't know how long he'd been standing there or how much he'd heard. She could only hope he'd come outside as Sutton was leaving, and she was pretty sure that was the case. If he'd heard Sutton's words, he would, at the very least, have confronted her about it. Most likely, he'd have caught up with Sutton and knocked him down. Then what would have happened to Blake? At the thought, fear rose up in her throat and her fingers tightened on the menu.

"Don't choke the poor menu to death." Blake grinned at her. "What has you so tense?"

"Oh, I don't know. Opening night is less than a month away. I guess I'm just worried."

"You'll do fine. I promise. You own Peg." He reached over and touched her hand then drew back. He didn't want to scare her off again.

After they'd eaten, they ordered coffee and Blake leaned forward. "I'm sorry if I offended you or frightened you last night. I can't help how I feel about you, but it was insensitive of me to blurt it out the way I did."

"You weren't insensitive." Her lips trembled. "I'm honored to know that you love me. You're a wonderful man. Any girl would be honored. I'm just not ready for love in my life yet. I have commitments you know nothing about. And problems that need to be solved before I can even consider that kind of relationship."

Blake took a deep breath. "Can't you share with me? Let me help you with whatever it is?"

She smiled tremulously and lowered her lashes. She knew if he looked into her eyes at that moment, all was lost. She'd never be able to hide the feelings coursing through her.

When she felt strong enough to control her feelings, she shook her head and looked him in the eye. "I have to work these things out for myself. But I'm grateful that you want to help. Right now, the best way you can help is to be my friend and not pressure me for information I can't give you. That would just make things more difficult for me."

"Very well, but I promised my mother I'd invite you to have Thanksgiving dinner with us. Just as friends, of course."

"Oh dear. I think Mrs. Kramer is planning to invite you."

He smiled. "Perhaps we'd better let those two ladies decide the matter between them."

At his relaxed manner, she saw with relief he'd accepted her terms. She glanced at the clock on the wall behind the counter and scrambled to her feet. "Look at the time. We'll be late if we don't hurry."

Blake jumped up and hurried to pay for their food, and they headed back to the theater.

Danielle only hoped Sutton would stay away from the afternoon rehearsal.

CB

Blake settled into his front row, center seat position, waiting for rehearsal to begin. So, his father was right. There were obstacles preventing her from returning his love. He knew in his heart that she did care for him, perhaps as deeply as he cared for her. If only he knew what the problems were.

Sutton. Suddenly, Blake remembered the look on Sutton's face when he'd watched Danielle perform that morning. Uneasiness washed over him. Although he'd pushed it away as his imagination, now he wasn't so sure. Had Danielle lied to him about her encounter with the man? Was it possible she knew him from before and he had some sort of power over her? If so, it must be pretty bad if Danielle refused to allow Blake to help her.

Heavenly Father, I need Your help. Show me how to help Danielle, and if Sutton is the cause of her problems, reveal that to me. I pray that truth will prevail and that You will protect and guide my precious Danielle.

Chapter 16

I have to get Jimmy out of there. I have to. Danielle shifted from one foot to the other as she peered around the edge of the shed and watched for Cobb. *If only Sutton would let Jimmy go, I could get us rooms in a respectable boardinghouse. But Sutton will never allow it. Maybe I can reason with him. How can one reason with an unreasonable man?* Thoughts knifed through her brain until she thought her head would burst.

Only two weeks remained until opening night. Although she'd questioned him over and over, Sutton still hadn't revealed his plan to her. Once more she peered around the shed, watching anxiously for Cobb. She was sure he'd have a pretty good idea of what Sutton intended to do.

She glanced around, suddenly nervous. Why hadn't they arranged a different meeting place? By now, Sutton was sure to know that she and Cobb met here.

She caught sight of Cobb just near the corner. Curious, she watched him shuffle up the sidewalk, his head down. This wasn't like him at all.

He stepped to the back of the shed where she waited and gave her an unaccustomed hug. She pulled back and stared at him, troubled at the look of concern on his face.

"What's wrong?"

"Nothing." Cobb averted his eyes.

"Something is."

He lifted his eyes, and a sick look crossed his face. "Danni, you know Sutton is planning a job for your opening night."

"Yes, and I need to know what it is so I can try to stop him."

"How do you think you're going to stop him? Don't be foolish." He wiped his hand across his head, and she noticed the worry lines on his forehead.

"I can call the police. That's what I can do."

"He's using Jimmy this time."

Stunned, Danielle stared at him. "Jimmy? But he's lame."

"Yeah, but Sutton has a plan. And he don't trust you. He said if Jimmy's involved you won't turn us in."

Hopelessness washed over her as she stared silently at Cobb.

"C'mon, Danni. You ain't gonna cry, are you? You never cry." He gave her an awkward pat on the shoulder.

"Tell me what he has in mind."

"All right, but don't let him know I told you anything. He's been in such a rage lately. He's liable to kill me." He inhaled deeply then exhaled a loud *whoosh* of air.

"We're gonna be all over the place during intermission. Lifting anything we can get our hands on. Watches, wallets, anything we find. But it's all just a distraction. Sutton won't tell me what he'll be doing while we keep the cops busy. But it must be something big."

"And Jimmy?"

Cobb licked his lips. "He's gonna have Jimmy with him."

Despair washed over her and she wrung her hands. "God, please show me what to do."

"It ain't no use." Cobb shook his head. "There ain't nothin' you can do."

Sudden anger rose up in Danielle, and she stiffened. Nothing she could do? She'd think of something. She'd get Jimmy out of there and make sure Sutton was put in jail so he could never bother them again. She didn't know what or how, but God would show her the way.

⍟

"I don't know where she went, Blake." Hannah threw him an apologetic wave and sailed past him. "Sorry. Gotta get home and spend some time with my kids before afternoon rehearsal."

He spotted Rhonda as she entered the lobby and grabbed her as she walked toward the exit. "Did Danielle tell you where she was going?"

"Why?" She frowned. "Did you have a date for lunch?"

"Well no, but. . .we've been lunching together nearly every day. I waited for her in the lobby, but she never showed up."

"Hmm. A little presumptuous, aren't we?" She laughed and walked on.

Blake felt his face blaze and wanted to kick himself. Of course he'd been presumptuous. Why hadn't he asked her this morning to have lunch with him? He supposed he'd taken her for granted. He hadn't realized. Where could she be?

Bosley had ordered lunch for himself and all the business partners, and they were all back in his office. Blake had checked to make sure Sutton was there, too. At least he didn't need to worry about that.

Feeling foolish, he headed for the café on the corner, the cold air almost taking his breath away, and ordered a sandwich and coffee. He ate without tasting anything then went back to the theater. He hung around the lobby for a while, watching for Danielle.

Sudden anger arose in him. He was acting like a lovesick kid. He had hung around hoping for crumbs from her long enough. Why should he wait when she obviously didn't want to see him? So, she had secrets. If she didn't want to share them with him, fine. Maybe it was just an excuse not to tell him she didn't care for him. Well, he wouldn't bother her anymore. And he wouldn't watch rehearsals, either. As a matter of fact, he was getting sick of the whole theater business anyway.

Wheeling, he left the theater, intending to go home, then stopped. Maybe she'd met that suspicious-looking character again. The redheaded so-called friend of hers. Where did she meet a rough-looking character like that in the first place? Worry oozed its way back in, pushing out the anger.

He'd about made up his mind to go take a look around the docks when Danielle came around the corner, huddled against the wind. With one hand, she held onto her large-brimmed hat, and with the other she attempted to hold down the folds of her coat. Head down, she brushed past him and into the building.

He turned, stunned, and followed her through the door, almost knocking her over when she stopped in front of him. He grabbed her arms to steady her.

Jerking free from him, she whirled, eyes blazing. "My goodness, Blake. You just about scared me to death."

"Sorry."

"I guess my stopping was rather abrupt. But why were you following so closely?"

He stood, not knowing what to say without sounding like that lovesick kid again.

After a moment she blushed. "I'm sorry I rushed away without saying goodbye. I had an appointment."

She didn't explain what the appointment was, and he didn't want to risk crossing the line again.

"It's quite all right. You aren't accountable to me. If you're free for lunch tomorrow, I'd like to take you to a little place I discovered the other day. They make a very unique sandwich."

"Sounds interesting. But tomorrow is Thanksgiving, remember? No practice, and we'll all be eating at your house." She waved and headed toward the dressing rooms.

Blake's gaze continued to rest on the doorway long after Danielle was no longer in sight. She seemed worried, or at least distracted, and once more unease weaved its way into his mind. Or was he imagining things again? Perhaps he needed to stop being so suspicious. Apparently he had a trust problem. Maybe he needed to talk to someone about it.

Afternoon rehearsal went off without a flaw. Blake, sitting in the darkened theater, watched Danielle bring Peg to life once more.

After the practice, he drove her home, promising to come over for a run-through of her lines later that evening. He didn't think she needed it, but it gave him an excuse to spend more time with her.

When he arrived at home, he gave his mother a kiss on the cheek and turned toward the stairs.

"Son, you've been awfully quiet lately." At his mother's voice, he turned. "And you're spending so much time alone in your room. Is something troubling you?"

"I'm fine, Mother." He gave her what he hoped was a convincing smile. "I'll be down shortly."

"Very well. Hilda made fried chicken. And chocolate cake."

"Sounds wonderful."

He started upstairs but then stopped and turned. "Mother, would you have someone call me when Father arrives? I'd like to talk to him before dinner, if he has time."

"Of course I will."

A half hour later, Blake sat across from his father in the library. "I feel helpless. I know something is wrong, and I think it has something to do with James Sutton."

His father looked alert. "What makes you think that?"

"I'm not sure. She seems nervous when he's around."

"Couldn't that be because he's the one providing most of the money for the show?"

"Maybe. But I don't think so. He looks at her as if he knows her. And as though he expects something of her. Almost like a spider with a captive creature in its web."

His father narrowed his eyes and puffed on his pipe. "What would you think of putting a tail on the man for a while? See if anything turns up. Maybe a background check would be in order, as well. There's no telling what he's been up to since his button business shut down. He has to be getting his money somewhere."

Blake took a relieved breath. "I've been thinking the same thing but thought it might be extreme."

"Not extreme at all. If there's any chance this man is harassing Miss Gray, you need to take care of it."

03

"Boys, you're getting a little bit rowdy now." Mrs. Kramer spoke quietly with a good-natured lilt to her voice. Danielle noticed, however, the twins stopped wrestling on the parlor floor at once.

"Sorry, Mother." Georgie ran a hand over his unruly hair.

"Sorry, Mother." David brushed at his jacket.

Danielle grinned. Some inexistent dust, she supposed.

David spotted the grin and flashed one of his own. "Miss Gray, would you read us a story before bedtime?"

"Now, David, Miss Gray has to practice her lines," Mrs. Kramer admonished her son.

"Oh, I don't mind. Blake won't be here for another ten minutes." She smiled at the boys who had scooted over to her chair and looked eagerly into her eyes. "What would you like me to read?"

" 'The Night Before Christmas,' " Georgie exclaimed.

"Yeah. 'The Night Before Christmas,' " his twin echoed.

"Now, children, you know your father reads that to you on Christmas Eve."

"Oh."

The boys finally settled on a story, and Danielle read it to them, portraying the voice of each character to their delight.

As Mrs. Kramer held Georgie's and David's hands and led them upstairs, the downstairs maid opened the door and Blake came in. A cold burst of air followed him into the foyer.

Danielle's heart lurched as he came toward her with a smile. How she wished things were different. If only she and Jimmy had grown up in a normal home, then she could accept Blake's love and return it gladly. It was only a matter of time before the truth came out. Sutton would see to that if she didn't cooperate with him. He'd find a way to reveal the truth without revealing his part in her upbringing. She shivered. That is, if he didn't kill her and throw her body in the river as he'd threatened.

As she went through her lines, she was hard pressed not to burst into tears. Would she and Jimmy ever escape? Would they ever be able to live normal lives?

Suddenly Blake took both of her hands in his. Oh, how wonderful his touch felt. But she couldn't allow him to do that. She started to slip her hands away.

He held on firmly with one hand and lifted her chin with the other. "Danielle," he whispered her name and gazed into her eyes.

She knew she should pull away but couldn't bring herself to abandon the touch she'd so longed for. She closed her eyes. If only she could stay this way forever.

"I don't know what or who is troubling you." Blake's voice trembled. "But I know something is terribly wrong. I want you to know that whatever it is I'm going to do my best to take care of it."

She felt his lips brush her across her closed eyelids and then he was gone.

Chapter 17

The piano tinkled a random tune beneath Blake's restless fingers. For the first time in a long while, he had no interest in writing music. All he could see was Danielle's long lashes against her cheek as he'd kissed her closed eyes.

After last night's sleepless round of tossing and turning, he'd come to a startling discovery. As much as he loved to write musical comedy, he couldn't see himself making a career of it. Besides, if he proposed to Danielle, as he had every intention of doing, shouldn't he have a solid future to offer her? He also had to admit he missed law school. Maybe it was time to go back.

When he went downstairs, he was surprised to find his father still at the breakfast table. Usually, he was out and about early, even on holidays.

Blake filled a plate from the sideboard and sat at the table. "Good morning, Mother. Anything interesting in the paper this morning, Father?"

"Not really." Blake's father laid the paper down and picked up his coffee cup. "I do have some news for you, though. I've heard from the private detective Alan Hite, whom I hired to track James Sutton."

Excitement coursed through Blake. "So what has he turned up?"

"Sutton spends a lot of time at a house across the river, near the docks. He asked around and it turns out Mr. Sutton owns the place." He frowned before continuing. "Which is a little strange, since most of the people in and out of there are young people. Hite said he's counted around twenty of them who appear to range in age between about nine and the early twenties. There's also a drunken old crone who says she's the cook. He couldn't get any information out of her. Said she's only been there a couple of months and doesn't know anything."

Blake jumped up. "So what do we do next?"

"Nothing yet. Hite has one of his people on surveillance night and day. But until we have a valid reason, we can't go bursting into the place."

"But what about all the kids?"

"Sit down and eat your breakfast. For all we know, the children are cousins or nephews he's caring for. Maybe neighbor kids who simply happen to like to hang out there."

Blake snorted.

"I know, I know. But until we have something more to go on, there's nothing we can do."

"All right. Are you going to church for the Thanksgiving service this morning, Father?"

"Actually, I thought I would."

"Good. By the way, I'm thinking about taking my last two classes."

His father's eyes lit up. "You mean your law school classes?"

"Yes, sir." Blake grinned. "I thought that would make you happy."

"You thought right. I'm more than happy. Does that mean you'll come in with the firm?"

"Well, I haven't completely made up my mind, but yes, if I do decide to practice law, of course I'll join the firm, if you'll have me." He grinned. "You can help me get ready to pass the bar."

His father laughed and clapped him on the shoulder. "Would this change of heart have anything to do with the pretty Miss Gray?"

"Well, yes. In a way. But to be honest, I actually miss poring over law books until three in the morning. And the challenge of mock trials. Writing music is wonderful, and I don't think I could ever give it up completely, but I'm not so sure anymore it's my life's work."

"I know you have show business in your blood, son. Nothing wrong with that. But I'm glad you're considering law as your career choice. And I'm more than glad you wish to join the family business." He grinned then stood and squeezed Blake's shoulder. "I'm going to get ready for church."

Blake turned to his mother, who watched him intently. "What do you think, Mother?"

"You're serious about this?"

"Yes, I think I need to at least finish law school."

A smile burst across her face like sunshine, and she clapped her hands together. "I'm so happy for you. I know you have a wonderful talent and God will be sure to use it, no matter which choice you finally make. But I'm thrilled you didn't wait ten years or so and then realize you should have finished law school."

"I appreciate how you've supported me in my choices, Mother."

"It has been my pleasure to watch you exercise your gifts, of which the practice of law is one, I have no doubt."

"Thank you, Mother." He reached across the table and took her hand.

"Are you escorting Danielle to church?"

"No, but I'm driving her over here afterward." He grinned.

"It's so nice the Kramers agreed to come. I don't think we've ever done Thanksgiving together in all the years we've been friends. I don't know why we haven't done this before."

ɔ3

Danielle leaned back in the porch swing, her shoulder against Blake's. She'd had a wonderful time with the Nelsons. She'd already known she loved Blake's mother, but she'd finally gotten to know his father better. Their open-armed acceptance of her had touched her deeply. But they didn't know her past. Neither did Blake. And she shouldn't let this go any further until things were settled with Sutton.

She shivered. "We must be crazy to sit out here. It's freezing."

"Not quite freezing. But it will be before morning." Blake curled his fingers around hers.

She considered pulling her hand away, but instead, with a contented sigh, she let it rest in his. She didn't know what would come tomorrow or the next day or next week. But no matter what happened, they would have this moment.

ଔ

Danielle tried to sit up straight, but the inviting depth of Amelia Kramer's boudoir sofa seemed to draw her in until all she wanted to do was sink into the plush cushion. She hadn't realized how tired she was until this moment. A tea service for two sat on a silver tray on the table in front of the sofa.

Mrs. Kramer, sitting next to her, smiled and reached for the teapot. "You just sit back and relax, dear. I'll pour and then we'll have a nice chat."

Danielle took a deep breath. Was this a mistake? After her tender moment with Blake last week, she knew it was time to make her move to get Jimmy out of Sutton's clutches so he couldn't use him against her any longer. But she also knew that she couldn't go into the man's lair without letting someone know her story. Otherwise, if something happened to her, Sutton would continue his evil plans. She'd considered speaking to Mrs. Parker, knowing that the lady would be kind to her no matter what she'd done, but after praying and sincerely asking God what He wanted her to do, she knew the time had come to be truthful with her benefactress. If she turned her out of the house, or even over to the authorities, Danielle would simply have to deal with it. She'd waited long enough. And she had to have some help for Jimmy's sake, even if it meant spending time in prison. So, this afternoon, after she'd arrived home from rehearsal, she'd asked to speak to Mrs. Kramer privately.

The hot tea soothed her throat and stomach, as well as her mind, and soon she relaxed and sank back. She wished she could close her eyes and go to sleep. Perhaps off to some dreamland where she never had to face the reality of her plight.

She sat up straight again and cleared her throat. "Mrs. Kramer. . ."

"Amelia. I've told you many times you could call me Amelia." She shook her finger playfully.

"Amelia, then." She cleared her throat. "I have something to tell you. Something that will probably cause you to hate me."

Consternation crossed Amelia's face. "Oh no. I've come to love you like a sister. The little sister I always wanted. I could never hate you."

Just wait until you hear. A tremor ran through Danielle's body. She knew she had to get it out now or she never would.

"I lied about the robbery. I was part of the gang." She took a deep breath and threw a fearful glance at Amelia.

Surprised, she saw Amelia's smile widen. Hadn't she heard what she said?

"Why, I know that, silly. I've known it all along."

"Wh–what?"

"Perhaps you could fool Officer Brady, but I saw right through your performance. That's why I wasn't a bit surprised when I heard how well you were doing in Blake's show."

"But, why in the world did you bring me home with you, if you knew I was guilty?"

Amelia reached over and patted her hand. "Because I could see you were scared half to death. Besides, God told me to."

Danielle gasped. "What do you mean? I didn't hear Him say anything."

A trilling laugh emitted from Amelia's throat. "I don't mean I heard Him with my ears. But I heard His voice deep inside me. And I knew you needed help."

"But why didn't you say anything?"

"Because I wasn't sure what God had in mind, and I didn't want to mess it up. But I had an idea you'd tell me the true story someday." She smiled encouragingly. "How about now?"

"I hardly know where to begin." Dear God, was it true that she'd known all along? She knew and didn't turn Danielle in to the police.

"I'd say the beginning would be the best."

Danielle let her mind drift back. When she began to speak, she felt as though she were in a dream. "My father died at sea when I was nearly ten and my brother was three. Mama was expecting a baby and we had no means of support. We moved in with a friend of Mama's who owned a boardinghouse. Mama and I both worked for her in exchange for a room and our meals." She stopped as memories of her parents bombarded her mind.

"Take your time, dear." Amelia patted her hand.

Danielle felt tears behind her nose and eyes. She gulped and cleared her throat. "Mama and the baby both died. And Aunt Mary turned us out."

"Oh, how heartless. You poor child. Is that when you and your brother went into an orphanage?"

At the sympathy in Amelia's voice, Danielle glanced over and saw her friend's eyes flooded with tears. Shame washed over her at the lies she'd told. "No, ma'am. I lied about that, too. Jimmy and I were never in an orphanage. And while I'm at it, I need to tell you my brother isn't dead, either."

Amelia looked at her with concern. "Then where is he? He must still be very young."

"Yes, he's twelve and has a crippled leg."

"Oh dear. An injury?"

"No, he had an illness when he was two. I'm not sure what it was. But it left him lame."

Amelia sighed. "I'll stop interrupting. Tell me what happened next."

"It was very cold and windy that day, and Jimmy and I hadn't eaten since the day before. We hid behind a crate on the docks and watched some men unloading a boat." She hesitated then confessed. "I stole some food from one of them. He chased us down the street. I had to half carry Jimmy. I can still hear the thumping and bumping of his crutch. Then a boy helped us get away. He took us to a house and introduced us to a man named Sutton. It looked like heaven to me at the time, and Sutton was our guardian angel. But he turned out to be the head of a gang of thieves, most of them children."

"Do you mean he made the children steal for him? Is that it?" Something like fury crossed Amelia's face.

"Yes, ma'am. But he felt sorry for Jimmy and took a liking to me. He never sent us out. I helped around the house. And Jimmy did a few little odds and ends, like shining Sutton's boots."

"So, if he didn't send you, why were you with the gang that robbed the bank customer?"

"Sutton made advances to me one day. When I slapped him, he was furious. He sent me out on the job to teach me a 'lesson.'"

Amelia closed her eyes. When she opened them, they were full of grief. "Danielle, did you steal anything?"

"No, I was the decoy so they could get away. I was supposed to walk away in the other direction, but I got scared and ran after them."

"I see. And that's when you and Blake collided. Does he know?"

Danielle's stomach sank. "No," she whispered.

"Well, maybe we'll keep your secret a little while longer until I think this through."

Danielle wanted so badly to stop now and leave things at this point. But she knew she owed it to Amelia.

"There's something else." Tears filled her eyes and she blinked hard. "When I was trying to keep Sutton appeased, I sent him the pearl necklace your mother gave me. I'm so sorry. I can never replace the sentimental value of her gift to me. But I'll pay her back for the cost of it."

For a moment pain filled Amelia's eyes, then blinking, she smiled. "The cost doesn't matter, my dear. You did what you felt you had to do at the time. Mother loves you and she'll understand. Don't worry about it."

Danielle fell into her gracious friend's arms and cried.

Chapter 18

Danielle stood at the end of the alley and hesitated. Should she really go through with this? But she had to. The play would open in less than a week. If she could convince Sutton to allow Jimmy to go with her, perhaps she would be able to think of some way to prevent him from implementing his plan, whatever it was.

Would he perhaps rob the theater? But that didn't make sense, since he was the main investor. And Sutton wasn't about to rob himself. She took one step down the alley and then turned and rushed back toward the theater. Maybe she'd been too hasty. She needed to pray and think things through some more before she did something she might regret.

She made a short detour and stopped at Tony's Sandwich Shop. Since Blake had introduced her to Tony and his unique Italian beef sandwich, she'd developed a craving for the things. She sat at a table and ordered. When her food arrived, she leaned over the table in a most unladylike manner to prevent the juices from dripping on her white blouse. Sometimes she wondered if they were worth the mess, but she'd been back a couple of times. Once with Blake.

Blake's appointment today had made it easier for her to slip away to the docks, but she needed to get back before he did. She didn't want him to start wondering again.

She sighed. Why was she such a coward today? She should have gone through with her plan. *God, please show me what to do.*

But either He didn't speak or she was too tense to hear His voice. She glanced at the clock behind the counter. She still had thirty minutes before rehearsal started.

Jesus, please be with me.

With determined steps, she headed back to Sutton's place, this time walking down the filthy alley and knocking on the door. Her heart thumped loudly as she waited. Maybe Sutton wouldn't be there.

The door swung open and Tay, one of the younger boys, stared at her, wide-eyed.

"Who is it, Tay?" Sutton's voice dashed her hopes that she could turn and leave.

Danielle smiled at the boy and stepped inside, laying her hand on his shoulder in passing. "It's me, Sutton."

"Ah, Miss Gray, is it?" His mocking voice cut through her soul like glass.

"Her name ain't Miss Gray." Tay scrunched his grubby face up and peered at her. "It's Danni. Danni Grayson. Ain't it, Danni?"

Danielle heard laughter.

"Stupid kid." Several of the older boys were playing cards at a table in the corner. The boy who'd spoken leered at Danielle.

"He's not stupid," she snapped then flashed the child a smile. "Sure it's me, Taytay. I couldn't fool you, could I?" She turned to Sutton. "I want to see Jimmy, and then I need to speak to you privately."

"Of course, my dear. Your wish is my command." He turned and nodded at Cobb, who'd just come into the room. "Get Jimmy for us. His sister has come to visit."

Suspicious of Sutton's honey tone, she peered at him through narrowed eyes.

"Danni?" At the frightened near-whisper, Danielle turned and saw Jimmy standing in the doorway, leaning heavily on his crutch. He blinked his eyes, but tears remained.

"Jimmy." She sailed across the room and took her brother in her arms. "Are you all right?"

He threw a quick glance at Sutton and nodded.

Danielle looked him over. As before, there was no sign of physical abuse. She could only hope Sutton had stopped the mental abuse as well, but the haunted look in Jimmy's eyes didn't give her much hope. She squeezed his shoulder. "I need to talk to Sutton alone, then I'll see you again. Is that all right?"

He nodded, but his eyes held worry and doubt.

Heart heavy, Danielle followed Sutton into the spacious room he used for an office.

Unlike the rest of the house, this room was scrupulously clean. The walls were covered with brocade. The oak furniture was waxed and shining.

Sutton indicated that she should sit on the sofa, but she shook her head. She stepped across the Turkish carpet to the chair in front of Sutton's desk and sat down.

With an amused smile, Sutton shrugged and sat in his desk chair. "Now," he said, dropping the smile and pretense of kindness, "what are you up to?"

Danielle pressed her lips together tightly to keep from licking them nervously. "I want to make a deal with you."

He raised an eyebrow and reached into a wooden box for a cigar. Striking a match, he lit it and leaned back in his chair. "A deal. What do you have in mind?"

"A deal that will be to your advantage." At his silence, she took a deep breath and continued. "If you'll let me take Jimmy away from here, and leave us alone, I'll pay you out of every check for as long as you say. Even if it's forever."

There. She'd done it. She sat on the edge of her seat and stared at him for some sign of response.

He pursed his lips around the cigar and took puff after puff while he stared silently. He sighed. "But, my dear, don't you know you're worth so much more to me right where you are? And if I allow Jimmy to leave, you'll never do what I ask."

He looked at her silently once more. Then a sound emitted from his lips. At first it was so slight she wasn't sure it was a chuckle. Then it grew louder until booming laughter filled the entire room.

Danielle covered her ears. If she could, she'd cover her whole self to escape the taunting, mocking laughter. She jumped up and headed for the door. Slinging it open, she rushed into the front room and grabbed Jimmy by the arm. "C'mon. We're getting out of here."

They were halfway to the door when Sutton's hand grabbed her arm tightly, jerking her to a stop. Jimmy fell backward but caught himself with his crutch.

"Where do you think you're going?" Sutton's voice thundered throughout the room.

"Away from here, and I'm taking Jimmy with me. I'll never steal for you, Sutton. And neither will Jimmy. If you try to make me, I'll turn you in to the authorities."

The blow hit her so hard she fell backward to the floor. Her head spun and her ears rang.

"You leave my sister alone." She realized the shadow that flew past her was Jimmy, and then she heard a loud slap.

"Bring them," Sutton yelled.

Rough hands lifted her and dragged her across the room. Then she was flung forward and onto the floor, with Jimmy landing beside her. A door slammed and darkness surrounded her. She heard the snap of the bolt.

She gasped, trying to get a clear breath, and fought against dizziness. At a moan next to her, she felt around until her hands found her brother. "Jimmy? Are you all right?"

"Yeah. I think so. I must have passed out for a minute. Where are we?"

"The kitchen pantry, I think. He locked us in."

"Oh."

"I'm so sorry, Jimmy. I shouldn't have made him mad. It's my fault we're in this fix."

He squeezed her hand in the darkness. "At least we're together."

℃〇

Blake paced the lobby and looked at his watch again. Where was she? She was more than an hour late for rehearsal, and that wasn't like Danielle. Frustrated, he crammed the watch into its tiny pocket and went outside where he peered in one direction then the other, down the near-empty sidewalk.

The afternoon was getting darker as clouds moved in. It looked as though it might snow.

Where was she? He'd phoned the Kramer house a few minutes earlier, but the maid said she hadn't been there since morning.

And where was Sutton? He almost always showed up for the afternoon rehearsal.

A chill washed over Blake and he walked at a near-run to the stable. Without waiting for the stable boy, he hitched the horse to the carriage. Jumping in, he flicked the reins and took off. He crossed the Clark Street Bridge and turned away from the docks.

For over an hour he searched the narrow streets and back alleys, his eyes scanning the area for her. He felt a rush of panic and his heartbeat raced as realization dawned. The guy she'd met. His eyes began to search for the mop of red hair that would identify her friend. Maybe he would know where she was.

Finally, dejected and feeling helpless for the first time in his life, he gave up his quest and headed for his father's office. He pulled up in front and threw his reins to the boy who'd hurried out of the building for that purpose. He entered the front office.

Charlie Jenkins, the firm's white-haired secretary, looked up from the front desk.

"Is Father with a client, Charlie?"

"No, but Mr. Crier will be here in about ten minutes."

"Okay, I just need to see my father for a minute." He headed down the aisle between neat rows of desks where the assistant secretary and seven clerks worked.

He tapped on his father's door then walked in.

"Blake, good to see you here. Getting the feel of the place?"

"I wish that was the reason. Danielle didn't come to rehearsal this afternoon and she's not at home. Sutton never showed up, either, and he seldom misses afternoon rehearsal."

"Hmm." His father's brow furrowed and he stroked his chin. "What are you thinking, son?"

"I need the address Hite turned up. I'm going to see if she's there."

"You know if you go barging in there you may be arrested for breaking and entering."

"I intend to be invited in. After all, he is a business partner."

"Yes, well, since you're not supposed to know he has interests in the house by the docks, he might get a little suspicious. Don't you think?"

"I don't know. But if Danielle's there, I'm going to find her. Then I'll find out why. Maybe she wants to be there for all I know."

Blake's father peered at him a moment then reached inside a folder that lay on his desk. "Here. This is the address. Hite still has a man stationed there. See if you can spot him. He might be needed."

The phone on the desk shrilled and Blake's father picked it up. "Sam Nelson. Yes, he's here." He listened intently then whistled. "You don't say. Thank you, Amelia."

"What is it, Father? Was that Amelia Kramer? Has something happened to Danielle?" Fear knotted Blake's stomach.

"The maid told Amelia you had called inquiring for Danielle. Amelia's worried because the girl has had some past dealings with Sutton. She said if Danielle was missing, you should find Sutton." He tapped his pencil on the top of the desk then added, "According to what Danielle told Amelia, Sutton has a bunch of kids robbing for him. Danielle and her brother, Jimmy, have been living with the man for years."

"What?" Blake stared at his father in unbelief. "But I thought she grew up in an orphanage."

"Apparently she made that up."

"So I was right all along." Disappointment and pain knifed through Blake, and nausea rose into his throat. How could someone as lovely and sweet-appearing as Danielle be involved with a thief who exploited children? Well, he was done. He'd find another actress to finish up the show. But. . .he remembered the fear in her eyes when Sutton had spoken to her. Was it possible she herself had been one of those exploited children? He looked at his father. "Is there anything else?"

"If there is, Amelia didn't tell me. I think she wanted me off the phone so we could go find Danielle."

"We?"

"Yes, you and I and as many police officers as they'll send with us." He reached for the phone and dialed.

cs

Danielle pushed against the door to no effect. The clatter of pots and pans was evidence the cook was getting ready to prepare dinner. It must be late. What had they thought when she didn't show up for rehearsal?

A loud pounding reverberated through the house and vibrated the floor beneath Danielle's feet. Something crashed, and Danielle could hear shouts and curses.

"Danni, what's happening?"

"I don't know, but I hope someone has come who will set us free."

"Danielle, where are you?" That was Blake. Joy and dread battled inside her. Amelia must have told him about Sutton. But how had he found the house?

She pounded on the door and called out loudly, "In here. We're in here."

More scuffling and shouts were heard. Then suddenly the lock snapped and the door swung open. Blake breathed heavily as he looked down at her. A storm of emotions battled in his eyes. He reached his hand toward her.

She stood. When she once more looked into his eyes, they were unreadable.

"Let's get out of here." The words were clipped, his voice cold.

Danielle's heart fell.

Chapter 19

Nearly a week had passed since Blake and his father had rescued Danielle and Jimmy from Sutton. The Kramers had opened their arms and their home to Danielle's little brother, just as they had to her.

When Mr. Kramer had mentioned having a doctor examine Jimmy to see if anything could be done for the infirm leg, Danielle had been stunned. She'd never imagined the possibility that Jimmy's leg could be fixed.

Jimmy trembled on the carriage seat beside Danielle. She didn't know if it was from fear or the shaking of the carriage as they drove through Lincoln Park.

Amelia smiled from the seat facing them.

The carriage turned down Fullerton and stopped in front of a cluster of stately buildings.

Jimmy straightened from the slumped position he'd held most of the way. "Is this it? I won't have to stay here, will I?"

Danielle felt cold fingers squeeze her heart as his voice broke. "No, of course not, Jimmy." Amelia's voice was full of sympathy. "We're just going to let the doctor examine your leg and then we'll go back home."

Jimmy took a deep breath and his voice, when he spoke again, was nonchalant. "Oh. I just wondered. I'm not scared or anything."

They stepped out of the carriage and walked up the broad walk to a massive door. Amelia opened it and they went inside. The room was spotless, its white walls gleaming. Several chairs stood neatly in rows. About half of them were occupied.

A white-clad nurse behind the front desk directed them down a hall and to the right. They found Dr. Paulsen's office quiet, with only a few people in the waiting room. Danielle gave the young woman at the desk their name and sat to wait.

When Jimmy's name was called, Amelia turned to him. "Would you like for me to wait here while you and your sister go in?"

"Yes, ma'am. I only want Danni to go in with me." His face turned red. "It's not that I don't like you or anything like that."

"That's all right. I understand. You don't need me in there. I'd probably be in the way."

Danielle and Jimmy followed the nurse down a short hallway and into a cold, sterile examining room. Danielle noticed Jimmy's nervous glance around the room and reached over and patted his hand. They'd only waited a few minutes when a man with steel-gray hair came in, looking at a chart. He took the chair across from Jimmy. "Well, young man. My friend, Kramer, tells me your leg isn't working quite right."

"Yes, sir. I mean no, sir. It never has."

"You were born this way?"

Jimmy looked up at his sister. "You tell him, Danni."

Dr. Paulsen peered at Danielle over his steel-rimmed glasses. "And you are?"

"My name is Danielle Grayson. I'm Jimmy's sister. Our parents are deceased."

Sympathy crossed the doctor's face, but only for a moment. "I see. Well, Miss Grayson, Kramer didn't tell me much. I need to know how your brother became lame and any other information that might help make a proper diagnosis."

"He had some sort of illness when he was two. I don't know what it was. But it left him lame. We didn't have money for doctors."

"I see. It could have been any number of crippling diseases. But we'll go with what we have. If you'll step outside, Miss Grayson, I'd like to examine Jimmy." He glanced over at Jimmy. "That is, with his permission."

Jimmy nodded and gave a nonchalant wave in Danielle's direction. Knowing it was only a brave front, she threw him an encouraging smile and returned to the waiting room.

Amelia's needles clicked and bright yarn of red and green cascaded across her skirt. She reached over and patted Danielle's hand.

Danielle sent her a grateful smile. "Waiting is hard."

"I know it is, my dear. Would you like to help with this scarf to pass the time?"

Danielle blushed. "I'm sorry. I don't know how to knit." She darted a glance at Amelia to see how she'd take that piece of information.

"Well, of course you don't, being raised without a woman to teach you. Crochet?"

Danielle shook her head. "No, I can barely sew on a button where it will stay."

"Ah. I think perhaps we need to have some lessons, my dear, before you get married."

Startled, Danielle stared at Amelia. "Married? What makes you think I'm getting married?"

A knowing smile tilted Amelia's lips. "Some things are pretty obvious. Such as the way you and Blake look at each other when you think no one is watching."

"Oh. Well, if Blake had any affection for me before, it's gone now. He hardly even looks at me since he found out I was part of Sutton's gang. We ride to the theater and back in silence, except for a polite hello and good-bye."

"Now, dear, I'm sure Blake doesn't blame you for what happened to you when you were a child. Look how he insisted the Nelson Law Firm defend your friend, Cobb."

All the children twelve and under had been placed in a children's home, except for Jimmy. The judge had been kind and allowed Jimmy and Danielle to stay with the Kramers while he investigated the situation. Danielle had confessed her intended part in the bank case, but since she'd actually done nothing, in the end, he found nothing to charge either of them with, and the exploited children would be cared for. The boys between ages thirteen and seventeen had been placed in a boys' home, pending individual investigation. Most would more than likely be cared for until age eighteen and then released.

Sutton was being held in jail awaiting a hearing, and to Danielle's sorrow, so was Cobb and all the other adult members of the gang. Mr. Nelson had agreed to represent Cobb in court, but he said the young man would probably be found guilty and serve some time in prison.

"I know. Blake's been very kind to the children. But I don't think he can forgive me for lying to him."

"And I think you're very mistaken."

Danielle hoped Amelia was right. But she didn't hold out much hope, and her heart was sick over it. She hadn't realized how much she loved Blake until now.

The doctor called Danielle back into his office. "I will, of course, need to run some tests to make sure, but there is a fair chance surgery will restore your brother's leg. The nerves responded well and that's always a good sign."

Jimmy's face tightened. "Will I have to stay here for those tests?"

"No. I'll schedule an appointment with the laboratory. They should be able to get them all done in one day. But if surgery is an option, you'll have to be in the hospital for a week or more." He peered at Jimmy. "Can you manage that?"

"Well, if it'll help me to walk right, sure I can."

Joy shimmered through Danielle, and with a lilt in her voice, she thanked the doctor. Then she and Jimmy hurried out to tell Amelia the good news.

☙

Blake sat in his front row seat in the darkened theater and watched the dress rehearsal for *Peg in Dreamland*. It was the evening before opening night, and the perfection nearly took his breath away. At any other time he would have been puffed up with pride and delight, but now he sat with despair on his heart.

Every time he thought of the tragic circumstances that had surrounded Danielle and her brother for years, he wanted to hit something, hard. When he opened the closet door and saw them sprawled on the bottom of the dark closet, he'd wanted to take her in his arms and never let her go. Make sure nothing evil could ever touch her again.

But mixed in with his sympathy and love was a thread of anger and disappointment that she'd lied to him. Hadn't trusted him at all. Her lie about her brother hit him the hardest. How could she pretend the boy was dead?

A picture of her lying in the fallen leaves the day he'd met her washed over him. Now that he knew her story, he realized she must have been terrified that day. He could understand that. And all he'd done was to make accusations and demand an interrogation.

But what about all the months since then? Surely she knew him well enough now to trust him. Why hadn't she confided in him?

He took a deep breath. Well, at least she'd received some good news. Jimmy's tests had shown that surgery should make his leg almost as good as new. He'd wanted to take her in his arms and whirl her around with the joy of it, but his uncertainty about their whole relationship held him back.

Anyway, she didn't need him. Tomorrow was her big day. Opening night. He was quite sure her performance of Peg would launch her into a successful acting career. She'd be able to take care of herself and Jimmy very well.

He turned his attention back to the stage and shock zipped through him. She was staring at him with a sad, questioning look on her face. When his eyes met hers, she turned and looked away.

He glanced up as Pop sat down beside him.

"How much did I miss?" He was breathing rapidly as though he'd rushed to get here.

"Just the first half of act 1. It's really good, Pop. They're doing a fantastic job."

"Ah yes. *Peg in Dreamland* will be a big success. I'm sure of it. So why are you sitting here like a dog who has lost his last bone?"

Blake didn't answer. Couldn't answer.

"Don't be so hard on her, my lad. Her life hasn't exactly been a fairy tale. She's been through a lot."

How did Pop always read him so perfectly? How did he know?

"Why couldn't she have trusted me?"

"Nelson." Blake glanced up to find Bosley glaring at him. "We're trying to have a dress rehearsal here. Keep the voices down."

Pop leaned closer and whispered, "If you'd been orphaned at ten, thrown out in the cold with a little lame brother to care for, and raised by an evil exploiter and mountebank like Sutton, maybe you'd find it hard to trust anyone, too."

A vice squeezed Blake's stomach. Was Pop right? How could Blake know what drove a child who grew up in circumstances such as Danielle's? He'd been loved and cared for since the day he was born.

"Have you told her you love her?"

"Yes, weeks ago. She ran away from me." The memory cut through him as though the event had just happened.

"Ah, but that was when she was in the throes of her trouble. James Sutton is an evil man and he had young Jimmy in his clutches. Besides, I'm sure he made threats against her friends as well as her brother."

"Do you think so, Pop?" If that were true, it could explain why she hadn't confided in anyone.

"Well, if I were in your shoes, I'd be finding out. Don't throw away your chance with the woman you love because of your supposing."

Blake looked at Danielle again. This time he gave her a hopeful smile.

Her eyes lit up and she stumbled over a word.

"Danielle, would you get your mind on the production and see if you can stay in character?" Bosley snapped then threw Blake a disgusted glance. "Stop making eyes at her, Nelson. We're trying to get through a dress rehearsal here."

Danielle blushed and averted her eyes as chuckles broke out among the rest of the cast.

Blake's heart pounded. Could he have been wrong? Did they have a chance after all? He forced himself to concentrate on the rest of the cast, everyone but Danielle.

The remainder of the rehearsal went smoothly, and Blake took the whole cast out for a late supper at Tony's. Pop excused himself and went home, despite the pleading of the entire cast that he join them.

Later, as the carriage rolled down the dark streets on the way home, Blake argued with himself about what to say to Danielle. He pulled to a stop in front of the Kramer house. "Uh, Danielle?"

"Yes, Blake?" She turned and spoke breathlessly.

Her soft lips were so close, and the thought of the kiss they'd shared a few weeks earlier hit him like a hammer. If he moved his head just slightly, he could touch her lips with his own.

He'd never been shy or tongue-tied around women before, but fear that she'd reject his love washed over him. He swallowed. "Do you need a read-through tonight? I'd be more than happy to help."

Her eyes clouded. Was that disappointment he saw in them?

"No, thank you. I'm very tired. I think I should go to bed and get a good night's rest."

"Of course. I should have realized." He jumped from the carriage and hurried around to help her down.

She smiled slightly and, ignoring his proffered arm, ran lightly up the steps and went inside.

Blake stared after her for a full moment before getting back into the carriage and driving down the street to his house.

Stupid, stupid, stupid. He continued to berate himself all the way into the house.

"Blake dear, your grandfather said rehearsal went very well."

"Yes, ma'am. It was a good rehearsal."

"I'm so excited about opening night," she chattered, her voice full of excitement. "Oh, and I forgot to tell you, but the Kramers are hosting an opening night party after the show."

Blake's eyes gleamed and he threw his arms around his mother in an enormous hug. Tomorrow night, he would ask Danielle to marry him.

Chapter 20

A thunderous roar of applause shook the theater as the crowd rose to their feet.

Danielle stood in the spotlight, blinking, trembling as she bowed to the audience.

The curtain went down with a *whoosh*.

Heart pounding, Danielle forced herself to stand there and smile as the other cast members joined her. The curtain rose again and the applause never diminished as the cast took their bows. Then, the curtain fell once more and Danielle leaned against Rhonda as they exited the stage.

"Honey, you were fantastic," Rhonda gushed.

Surrounded by the joyful cast, Danielle tried to get her bearings. "It was everyone. You know you all did great," she protested.

Bosley appeared from somewhere. "Congratulations. Great job. All of you."

Somehow, with Rhonda and Hannah on either side of her, she reached the ladies' dressing room.

"You'll be having your own room with a star on the door after this."

Startled at Hannah's sudden proclamation, Danielle stared at the actress.

"No, I will not," she protested. "Stop teasing."

Laughter filled the room, but several added their assurances that her status had changed.

A knock on the door interrupted the good-natured chatter.

Hannah flung it open to find a delivery boy, his arms filled with several large bouquets. All roses, mostly red, with a few pink interspersed among them.

"These are for Miss Danielle Grayson," he grinned. "Heard you had a smashing show."

Danielle got a coin from her purse and handed it to him. "Thank you."

The door had no more than closed after him when another knock came.

"Oh, my goodness, Danielle. Would you look at this?" Hannah's voice rang with excitement as more bouquets were presented.

Rhonda stuck her head out and called to one of the stagehands. "Would you stand guard and not let anyone knock so we can get dressed?"

The young man waved and nodded then deposited himself on a chair by the door.

Danielle glanced eagerly through the cards that accompanied the flowers. The Kramers, the Nelsons, several friends of both families were represented. Breathlessly, she continued to look. Then, disappointed, she sighed and went to change. Of course, Blake was included in the roses his family had sent, but she'd hoped. . .

The Kramers, Mrs. Parker, and Jimmy waited for her in the lobby, which sparkled with white lights and red roses for the occasion. She'd be riding home with them in the family carriage.

The ladies converged on her with hugs and kisses.

Nearby, Jimmy leaned on his crutch, a look of shining pride on his face.

Danielle hurried over to her brother and hugged him tightly. Soon, perhaps, he could throw the crutch away. Waves of joy washed over her at the thought.

"You were great, Danni. You're the best. I'll say you are. Hey, I almost thought you really were that girl, Peg."

Amid laughter, Danielle glanced around for a glimpse of Blake. She'd thought sure he would be waiting. This was his victory night, too.

With congratulations bombarding her from all sides, she allowed herself to be led from the theater. Their carriage was brought around and they all piled in and headed home.

The house was blazing with light. The servants had everything ready for the guests, and most of them stood in the foyer grinning as Danielle trailed in after the rest of the family.

"Congratulations, Miss Gray." Sally beamed and took a step forward.

"Miss Gray? Since when have I stopped being Danielle?"

"Since you became a star, miss."

The news had traveled fast, it seemed.

"Well, I don't know about that, but I'm still just Danielle, if you please."

Sally's shoulders shook with laughter. "If you insist."

Danielle smiled and headed up the stairs to get changed for the party. Halfway up, she turned around. The servants had scattered, all but Sally, who stood speaking to Mrs. Kramer.

"And Sally. . .by the way, Gray is my stage name, but my real name is Grayson." With a grin, she whirled around and continued up to her room.

Her new dress lay spread on the bed in all its blue velvet glory. A narrow silver box sat beside it. Surprised, Danielle picked up the box and removed the lid. The lights that sparkled from the diamond necklace took Danielle's breath away.

She had no doubt it was from Mrs. Parker. Amelia must have told her about the pearl necklace. This was the sweet lady's way of assuring her it was all right.

She dressed and redid her hair then went downstairs.

Amelia was greeting a guest in the foyer. She turned and her eyes met Danielle's. Smiling, she nodded.

"Danielle, my dear girl, what a little actress you are." Mrs. Carlton, socialite number one in the city, kissed the air on both sides of Danielle's face then, with nose in the air, pushed on by her. Danielle heard the woman say in stilted tones to Wanda Fullerton, "Don't you think there's something a little disreputable about performing on the stage?"

Coldness knifed through Danielle. Was that what everyone thought of her? No wonder Blake had withdrawn any feelings he had for her. That and the fact he thought her a liar and a thief. He was probably sorry he'd told her he loved her.

"Pay her no mind, my dear." Mrs. Parker had come up behind her. "She's more than likely jealous. She had hopes that her daughter, Susan, would capture Blake's affection. Now, there are some friends here who would like to see you."

Danielle turned to find the Nelsons smiling from a few steps away. Mrs. Nelson stepped forward and took her in her arms, giving her a real kiss on the cheek. "You were marvelous, Danielle. You made me want to be on the stage again. But I was never as good as you."

"I beg to differ there." Mr. Nelson gave his wife a tender smile. "Why do you think I sat and watched you perform night after night for months if you couldn't act?"

"Because you were in love with me, of course." The lady winked at Danielle, and she and her husband joined the crowd in the drawing room.

"Hello, Danielle." Blake stepped forward, a huge bouquet of deep red roses resting in the curve of his arm. "I tried to get backstage after the show, but the hallway was so full of admirers and delivery boys, I decided to wait."

"I wondered why I didn't see you earlier. I wanted to congratulate you on the success of *Peg in Dreamland.*"

His hand brushed hers as she took the roses, and a thrill ran through her.

"Thank you, Blake," she whispered. "They're the most beautiful roses I've ever seen."

"For the most beautiful woman I've ever seen." Blake smiled, but when he spoke again, his tone was serious. "I wonder if I could have a word with you in private a little later."

He'd called her beautiful. "Yes, of course. Perhaps after everyone settles down a bit."

The smile he flashed her could only be called adoring.

CB

Blake tapped his foot as he stood in the middle of a group of his friends. He wondered how soon he could excuse himself without seeming rude.

"So this is what you quit law school for." Donald Wilson shook his head. "I'll have to admit, legal terminology is quite boring compared to your masterpiece."

Blake threw his friend a wry smile. "Hardly a masterpiece. But thanks for the very kind words."

All his friends had been effusive with their congratulations on the success of *Peg in Dreamland.*

"I was especially impressed with the lovely young thing who played the part of Peg." Tom Ferrell whistled. "She's quite a doll. I believe I saw her here a minute ago. How about an introduction, Blake?"

Blake stiffened and glared at his friend. "Miss Grayson is a lady. Don't get any of your ideas about her, Tom."

Tom and the others burst out laughing.

"Sorry. We had a bet going to know if you were in love with the young lady and decided this would be the best way to find out. I won the bet. Thank you very much."

Blake endured the good-natured teasing for a while then excused himself and went in search of Danielle. He'd waited long enough.

After searching the drawing room and library, he stepped out onto the veranda.

She leaned against one of the round white columns, staring up at the few stars that peeked through the dark clouds. When she heard his footstep, she turned. "The stars are beautiful tonight, but clouds are coming in fast. Do you think it might snow?"

Blake stood beside her and looked up. "Maybe. Would you like that?"

"Yes. I don't usually like snow. The floor was always such a mess at Sutton's because of the boys tracking the stuff in." She paused. "Sorry. I didn't mean to bring that up."

"You don't have to apologize, Danielle." Pain stabbed his heart. Had he been that unreasonable that she'd think she couldn't mention her past? "I want to know every detail about your life. That is, of course, only the details you want to talk about." He was rambling like an idiot.

She smiled and ignored his clumsiness. "I don't think I'll mind the snow this year. It might be nice."

"Danielle. . ." He whispered her name and she looked into his eyes, questioning. "I love you." There. *Please, God. Don't let her run away again.*

"You do?" Awe filled her voice. "Even now that you know I lied to you?"

"That was partly my fault. How could you know you could trust me?"

"Sutton made threats against you."

He inhaled sharply. Sutton had wanted her for himself.

"I was afraid. Afraid he'd hurt you or your family if I told."

"I know, sweetheart. Pop figured that one out."

"I finally told Amelia a little, but I even regretted that. I was afraid if Sutton found out he'd hurt her, too."

"It's all right. Nothing is going to hurt you again. Not if I can help it." He looked at her with longing. "Could you possibly love me, too?"

A look of surprise crossed her face. "I do love you. I thought you knew that."

Joy washed over Blake, and he drew her into his arms. "Sweetheart, you need to know I'm returning to law school."

Her eyes widened, and she leaned back in his arms and looked up at him. "You mean you're not going to write music anymore?"

He grinned. "I don't think I'll ever stop writing music. But it'll have to be a secondary career. Do you think you could stand being married to a stodgy attorney?"

"You could never be stodgy." She started to smile. Then a frown appeared between her eyes. "But, Blake, I have to take care of Jimmy."

"Of course. But it's *we* that will take care of Jimmy. I always wanted a little brother."

Happiness filled her eyes. "Are you sure, Blake, absolutely sure?"

"I've never been more sure of anything in my life. So. . .will you marry me?"

A glint of mischief sparkled in her eyes. "Can I still be an actress?"

"Do you want to be?"

"Only for a little while. I'd hate to stop being Peg just now."

He laughed. "Okay. That's settled. When *Peg in Dreamland* closes, you quit the theater and we get married."

"What if it goes on forever?"

"In that case, Bosley will have to find someone else."

"Look, Blake. It's snowing." Sure enough, big flakes were falling all around them. One landed on Danielle's nose. She giggled and brushed it away as Blake threw his head back and laughed.

"Hmm." She threw him a coy smile. "I wonder how it feels to be kissed in the snow."

Blake pulled her closer. "Let's find out."

SUGAR AND
SPICE

Dedication

With love, to my children and grandchildren. And to my precious great-grands, Lauryn, Braylon, Christopher, and Kezan. Special thanks to JoAnne Simmons, my editor at Heartsong, who gave me the opportunity to honor the victims of the *Eastland* disaster while writing a story of love and family. And my heartfelt gratitude to Aaron McCarver who helps me to make my books so much better. To the city of Chicago itself for its history and its people. To my faithful friends who encourage me and pray for me. To my readers who make this possible. Most of all, to my Lord, Jesus Christ, who loves unconditionally and forgives freely.

Chapter 1

Chicago, January 1915

Snow crunched under Jimmy's feet as he crossed the street to Nelsons' Law Firm. The cold late February wind whipped around his neck. Jimmy raised his collar against it and hoped Blake's response to his announcement wouldn't be as chilly.

Miss Howard, the firm's secretary, smiled sweetly. "Good morning, Mr. Grayson. Nasty weather, isn't it?"

"I'm ready for spring." Jimmy unbuttoned his coat. "Can I go on back?"

"Yes, he's expecting you."

Jimmy went through the swinging gate and headed down the hall to his brother-in-law's office, repeating in his head the words he'd practiced. He took a deep breath. Blake had always been kind to him, and he had no reason to think this time would be different. Except that Danni wasn't going to like the news, and Blake didn't like it when his wife was upset.

He tapped on the door and entered Blake's neat office. The smell of leather and Murphy's oil greeted his nostrils as he closed the door and stepped up to Blake's desk.

"Hi, Jimmy." Blake looked up and lifted his eyebrows. "What's so important it couldn't wait until after work?"

"I need to talk to you first, without Danni."

An amused smile crinkled Blake's face. "Uh-oh, it must be bad if you don't want your sister to know about it."

Jimmy swallowed hard. This wasn't going to be easy. "I want you to know. . ." He cleared his throat and started again. "Blake, you know how much I appreciate everything you've done for me. And I know Danni has her heart set on my continuing in your footsteps." He paused.

A cautious look crossed Blake's face, but he remained silent.

"I've enjoyed my year and a half at law school, but. . . ."

Blake stood up behind his desk. "Are you saying you don't want to be an attorney?"

Jimmy licked his lips and searched Blake's eyes. No condemnation. At least, not yet. Jimmy's shoulders relaxed. "I'm just not sure." Jimmy dropped into the chair in front of the desk, and Blake returned to his.

"I see."

"I like law. And I want to help people. I also know how much you've spent on my education this far."

Blake waved the comment away.

"Lately, I've felt there's something missing. Something I can't put my finger on."

"What is it, exactly, you want to do?"

"I'm not sure. Maybe I'll end up getting my law degree. But I need to know for certain." Jimmy hesitated. "I'd like to take a semester off." He leaned forward, awaiting his brother-in-law's reaction.

"And you think you'll find your answers in a semester?"

"I don't know, but I have to try." Jimmy gave Blake a steady look. "If I don't return to law school, I promise I'll pay back every cent you've spent. And don't think I'm going to live off you and Danni while I'm searching. I'll get a job to pay my own way."

"Money isn't what's important here, Jimmy."

"I know. But I'll feel better."

Blake inhaled deeply and tapped a pencil on his desk. "I wish you'd think about it a little bit longer. Maybe talk to your instructors at school, or even Reverend Martin."

Jimmy bit his lip. Why had everything seemed so reasonable a few minutes ago but now, under Blake's scrutiny, didn't?

"I have spoken to two of my professors about my doubts."

"And?"

Jimmy sighed. "They tried to talk me out of it. But Blake, this isn't just a whim. It's something I feel I must do. As much as I enjoy law, my heart isn't in it."

Blake sat back in his chair and once more tapped the pencil against his desk. Suddenly he sat up and grinned at Jimmy. "Did you know I once left the firm to write musical comedy?"

"Sure. The one Danni was in."

"That's right. My father was furious for a while. So who am I to stop another man from searching his heart? Don't worry about Danielle. I'll talk to her." Blake stood and held out his hand. "After all, you're twenty years old. It's time she realized that."

"Thanks, Blake. I hope she won't be too upset." Jimmy rose and took Blake's hand.

As he left the building, relief washed over him and he felt free for the first time in months. A light snow had begun to fall again. Jimmy stood for a moment, wondering what his next move should be. The warehouses near Clark Street, over by the docks, were always hiring. He started down the street toward the livery where he'd left his horse and buggy.

Ahead, two young women stepped out of a department store, arms full of packages. But Jimmy's attention fell upon only one. Golden blond hair, topped with a tiny blue-feathered hat, fanned out across the collar of her blue wool coat.

As she reached him, a parcel fell from her arms.

Jimmy picked it up and held it out to her as though presenting a gift to a queen.

Lovely blue eyes sparkled at him as her lips curved into a pouty smile. "Thank you, sir." Her musical words rippled through him and he caught his breath. She passed by, before he could think of a word to say, and continued down the sidewalk.

Jimmy turned and stared after the vision, hardly aware of her companion. He'd never seen such a beautiful girl.

The angry voice of a man shoving by him jerked Jimmy back to attention. Shaking himself, he laughed and continued down the street to the livery.

Jimmy, you idiot. She's just a girl.

Turning the corner, he stopped at the stable and got his horse and buggy then crossed the bridge and left them at a nearby livery. If he got a job in the area, he'd ride the streetcar to work. It was time he got around like the rest of the working class. He headed down the dirt street beside the Chicago River. Clumps of floating ice didn't stop the barges lined up at the dock, loading and unloading their goods.

Jimmy looked around, and a wave of nausea hit him as memories of his childhood came flooding back. He could easily find his way to the house where he'd first met Sutton, the man who'd held him and his sister captive for eight years, convincing them he was looking out for them.

Resisting a sudden urge to run, Jimmy forced himself to continue down the street to the warehouses. A little girl in a threadbare coat ran by, laughing. Her mane of blond curls caused him to think of the beauty he'd helped earlier that day. He wondered if he'd ever see her again. Probably not. There were a lot of people in Chicago. So how could he expect to see those gorgeous eyes and tantalizing lips again? He grinned and headed toward the nearest warehouse.

☙

Cici sat beside Helen on the slatted seat of the streetcar and cast a sideways glance at her friend, who shook her head and grinned.

"What?" Cici looked at her with wide-eyed innocence.

"What indeed." Helen shook her head again. "That was bold, my friend."

Cici laughed. "Okay. I dropped it on purpose. But how else was I to get his attention?"

"How?" Helen hooted with laughter. "Since when have you needed to try to get a man's attention? You already have all the young men of our acquaintance smitten. Leave a few for the rest of us, dear."

"Oh, don't be modest. Eddy Wright doesn't know I'm around when you're in the room."

"Okay, so one young man is impervious to your charm." Helen blushed. "Eddy is rather special. I'm glad he notices me."

Cici sighed. "I wonder if I'll ever see him again."

"Who? Eddy?" Helen looked at her in surprise. "You see him every Sunday at church."

"No, silly. I mean *him*. The man who picked up my package."

"Hmm. It looks like the tables were turned this time. So he got your attention, too." Helen nodded. "Serves you right."

Cici giggled softly. "He *was* handsome though. Did you notice those dark brown eyes?"

The girls chattered until they reached Cici's stop then said good-bye.

Cici walked the half block to the parsonage, struggling to hang on to her packages. Why in the world hadn't she taken a cab? She wrestled the packages through the front door, letting the screen door slam behind her.

"Is that you, Cici, dear?" Her mother's voice seemed to sing the words.

"Yes, Mama." Cici dropped the packages on the rug in the parlor and flopped down on the sofa, breathing hard.

"Goodness, you had your arms full." Caroline Willow came through the door from the kitchen, drying her hands on a dishcloth. "You didn't take the streetcar, did you?"

"Yes, I don't know what I was thinking."

"Well, get out of your coat and go change clothes. I'll make you a hot cup of tea. We have to bake for the Community Bazaar."

"All right. Just let me get my breath a minute."

"I don't know how you stand to ride those noisy streetcars. The one time I tried it, I felt absolutely nauseous."

After she'd changed and returned to the kitchen, Cici stood for a moment and watched her mother cutting sugar cookies. "Mama, don't you ever wish your life was more exciting?"

Mama chuckled. "I think it's exciting enough. We have to bake a dozen pies and six dozen cookies." She opened the oven door and put the pan of cookies inside.

"But that's not what I mean, Mama." Cici realized her voice had taken on a hint of exasperation, and she softened her tone. "Baking and cleaning and ironing. Don't you get sick of it sometimes?"

Her mother turned and gave her a puzzled look. "No, dear. I never get sick of it. Tired, sometimes, but I wouldn't trade my life for anything."

"Well, I want more out of *my* life." Cici gave a small stamp of her foot on the floor. Then realizing what she'd done, she reached over and put her arm around her mother's shoulders. "I'm sorry, Mama."

Mama smoothed Cici's hair back off her forehead. A small frown appeared on the older woman's face. "Cecilia," she said softly, "I don't know why God gave you such an adventurous spirit, but you can be sure He wants to use it for His glory. Wait on Him. Don't do anything rash. You aren't a little child anymore. You're a young lady of eighteen."

Cici leaned into her mother's hand and smiled. "My escapades gave you a lot of grief, didn't they, Mama?"

"You've never given me grief." Her mother spoke tenderly. "Worry maybe, but not grief."

Cici giggled. "Remember the time I turned Mrs. Gardner's chickens loose?"

"I think that's best forgotten, my dear, as well as the time you decided to whitewash Mr. Taylor's milk cow."

"He was so angry. But not nearly as angry as Mrs. Potts was when I put the garter snake in her desk drawer."

"That was very naughty, and the school almost lost a teacher over it. Which is what I meant when I said you should wait on Him. He can fulfill your need for adventure without your bringing grief to others."

"I thought you said I've never brought you grief." Cici's eyes danced.

"Well, you haven't. But you certainly brought grief to a lot of others."

"Papa might say I bring him grief."

"Grief? What have you been up to now, Cecilia?"

Cici glanced up as her father walked into the kitchen. "Not a thing, Papa." Cici stood on tiptoe and gave her father a kiss on the cheek.

"How is Mrs. Appleby, George?" Mama took Papa's coat and laid it on a kitchen chair.

"Not too well, I'm afraid." Rev. Willow kissed his wife on the forehead. "The doctor isn't sure she'll make it through the night."

"I'm so sorry, dear." She patted her husband on the cheek. "But at least we know where she's going. She's served the Lord faithfully for many years. I think she wants to go on to a better life."

Grabbing the last of the batch of dough, Cici rolled out a pie shell and placed it into a pan. As she mixed dough for another batch, she tuned her parents out and let her mind wander back to her morning. She smiled as she thought of the young man on the sidewalk. A lock of dark brown hair had fallen across his forehead as he bent to retrieve her package. But it was the look in his dark eyes that had piqued her curiosity. Excitement. Or perhaps anticipation of something about to happen. She wondered if she'd ever see him again.

Chapter 2

Jimmy grunted as he lifted his end of a gigantic crate and swung it over to rest on top of another.

"Whew." Eddy Wright wiped his forehead with a sleeve and grinned at Jimmy. "You're getting broken in the hard way today."

Bending over and resting his hands on his knees, Jimmy took a deep breath. "What's in these crates anyway?"

"I've no idea. Our job is to move them, not to look inside." Eddy moved to the next crate, motioning for Jimmy to pick up the other end.

The first few days on the job had been fairly easy, but the night before, this new shipment had come in. Jimmy had a new respect for the men who worked here day and night, practically all their lives.

After they had deposited the crate in its new location, they headed for their lunch break.

"Come on. Let's go watch the boats unload while we eat." Eddy grabbed his lunch bucket and Jimmy followed suit. His new friend, whose cheerful conversation had made the morning easier to handle, had stirred Jimmy's curiosity. Obviously no stranger to this sort of work, or to the neighborhood, he spoke in a way that proved him to be educated and well mannered.

A twinge of sadness hit Jimmy as he sat on an upended barrel and ate his lunch. The docks brought bad memories from his childhood, but he had earlier memories from before his mother died. Good memories of walks by the river and a soft hand holding on to his. Or were they really memories? Perhaps they were merely desires buried deep in his heart. He'd been so young. He should probably ask Danni. But he'd rather hang on to the memories, real or not.

A group of children ran up to Eddy, chattering and laughing. He laid his sandwich aside and gave all his attention to them. At one boy's joke, he threw back his head and roared with laughter. He opened his lunch bucket and looked inside. "Hmm, what's this in my lunch pail, I wonder." Reaching inside, he pulled out a paper parcel, which proved to contain cheese and sausages. He passed them out to the children, who bowed their heads and waited until Eddy had said grace.

Jimmy watched the children as they ate, thanked Eddy, and then ran off to play. "Do you do this often?" he asked.

"I try to at least twice a week. They're hungry, you know."

"Yes. . ." Jimmy felt his voice break. "I do know."

Eddy looked at him, curiosity on his face.

"My sister and I were orphaned when we were very young. I remember the pangs of hunger quite well."

"I'm sorry to hear that."

The old wounds had healed long ago, but the sincerity in Eddy's voice was like ointment flowing over the scar tissue that still ached at times. "Thank you. It was long ago, and we're fine now. We were luckier than most." With a rueful shake of his head, he added, "No one ever gave us lunch though. Not willingly, at least. Why do you do this?"

Eddy smiled. "God told me to."

"Oh." He gave a little laugh. "Now you sound like my sister, Danni. She says God talks to her, too."

"Do you attend church?"

"Yes, I go with my sister and her husband. Why?"

"What sort of minister do you have there?"

"Oh, the usual sort, I suppose." Now why would Eddy ask that? "You know, he talks about God, like he should."

Eddy chuckled. "That's good."

"Why do you ask?"

"Oh, I thought you might like to try mine some Sunday. It's a great church and you'd be welcome."

"What's so great about it?" After all, a church was a church.

Eddy smiled. "For one thing, our minister, Reverend Willow, is a godly man who loves to share life-changing sermons. Also," he said with a grin, "a lot of pretty girls attend."

Jimmy nodded solemnly. "Uh-huh. I see. Well, I might just have to try it out. . .for the sermons, of course."

The following Sunday found Jimmy seated next to Eddy in the small stone church. He'd been introduced to the reverend and several others, but so far no girls.

Just as Rev. Willow took the podium, Jimmy heard a scurrying and a young woman hurried down the aisle and sat in the second pew. His stomach lurched at the sight of golden blond curls.

Come on, Jimmy, what are the chances? There are probably hundreds of girls with hair just that shade.

Jimmy tried to focus on the hymn they were singing, and by the time the sermon started, he'd convinced himself the young woman in the second pew couldn't possibly be the girl he had dreamed about for the past week and a half.

Eddy was right about Rev. Willow. Jimmy didn't remember any sermon touching his soul this way before.

After the service, Jimmy glanced at the young woman as she stood and turned. His breath caught in his throat. He reached over and grabbed Eddy's sleeve, tugging frantically.

"What?" Eddy pulled his sleeve out of Jimmy's grasp.

"Do you know that girl?" Jimmy whispered.

Eddy glanced over and grinned. "Sure, I know her. Why?"

"Will you introduce us?"

"I might, for a price." He was enjoying this too much.

"Name it."

"Hey, I was only kidding. Come on."

Eddy led the way through the departing church members to where she stood.

As they approached, she smiled at Eddy. "Hi, Eddy. If you're looking for Helen, she's home with a cold." She glanced briefly in Jimmy's direction then lowered her eyes, her long lashes fluttering against her cheeks.

"I know." He threw a sideways glance at Jimmy. "Actually, I came to say hello to you and to introduce you to my friend, Jimmy Grayson."

She lifted her glance to Jimmy, her lips curving in an adorable little smile, and held out her hand. "Hello, my name is Cici. I'm happy you came to our service today."

Jimmy stared into her eyes as he held the soft, gloved hand in his. He hadn't been dreaming. She really was the most beautiful woman he'd ever seen.

"Not as happy as I am." Hardly knowing what he was doing, he lifted her hand and placed a soft kiss on the gloved fingers, then lifted his eyes and looked into hers.

A blush colored her cheeks and her lips turned up in a slightly shocked smile. "A chivalrous deed," she said. "A trifle bold, perhaps, but I think I liked it."

"Forgive me. I couldn't restrain myself."

"Well, we'd better go. Good-bye, Cici." Eddy grabbed Jimmy's arm and practically dragged him away.

Jimmy followed as though in a daze. Had he actually kissed her hand? "Why did we have to leave so fast?" he objected as they walked down the street.

"For your own protection."

"What?"

"If I'd known she was going to have that effect on you, I'd never have introduced you." He gave Jimmy a pitying look.

"What are you talking about, you idiot?"

"Cici is Reverend Willow's daughter, and she devours love-smitten fellows like you. One minute she's all sweet and girly; then the next she's giving a fellow a tongue-lashing. Sort of like sugar and spice, you know?"

ॐ

Helen sat straight up on her bed, then moaned and leaned back onto her pillows. "Are you kidding me?" She coughed. "It was the same man?"

Cici nodded. "The very same."

Helen's eyes widened and she grabbed a hanky from her bedside table and sneezed loudly.

"Goodness, maybe I'd better leave so you can rest."

"No, don't you dare. Tell me everything. Do you mean to say he kissed your hand, right there in church, with everyone looking on?"

"Mm-hmm," Cici said in a dreamy voice. "Well, not everyone. Nearly everyone had left, but I think Papa may have seen."

"Oh no. Did he say anything?" Helen's red-rimmed eyes rounded with excitement.

"Not yet." A niggling of worry bit at Cici's mind, but she pushed it away. "Anyway, what could he say? It wasn't my fault Jimmy kissed me."

"Kissed your hand," Helen corrected.

"But it seemed like more." Cici closed her eyes and could almost feel the touch of Jimmy's lips on her hand. She shivered.

"Watch out, Cici." Helen's lips tilted. "I think you've finally fallen for someone."

Cici opened her eyes and sat up. "Oh, it was just the novelty of it all. It was rather romantic though. I wonder if he'll be back."

"I'm going to ask Eddy about him." Helen gave a short but emphatic nod then grabbed another handkerchief and dabbed at her nose. "After all, you don't know the man at all."

"I know. But I don't think Eddy would be friends with someone who wasn't all right. Do you?"

"Well, no, but. . ."

Cici rose and bent to kiss her friend on the forehead. "You take care of that cold. I have to go now. I'm almost late for my appointment at Milady's Coiffure."

Helen sighed, a dreamy look on her face. "You're so lucky. I'd die to have my hair done there."

"Well, perhaps when you turn eighteen next month, your parents will allow it. Like mine did." She grinned. "I think it's their way of turning me from a tomboy to a lady. But I really, really must go. I'll drop by again tomorrow."

"Promise?"

"Promise." Cici gave a little wave and left.

Twenty minutes later, she sat in the chair at Milady's, her hair in tangled knots.

"The things we go through to be beautiful."

Cici turned, curious to see who'd spoken the laughing words. The girl in the next chair appeared to be a little older than Cici. Short brown hair framed a heart-shaped face. Lips pursed in a pretty pout were a little too pink to be natural. Not wishing to appear rude, Cici forced her glance away from the lips and met a pair of gold-flecked green eyes filled with amusement.

"Are you shocked because my lips are painted?"

Cici felt her face grow warm. "I really hadn't noticed," she lied.

The girl chuckled. "All righty, then." She leaned over and held out her hand.

"My name is Gail. And you are?"

Cici took the girl's hand. "Cici."

"Well, Cici, lipstick is growing quite popular. Almost everyone uses it now. You should try it."

A little bolt of excitement ran through Cici. To be honest, she'd wanted to try painting her face to see how she would look. "I wouldn't dare," she whispered.

"Why not?" Gail gave her the once-over. "You're quite attractive, but makeup would make you look even better."

"Do you think so?" Cici asked.

"Absolutely. You're very pretty, but with a little lipstick and mascara, you could look like a movie star."

"Oh, I would never use mascara." The very thought seemed daring yet exciting.

"Well, here, then. Let's try a little color on your lips." Gail slipped off her chair and produced a small cylinder. "Here, pucker your lips like you are about to be kissed."

Unable to resist, Cici closed her eyes and did as directed. Something smooth and moist glided across her lips.

"Now press them together to even it out and see what you think."

Her heart in her throat, Cici opened her eyes and looked in the mirror. Her eyes widened. Gail was right. The lipstick did make her look prettier.

"Well, what do you think? Shall we take it off?" Gail held up tissue.

Cici bit her lip, indecision battling inside her. She couldn't really wear it in public. Could she? "No." Cici held up her hand. "Don't remove it. Thank you very much."

"My pleasure." The girl grinned and sat back on her chair.

Cici took a closer look at her new acquaintance. Actually, Gail seemed quite nice, in spite of her painted face.

Gail chatted endlessly for the next hour and a half while the girls had their hair dressed and nails done. Gail was finished first but continued to chatter to Cici until she, too, was ready to go. By the time they left the salon together, Cici was totally enthralled with her new friend. They agreed to meet somewhere for lunch sometime soon.

"Here." Gail quickly scribbled on a piece of paper and handed it to Cici. "This is my landlady's phone number. I live upstairs. Just ask for me."

Excitement bubbled in Cici as she rode home. She'd never met anyone as intriguing as Gail. A twinge of guilt pinched at her as she thought of Helen, who Cici was sure wouldn't approve of Gail. But she didn't have to know. Cici ignored the second twinge.

As she neared her stop, she grabbed a handkerchief from her pocket and scrubbed, then reached into her handbag and removed a small mirror. Good, there was no sign of the lipstick, but her mouth was red from the scrubbing. She replaced the mirror and stuffed the hankie deep into her handbag, then pulled the bell cord.

She walked the half block home, and as she slipped through the door, her lips curved. What would that daring Jimmy Grayson think of painted lips?

Chapter 3

Jimmy lifted a heavy crate and stacked it with others intended for the same warehouse. He was glad he'd hired on to work on the docks until noon today. He loved it out here in the open, even with a cold March breeze from the river whipping around his collar. Maybe he should try to find permanent employment here instead of at the warehouse. A steam whistle blew and another boat pulled up.

What was it about this place that kept drawing him back? Children dodged and chased each other as they played on the crowded street. Every now and then, one would get too near the dock and a worker would run him or her off.

Jimmy was getting ready to leave when he saw a small boy being chased off by a stocky laborer who yelled at him to stay away. Something clicked in Jimmy's mind, and he took a closer look at the man. His stomach knotted as though someone had punched him. It was Cobb. The one who'd led Jimmy and Danni to Sutton that cold day so many years ago. Cobb had been a mere boy himself at the time, maybe twelve. By the time Jimmy and his sister were rescued, he must have been twenty or so. He had always been friendly to them, but still, Jimmy felt his heart chill. He turned to leave.

"Hey! Jimbo! Is that you?"

Jimmy groaned and turned to face the man who was sprinting toward him.

Cobb didn't look much different than he did when he was hauled off by the police eight years ago. Cobb grabbed him in a bear hug. "It is you. I can't believe it." He smacked Jimmy on the arm and laughed. "How've you been, kid? How's Danni?"

Jimmy swallowed and attempted a friendly smile. "I'm fine, and Danni's doing well. How about you?"

"Great, just great. I keep busy." He shook his head, grinning widely.

"So how long have you been working here?"

"A couple of years, I guess. Mostly I work in the galley on the *Eastland*. When we're docked, I work here to keep busy."

"They actually pay you to cook?" Jimmy laughed. He could still remember some of Cobb's concoctions; they were pretty bad.

"Yeah, I finally learned you don't add salt to corned beef and you don't put molasses in mashed potatoes." He guffawed.

Jimmy couldn't help grinning back at the friendly face. Why had he even tried to avoid Cobb? After all, he'd been as much a victim of Sutton's as Jimmy and Danni had. And he hadn't gotten off the way they had. He'd served time in prison.

Impulsively, he threw his arm around Cobb's shoulder. "Come on, let's go to lunch somewhere."

"Perfect timing. I just finished loading the *Swallow*. Let me get my stuff." Cobb walked away and was back in five minutes.

They headed down Michigan Avenue, with Cobb continuing to pound Jimmy on the back. "I've missed you, Jimbo. Didn't think I'd ever see you again."

"Yeah, I know. Here, how about this place?"

They entered the diner and found it packed, but they managed to get a table toward the back.

After they had ordered, Cobb glanced at Jimmy, curiosity in his eyes. "So how about you, Jimmy? You working by the docks, too?"

"Yeah, I'm at Henderson's Warehouse."

"Yeah? I worked there a couple of times. Not a bad place. A little surprised to see you there, though. You were always daydreaming. Once that lawyer fellow took you in, I figured you'd get educated."

Jimmy hesitated. "Yes, I went to school. Then college. I'm actually taking a semester off from law school."

Cobb stiffened. "So why are you working as a laborer? Seeing how the lower class lives?"

"That's a dumb thing to say, Cobb," Jimmy retorted. "I grew up here, too, you know."

"Okay, okay. Sorry."

"I took time off to do some soul-searching. I'm just not sure I'm supposed to be a lawyer." He stared at the cup as he stirred sugar into his coffee. "I feel like there's something else I'm supposed to be doing."

Cobb looked puzzled. "Guess I just always figured I'm supposed to do what I have to to get by."

Jimmy nodded, not answering.

"Hey, Jimbo, I noticed you weren't limping. What happened?"

Jimmy hardly remembered anymore that he'd once had a lame foot. "I had an operation. The doctor said if I'd waited much longer, he wouldn't have been able to do much." He took a drink of his coffee. "I still favor it a little when I'm overtired."

"That's great. I thought it might get worse as you grew. Sure glad they could fix it."

Jimmy listened with interest as Cobb regaled him with stories of his adventures at sea. He had a feeling his former friend might be stretching the truth part of the time.

The *Eastland* was leaving the next day for a two-week cruise. They agreed to get together when Cobb returned.

Jimmy took the streetcar home to find a frantic Danni, her auburn curls escaping from the pins that held them back.

"You didn't forget we're having the Kramers and the Robertses over to dinner tonight, did you?"

Jimmy had forgotten, and Danni could read him like a book. As he looked at her frowning face, he grinned. "What can I do to help?"

He spent the rest of the afternoon picking up last-minute items for the dinner and helping Danni with cleaning. As he worked, he thought of the afternoon with Cobb. Should he tell Danni about it?

"Jimmy"—Danni touched his arm—"I have something to tell you. I want you to be one of the first to know."

"What is it?" She'd probably bought something new for the house. She knew she could count on him to praise anything she did around the place.

"Brother, you're going to be an uncle."

Jimmy's mouth fell open and he laughed in delight. He knew his sister had longed for a child. He gave her a gentle hug. "Danni, that's wonderful news. When?"

"Around the first of October." She beamed.

Jimmy felt a tug of emotion at the joy on her face. "You'll be the best mother in the world." And he'd definitely not tell her about Cobb.

"Are you going to services with Blake and me tomorrow," she asked, "or to your friend Eddy's church?"

Jimmy hesitated. And suddenly the adorable face flooded his memories. He'd attended a couple of services with Eddy but had only seen Cici from across the sanctuary. Perhaps that was for the best. He'd tried not to think about her. His future was too up in the air right now to get involved anyway. Maybe he should go with Danni and Blake. But he had promised Rev. Willow he'd be there for the monthly church dinner. "Uh. . .no, I. . .sort of committed to go to Eddy's church tomorrow."

ೞ

"Is he here?" Cici whispered to Helen. She wasn't about to turn and look, but she was dying to know if Jimmy was here. It had been five weeks since his first visit and he'd only been back twice. But her father had invited Jimmy to the church dinner after today's service, and he had promised to come.

"He's coming in now, with Eddy," Helen whispered. "Oh. They sat down two rows behind us."

"Well, turn around. Don't let him see you looking," Cici whispered fiercely. It wouldn't do to let him think she was watching for him.

Helen giggled and Cici swatted her arm. She didn't know why she was so attracted to Jimmy. He wasn't all that special. Well, he did have those gorgeous big brown eyes. But there was something about him that had caught her attention from the beginning.

She forced herself not to turn around but to focus on her father who was taking his place on the platform. Papa looked quite handsome today, she thought. His dark blue suit was perfectly pressed and his mustache waxed to perfection. He was starting to turn gray at the temples, but Cici thought that made him look very distinguished. She felt a little knot of pride for her father as he smiled and opened his Bible.

She tried to focus on the sermon, but she was too aware of Jimmy two rows behind her. Determined not to let her mind dwell on the handsome young man or the tantalizing kiss he had planted on her hand, she steered her thoughts to her new friend, Gail. Cici had called her a few days before and they'd agreed to meet a week from Tuesday for lunch. She wondered if she dared take the tube of lipstick she'd purchased and hidden in a bureau drawer in a pair of rolled-up stockings. She could apply it after she got on the streetcar. She pushed aside the twinge of guilt and forced herself to listen to her father's sermon. But her thoughts wandered again and again until the congregation stood for a final hymn and then her father closed in prayer.

Picking up her Bible, Cici stepped into the aisle. She and Helen headed for the basement to help set the tables and get the food ready to serve. She used to love church dinners, but for the past couple of years she'd found them boring. Today, however, she felt an excitement she hadn't felt about a church event in a long time.

She'd just served Mr. Gladstone a double portion of mashed potatoes, when out of the corner of her eye she observed Jimmy and Eddy walk in. When they came through the line, she found her hands were trembling.

Jimmy stopped in front of her. "Hi, Cici."

"Oh. Hello, Jimmy. It's nice to see you again." She hoped her voice didn't sound as nervous to him as it did to her own ears.

"It's very nice to see you again, too."

Hmm. He sounded nervous, too. And something else. Was it possible he'd lost interest? Or had she only thought he was interested? Perhaps she should be aloof. It wouldn't do for him to think she cared if he didn't.

"Hi, Helen, Cici. Would you girls join us for lunch?" Eddy asked with a grin.

Helen smiled and nodded. "Thank you. That would be lovely. We'll just be a few more minutes."

Jimmy's eyes found Cici's. He smiled but still had that nervous look on his face. "Is that all right with you, Miss Willow?"

"Yes, I suppose so." She and Helen finished serving then filled their own plates and joined Jimmy and Eddy. She was glad to find that after a few moments with Jimmy, her nervousness disappeared. He seemed to relax also.

After a while, Eddy and Helen wandered off. Cici grew suddenly tongue-tied and groped around for something to say. "What do you think of our little church?"

"I like it a lot. I find Reverend Willow's sermons very inspiring." He glanced across the room to where her parents were visiting with some other couples. She noticed respect in his eyes as he looked at her father.

But she certainly didn't intend to spend the afternoon talking about her father's sermons. "Tell me, Jimmy, what sort of work do you do?"

He hesitated and a trapped look crossed his face; then he relaxed. "To be honest, I'm trying my hand at several things. I work at the warehouse with Eddy through the week. Yesterday I worked on the docks."

"Really? How exciting. My parents won't allow me to go near that district."

"That's probably wise of them. It's no place for a young lady to go alone."

"Tell me about it. What goes on down there?"

"It's usually teeming with people. From passengers boarding steamboats to dockworkers." He smiled. "Children everywhere, and of course there are warehouses and other buildings all along the river. You weren't too far from there the first time I saw you."

"I know, but I was only shopping. Please, tell me more."

She listened, uncomfortable, as Jimmy told her about the poverty of the people who lived in the area.

When Helen and Eddy rejoined them, Cici welcomed them eagerly. She didn't want to hear about poor people. She wanted to hear about adventure and excitement.

The afternoon sped by, and before they knew it, the party was breaking up.

Cici had cornered her parents shortly before and received permission to invite Helen and the boys to dinner the following Sunday.

They all accepted and the boys left, while Cici and Helen helped clean up.

When Cici went to her room that night, she felt happy and eager to see Jimmy again. As she got her night things out, she saw the stockings with the lipstick and suddenly she wasn't sure about her new friendship with Gail. Well, she was going to lunch with her soon. She'd see how she felt about it then. And there really wasn't anything wrong with a little lipstick, was there?

But her conscience answered, *What about deceiving your parents and friends?*

Chapter 4

Commit thy works unto the Lord, and thy thoughts shall be established.' " Jimmy inhaled sharply, the softly spoken words penetrating his mind and heart like a knife. Did Rev. Willow know about the confusion in his head? But how could he? He hadn't spoken of it to anyone but Blake and Cobb.

"How many times have we skimmed over these words, scarcely noticing them? Do we remember this scripture when we make decisions in our daily lives? Do we even know what the words mean?"

Jimmy leaned forward, eagerness tightening his chest and throat.

"It is really quite simple." Rev. Willow cleared his throat. "It means exactly what it says. Is there an important decision you have to make? Whom to marry. Which house to buy. A career choice."

Yes, yes. But how did he know?

"In these decisions, we must get down on our knees. Discuss the situation with our heavenly Father. Give it to Him. Ask Him what His plan is in the situation. According to God's Word, if we do this, our thoughts shall be established. We will know what to do."

Jimmy frowned and crossed his arms. Was it really that simple? Danni prayed a lot. And Blake always said a blessing over meals. But Jimmy had never really given God much thought other than attending church on Sunday mornings. He wasn't sure he knew how to go about discussing things with God. Maybe he'd get a chance to ask the reverend about it after dinner. He was glad he and Eddy had been invited.

The service over, Jimmy rose. Cici and her friend stood in the aisle by his pew. Startled, he realized he hadn't thought about her during the service even once. Now, as she turned her glance in his direction, he was once more mesmerized by her loveliness.

"Let's go, Jimmy." Eddy shoved him from behind and they moved out into the aisle.

"We may as well walk to the parsonage together, right?" Eddy flashed a grin at the girls.

"Of course." Cici smiled and waited.

"Oh, forgive me." Heat rose in Jimmy's face as he realized the girls were waiting to be escorted. He offered his arm, and Cici slipped her hand inside the crook of his elbow.

The walk to the house next door was much too fast. They stepped inside, and Jimmy felt a twinge of disappointment as Cici removed her hand from his arm.

The girls removed their wraps and went to help Mrs. Willow.

"Come." Rev. Willow motioned toward the chairs by the fireplace. "We might as well visit while we wait."

Supposing this might be the time he could ask the minister about the morning's scripture, Jimmy was a little disappointed when the minister began to regale them with stories from his last hunting trip, then proceeded to tell a joke he'd recently heard. Soon Jimmy found himself roaring with laughter, along with Eddy. Then Cici announced that dinner was served.

They sat down at the food-laden dining table, and Rev. Willow stretched his hands out to his wife and daughter, who sat on each side of him. Jimmy, seated next to Cici, took her extended hand as her father blessed the food.

Although he'd expected the dinner conversation to reflect the morning's sermon, the room rang with laughter. Apparently he had a lot to learn about preachers and their families.

After dinner, Rev. Willow invited Eddy and Jimmy to his library. Leather- and cloth-bound volumes lined two walls. Their host walked over to a book-lined shelf.

Jimmy followed. He scanned the titles, but nothing seemed familiar.

"Ah, those are all books on theology." The reverend ran his hand along the spines in an almost caressing manner. He turned and motioned to the book-laden wall across from them. "Those might be more to your liking."

The two younger men followed him across the room.

"*The Three Musketeers*." Eddy laughed and slipped the book from the shelf. "This was my favorite when I was a lad."

Jimmy found many old friends in the collection, but his eyes kept going back to the shelves on the other wall. He felt drawn to the books and had no idea why. He glanced over and found Rev. Willow studying him with a curious expression on his face.

"Are you interested in theology, Jimmy?" The older man lowered himself into an overstuffed chair and motioned the boys to the sofa across from him.

"I really know very little about it, sir." Jimmy hoped he didn't sound as ignorant as he felt.

"Most people don't. They prefer to leave that to their ministers. But there's a world of wealth in those old tomes. Anytime you would like to borrow one, please feel free to do so."

Excitement gripped Jimmy. "Thank you. That's very generous."

"Nonsense. My offer is purely selfish. I seldom have anyone with whom to discuss my books. It would be a rare treat." He smiled and waved toward the door. "I'm sure the ladies have finished cleaning the kitchen. Cici and Helen won't be happy with me if I keep you here any longer."

Jimmy and Eddy thanked their host and joined the girls. Jimmy hoped to have

SUGAR AND SPICE

a few moments of private conversation with Cici, but after a rousing game of croquet, Helen suggested they play checkers. Before they knew it, Mrs. Willow entered the dining room with a platter of sandwiches and fruit. They ate and then headed back to the church for the evening service.

Afterward, Jimmy managed to speak to Cici on the front step of the church. "I enjoyed the day, Cici. You have a wonderful family. Thanks for your hospitality."

A pretty pink blush appeared on her cheeks. "It was my pleasure. Thank you for coming."

"Do you think. . . ?" He cleared his throat. "That is, perhaps I can return the hospitality someday soon and you could have dinner at my sister's home."

"Perhaps." A dimple appeared at one corner of her lips. "I'd have to get permission from my parents."

"Of course."

She offered her hand. He took it and then wasn't quite sure what to do with it. Finally, he gave it a slight shake, bowed, and left.

"You dunce," he berated himself. "She probably expected you to kiss her hand like you did before."

"Hey, Jimmy, wait a minute." Eddy huffed after him, his cheeks red from puffing. "Well," he panted, "seems you decided to ignore my warning about Cici."

Jimmy glared. "I don't know why you don't like her. She's perfectly delightful, and your description of a siren doesn't fit her at all."

Eddy threw his hands in the air. "Okay, buddy. Sorry I said anything. I wish you well."

They headed for the streetcar, where they said good-bye, since they were going in different directions.

Jimmy rode to the elevated train station. On the way home, his mind kept jumping from Cici to the morning sermon. The chance to talk to Rev. Willow about the scripture hadn't arisen, but he determined to speak to the minister about it the first chance he got.

ᛒ

Cici sat on the seat of the wobbling streetcar, her back rigid. She'd told her mother she was going to lunch with a friend and rushed out of the house before she could ask for more information. A niggling thought worried her mind. She'd never felt the need to be evasive about her friends before. But somehow she knew her parents wouldn't approve of Gail. Cici took a deep breath and shoved the thought away. After all, she wasn't a child. She was plenty old enough to choose her friends. And there was nothing wrong with Gail. Cici was sure of it.

The streetcar carried her to the downtown district, past department stores and salons. After a few blocks, she pulled the cord and got off. She glanced around, consternation rising in her. The neighborhood was rather rough looking. She bit her bottom lip and wondered if perhaps she should turn around and go home. A surge of fear shot through her, but with it came a thrill of excitement. Her eyes scanned the nearby buildings and came to rest on a sign that proclaimed Tony's Place.

She swallowed and ran her tongue over her dry lips. She'd never felt timid or fearful before and didn't intend to start now. She took a resolute step forward and walked down the street to the café. There, that wasn't so bad. She reached out for the doorknob, but a laughing couple shoved past her and opened the door.

Cici gave an indignant glare to the retreating couple, then stopped inside the door and glanced around. The room sparkled with bright lights, and a small orchestra played merry music in a rear corner. Her nose inhaled the smell of smoke and perfume mingled with the zesty aromas drifting from the kitchen.

"Cici, over here."

She turned.

Gail beckoned from a small round table.

With relief, Cici headed in her direction.

"Hey, I'm so glad you came. Put your coat on the extra chair. They never have enough coatracks here."

Flustered by the daring adventure and Gail's exuberance, Cici sat across from the laughing brunette.

A waitress came with menus and glasses of water.

Cici scanned the selections and the girls placed their orders.

"I wasn't sure you'd come." Gail tossed her a sideways grin.

"Why? I said I'd be here."

"I know. I just thought you might change your mind and back out."

"Well, I almost did when I saw the neighborhood." She glanced around nervously. "Are you sure we're safe here? It doesn't look quite respectable."

"Nonsense. Don't be a baby. Some very interesting people come here. You know. . .show business folks and such."

"Really?" Cici forgot her fears at this exciting news. "Have you ever met any?"

"Sure. All the time. Some of the cast of *The Scarlet Lady* hang around here a lot."

Cici gasped. "What's that? It doesn't sound nice."

"Sure it is. Upper class and all that."

"Well, if you say so." But dread tightened her chest.

"Gail sipped from her water glass. "You look very pretty today. I'm glad to see you painted those lips."

"Yes," Cici whispered, looking around. "Is it noticeable?"

"Of course. It's supposed to be noticed. Why else would you wear it?" She gave a little laugh.

Indignation flooded Cici. Was Gail mocking her?

"Oh dear. That was rude. I'm sorry, Cici. Sarcasm just seems to come naturally to me."

"It's all right. You weren't rude. I tend to be overly sensitive at times."

"Well then, good. We're still friends." Gail reached over and patted her hand.

Their food arrived and Cici bowed her head and said a silent prayer. She looked up and found Gail staring at her. "What's wrong?" Didn't Gail give thanks for her food?

"Nothing." Gail picked up her hamburger and took a large bite. "Mmm. Don't you love hamburgers?"

"They're all right, I guess." Cici bit a small corner off her ham sandwich and tried not to look at the grease on Gail's mouth. They chatted between bites. Finally, Cici pushed her plate back.

"How about some pie?" Gail looked around for the waitress.

"No, I couldn't eat another bite." She glanced at the watch at the end of her neck chain. "I should probably be going."

"Stay awhile longer. We've hardly had a chance to talk yet."

"Well, maybe a few minutes."

"Gail! Darling! How nice to see you." An older man had stepped to their table and stood smiling at Gail.

The girl flung her head back and looked up with a saucy grin. "Well, Sutton, it's been a long time. Where have you been keeping yourself?"

"I've been directing a show in Paris, my dear. I arrived home last week." He glanced at Cici. "And who is your charming companion?"

"Oh, forgive my bad manners. Cici Willow, I'd like to introduce you to James Sutton, an old family friend." She glanced back at Mr. Sutton. "Cici and I, on the other hand, met only recently, but I believe we're on our way to becoming best pals."

Cici blushed and offered her hand to the gentleman. He lifted it and let his lips linger on her fingers for a moment. Startled, Cici jerked her hand away, heart hammering.

His lips tipped in an amused smile. "Ah. Forgive my clumsiness, my dear. Your beauty quite overcame me for a moment."

"Won't you join us, Sutton?" Gail interrupted. "Tell us about the Paris show?"

"I would be delighted. That is, if your young friend has no objection." He turned his eyes on Cici. Deep, dark eyes that seemed to search her entire being.

What was it about him that fascinated her so? He was as old as her father. And the feelings he elicited in her were certainly not romantic. Yet she found herself wanting to stay in his presence. To hear his deep, soothing voice.

She cleared her throat. "No, I have no objection. I'd love to hear about the show, Mr. Sutton."

Chapter 5

B ut Danni, I love working on the docks and couldn't pass up the opening."
He stared down at his weeping sister, helpless at the unusual sight. "It'll
be all right."

She wiped her eyes and sniffled. "Jimmy, have you forgotten so soon? How
could you enjoy a place that is so wicked and cruel to children? Even before
Sutton got us in his clutches, don't you remember how we walked the streets till
we were exhausted, then hid on the wharf, cold and starving, even to the point
of my stealing someone else's lunch?"

Jimmy patted her shoulder, wondering how to explain. "I do remember, Danni.
But for some reason, I feel drawn to the area. I love the excitement of the harbor
and the ships that moor there."

"Oh, Jimmy."

"But it's not just that." He walked to the window and glanced out. Late afternoon shadows fell across the opulent green lawn. Like the shadows that had
reached out to him in his dreams, bringing him to his latest decision. Should he
open up to her? Mention the children whose hungry eyes haunted his dreams
and waking hours? Should he tell her of the cries of his heart to help them?
"There are the children."

She glanced up, a startled look in her eyes. "Is that what this is about? Have
you been helping the children?"

He returned and sat beside her on the settee. "Not much. I'm not sure what I
can do besides offer a bite of something now and then. Eddy is the one they flock
to. They're drawn to him like a bug to light, but he's only there for an hour and
sometimes he can't make it."

She bit her lip. "So it is the children."

"Not just the children. If you could see the hopeless looks on the faces of the
mothers. . ."

She laid her hand on his and looked into his eyes. "Please, Jimmy," she whispered,
"there are other ways to help these people. You know I'm part of a charitable foun-
dation to help the poor of the city. I'll try to get more people interested in helping
out around the wharf area. Go back to school. Don't throw your future away."

He groaned. "Maybe I'm losing my mind, turning my back on a career in the
Nelson firm. You and Blake must think I'm completely ungrateful, and I'm not.
It's just. . . I don't know, Danni. I'm sorry to make you cry. But I can't leave the
docks. At least not yet."

She turned, her face ashen, and walked from the room.

Jimmy hit his fist against the windowsill. *Idiot. Why'd you tell her? Of course she'll worry.*

He took a deep breath. At least he hadn't mentioned Cobb, who'd actually introduced him to the dock supervisor.

It had taken a few days to work out a system where he could help without compromising his job. He'd followed Eddy's lead and made sure he had extra food in his lunch pail, but most days, he gave it all away. He chuckled. Cook must wonder about the enormous quantities of food he stuffed into his lunch pail, as well as the amounts he consumed at breakfast and dinner.

He headed upstairs to get a book from his room. He had intended to join the family for dinner before going to Rev. Willow's for a Bible study, but under the circumstances, it might be best if he left early. Tonight they planned to discuss the topic of salvation by grace. Jimmy had accepted Jesus as his Savior when he was twelve, but in spite of the fact that Danni and Blake had a close relationship with God, Jimmy had never really studied the Bible for himself. The reverend had been teaching him the fundamentals of Christianity, and it had opened up a world of truth and light to him. He couldn't seem to get enough. He couldn't understand the insatiable hunger that seemed to drive him to more and more spiritual understanding; he could only follow it.

The fact that he was thrown more and more into Cici's presence was an added joy and benefit.

୧

"Cici, see who is at the door, please. I think Papa is expecting Mr. Grayson."

"Yes, Mother." Cici laid her book on the table by her chair and went to the door. Why hadn't Papa told her Jimmy was coming? She was supposed to meet Gail and some other friends at Tony's at seven.

"Hello, Jimmy." She opened the screen door and let him in.

"Cici. It's nice to see you." He cleared his throat. "It's such a wonderful evening, I was wondering if you'd like to go for a walk after the Bible study."

Now what should she do? Gail and her crazy gang of friends were so exciting. She couldn't remember when she'd had so much fun. But Jimmy, well, Jimmy made her heart go wild, just as it was doing right now. Why did he have to be so handsome? But she'd had handsome beaux before. So what was it that made Jimmy so special? "Thank you. That would be nice, if it's all right with Papa."

"Would you like for me to ask him?"

"If you'd like. I have to go out for a while, but I'll be back before your meeting is over."

She smiled as Jimmy went to join her father in the study. Of course. The Bible study would last a couple of hours. She could go to the café and be back before then. She breathed a sigh of relief and went into the parlor, where her mother was mending the lace on a collar. "I'll be back soon, Mother."

"Very well, dear. Tell Helen's mother hello for me."

"Yes, ma'am." Guilt tugged at her heart as she kissed her mother and headed for the door. But she hadn't said she was going to Helen's. Not tonight or the other times she'd gone out with Gail. So she hadn't lied. Cici stood at the corner and attempted to brush away the thoughts running through her head. Maybe she hadn't lied with words, but she was practicing deception. She breathed a sigh of relief as the streetcar came rumbling down the street.

The café was thick with smoke. She hadn't noticed it being this smoky before. She hoped it wouldn't cling to her hair and clothing.

"What's the matter, Cici girl? Why so glum?" Carl Foster, one of the young men in her new circle of friends, took her hand and began to lead her to the long table where the others waited.

"Don't sit down, you two." Gail jumped up. "We were just about to head over to the Blue Gardenia. You're just in time, Cici."

"Oh, but I can't stay long. Couldn't we remain here instead?" Cici had no idea how far away the Blue Gardenia was.

"There's no action here tonight. Besides, I promised Sutton we'd meet him there. He's recently returned from New York City."

Cici bit her lip. "But I have to be home by nine. I have another commitment."

"Don't worry about it. Someone will drive you."

"I would be honored to escort you home in my trusty flivver whenever you wish to go." Carl bowed, and as he lifted his head, Cici's nose twitched at the smell of alcohol.

"Flivver?"

Gail snorted. "He means his wreck of an automobile."

Carl frowned. "I resent that. And so does my flivver. And so do all the girls."

"Thank you, Mr. Foster, but I don't think so."

Gail and several others laughed. "Good choice, Cici. In another hour, he won't be able to drive anyway. Someone will take you home. Don't worry about it."

Cici allowed herself to be persuaded. After all, it would be rude to leave so soon. And besides, it would be nice to see the mysterious Mr. Sutton again.

When the party of six divided up between a carriage and Carl's automobile, Cici made sure not to end up in the latter. They rode several blocks, amid boisterous conversation, and pulled up in front of a brightly lit club. The front of the building sported a huge picture of a diamond and the name in large blue letters below.

A shiver of excitement offset the twinge of fear that ran through Cici as they pushed through the door of the club. She had accompanied them to restaurants that served liquor before and a few of them drank a little, but this was the first time she'd been inside an actual nightclub. Cloth-covered tables encircled an empty space where couples danced. The room was nearly dark, the only lights an occasional shaded oil lamp and a few low-burning gaslights spaced on the walls.

A waiter approached and led them to a table toward the rear of the room. As they neared a large round table, James Sutton rose and bowed, motioning them to chairs. Somehow when they were all seated, Cici found herself next to their host with Gail on his other side.

"The delightful Miss Cecilia Willow. How very nice to see you again." He leaned his head toward her and smiled. "I hope you've been well."

Cici swallowed. "Yes, I'm very well, thank you."

"I'm most happy to hear it, my dear." His voice rolled over her like silk, and she felt herself relax. What a nice man. And so charming.

Raucous music blared across the room. Cici started and put her hands to her ears.

"Hey, Cici, c'mon. Let's cut a rug." Carl had jumped up from his chair across the table and stood at her side, his hand extended to her.

"What?"

"Aw, honey, haven't you ever heard of ragtime?" He danced a few strange dance steps where he stood; then he grinned.

"I don't dance, Carl. You'll have to excuse me."

"Don't dance? Of course you do. Everyone dances." His words slurred, and Cici was thankful she wouldn't have to ride home with him.

"Miss Willow doesn't wish to dance, Carl." Sutton's voice was firm and his smile grim, and something in that smile, Cici wasn't sure what, passed between the two men.

"Oh, I see." Carl's face had turned ashen. "I mean, sure. That's fine. I'm sorry, Cici. That is, Miss Willow." He stumbled across to one of the other girls, and the two of them made their way to the dance floor.

Cici sat stunned, not sure what had just happened but glad Carl no longer bothered her.

Sutton turned to her with a smile, quite unlike the one he'd given Carl. "I'm sorry if he annoyed you with his attentions, my dear."

"Thank you. I don't think he meant any harm though."

"You may be right. The young man has had too much to drink." He smiled then turned to Gail. "Now to a more pleasant subject. I would like to extend an invitation to all you young people to accompany me down to my friend John Cowell's lake house for an evening of symphony and excellent dining."

Gail's eyes were bright. "Wonderful. Mr. Cowell always throws a great shindig."

"Yes, well, I think this will be a little more refined than a shindig." His expression had grown stern.

"Sorry. Of course, I meant to say soiree, not shindig." The girl's face flamed.

What was it about Sutton? He could be charming one moment and almost threatening the next. He patted Gail's hand. "Of course you did, my dear." He turned to Cici. "I would be very pleased if you would accompany us. That is, if you're free on Friday night of next week."

"Why, I don't know." Should she?

"We will take a passenger boat from the Clark Street dock, sail downriver, then across the lake to the Cowell mansion."

A mansion? Cici's heart hammered at the enticing idea. But would she dare?

"It's very kind of you to invite me, Mr. Sutton. I'll have to let you know." She stood. "I really must go now."

"Let me find someone to take you, Cici." Gail rose.

"No need for that." Sutton tossed a wad of bills on the table and rose. "I would be honored to drive you both home."

Cici was relieved when he drove her home first. He made no comment when she asked to be let off at the streetcar stop. She hurried down the street to her house and rushed upstairs to her room. She must shed these smoke-saturated clothes before anyone saw her.

☙

Jimmy offered his arm to Cici and they strolled down the sidewalk. The girl, who had been so quiet earlier, seemed fidgety. "Have I done or said something to offend you?"

"What? I mean, excuse me? What did you say?"

"You seem distracted. I thought perhaps I'd said something to offend you."

She peered up at him. "Oh no. I seem to have a slight headache. That's all."

"Oh. Forgive me." Jimmy stopped and turned to her. "Would you prefer to postpone our walk for another time?"

"No, I think perhaps the fresh air might help." She blushed and Jimmy's heart turned over. What a sweet, precious girl she was. They continued down the sidewalk.

"How is the work on the docks going? Do you still enjoy working there?"

"Yes, but it's difficult to see the poverty-stricken children." He frowned. "There's so much I want to do for them, and so little I can."

"You're very sweet, Jimmy, to want to help them." Her voice had softened. "But there are so many of them. What can one person do?"

"I don't know, Cici. But I have to try. My sister's charity group is going to help. So that's a start."

"Perhaps the church could help, too."

Jimmy looked at her in surprise. This was the first time she'd shown any interest in the conditions of the residents in the dock area. Encouraged, he talked as they strolled along, until finally they arrived back at the parsonage.

They stepped up on the porch and Jimmy glanced at the swing. "Could we sit on the swing for a while and talk?"

"Yes, I'd like that." Her eyes crinkled as she smiled.

Jimmy's heart flopped in his chest. Had there ever been a sweeter, prettier girl? Eddy must be crazy. He and his warnings. Probably jealous.

They leaned back. Would he dare take her hand? Better not.

"Oh, Jimmy, would you look at those stars? I don't think I've ever seen anything so bright and lovely. They about take my breath away." Her lips parted and her eyes widened in delight.

"I have." Uh-oh. He hadn't meant to say that aloud. But since he had, he might as well go ahead. "Your eyes are even brighter and lovelier."

He watched, captivated, as pink washed over her face. Her lips began to tilt and she straightened them, pressing them firmly together.

"I hope I haven't offended you, Cici."

She faced him, and this time her lips curved in a sweet smile. "Only if you didn't mean it."

A bubble of pleasure swelled his chest and he laughed. "I assure you I meant it."

"In that case, thank you very much." She rose and tossed him a saucy grin. "And now, I believe it's time for me to say good night."

He stood. "Must you?"

"Yes, I must. Good night, Jimmy." She slipped inside and the door shut softly behind her.

Jimmy stood for several moments, unable to stop the idiotic grin he knew was on his face. He walked to the streetcar stop, his heart light. What an evening. The Bible study had been enlightening and uplifting. And to top it off, a stroll around the block and a private conversation, albeit very short, with the sweetest girl in the world. And the most delightful "good night" he'd ever known.

Chapter 6

The dock teemed with activity. Almost as much as in the daylight hours. Stevedores yelled at each other in their haste to get cargo loaded and stacked. But most of the action came from passengers waiting to board the two huge ships hugging the harbor.

Jimmy stretched his aching back and wiped a sleeve across his forehead. In spite of the cold late-April wind blowing off the water, he'd worked up a river of perspiration. He'd been glad of the extra hours when Stephen had asked him to cover his shift. But fourteen hours of hauling heavy crates and boxes was taking its toll on him. He slipped his watch from his pocket. Eight o'clock. His shift wouldn't end till two. He sighed. He'd make it through.

"Hey, Jimbo. Here's the last one." Cobb hauled a heavy crate over the deck, and Jimmy grabbed one end. Together they maneuvered it down the stairs to the galley supply area and battened it down.

"Whew! What's in that one anyway?" They'd all been heavy, but that one was a doozy.

"Wine for miladies and gents." Cobb gave a mocking bow and laughed. "C'mon, let's go eat some supper."

They grabbed their tin pails from the dockworkers' shack and headed for a couple of upturned crates at the other side of the dock. Jimmy had learned, these last two weeks, that if he stayed too close to the loading area, his break was likely to be cut short by someone needing a hand.

Cobb opened his pail and retrieved a hunk of cheese and a piece of bread. "I don't get you, Jimbo."

"What do you mean?"

"Well, I know why I'm breaking my back with all the extra work I can get. But why are you down here at night when you could be having fun with your little clean-cut pals?"

"You don't think I need to earn money?" Ignoring the remark about his other friends, Jimmy pried the lid off his bucket and looked at Cobb.

"Not like I do, old boy." Cobb spoke around an enormous bite of cheese. "I mean, you live with Danni and that rich lawyer husband of hers. It ain't like you have to earn a living."

"Believe it or not, my friend, I don't wish to be dependent on my brother-in-law forever. I figure it's high time I start earning my own way."

"Prob'ly shoulda stayed in law school, then, buddy. You'd get there a lot faster."

Jimmy pulled a cloth-wrapped sandwich from his pail, his mouth watering at the smell of ham and cheese.

A faint cough drew his attention. Two small boys stood at the top of the steps leading up to the dock, their eyes wide, watching Cobb as he crammed another hunk of cheese in his mouth. The Daly boys, six-year-old Patrick and his little brother, Mike, who wasn't more than three. A little late for them to venture out.

Jimmy smiled and crooked his finger, motioning them over.

They grinned and broke out in a run, stopping in front of him.

"I wonder if you boys could help me out here." Jimmy pursed his lips and gave them a very serious look. "You see, my sister loaded my lunch bucket down with so much food I'll never be able to eat it. It'd be a shame to throw this good stuff away. But if I take it back home, she might think I don't like it."

Both boys nodded their heads, causing their filthy blond curls to bounce.

Jimmy shook his head. "I'd sure hate to hurt her feelings like that."

More nods. This time eager, hopeful nods.

"Do you think you could help me out here and eat some of it for me?"

"Yes, sir." Little Mike's excited voice tugged at Jimmy's heart.

Cobb snorted.

"Yeah, we wouldn't want your sister's feelin's to be hurt or anything." Patrick ran his tongue across his cracked lips.

Jimmy tore a sandwich in half and gave an exaggerated sigh of relief. "Well, I sure do thank you both. Here. See if you can take care of this for me."

Their red, chapped little fingers clutched at the food he handed them.

"Now, don't gobble it down too fast. I wouldn't want you to get a stomachache when you're only trying to help me out."

They took small bites and chewed slowly. Still, the sandwiches were gone all too soon. Jimmy reached inside his bucket and produced a banana. He divided it and handed the two pieces over to Patrick and Mike.

When they'd finished, he took some coins from his pocket and handed them to Patrick. "Would you take this to Bridget and tell her to buy food?"

"Yes, sir. Thank you, sir." Patrick crammed the coins into his pocket and grabbed Mike by the hand. They ran down the steps and toward the tenement-lined street.

Jimmy winced as he saw the soles of their shoes flopping loose against the dirt street.

"Okay. I take back everything I said. I see now where yer money's going." Cobb shook his head. "Jimbo, Jimbo. When are you gonna stop trying to save the world? Look out for yourself. That's what I always say."

"The boys are orphans. Their sister is raising them."

Cobb shrugged, took an apple out of his bucket, and wiped it on his dingy pant leg. "So what? Some kids don't have a sister to look out for them." He grinned. "Maybe it's the sister you're interested in?"

"Bridget is ten years old."

Cobb's hand stopped in midair, halfway to his mouth. He dropped his arm and stood. "Let's get back to work." He laid the apple on the box and headed toward the loading area.

Jimmy pushed the bucket lid down and got up. Halfway across the dock, he stopped still, his heart thumping fast. What was she. . .

Cici had just stepped on the gangplank of the *Lady Fair*. She seemed to be part of a group of several young people. A young man put his hand on her shoulder. She shrugged it off. The girl beside her leaned over and said something. Cici laughed and turned her head, her eyes staring straight into Jimmy's. She froze, her eyes rounding and her rosebud mouth dropping open.

Jimmy nodded.

She clamped her mouth shut and gave a little wave, then hurried up the gangplank after her companions.

Why was Cici boarding a tour boat this time of night? And who were the people she was with? They certainly weren't members of their church. Was she in some kind of trouble? Should he go after her? But she had seemed to know the young man and woman.

"Hey, Jimbo, you coming? We gotta load the *Monarch*." Cobb, waving both hands, stood on the deck of the cargo ship.

"Coming." He scanned the deck of the *Lady Fair* but saw no sign of Cici. He was more than likely making a mountain out of a molehill, as the saying went. Surely her parents wouldn't have allowed her to go off on a boat with people they didn't know and approve of. Laughing at his own imagination, he hurried up the *Monarch*'s gangplank.

CB

Silver tinkled against crystal, drawing Cici from her reverie. They had seated her next to Sutton who sat on the host's left. Gail sat across from her next to an older man who'd been introduced as Mr. Cowell's brother, William.

Cici smiled at the tall, thin waiter who had just placed a generous slice of chocolate cake, covered in some kind of sauce, in front of her. He nodded and stepped over to serve Carl.

When he moved away, Carl turned to her. "Hey, this is real Haviland china. Don'tcha think?"

Cici nodded and took a small bite of the rich concoction. What terrible luck that Jimmy had been working tonight. What must he think? She swallowed and took a deep breath. If her parents found out. . . Well, that simply could not happen. She must get to Jimmy and ask him not to say anything around them. She'd have to try to think up some reason. Her heart sank. Up to now, she'd managed to keep seeing her new companions and still avoid outright lying. It might not be possible this time. How had she gotten herself into this situation? Why was she hanging out with such a worldly group of people anyway?

Sutton's smooth voice invaded her thoughts. "Have you enjoyed your dinner, my dear?"

She forced herself to smile. "Yes, thank you. Very much."

"I believe everyone is about to retire to the drawing room. I must speak privately to our host, but I'll join you shortly. It's only a business matter that will not keep me for long." He rose, bowed, and followed Mr. Cowell out of the room.

Several of the guests departed, leaving Cici and Gail and their group alone. A servant entered the room and asked them to follow him.

The drawing room turned out not to be a drawing room at all, but some sort of gaming area. Tables were positioned around the room. Each held decks of cards, dice, and other objects. Cici felt suddenly faint. Two of the tables were already occupied by men and women who'd apparently been there for some time. Glasses containing what Cici was sure was liquor rested next to them.

"Hey, what's wrong? You're white as a ghost." Gail stood by her side, a frown on her face.

"Gail, those people are gambling." Her voice had risen, but at the moment, she didn't care.

"Of course they are, silly. What's wrong with that?" Lines appeared between her eyes. "Don't tell me you're going to make a fuss because of some old-fashioned sense of guilt. Everyone gambles nowadays, Cici. Even refined folks like the Cowells."

"I. . .I hadn't intended to make a fuss, of course. I'm simply not sure I should stay."

Gail huffed. "Cici, you have no choice. The boat won't be leaving for at least two more hours. If you don't wish to play, you don't have to. As you can see, there are sofas and chairs by the fireplace. You can sit there. Chances are, someone will join you, so you won't have to sit alone all evening."

"Couldn't you sit with me?" She shouldn't have said that. It sounded immature even to her own ears. "Never mind. I'll be fine."

She found a magazine and sat on the edge of a chair that turned out to be hard and uncomfortable.

If only she had stayed home tonight. Her parents thought she was spending the night at Helen's when she actually planned to stay at Gail's. Cici sincerely hoped the girl wouldn't drink much.

She took a deep breath and her heart fluttered. She didn't belong here. Her parents had taught her better. Why couldn't she be faithful to God and her upbringing? The night she and Jimmy had sat on the porch and looked at the stars had been so sweet, so innocent. She really thought she might be falling in love with him a little. So what was wrong with her? Why had she come with these people?

As the evening dragged on, the room filled with smoke from cigars and cigarettes. Cici slipped out the French doors and sat on a cushioned wrought-iron bench. She shivered as the cold wind off the lake swept over her, wishing she'd slipped her wrap on. But anything was better than the stuffy drawing room. Stars flashed and twinkled in the dark night sky, reflecting on the surface of the lake. She leaned back and wrapped her arms around her shoulders.

"So there you are. I thought perhaps I'd find you here." Sutton's tall form appeared in the doorway, her wrap over one arm. He stepped through and shut the doors behind him. "I was getting concerned."

"I needed a breath of fresh air." She thanked him as he slipped the stole around her shoulders.

"Of course you did. The drawing room has become abominable. I think we must leave soon."

Cici didn't answer, but waves of relief washed over her. She'd thought the night would never end.

"I hope you aren't offended by the card playing. I know your father is a minister."

Cici started. "I'm surprised you're aware of that. I don't believe I've told anyone." In fact, she was almost certain she hadn't.

"Perhaps you've forgotten. I believe Gail mentioned it." He sat next to her and leaned back, his shoulder pressing against hers. Uncomfortable, she moved, leaning as close to the end of the bench as she could.

He shifted and straightened.

She shrugged. Perhaps she had forgotten as he suggested.

The *Lady Fair* pulled into the Clark Street dock after midnight. Tired and disturbed about the evening, Cici wished she could go home. But what would she tell her parents? Having no other recourse, she got into a carriage with Gail and went home with her as planned. Cici almost gagged in the enclosed space at the smell of liquor on Gail's breath. As they climbed the stairs to Gail's apartment, the girl stumbled and cursed.

Later, Cici lay on her side on a narrow cot in Gail's bedroom. Drunken snores rumbled throughout the room. Suddenly Gail didn't seem so exciting. She only seemed pathetic.

♋

Disbelief clouded Jimmy's mind. Surely Cici wasn't asking him to keep secrets from her parents. As he stared at her, a pink blush tinged her cheeks.

He'd been about to walk into the church for the morning service when she'd appeared as though out of nowhere, in a sky blue dress that brought out the deep azure of her eyes, and asked to speak to him. His heart had beat double time, eagerly awaiting her words. But never would he have expected this.

"Oh dear. I know you must think I'm horrid, Jimmy. You see, I spent the night with Helen and forgot to tell Papa and Mama we were visiting friends upriver. Please don't misunderstand."

"But Cici, don't you think you should simply explain to them?" Confusion clouded his mind.

"But you see, they worry so. And if they knew I went somewhere without their knowing, they'd worry themselves sick about what might have happened." She bit her lip and sent him a pleading look. "And I'm not asking you to lie about anything. Just don't mention it unless the matter should come up."

Okay, that really made things clear. Surely the Willows would want to know about this. But it wasn't his place to tell them unless they asked, and that wasn't likely.

"Please, Jimmy. Papa has so much on his mind. And Mama had heart palpitations a few days ago. She said it was nothing, but I can't help but be concerned."

He inhaled deeply.

Tears had formed in Cici's eyes and she blinked hard to hold them back. She must be very worried about her mother. And what if she was right? What if he told them and Mrs. Willow had a heart attack or brain seizure?

"All right, Cici. I think you're making a mistake, but an honest mistake, so I'll honor your request. I doubt there would be an occasion for the subject to come up anyway." Jimmy's heart raced at the relief that swept over her face.

"Oh, Jimmy, thank you so much. I promise I'll never forget to tell them where I'm going again."

His heart jumped as she reached a hand out and placed it on his cheek. Of course, there was nothing wrong with what she asked. She'd simply made a mistake and was concerned about how it would affect her parents. Totally reasonable. He reached up and took her hand in his.

Chapter 7

I've taught you all the basics, Jimmy, and you've learned well. Your hunger for knowledge of the Word amazes and thrills me."

Warmth flowed through Jimmy at Rev. Willow's words of praise.

"Thank you, sir. I don't know how to thank you for all your help. I thought I knew the basics of Christianity but discovered I knew very little. I'm sorry to see our studies end."

"Actually, Jimmy, they needn't end. I plan to begin a series of in-depth Bible studies starting next Tuesday night at the church. If you're interested, you're welcome to join us."

"I'm very interested." Jimmy couldn't believe it. There was so much he wanted to know, and he felt totally unready to start out on his own. Sometimes the Bible seemed like a great mystery that he'd never understand. But he'd learned the past few weeks that God wanted to reveal those mysteries to His children.

"Good. Then be at the church at seven. We have a number of people signed up. I believe you'll find a group study very beneficial."

"I'm sure I will, sir." He shook the reverend's hand and left the study. Disappointed not to see Cici, he stepped out onto the porch. Moonlight washed over her and the wicker porch swing.

"Hi, Jimmy." She smiled and patted the seat next to her. "So this was your last study, wasn't it?"

He leaned back in the seat beside her. "Yes, I was feeling rather lost about that. But then your father told me about the new Tuesday study at the church."

"You're not going to join?" Wrinkles appeared between her eyes and disappointment filled her voice.

Confused, he stared at her. "Well, yes, I thought I would. Why?"

"We hardly see each other at all, Jimmy. Sundays at both services and sometimes Sunday afternoons for dinner. I'd hoped perhaps you would save that time slot for me." She blushed and turned away. "Forgive me for being so forward. Perhaps I've misunderstood. I thought you'd want to spend more time with me."

"Not at all. I mean you haven't misunderstood. I want nothing more than to spend time with you." Puzzled, he peered at her. "There are other evenings, Cici. What does one thing have to do with the other?"

Cici bit her lip. "You're right. I don't know what I was thinking." She stood. "I really must go inside. I'm not feeling well. Good night, Jimmy."

Jimmy stared after her then headed down to catch the streetcar. Now what was that about? If she liked him, as she'd implied, he'd have thought she would want him to learn as much about the Bible as he could and grow spiritually. After all, she was a minister's daughter.

CB

"What's wrong with you today, Grayson? Get a move on."

Jimmy looked up to see the first mate of the *Heron* leaning over the rail and shaking his fist.

"Sorry, I'm coming." He couldn't really blame the man for yelling at him. He'd had Cici and her strange behavior on his mind all morning and had probably been dragging his heels. He practically ran up the gangplank and went to help a couple of stevedores stack crates to make room for more.

"Okay, Grayson, get back dockside and bring another one up. Go help him, McDugan. These crates are heavy."

Jimmy started down the gangplank when a figure down below caught his eye. A chill ran through him. The man's tall stature, the set of his shoulders, and the way he sauntered across the dock were all too familiar.

Jimmy frowned. No, it couldn't be Sutton. He had two more years to serve. They'd said he wouldn't be eligible for early release. But it sure looked like. . .

The man turned.

Jimmy clamped his teeth together. Anger rose like bile inside him. It was Sutton. Jimmy watched as the man who'd exploited him and Danni and many other children strolled down the side street parallel to the bridge as though he hadn't a care. The same street Danni and Jimmy had raced down with an angry dockworker in pursuit. And there was the alley where Cobb grabbed them and jerked them out of sight. Sutton was headed to the run-down house where he'd operated his child crime ring.

Another stab of anger pierced him. Would the man be stupid enough to have another gang of children stealing for him? Surely not. The authorities must be keeping an eye on him.

"Hey, Grayson. What you standin' there for? I ain't loading this doozy by myself."

Sutton had moved on down the street, out of sight.

Jimmy joined McDugan and went back to work. When he broke for the midday meal, he headed for the part of the dock next to the street. Craning his neck, he looked as far as he could see, but no sign of Sutton remained.

"Jimbo, what you gazing at?" Cobb joined him, his lunch pail swinging from his hand.

"You won't believe it. I just saw Sutton."

A shadow crossed Cobb's eyes, but he didn't reply as he sat on a crate and opened his bucket.

"Did you hear what I said? I saw Sutton walking down the street toward the old place."

"Aw, you must have been seein' things, Jimbo. Sutton's locked up. He ain't around here."

"No, it was him. I wasn't sure at first. Then he turned, and I saw his face." Jimmy sat but didn't move to open his lunch pail. "It was him all right."

"Hmm. I'll ask around. But I think you're imagining it, old man." Cobb laughed, but his laugh was shaky. "You were just a kid last time you saw him. Easy to make a mistake. You probably wouldn't even recognize him if you saw him now."

Jimmy stared at his friend. Why was he so sure it wasn't Sutton? Or maybe he knew it was. Could Cobb be involved with Sutton again? After all the trouble he'd caused him? Jimmy hoped not. He and Cobb had always been friends, but even more so in the last few months. He'd hate to see him get into trouble again.

He ate in silence. What should his first move be? He needed to tell Blake right away. That much went without saying. Sutton might be after Danni. He'd threatened her once before. She could be in danger.

☙

Cici laughed as Jimmy and Eddy chased the soccer ball around the back lawn. May had brought long-awaited springlike weather, and the young people had decided to take advantage of it.

Helen leaned back in her lawn chair and yawned. "It's nice to see the boys having some fun for a change. Jimmy's been so serious lately."

"What's wrong with that, I'd like to know?" Cici had thought the same thing many times and had no idea why Helen's words had brought on the defensive response.

"Why, nothing, I suppose. I wasn't criticizing him."

"I know, I know." Cici frowned and studied Jimmy as he dodged the ball that had flown by his head. "I've no idea what they think they're playing."

Helen giggled. "Me either. Guess they're making up their own game."

"Jimmy *is* rather serious lately. He spends as much time with Papa as he does with me." She bit her lip and cast a sideways glance at Helen.

"Hmm. That's odd." She thought for a moment then sat straight, her eyes wide. "Cici, you don't think. . ." She flopped back against the chair. "Nah. That couldn't be it."

"What couldn't be it?" Cici frowned.

"I just wondered if maybe Jimmy was thinking about the ministry."

"Thinking what about the ministry?" What in the world was she getting at? A chill ran across Cici's skin. "No. No, Helen. Jimmy is going back to law school. I'm sure. This manual labor thing is just a phase he's going through." She laughed, but the sound was unconvincing, even to herself. "He would have told me if he had anything like that in mind."

"Maybe he doesn't know."

"Well, don't you dare say anything."

☙

Jimmy and Cici sat on the porch swing and watched as Eddy and Helen walked toward the streetcar hand in hand.

Cici took a deep breath. "Jimmy, have you decided whether you're going back to law school or not?"

He frowned and shook his head. "I know I need to make a decision soon." He reached over and took her hand, rubbing his thumb over the smooth skin.

Cici shivered but left her hand in his. She ran her tongue over her lips. "Of course, it's none of my business. I shouldn't have asked."

He smiled. "Cici, I hope you will consider my business yours. I care a great deal for you and your opinion."

She inhaled deeply. She cared about Jimmy, too. But how much did they really know about each other? Obviously, there was way too much he didn't know about her. And lately he'd been way too religious. Could Helen possibly be right?

୬

Jimmy stepped onto the streetcar and sat on a slatted seat near the front. Cici's face appeared in his mind as it tended to do when he was quiet. They had been spending a couple of evenings a week together. They'd had some nice long talks and had grown closer. But something seemed to be on her mind. Was she growing tired of him?

He groaned. As if he didn't have enough on his mind. It had been a week since his glimpse of Sutton. Blake had made a phone call and confirmed that Sutton had been released early. The prison was overcrowded and his good behavior had precipitated the decision. Yeah, good behavior. Sutton knew how to manipulate, all right.

Jimmy's mouth tightened as he recalled the fear that slid across Danni's face when they told her. She'd readily agreed not to leave the house without her husband for the present.

If Danni didn't have so much to worry about, he'd talk to her about Cici. Or maybe it would be good for her to get her mind off Sutton for a little while.

୬

"Why must he be so religious?" Cici stepped into Tony's Place with Gail close beside her. "I mean, it's one thing to go to church. Of course I want him to do that. I wouldn't dream of missing a Sunday service myself."

Gail seated herself at their usual table and waited for Cici to sit across from her. She patted a yawn with the back of her hand. "I don't know what your problem is. Why don't you just break up with the guy?"

"What?" The possibility of breaking up with Jimmy had never crossed Cici's mind. The thought of it sent a chill over her. "How can you say that? You know how much I care about him."

Gail gave a little laugh. "If you say so. But I could point out plenty of fellows who'd love to step in and take his place."

Shaking her head, Cici turned to the waiter who'd come to take their order. "Just a cup of tea, please."

Gail ordered coffee, and when the waiter had left, she leaned forward on her elbows. "To be quite honest, my dear, I think you're something of a hypocrite."

Shock bolted through Cici and heat flooded her face. "Excuse me?"

Gail laughed and leaned back in her chair. "You don't need to act so indignant. You're too good for the likes of Carl, who'd give his eyeteeth for one of your smiles. But on the other hand, you think Jimmy is a little too honorable and dull."

"I never said any such thing." Cici frowned. "I merely said he was spending too much time with Papa, studying the Bible."

"Oh well. It doesn't matter to me. If you can get by with living in two worlds, more power to you." She smiled. "Personally, I wouldn't want anything to do with the religious life."

"But Gail, you believe in God, don't you?"

A shadow slid across Gail's eyes and she shrugged. "Used to. Not so much anymore."

"But why?" Cici stared across at her friend.

"It doesn't matter. Now, see? That's what I mean about you being a hypocrite. You're doing everything you can to get away from the religious life, but you're trying to push it on me." She clamped her lips shut as the waiter came with their drinks.

Cici reeled from the words Gail had thrown at her. Was she a hypocrite? She didn't mean to be. She simply wanted to have fun. But she still loved God. At least, she thought she did.

A sick feeling clutched at her stomach and she took a sip of the steaming tea. Was she changing? For the worse? She looked across at Gail. She'd never met anyone who didn't believe in God. Maybe that was the reason for their friendship. Perhaps she was supposed to help Gail regain her faith. Yes, that must be it. This was all part of God's plan.

Chapter 8

Jimmy Grayson!" Danni stood, hands on her hips, staring daggers at him. "Do you mean to tell me you've been seeing a girl for three months and didn't tell me?"

Uh-oh. Jimmy hadn't expected this. Danni had been trying to pair him up with girls for ages. She should be shouting for joy. "Well, I met her about that long ago. We've only been seeing each other for a few weeks. Sorry, Danni. I didn't think about telling you."

Laughter burst from Danni's lips, and she threw her arms around him and hugged him. "I was only teasing. I'm not mad. I'm very, very happy for you."

Jimmy grinned and returned the hug. "Whew. You had me going there for a minute."

"Sorry, little brother. You should have seen the look on your face." Her tinkling laughter filled the room. "So her name is Cecilia Willow?"

"Yes, but everyone calls her Cici."

"What a sweet name. And I'm sure she's just as sweet."

"Yes, she is, sis. I can't wait for you to meet her." Should he tell Danni about the way Cici had been acting lately? Maybe not. He was probably exaggerating the problem.

"Well, we're planning a family picnic a week from Saturday. Why don't you ask her to come so we can meet her?" She pursed her lips and tapped a finger against her cheek. "Blake's parents will be there. And Pops. And the Kramers."

The Kramer family had taken Danielle under their wing when she was trying to get away from Sutton. And they'd taken Jimmy in just as readily. They'd been like family ever since.

"Sounds like a good idea. I'll ask her right away."

She bit her lip. "I hope Pops will behave himself."

Jimmy snickered. "He just likes to have fun. He'll be okay."

"Well, you know how he gets when he starts talking about his vaudeville days."

He bent over and kissed her on the cheek. "You worry too much. Cici will love him."

She smiled. "I know. Do you want to invite some of your friends? She might feel more comfortable with people she knows there."

"Hmm. Not this time. Just Cici." He grinned. "You're a great sister. I don't deserve you."

"I know." She smiled and patted his cheek. "I don't deserve you either."

"And neither of you deserve me." Blake stepped out of the library, laughing, and put his arm around Danni's shoulders. "Now what's going on?"

"Jimmy has a girlfriend, a minister's daughter. Her name is Cici, and Jimmy's going to invite her to the family picnic." She gave an excited giggle.

Jimmy and Blake exchanged amused glances.

"Well now, I don't know if you could say she's my girlfriend. We haven't even seen each other except at church and the parsonage." Jimmy frowned. Maybe Cici wouldn't like being called his girlfriend.

"Well, she's a girl and your friend, right?" Blake grinned and slapped him on the back. "What's her father's name?"

"Reverend Willow. He's the pastor of the Hope of Heaven Community Church."

"Oh yes. I've met him. I understand he's a fine man. Very well respected in the community."

"He is a fine man. And a great teacher. You should come and hear him some Sunday."

"We might just do that."

A maid appeared in the doorway. "Dinner is served."

"Thanks, Marie. We'll be right in." Blake smiled at the girl and she nodded and left.

As Jimmy followed Blake and Danni to the dining room, a picture of Sutton crossed his mind for the first time that evening. He prayed Danni's thoughts wouldn't go there. She appeared more relaxed than she'd been since she first found out Sutton had been released.

The next morning he stepped off the streetcar at the end of the Clark Street Bridge and onto the dock. He spotted Cobb just arriving also. He carried his duffel.

"Hi, Cobb. You shipping out?"

"Yeah. *Eastland*'s leaving on a three-day tour. Can't get along without their head cook." He grinned.

Cobb still denied having seen Sutton, although Jimmy had told him the man was out of prison. It was hard to believe he hadn't run into the man by now if Sutton was hanging out in the area. But then, Jimmy hadn't seen him again either, so maybe he'd only been in the neighborhood to see someone that day. Jimmy wanted to believe his friend was being honest.

"Yeah, I guess not." He grinned. "Don't give them ptomaine poisoning."

"I'll try not to." Cobb waved and headed for the *Eastland*. Passengers were already standing in line to board the big tour boat.

The *Lady Fair* was docked nearby. Jimmy scanned the deck then shook his head. Why did he watch for Cici every time he saw that boat? She'd only been visiting a friend the day she'd boarded the *Lady Fair*.

The morning passed in a hurry and Jimmy headed for his usual spot, lunch in hand. He'd just sat down and opened his pail when Bridget and the boys stepped onto the dock. "Hey, come on over." Jimmy motioned to them. "Glad to see you."

"Hi, Jimmy." Bridget's voice was strong. She grabbed Mike as he started to walk away. "No, Mikey. You stay right by my side. You're not going to get lost again."

"He got lost?" A vise of fear clutched at Jimmy's heart. A tiny boy alone in this neighborhood could get hurt bad.

"Yes, he got away from Patrick. Mrs. Baker found him and brought him home." Her voice didn't falter on the word *home*, although Jimmy knew that home was a discarded, three-sided booth someone had once used to sell vegetables. Somehow, Bridget managed to make a home for them there.

"Did you get the blankets I left at your place?"

"Yes, sir. I thought they must be from you. I had to leave to find food for breakfast."

Jimmy reached in and removed two sandwiches from his pail. He tore one in half and handed the halves to the boys, then held the other sandwich out to Bridget.

She put her hands behind her back and shook her head. "No, sir, I don't need anything for myself. I know you've been feeding my brothers and I didn't want them coming out alone after Mikey getting lost."

Jimmy's eyes burned as he blinked back tears. "Bridget, honey, I'd be honored if you'd share my lunch."

She shook her head, but hunger screamed from her eyes as they darted to the sandwich.

"Do you like stories, Bridget?"

Startled, she turned her eyes from the ham and cheese that stuck out between the slices of bread. "I guess so. Haven't heard any since Ma died."

"Well, I'll tell you what. I'm going to be telling stories to some children this weekend, and I'd appreciate it if you'd let me practice on you so I won't make a fool of myself."

"Oh sure. I don't mind."

"Good." He glanced at the sandwich in his hand. "Well, here, I've already unwrapped this and I can't eat and talk at the same time, so why don't you have it, and when I finish my story, I'll eat the one still in my pail."

She nodded and her little pink tongue darted out and licked her lips as she accepted the food.

Jimmy stretched the story of Jesus feeding the five thousand as long as possible, dividing the other sandwich and a large piece of cake between the three children.

When they turned to leave, little Mike stopped and ran back to Jimmy. "Are you Jesus?"

"Oh no, Mike. I'm Jimmy, remember?"

"But he's like Jesus, Mikey." Bridget smiled and took the little boy's hand

and led him away.

ଔ

Cici rocked back and forth in the wicker rocker on Helen's front porch. She felt like she'd explode if she didn't tell Helen right now. She grinned at her friend.

Helen laughed and, leaning over, put her hand on the rocker's arm to slow it down. "Cici, you're going to fly right out of that chair if you don't calm down."

"I feel like I'm flying, Helen. He's asked me to join his family for a picnic."

"Yes, you said that a number of times. I think I've got the idea. And what if he did? He's had dinner with your family many times."

"That's not the same, and you know it." She shook her finger at Helen, who grabbed it and pushed it away.

"No, I suppose it's not the same. Men don't usually ask you to meet their families unless they care for you a great deal."

"Exactly." Cici nodded and rocked the chair again.

"But of course you must have known anyway. Else you wouldn't have been sneaking off with him." She shook her head. "What I can't understand is why you found it necessary. Your parents like Jimmy. They wouldn't have objected to his taking you on a date."

Cici stared, confused. "What are you talking about? Jimmy and I haven't been sneaking around."

"Oh, come now, Cici. You might have let me in on it though. I had to do some fast thinking when your mother asked me if we had fun the night you slept over." She smiled. "Now, I know you two didn't spend the night alone, so where were you and with whom?"

Cici swallowed. Oh no. How stupid she was. Why didn't she think about the possibility of her mother saying something to Helen? Her mind darted here and there in an attempt to come up with something. If this got back to Jimmy. . . There was only one thing to do. "Oh, Helen."

"What? What's wrong? You're white as a ghost."

"Helen, I have to tell you something. But you have to promise not to tell anyone."

"Well, of course. You know I wouldn't tell a secret." A worried look crossed her face. "Cici, you're scaring me. What's wrong?"

Cici attempted to swallow but her throat tightened. She forced herself to relax. When she managed to speak, her words were only a whisper. "I wasn't with Jimmy that night."

"Then where. . .who?"

"Let's go for a walk. I don't want your mother or sister to hear."

As Cici bared her soul to Helen, she experienced a freedom she hadn't had since she'd first met Gail and begun her journey of dishonesty. Why had she ever thought a life of worldliness and deceit was exciting? All it had brought her were fear and guilt.

"Oh, Cici, why didn't you tell me?"

"I was too ashamed. I felt as though I was betraying our friendship. And...well, I'll admit, I was afraid you'd tell my parents." She darted a questioning look at Helen. "Would you have?"

"I don't know, Cici. I might have." Her brow furrowed and she peered into Cici's eyes. "Have you stopped seeing those people?"

"Well, it's been a couple of weeks. And I've decided not to meet them again."

"I hope you mean it."

Heat seared her face at the accusation. Then pain shot through her. What had she become that her best friend couldn't trust her? She sighed. "Yes, I mean it. But to be honest, I don't know if I can stick to it."

"Cici, I'm sorry, but I don't understand. Just don't do it anymore. It's that simple."

"It's not that easy, Helen. I feel like I'm being pulled in two directions." She blinked back tears as they arrived back in front of Helen's house. "I have to go."

"No, Cici, don't leave mad. I'm sorry."

"I'm not mad. Pray for me, Helen." She hurriedly walked away and headed for the streetcar stop. Fear gripped her, clutching and clawing. What kind of horrible person was she? She knew the scriptures. *Resist the devil, and he will flee from you.* So why was the temptation still there?

As she tossed and turned in her bed that night, fear rose again. She never should have told Helen. She'd probably lose her friendship. Her breath came in sobs.

Then she stopped and took a deep breath. Wait. She had almost forgotten. Hadn't God arranged her friendship with Gail so that Cici could help her spiritually? Yes, she couldn't desert Gail. This was a thing from God.

But what if Helen decided to get even and tell her parents? Guilt bit at her conscience. Helen wasn't like that. Once more, tears fell, soaking her pillow. She tossed it aside and slid another under her head.

Finally, in the wee hours of the morning, she fell into a fitful sleep.

Chapter 9

Michael O'Shannon, the old man Jimmy called Pops, laid his chicken leg on the plate and turned to Cici, pointing his thumb in Jimmy's direction. "Well, lass, and what would you be seeing in this young rapscallion?"

Rapscallion? Jimmy? Cici choked back a laugh. "Well, my papa says he's a fine young man. So it must be so."

"Ah, and it's honoring your father's views, you are. That's a good girl. And your father is absolutely right." He patted her hand then lifted a forkful of potato salad. "You'd best be eating now. You could use a little meat on those bones."

"Papa!" Blake's mother pressed her lips together and threw her father a warning look.

"Don't be twitching your nose at me, Katie O'Shannon." He took a bite from the drumstick.

"Nelson, Papa. Nelson."

"Ah, so it is, Katie girl, and well I know it."

Cici laid her napkin next to her plate and glanced around the long table. Blake and Jimmy had set it up on the lush green expanse of the senior Nelsons' front lawn. Two apple trees blossomed nearby. She closed her eyes for a moment, inhaling the fragrance.

"Lovely here, isn't it? I never get used to it."

Cici opened her eyes. Danielle stood next to her, a pitcher of lemonade in her hand.

"Yes, it's very n—nice," Cici stammered, suddenly shy around this sister whom Jimmy adored so.

"Would you like more lemonade?" Danielle motioned with the pitcher toward Cici's glass.

"Oh yes, thank you." She held the glass steady while Danielle poured.

"I hope we'll have a chance to visit before you go home."

Danielle's sincere smile wrapped Cici like a warm shawl, and she relaxed. "Yes, I'd like that very much." She took a deep breath and smiled at Mr. O'Shannon, who winked at her. Jimmy had told her he used to be onstage, and she hoped the subject would come up. She'd never actually met an actor before.

When the meal was over, Cici followed the ladies over to a group of lawn chairs the men had brought out. She watched, amused, as Jimmy, Blake, his father and grandfather, and the Kramers' fifteen-year-old twin boys laughed and argued while they tossed horseshoes until their arms grew numb. Finally, tired of the game, they joined the ladies.

The twins threw themselves onto the ground, and Jimmy flopped down on the chair next to Cici. "Whew." He winked at Cici and her heart fluttered double time.

"Uh-huh," Mr. O'Shannon cackled. "You lads can't keep up with the men, now, can you?"

Cici grinned. The older man was huffing and puffing, but she was pretty sure no one would mention it.

"Yeah, Pops. Guess you're right." Jimmy grinned and Pops smiled back.

Warmth swept over Cici. Obviously the two had a lot of affection for each other.

"Hey, Pops." Jimmy peered around Cici. "I think Cici would like to hear about your acting days."

The old man's eyes widened and sparkled. "Ah, she would, would she?"

Cici heard a groan and giggled when Blake's mother shook her head and frowned at Jimmy.

"Yes, Mr. O'Shannon, I'm dying to hear all about it." Cici leaned forward.

"Well now, on one condition." He gave her a mock stern look. "There'll be none of this mister stuff. You'll be calling me Pops the same as all the other young folks do."

"Yes, sir. Pops it is." She grinned. He must have been quite a charmer in his heyday.

He coughed and cleared his throat. "You see, I was just a young lad when I got my first job in a small theater in New York City. A stagehand I was. Repaired ropes and hangings and made sure everything was in tip-top shape. To me, it was a magical kingdom. The costumes of every color of the rainbow and the story that came to life. Then there was the smell of greasepaint and the stage settings. Nothing like the theater had ever entered my realm of existence before."

Cici sat mesmerized as he gazed off across the lawn as though he'd entered another world.

"The star of that first show was Ferdie Swaine. He made me believe he was every character he played. Never in my wildest dreams did I think I'd ever be on the stage myself. Then Ferdie's valet came down with a fever, and Ferdie asked me to take his place until he was well again. One of my duties was to read off all the other parts as he practiced his lines." A fit of coughing overcame him for a moment, and Jimmy poured him a glass of water.

"Ah, thank you, my boy." He drank and set the glass down. "Now, where was I?"

"Reading lines, Pops." Blake grinned and his grandfather threw him an affectionate smile.

"But you can stop if you're tired, Da." A burst of laughter followed Mrs. Nelson's remark.

What a loving and fun family they all were.

Jimmy leaned over and whispered in Cici's ear, "You notice she's switched from Papa to Da. She does that every time he tells stories of the old days. I think it takes her back to her childhood."

"That's all right, daughter. I'll go on." He patted Cici's hand again. "Don't want to disappoint this pretty lass."

Cici smiled, in awe of the former vaudeville star. "Thank you, Pops."

"Now, I've lost me train of thought again." He frowned and threw his daughter a scolding look. "Ah yes. I was reading lines for Ferdie, I was. Well, I got to liking it, I did. And Ferdie kept bragging on me to the manager. When it came time for tryouts for the next show, he asked me to read for a small part, so I did. And got the part. Soon they discovered I had a knack for song and dance, and that's when my vaudeville days began."

"Tell her about the Irish troupe, Pops." Blake pursed his lips and Cici had a hunch he was egging on his grandfather to tease his mother.

"Ah yes. She'll be wanting to know about that." Shadows clouded his eyes for a moment. He cleared his throat. "After my wife passed away, I brought my young daughter to her grandparents' farm and came to Chicago looking for work. Vaudeville hadn't reached the area at that time, but the theater district was booming. I was hired by Harrigan's Music Hall and Theater. An Irish troupe they were, with all the old Irish song and dance and musical comedy thrown in. Harrigan himself was a fine Irishman, with a song in his heart and music in his toes. He knew how to put on a show, he did. The Irish weren't too well thought of in this city at that time, but everyone, rich and poor, loved Harrigan and his Irish troupe." His speech slowed and his eyes drooped. "Ah yes, there never was a man like Harrigan. . . ."

A soft snore reached Cici's ear. Why, the old dear. He'd gone to sleep right in the middle of his story.

Dusk was falling as Cici sank back into the seat of Blake's automobile. He'd insisted Jimmy use it to take her home. It had been a full, wonderful day, but the excitement of meeting the extended family had been tiring, and Cici sighed as relaxation engulfed her body.

"Tired?" Jimmy smiled and took her hand.

"Mm-hmm." Then she sat up straight, wide awake. "Shouldn't you have both hands on the steering wheel?"

He bit his lips and grinned but put his hand back on the wheel. "I'm only going about five miles an hour. I don't think we'll crash. But I'm sorry if I made you nervous."

She scooted a little closer to him. "It's all right. I'm not used to automobiles. I'm sure you wouldn't do anything unsafe."

They pulled up to the curb in front of the parsonage and Jimmy came around to Cici's door and helped her out.

As they stood in front of the door, Cici looked up into his eyes. "Thank you for inviting me to the picnic. Your family is very nice."

"They like you, too, Cici. I could tell." He took her hand and smiled. "Is it okay now that I'm not driving?"

She blushed. "Sorry I overreacted."

"I was teasing. You had every right to react to careless driving."

She swayed and he steadied her. "Oh, I must be more tired than I thought. I'd better get inside."

"Thank you for coming with me to the picnic. I'll see you at church in the morning."

"Yes, I'll see you then."

"Don't forget we're going out for lunch."

"I haven't forgotten." She smiled a rather sleepy smile. "Good night, Jimmy." She slipped inside and leaned against the door, listening to his footsteps as he walked across the porch and down the steps.

‰

Jimmy laughed. What a great weekend. He lifted a box and stacked it on some others near the loading area. The picnic had been a great success. Everyone loved Cici and she'd seemed to return the feeling. She'd laughed and talked about Pops all the way home in Blake's new Ford Runabout. He'd almost kissed her good night but decided he'd better not. He didn't want to ruin a perfect day by possibly offending her.

He looked up as the *Lady Fair* bumped against the dock then watched as the crew lowered the gangplank. The *Lady Fair* was cargo-only this trip, so no passengers disembarked. Jimmy and several other stevedores walked on board and began to unload crates.

After church on Sunday, Jimmy and Cici had gone to a restaurant with Eddy and Helen. The girls had been silent most of the evening and rather cool, though polite, to one another. But then after they'd parted company with the other couple, Jimmy and Cici sat on her front porch late into the night, discussing their families and the picnic. Cici told him how much she admired Danielle.

Jimmy had forgotten his concern about Cici and Helen. But now it wormed its way into his thoughts. They'd probably just had a disagreement about something. Jimmy grinned. Girls. Yes, it had been a perfect weekend.

The *Eastland* was coming into the harbor. Good. He hadn't seen Cobb in days. Maybe they could eat their midday meal together. After the *Lady Fair* was unloaded, Jimmy and two others reloaded the ship. Then Jimmy grabbed his lunch bucket from the shack and went looking for Cobb.

A streetcar stopped at the end of the bridge and a tall man stepped off.

Jimmy took in a sharp breath. Sutton. Jimmy's eyes followed him as he hurried down the street in the direction of his old headquarters. Did he still own the place? Jimmy's chest tightened. He turned and almost ran into Cobb, who reached out a hand to steady him.

"Whoa, Jimbo, easy there. What's got you riled up?" Cobb pushed his hat toward the back of his head.

"I just saw Sutton. And there's no mistake. It's him, all right."

"Jimmy, Jimmy. Don't you think I'd have run into him by now if he was in this area?"

"I don't know, Cobb. But it was him," Jimmy snapped. "Why don't we go to the old place now and see if he's there?"

Near panic crossed Cobb's face. "Sorry, Jimbo. We're leaving out again in a few hours. I have to restock the galley. I'll see you when I get back. Maybe we could check it out then." He took off across the dock.

Jimmy's stomach clenched. Cobb was keeping something from him. What if he was mixed up in something illegal with Sutton again?

At least ten children, of all ages, were waiting at the edge of the dock.

Uh-oh. He'd brought a lot of food but didn't know if it would stretch that far. "Hi, gang." He grinned and sat on the old barrel.

A chorus of hellos answered. Bridget and her brothers drew close. At least their lips weren't blue from the cold anymore.

Jimmy managed to find enough for everyone to have a few bites. The children nibbled their food and listened eagerly as Jimmy told the story of David the shepherd boy.

"And he really killed the old mean giant with a little rock?"

"Yes, he really did." Jimmy smiled at the thin, ragged boy who'd asked the question. "But you have to remember, Tom, no one could kill a giant with a stone without help from God. David loved the Lord with all his heart. He knew the Philistines were evil men, out to destroy God's people. He trusted God to help him."

"Why don't God help me, Jimmy?" The little girl was only four. Her mother managed to bring in a little money doing people's laundry, but her husband squandered most of it at a local saloon.

Bridget put her arm around the child's thin shoulders. "But He does help you, Sally. He helps all of us. He sent Jimmy to us, didn't He?"

Jimmy's heart lurched. He had to do more. These children needed more than he could give them from his lunch pail.

God, show me what to do.

Heart heavy, he rode the streetcar home. He'd talk to Rev. Willow. Maybe he'd have some ideas. Or perhaps some of Blake's wealthy friends would be willing to help. He hated to ask, but the children needed so much more than he could give them.

Every time he looked into a hungry face, he remembered that day on the dock after his mother had died and he and Danni had been tossed out onto the street by the woman who had claimed to be her friend. Danni had stolen food that day. She'd done it for him. And Jimmy had never forgotten.

Chapter 10

Sir, I've never experienced this before." Jimmy paced the floor in the parsonage study and searched for the words to convey his thoughts to his spiritual mentor and pastor. He'd struggled all morning with a restlessness he couldn't explain as he helped load the *Midnight Maid.* His thoughts whirled. What was wrong with him? "Maybe I'm not really saved." He flung himself into the chair in front of his pastor's desk.

Rev. Willow steepled his hands and studied Jimmy. "So are you saying you're unsure of your salvation?"

Jimmy sighed and rubbed his finger across the bridge of his nose. "No, no. Not really. I know better. I meant it when I asked Jesus to be my Savior."

The reverend was silent, waiting for Jimmy to gather his thoughts.

"I don't understand why children must suffer. My heart has a longing. A longing to do something meaningful. To show people, especially children, the way out of their misery."

"Rescue the perishing perhaps?" Rev. Willow spoke softly. "That's more than a hymn, you know. It's a direct command from our Lord."

"Yes, maybe that's it. But in more than one sense. It's hard to make children understand that Jesus loves them when their stomachs are hollow from lack of food. Or to help a mother believe when she has no warm blanket for her child."

"It sounds like you have a missionary's heart, Jimmy. Perhaps God has placed this call on your life."

"You mean like going to Africa?" Jimmy's heart fell. He had no desire whatsoever to go to Africa.

"No, no, not necessarily." The reverend smiled. "There's a mission field right in front of you. There in the tenements near the docks. As you say, it's difficult for a starving child, or adult for that matter, to concentrate on spiritual things."

Jimmy sat up straight. A missionary to his people. For they were his people. Always had been. His eyes brimmed with moisture. Soft laughter rolled from his throat. "Reverend Willow, that's it." He smiled at his teacher. "Thank you."

"I did nothing, Jimmy. God led you to this moment. He used me only as a tool."

"What do I do next?" Jimmy laughed. "I have no idea how to be a missionary."

"You are already a missionary. Every time you feed a hungry child or tell one of your Bible stories, you are doing the work of missions. I suggest you continue with your studies. Spend much time in prayer and praise to God. Listen for His voice. Watch for opportunities to serve. Our Lord will let you know when it is time for the next step."

"Seminary?" Jimmy whispered.

Rev. Willow nodded. "I believe so. Unless God tells you otherwise. There is a very good missions program at my old seminary, and it is only a few miles away. If you would like, I'll refer you when the time is right."

"I'd like that very much." Jimmy felt a grin forming. He couldn't wait to tell Cici.

The reverend gazed deep into Jimmy's eyes. "Don't think this is going to be easy, son. You must be very close to God so you can hear His voice. People need help. But their self-esteem must not be crushed."

Jimmy nodded. "How do I prevent that, sir?"

"See them as Jesus sees them. Love them with His unconditional love. Follow His voice and trust Him with the results."

Jimmy jumped up and shook the reverend's hand. "I have to get back to work. Thank you, sir."

He turned away and almost bumped into Cici as he left the room.

Her face was pale and tears filled her eyes.

"Cici, what's wrong?"

"Nothing's wrong. I. . .I must have gotten something in my eyes when I was outdoors."

Without thinking, he grabbed her shoulders. "Cici, you'll never guess. I'm pretty sure I'm supposed to enter seminary and become a missionary."

"A. . .a missionary?"

"Yes, to the poor people of our own city. Isn't it wonderful? God is marvelous!"

A tremulous smile appeared on her face. "Yes, yes, of course. Wonderful, Jimmy."

"I have to get back to work. Do you mind if I come over later so we can talk?"

"Oh. . .I'm sorry, Jimmy. I'm not feeling well. I should probably go to bed."

"Oh, my dear, I'm so sorry. Of course you need to rest and get better." He gripped her hand for a moment then slipped out the front door.

⟡

She couldn't believe it. Jimmy had so much going for him. And he wanted to throw it all away to be a preacher? A pang of guilt shot through her. Her father did so much good. There was no doubt he was called to be a minister. But that was different.

Cici got off the streetcar and made her way to Tony's Place. She'd already tried Gail's apartment and several of their friends' homes. This was the last place she could think of where Gail might be. And Cici absolutely had to talk to her.

She pushed through the door, barely missing a waiter in her rush. The tray he held aloft wobbled before he got it balanced. "I'm sorry." Cici gave him an apologetic smile and got a frown in return.

Gail looked up from their usual table and spotted Cici bearing down on them.

She said something to the man across from her.

He laughed and left the table just as Cici reached them.

"Well, Cici, sit down and cool off. You look upset."

Cici dropped into the chair the man had vacated and huffed.

"Okay, what's he done this time?"

"Who?"

Gail laughed. "The only one who can get you that stressed out is dear Jimmy. So what's he done?"

Cici waited until the waiter had taken her order for coffee before answering. "I don't know what Jimmy is thinking. I don't understand him at all."

When Gail was silent, Cici sighed. "He's thinking about becoming a missionary."

Laughter exploded from Gail's lips.

"It's not funny, Gail." Cici frowned her displeasure and Gail pressed her hand against her mouth.

"Okay, okay. Sorry." She reached over and patted Cici's hand. "Now, tell me all about it. What else?"

"What else?" Cici straightened and frowned. "Isn't that enough?"

"So do you mean he's going over to Africa to convert natives?"

"No, no. He thinks the docks and all that tenement area is his mission field."

"Oh, well, he already does that. What's the big problem?"

"He's going to seminary. He wants to be a full-time missionary." The despair in Cici's heart rang out in her words.

Gail shook her head in disbelief. "I thought he was supposed to be some kind of lawyer."

"A law school student. A year and a half and he's throwing it away. I thought for sure a few weeks working on the docks would bring him to his senses, but. . ." Cici's words faded and she bit her lip.

"Hmm. I understand why you're so upset. A lawyer's wife has a lot more going for her than a missionary's wife. Don't you think it's time to look around at other options?"

"What? Oh, you mean the fellows in our crowd. I told you before, I'm not interested."

Gail's voice dropped in a conspiratorial manner. "Maybe I meant someone else."

"Who?" Not that she cared, of course. She wasn't interested in anyone but Jimmy. Gail didn't understand. It wasn't so much that Cici wanted to be married to a lawyer. She simply did not want to be married to a preacher. No matter what he called himself. She'd spent all her life so far as a preacher's daughter. Everything was "Don't do this. Be careful what you say. Don't offend anyone. Don't bring shame on your Lord. Don't. Don't. Don't." Maybe her mother liked being a preacher's wife, but Cici wasn't her mother. Pain shot through her. If only she were more like Mama.

"Never mind who." Gail no longer whispered. She smiled. "Hello, Sutton."

Cici looked up.

Sutton stopped beside their table. "Good afternoon, ladies." He bowed over Gail's hand then took Cici's and lingered over it for a moment. "How very nice to see you, Cecilia."

The pulse in Cici's wrist fluttered, and she cleared her throat. "Hello, Mr. Sutton."

"Tsk-tsk. Now what have I told you? James, not Mr. Sutton." He waved a finger in her direction.

"James." Cici blushed. She had been taught it was disrespectful to address older persons by their given names. Probably another old-fashioned rule she needed to get past. Anyway, Sutton didn't seem all that old.

He seated himself and asked the waiter for a glass of water. "I understand you are interested in the theater, Cecilia."

"Oh, I suppose I am." She had never been to a show in her life until she'd met Gail, and some of those made her uncomfortable. "An acquaintance of mine used to be in vaudeville. And my friend Jimmy's sister was in a musical comedy a few years ago. Written by her husband."

His eyes flickered and he stared at her. "Oh? And do you by any chance know the title of this musical comedy?"

"Yes, *Peg in Dreamland*. It was the only one he ever wrote professionally."

Anger flared in Sutton's eyes then was gone.

Had she imagined it?

He took a deep breath and seemed to study her. "That is very interesting, my dear. Perhaps you have entertained thoughts of acting as well?"

Now, how had he guessed that? She'd thought of hardly anything else since she'd met Michael O'Shannon and the Nelsons. That is, until Jimmy had told her about his intentions. Why couldn't he have had stars in his eyes about the theater or something like that? Why did he have to be a missionary?

"Cecilia?"

She started, and heat washed over her face. "Oh, I beg your pardon. My thoughts wandered for a moment."

"That's quite all right, my dear." He smiled.

"In answer to your question, I must admit the thought has crossed my mind. But of course it's just nonsense. I could never be an actress."

"Nonsense." His eyes gleamed. "With your beauty and your lovely voice, you could be a star in no time. Perhaps you simply need the right contacts."

"Sutton?" Gail leaned forward, a worried expression in her eyes.

He turned to her, his eyes darkening. "Yes, Gail, dear?"

"N—nothing."

Was that fear in Gail's eyes? But why?

He nodded and a chill went over Cici as he turned his attention back to her. Oh, she was only being silly. Why would Gail be afraid of Sutton? They were very close friends.

Sutton called a waiter to refill their glasses. After the waiter had left, Sutton turned to Cici. "While I have focused my directing talents on European cities, I do happen to have several contacts who, I am quite certain, would love to help you find a place in the theater. That is, if you are interested."

Heat washed over Cici. It started at the top of her head and slid downward until even her toes tingled. She stared at him. "Are you serious?"

"Very serious." He took her hand. "Your loveliness would grace any stage, my dear."

"But I've no experience. I've never acted in my life."

He shrugged. "Acting can be taught. You have beauty and presence. That is enough to begin with."

Visions swirled in her thoughts. Her? On the stage? Wearing beautiful dresses? Wined and dined by admirers, flowers thrown at her feet? But what would Mama and Papa say? This wasn't something that could be hidden the way she had hidden her new friends. They would know.

Dread clutched at her stomach, pushing out the excitement that had shot through her a moment before. Mama and Papa would be mortified if word got around, which it surely would. But Danni had been on the stage. And Danni was a wonderful Christian. Mama and Papa were very old-fashioned. Not that there was anything wrong with that. But Sutton cleared his throat and she looked up, startled. "So what is your decision, my dear? Would you like me to look into this for you? It's entirely up to you."

Cici licked her lips. "Could I think about it awhile?"

"Of course." He laughed. "There is no time limit, my dear. My theater contacts will not go away. Take all the time you like."

 C8

Jimmy stood by the dock, a large cloth-covered basket on his arm, and peered down the street. He put his hand above his eyes to shield them from the glare of the setting sun that had yet to slip below the horizon.

In the middle of the next block, a group of children huddled around something.

Jimmy couldn't tell what. Laughter reached him and he breathed a sigh of relief.

A head popped up and looked his way, revealing Patrick's grinning face. When he caught sight of Jimmy, he yelled and came running. By the time he reached Jimmy, the others had caught up with him. "Hey, Jimmy. Whatcha doin' down here?"

"Whatcha got in the basket, Jimmy?"

A cacophony of shouts almost drowned each other out.

Jimmy laughed and looked into the basket. "Bread and soup beans. I had extra and wanted to share. Would you mind taking some home with you?"

At the sound of silence, he looked up into blank faces. One of the older boys turned and walked away. Another followed.

"Hey, Walter, where are you going? What's wrong?"

Walter stopped and looked at Jimmy. "My pa'd skin me good if I came home with charity stuff."

"What?" He glanced around. What had he done wrong? "Patrick?"

Patrick licked his lips and looked at the bread. He lifted his eyes to Jimmy's. "Some of the pas don't take nothin' from no one."

Marty Woods, a ten-year-old with a club foot, nodded and shifted on his crutch. "My pa says we may be poor, but we ain't beggars." He hobbled down the street and turned into a narrow alley.

Jimmy glanced around at the children who had remained. "I'm sorry if I've done something wrong. I didn't know."

Lily Rose, a seven-year-old, gave him a sweet smile. "It's okay. Most of us don't have pas." She looked at the basket. "That bread smells mighty good."

He divided the food between the few remaining children. "Hey, Patrick, where's Mike and Bridget?"

"Bridget had to clean some fish heads someone gave her for soup. She won't let Mike out of her sight since he ran away."

"Well, there should be enough bread here for a couple of days. Does she know how to make beans?" He wasn't taking anything for granted anymore.

"Sure, she makes the bestest beans in the world." He reached a finger through his greasy locks and scratched.

Jimmy forced himself not to grimace as his scalp crawled in response to the sight. Did the boy have lice?

After the Bible story, the children shouted their good-byes and scattered.

Jimmy tromped to the bridge to catch the streetcar. He'd made a mistake today. It didn't matter that he had good intentions. Why had he thought God had called him to feed the hungry and save their souls? It must have been his imagination. How could he help anyone when he had no idea what he was doing?

His heart lurched at the memory of Lily Rose's tiny hand on his. And Patrick and the other children had sat still, their eyes wide as he told them the story of the boy Jesus in the temple.

Hope shot through him. He absolutely was called to help these people. He simply needed someone to guide him.

There used to be a church around here somewhere. Mama used to take him and Danni. They'd know the minds of these people. But where was it? Maybe Danni would remember. Yes. He'd ask Danni.

Chapter 11

Thank you for inviting me to lunch, Danielle." Cici smiled and sipped her tea.

"It's my pleasure entirely, I assure you." Jimmy's sister put a cube of sugar in her cup and stirred. "I was so disappointed we didn't get a chance to talk alone at the picnic."

"Me, too. But I must admit I enjoyed Mr. O'Shannon's, or rather Pops's, colorful stories of his vaudeville days."

Laughter exploded from Danielle's lips. "I should warn you, the stories often vary in detail. I believe he may have forgotten which versions are the true ones. But he's a wonderful man with a great big heart."

"Yes, I'm sure he is." Cici stirred her tea. Should she broach the subject of Danielle's short acting career? Or would that be rude?

"Is something bothering you?" Danielle pursed her lips, and twin furrows appeared between her eyebrows.

"Oh no. I was just wondering. . .that is, I understand you and your husband were involved with the theater as well."

"That's right. We were for a short while. He wrote a musical comedy and I played the lead." She grinned. "But then we fell in love and he decided he should return to law school and his father's firm."

"He quit law school, too? Like Jimmy?"

"Mm-hmm. He had his heart set on a career in music and the theater. He still loves it but soon came to realize he loved law just as much." She grinned. "His mother was in a show once, too."

"Really? Mrs. Nelson? I mean the senior one?"

"That's the one. She was employed at Harrigan's with her father until the fire wiped everything out. By that time, she realized all she really wanted to be was Sam Nelson's wife. So she gave it all up."

"He gave her an ultimatum?" Cici felt a spark of anger.

"No—goodness, no. Sam Nelson would have given Kathryn O'Shannon the moon if she'd asked for it. It was all her idea. When the theater was rebuilt, Pops went back though."

"I don't remember ever hearing of Harrigan's. Is it still around?"

"No, I believe there's a nightclub in that spot now. About five years after the fire, Harrigan and his Irish troupe began touring all over the United States and Europe. That's when Pops gave it up. He didn't want to leave his little grandson, Blake." She smiled and winked. "They've always been very close."

Cici took a sighing breath. "I had hoped Jimmy would return to law school."

"Yes, me, too. In fact, I almost begged him. But if he really has a call of God on his life, we wouldn't want to interfere, would we?" Danielle's eyebrows lifted.

Huh. A twinge of guilt shot through Cici. She would interfere in a heartbeat if she thought it would do any good. And she wasn't giving up yet. She took another deep breath and smiled. "I suppose not. But tell me, how could you stand to lay it all down? I mean, your career?"

"Oh dear. I have everything I want. Blake is the most important thing in my life, and now"—she smiled and leaned forward, close to Cici—"I'm going to have a baby in October."

"Oh, how exciting. Does Jimmy know?"

"Yes, and he's going to be a wonderful uncle. I know it."

The clock on the mantel chimed twice. Cici smiled and stood. "I really must get back to the parsonage. I promised to help Mother mend choir robes this afternoon."

"Oh dear, and I never got around to asking you."

"Asking me what?" Cici's heart pounded. Had Danielle found out about Gail? But how?

"My church ladies' benevolence group has agreed to sponsor Jimmy's charitable activities in the tenement district." She stood and faced Cici. "We're going to open a soup kitchen down near the Clark Street docks in the near future. When we get more information about the families, we'll be distributing food baskets. I thought perhaps you might like to be involved."

Cici relaxed and smiled. She wasn't really that excited about the idea, but she would have agreed to anything just now. "Yes, I'd like that very much."

"Good, then that's settled. Our first meeting is next Tuesday. I'll pick you up in the carriage." She gave Cici a wide grin. "Blake won't let me touch his Ford, and personally I think it's way too loud anyway."

On the way home, Cici stared out the streetcar window and frowned. How did she let herself get talked into working with the poor? But there was one thing in its favor. Perhaps if she got to know more about the people Jimmy was so concerned about, she'd get some ideas of how to change his mind. After all, she was only thinking about his future. He'd thank her someday. She leaned against the seat and smiled. Yes, this was a good thing.

♋

The little church stood, small and obscure, between two tall buildings, its stones black from grime. Danni said she came here a few years ago. The pastor was new, but he was kind. Perhaps, living in this area, he would understand the people.

Jimmy gave a short laugh. He'd spent the first twelve years of his life here. But after they'd gone to live with Sutton, everything had changed. They were kept pretty close and weren't allowed out much except for the games, sometimes. And then they were in groups. Most of the time, the games were inside. A queasiness came over Jimmy. Games, Sutton called them. Lessons in stealing, that's what they were.

Jimmy knocked on the door. The sun bored into his shoulder blades.

"Come on in. Door's open." The shout echoed from somewhere inside.

Jimmy turned the doorknob and pushed open the door. The smell of paint assaulted his nostrils. The room was dark, shaded by the tall buildings on each side. Benches stood in rows. Pretty rickety. Most of them looked like they were on their last legs. Jimmy scanned them, frowning. Why hadn't anyone fixed them?

"Be right there." The words issued from a narrow door standing open at the rear of the room.

A moment later, a man stepped through. His overalls were spattered with white paint. He came forward, his hand outstretched. "Hello, I'm Brother Paul Norell. How may I help you?"

Jimmy shook the man's hand. "Jimmy Grayson. I work on the docks."

"Grayson." A thoughtful expression crossed his face. "Sounds familiar. Have we met?"

"No, sir. I believe you met my sister, Danielle, a few years ago."

His face lit up. "Of course. Danielle Grayson. And you are her younger brother. She mentioned you."

"Yes. I hope I haven't come at an inconvenient time. I hurried over here when we broke for lunch."

"Not at all. I was about to take a break from painting the kitchen anyway. You've given me the excuse I needed. Here, let's sit." He led the way to a bench up near the pulpit. When they were seated, Brother Paul smiled. "We're not likely to be disturbed. My wife is out replenishing our larder, and seldom does anyone come during the noon hour."

"Er. . .Brother Paul. . ." Jimmy hesitated at the unfamiliar terminology.

"Jimmy, please feel free to call me Paul. We don't stand on formality."

"Paul, then." Jimmy grinned then paused. "I believe I'm called to do missionary work among the people of this area."

Interest sparked in Paul's eyes and he nodded. "Go on."

As Jimmy shared the things on his mind and heart, lightness seemed to lift him from the helplessness he'd walked in the past few days. When he'd finished, relief washed over him and he glanced at Paul.

Paul blew a puff of air from between pursed lips. "Jimmy, you've learned one of the first lessons necessary for ministering to poverty-stricken people. I don't speak of the bums who think the world owes them a living, but people who want with all their hearts to take care of themselves. The only thing they have is their faith in God and their self-respect. As long as they can set a meal on the table for their families, they can keep both. And we mustn't ever intrude on that no matter how much we want to help. Because once they lose their self-respect, their faith soon follows, and after that there's nothing for them to do but give up in despair. Do what you can to protect their self-respect."

"Then what can I do to help them?"

"Pray for them. Feed the children whenever possible. Help those widows and abandoned mothers. Be ready to give an encouraging word to the men, and if an opportunity to help without breaking them should arise, follow the Lord's leading. Assist them to find jobs whenever possible. Most of them will work extra when the chance comes. Do what you can to stop the unfair wages and working conditions. Let God love and help them through you." He paused and took a deep breath. "It isn't easy, Jimmy. Your heart will be broken over and over again. And your patience will be tested time and time again. Be very sure, my friend. And remember, God loves these precious people more than you do. I'll be here to encourage you, pray for you, and help you in any way I can."

"Thank you, Paul. I do have one other question. My sister's church is thinking about opening a soup kitchen and distributing food baskets. Do you think that's a bad idea?"

"On the contrary. It's a very good idea. You will be there for those who want and need help. But you won't be intruding on those who don't. Even the proudest of men will not likely object to their families having bowls of soup for their midday meals as long as they aren't brought into the homes and put before their faces." An eager smile appeared on his face. "I'd like very much to help with this project in any way I can."

Jimmy went back to work with a clearer idea of what was before him and a sense of direction. He'd make mistakes. No doubt of that. But he could see the path now, and having Paul's prayers in addition to Rev. Willow's gave him a sense of peace he hadn't had before.

And faith. Paul's comments about the men and their faith in God had impressed him. If these poor men could have faith in God in their situations, he could certainly learn to trust the Lord in his. And Paul had said the same thing Rev. Willow had. God loved these people more than he did. He would be there to lead and guide in this endeavor.

Two small girls waved from a dingy hallway where they were weaving colored strips of fabric through each other's hair.

"Hi, Jimmy. Where you going?"

Now, what was her name? Oh yes. "Back to work, Brenda. You sure look pretty today. And you look pretty, too, Janey Lee."

Both girls giggled. "Thanks for the cheese and apples you gave us." The little brunette grinned, and the other, with stringy blond hair, nodded and smiled.

"You're very welcome, Janey Lee. You, too, Brenda. See you later."

"See you later, Jimmy," Janey Lee shrilled.

"See you later, Jimmy," Brenda echoed.

Ↄ

Why did Danni keep looking at him like that? She'd been throwing him furtive glances all during dinner.

"Is something wrong, Danni?"

She bit her lip and pink slid over her face. She gave a little shake of her head and focused on the enormous slice of chocolate cake that had already shrunk to half its size.

Jimmy shrugged. His imagination more than likely. He resumed his narrative of his midday conversation with Paul Norell.

"That's interesting, Jimmy." Blake, always the encourager, had been on Jimmy's side from the beginning in spite of his disappointment that his brother-in-law wouldn't be practicing law with him. "My father told me a story once about his experiences with the Chicago poor before the great fire, especially immigrants. Many people, including Dad, were under the false impression that they were shiftless people. He discovered most of them weren't. Rather, they were hard-working people forced to live and work under abominable conditions. Things aren't as bad now as back then, but it's still very hard for poor people to earn a living there."

"Yes, there will always be those who take advantage of the less fortunate." Jimmy lifted a bite of his cake to his mouth. A picture of Patrick, Mike, and Bridget came to his mind and he put the fork down.

"Jimmy"—Danni's eyes swam with tears as she stared at his plate—"it won't help any child for you to do without food."

He took a deep breath. "I know. I have to learn to deal with my thoughts though."

"Let's have our coffee in the parlor and talk awhile. We haven't seen much of you lately."

Blake laughed. "Now, Danielle, don't be a mother hen. Remember when we were courting?"

"Humph. I remember when you drilled me for hours on my diction and the position of my head."

"Huh?" Jimmy stared at his sister.

"Don't mind her." Blake snickered and gave a little yank to one of Danni's curls. "She's still holding an eight-year grudge over my coaching techniques for *Peg in Dreamland*."

"I am not."

Danni and Blake stepped into the parlor, laughing while Jimmy trailed behind, shaking his head. It was great the way those two still laughed and teased each other. Would he and Cici be like that when they'd been married that long? He froze. Where did that thought come from? He and Cici hadn't spoken of marriage. But in his heart, he dreamed.

"Come on, Jimmy. Why are you standing in the doorway?"

He laughed and stepped into the room. "A lot on my mind, I guess." He sat in a corner chair by the open window. He leaned back and yawned, closing his eyes for a moment.

"Jimmy."

He jerked up. "Sorry, I must have drifted off to dreamland. Didn't see Peg there."

Blake snorted. "Good one."

Danni wasn't laughing.

"C'mon, Danni. You've been giving me strange looks all evening. What's wrong?"

"I'm not sure if anything is." She bit her lip. "Are you serious about Cici?"

"Danni, that's Jimmy's business." Blake held up both hands at her glare. "Okay."

Jimmy swallowed. "Well, yes, I guess I am. Yes, I am serious. I want to marry her. Haven't proposed yet though. I'm sure she'd think it was much too soon. Besides, I can't really support a wife on a dockworker's salary."

She frowned. "But you'll more than likely have support from a church after seminary, won't you?"

"Yes, hopefully." Jimmy knew he was going to get depressed if this conversation continued.

She bit her lip. "That's not what I wanted to talk about. What I was wondering is, have you talked to Cici about your ministry?"

"Some. Why?" Now what was she getting at?

"Are you sure Cici shares your enthusiasm for helping the poor?"

Jimmy's heart seemed to drop into his stomach. Was he sure? She'd smiled and said, "That's wonderful," when he'd told her his decision. But her eyes had seemed to say something different.

What if she didn't share his desire to minister to hurting people? He took a deep breath. "I suppose it's time to find out, before it's too late." But was it already too late? Was he willing to give her up for this call on his life?

Chapter 12

Jimmy and Cobb stared after the family struggling down the street. The man's brow was still furrowed with anger as he pushed a wheelbarrow piled high with boxes and bags. Pots and pans stuck out, in danger of falling to the street. The man's exhausted-looking wife carried several crammed-full pillowcases, and the three boys each had a corner of a bulging tied-up sheet that threatened to spill its contents. Other pedestrians avoided the family's eyes as they hurried past, probably thankful it wasn't them.

Jimmy followed, determined to try one more time. "Hawkins, if you won't allow me to give you the money, at least accept a loan."

"Get away from me." He dropped the handles of the wheelbarrow and turned a face filled with fury upon Jimmy. "I don't need your help. It's my family, and I'll take care of them. A man has to take care of his own."

Jimmy stepped back. What could he do? As soon as he'd heard the Hawkinses were being evicted, he'd gone to their home and offered his assistance with the rent. An offer that was promptly refused with a counteroffer to kick Jimmy out the door.

Cobb clapped his hand on Jimmy's shoulder. "Let them go, Jimbo. There ain't nothing you can do."

"But where will they go?" Confusion clouded his mind and grief cut into his heart. Where could they possibly go?

Cobb inhaled a breath and blew it out with a loud *whoosh*. "Don't worry yourself sick over it. They'll find someplace."

"How will they do that? They have no money. God, show me what to do." The words came out with a groan. A groan that seemed to come from the depths of his being. "Those little boys, Lord."

"Okay, Jimbo"—Cobb faced him and grabbed his shoulders—"listen to me. There ain't nothin' you can do. Nothin' at all. Don't take it so hard. You can't help everyone."

The harshness of Cobb's voice penetrated Jimmy's mind. Realization hit like a sledgehammer against a concrete wall. There was nothing he could do. "I'm going home." Home where no one was cold or hungry or homeless.

"Now you're talking. Get some hot food in your stomach and a good night's rest. You'll feel better in the morning. Just wait and see if you don't."

Jimmy sighed. "Yeah, you should be a preacher, Cobb."

"Who, me?" A horrified, trapped expression crossed his face. "Why would I want to do that?"

"Don't look so scared. I was only teasing." He narrowed his eyes and peered at Cobb. "Wouldn't hurt you to go to church though."

"Yeah, that's what you keep telling me." Cobb grinned. "Maybe I will, one of these days. Who knows?"

Jimmy waved and headed for the streetcar line. He rode in silence, hardly noticing the other passengers. Had he only imagined the call of God on his life? He'd stood helpless and watched a family trudge down the street with nowhere to go. Maybe if he'd handled it differently. . ."

He groaned. He'd broken the first rule. Never intrude. Always protect a man's self-respect.

❧

Jimmy moved his fork around his plate, his mind wandering over the events of the afternoon. Emptiness swelled like a cavern inside him. It was over.

"Jimmy, what's wrong? You haven't touched your food." Danni frowned.

"Sorry, sis." He stabbed a piece of pot roast and lifted it to his mouth. The tender, succulent bite may as well have been burnt coal.

"Are you ill?" She pushed her chair back and rose.

"No, I'm fine." He motioned her to return to her seat. "I have some things on my mind. Nothing for you to worry about."

She cast him a glance that said she didn't believe a word of it then continued her conversation with Blake.

After dinner, Jimmy took his brother-in-law aside. "Could I speak with you privately?"

"Of course. Let's go to the study."

Jimmy followed him and they sat in leather chairs on each side of the empty fireplace.

"So it would appear Danielle was right. Something is wrong." Blake raised his eyebrows.

Jimmy drummed his fingers on the round table beside his chair. "I don't know, Blake. I'm having second thoughts about becoming a missionary."

"Are you? Hmm. I thought you were set on the decision." Blake peered at him. "What has brought on this new doubt?"

Jimmy cracked his knuckles, something he hadn't done in years. He took a deep breath. "Several things. I'm not sure I'm cut out for it. Maybe I imagined I heard from God. Besides, I'm seriously thinking of proposing marriage to Cici. How can I ask her to marry a dockworker who can't support her?"

"Okay, Jimmy." Blake leaned forward, his hands planted on his knees. "Something has brought this on. Do you want to tell me about it?"

Jimmy opened his mouth and the incident with the Hawkins family poured out. "All I could do was stand and watch as a whole family carried their belongings down the street, knowing they had nowhere to go."

"So this is about your feeling of helplessness?"

"Partly. But watching that proud man, knowing what his pain must be, I envisioned Cici. Because the same thing could happen to us."

"Jimmy, that's nonsense. You have a home with Danielle and me as long as you need or want it. Cici, too. In fact, Danielle and I sort of discussed it when we heard you wanted to be a missionary to the poor. We have plenty of room."

"I know you mean well, Blake." Jimmy attempted a smile that didn't materialize. "But a man has to take care of his own." He drew in a sharp breath. That was what Hawkins said. He jumped up. That settled it. He knew what he had to do. "I think it would be best for me to return to law school. I'm going to talk to Cici."

The streetcar ride to the parsonage seemed to take forever. Should he propose? But they hadn't really spoken of a future together. Perhaps she was only interested in a companion for recreational purposes. Still, she had agreed to meet his family and close friends and they all got on well. In any case, he'd need to get a ring before he proposed and nothing would be open this late. So that settled it. No proposal tonight.

Knots formed in his stomach as he knocked on the parsonage door. It was after eight. Perhaps the Willows would consider it too late for him to be calling.

"Jimmy, what a pleasant surprise. Come in." Mrs. Willow beamed as she opened the door.

"I hope it isn't too late for me to be calling. I'm afraid I wasn't thinking." Jimmy gave her an apologetic smile as he stepped into the hallway.

"Not at all. Are you here to see my husband or my daughter?" Humor shone from her blue eyes. Eyes so much like Cici's.

"Well, Cici. Of course, she may not be home. I shouldn't have assumed."

"I'm here. Hello, Jimmy." Cici's trilling voice matched the smile on her face. "Would you like to come into the parlor?"

"Uh, yes, I suppose so." If he didn't quit stammering, she'd think he was an idiot.

"Perhaps you young folks would prefer to sit on the porch swing. It's a lovely night." Mrs. Willow smiled again. "I really must return to my mending."

"The swing is a very good idea, Mama." Cici grinned and practically shoved Jimmy through the door.

He followed her to the swing, where they sat down together, their shoulders nearly touching, which didn't help Jimmy's nerves any.

"I'm so glad you came over, Jimmy. I was beginning to think you'd forgotten me." Her pink lips formed a pout that set Jimmy's heart thumping triple time. "I haven't seen you since Sunday."

Jimmy couldn't suppress a grin. "Today is only Tuesday, you know. Although I must admit it seems much longer to me. But to be honest, I didn't want to wear out my welcome."

Cici dimpled. "Does that mean you wanted to come over yesterday?"

"Of course. I'd be hanging on your doorstep like a lonesome dog if I thought I wouldn't get kicked off."

A peal of laughter erupted from her throat. "All right. I believe you."

"Good." He grinned then relaxed his face. "There is something I'd like to talk to you about."

"Oh?" She lowered her eyes, her lashes brushing her cheeks, but not before he'd seen a flicker of something that appeared to be dread. What was she expecting him to say?

"I'm seriously thinking of returning to law school to complete my studies. I only have six months to go. After that I can work at the Nelson firm while I'm studying for the bar."

Her eyes widened and her lips fell open. "Really? So you've decided not to be a missionary?"

"Almost. I'm still thinking things over."

"But why?" And why was she questioning his decision? Wasn't this what she'd wanted all along?

"I saw a poor family evicted from their home today. I might have helped them if I hadn't handled it wrong." He inhaled a deep breath.

Pain clutched him as he told her about the Hawkins family and about the man's reaction.

"Well, that just goes to show you can't help some people." Indignation filled her voice and a frown creased her forehead. "I know there are deserving people who can't help being poor, but that man was horrible to you."

"But. . .Cici. . ."

"Never mind." She reached over and touched his cheek. "The church ladies will be opening the soup kitchen and you can still give food to the children. That's probably all God ever intended you to do."

He lifted his hand and covered hers. A tingling sensation ran all the way up his arm. It was so precious of her to care about his feelings.

"Cici, I'd like to spend more time with you."

"You would?" A flash of excitement filled her eyes. Why hadn't he bought a ring before now? Perhaps she would have accepted his proposal.

"Yes." He took a deep breath. "I care deeply for you."

A pretty pink blush stained her cheeks.

"Is there any possibility you could return my feelings?"

"I care for you, too." Her whispered words sent joy ringing through him, and he grabbed both her hands and brought them to his lips.

She giggled. "I was beginning to wonder if you'd ever kiss my hand again."

He smiled and lifted her chin. "Not only your hand."

Her lips trembled and he caught his breath. "Cici." He lowered his lips and brushed hers in a soft kiss.

Ↄ

Cici wrapped her arms around herself as she stared out her window into the moonlight.

Thank You, God. You never meant Jimmy to be a missionary, did You?

Of course He didn't. And now that Jimmy was back on the right track, Cici would be sure to serve God. Yes, she would. The first thing she would do tomorrow would be to call Gail and bow out of her planned afternoon on the *Eastland* with Gail and Sutton. After all, she was quite certain Jimmy would propose soon, and an attorney's wife had to watch her reputation. She hugged herself then whirled around the room, her arms flung wide.

ଓ

Jimmy stepped off the streetcar, still nearly floating from the time he spent with Cici. He gave a little skip as he headed down the sidewalk. She loved him. He knew she did. If he'd had a ring, he would have proposed and she would have accepted. He was sure of it.

In the morning, he would send word that he'd be late to work and would make the necessary arrangements for returning to school next term. He laughed. Danni would be thrilled. The missionary idea had been a foolish dream.

The faces of Patrick, Mike, and Bridget popped into his mind and he slowed. But of course, he would still do what he could for the children. He would never desert them. And as Cici said, the women's group would have the soup kitchen and the food basket program. But. . .who would sit and tell Bible stories to the children? Who would offer hope for the future?

An agony Jimmy had never known knifed through his heart. Could he walk away? After all this time? He stopped.

"God! What do You want from me?" He hadn't meant to speak out loud, didn't realize he had shouted until an upper shade flew up in the house he faced.

A man leaned out the window. "Quiet down! People are trying to sleep!"

Jimmy lifted his hand in silent apology and resumed his walk home.

The light was still on in the parlor. Jimmy went inside and found Danielle sitting in her rocker with her Bible in her hand. She looked up, a troubled look on her face.

Jimmy flopped down on the sofa across from her.

"Jimmy?"

"Danni, what's wrong with me? I keep making decisions and then having second thoughts." He put his head in his hands.

"Blake told me you were thinking of returning to law school?" She peered at him.

"Yes, I even told Cici."

"And what did she think about the idea?"

"Oh, she was happy. Agreed it would be best. She had a lot of sensible things to say." He took a deep breath. "I could still help the children."

"Uh-huh." She laid the Bible on the side table.

"And your ladies' group is going to help with food and clothing."

"Yes."

"I thought you'd be jumping up and down with joy." He could hear the exasperation in his voice. "Sorry, sis. Didn't mean to snap."

"It's all right, Jimmy. I know you're under a lot of stress right now. Indecision will do that to you."

"I don't know what to do." He groaned, angry with himself for his inability to stick to his plan.

"Jimmy, what do you think is causing this struggle?" She gazed into his eyes.

He lowered his eyes. "Like I told Blake, I feel inadequate for missionary work."

"But you haven't even begun, really. Just because one man rejected your help, you're giving up the dream God placed in your heart?"

"I thought you wanted me to go back to law school." What was wrong with everyone anyway?

"I do. But only if it's God's plan and you want it with your whole heart." She paused. "I've never seen you so happy as you've been lately, Jimmy."

He jumped up. "Thanks for listening, Danni. I'm going up to bed." He kissed her on the cheek and went to his bedroom.

She was right. He had been happy. Why had he let this one incident change his mind? He dropped into a chair by the window and looked out at the moon. The same moon that had looked down as he kissed Cici's soft lips. And the truth hit him.

Will she love me if I don't return to law school? Will she agree to be the wife of a missionary?

Chapter 13

Rain fell in sheets, slapping the parlor window where Jimmy stood. A flash of lightning speared the ground, followed by a clap of thunder that shook the room.

"Great, just great." What else could happen? Just before his shift ended, a badly tied-up barrel had fallen from the mast of the *Eastern Sun*, bursting its contents, which happened to be molasses, all over the deck. And naturally he had to help with the cleanup. The jeweler had been locking up when Jimmy arrived and it had taken ten minutes to talk the man into letting him purchase a ring. Only when Jimmy had pulled out his money did the store owner relent and let him in.

Jimmy drew in a deep breath and let it out with a huff. He pulled the little blue box from his vest pocket and looked at it again. Would Cici like it? Was the stone big enough? He'd had a little money saved up. But when he'd glanced over the rings and seen the prices, he'd almost walked out. He'd finally chosen one he thought she'd like that hadn't been too much more than he'd planned to spend. Now that he examined it more closely, he wasn't sure. It was the new Edwardian style with a platinum band. He sighed and put it back in his pocket. He never would find out, if the rain didn't stop. He'd thought of making a run for it, but he'd be soaked before he got to the streetcar line. Maybe he'd better call Cici and tell her he couldn't make it.

"Jimmy, why are you standing in the dark?" Blake turned on the gas lamp on the wall by the door. "I thought you'd already left."

Jimmy shook his head. "In this downpour? I'd be half drowned before I got half a block."

"You can take the carriage. I've told you before to feel free to use it anytime Danielle doesn't need it."

"Maybe I'll wait until it slacks up and take the umbrella." Jimmy preferred the more modern style of transportation. It freed him from making arrangements for the horse. And Blake sure hadn't offered his automobile. Probably afraid Jimmy would wreck it on the slippery streets.

"Okay, I offered." Blake sighed and shook his head. "Oh, all right. Take the Runabout."

Jimmy grinned and looked out the window. "Nah, it's letting up. I think I'll make a run for the streetcar. See you later."

He grabbed his umbrella from the stand in the foyer and took off down the street. He'd only been waiting a couple of minutes when the streetcar arrived.

Maybe his luck was turning. Or. . .maybe God had something to do with it. Uneasiness churned in his stomach as he climbed aboard the public conveyance. He hadn't been spending much time with God. It wasn't that he was turning away from Him or anything like that. He'd just been busy. Too busy to spend an hour or even a few minutes with God? He hadn't had his Bible open all week except at church. He pushed the thought aside and took a seat in the empty car. Apparently he was the only one crazy enough to come out in this weather.

By the time he got off near the parsonage, the rain had increased again, so Jimmy opened his umbrella and ran down the sidewalk in the deluge.

Cici's eyes widened as she opened the door for him. "Jimmy, I didn't think you'd come."

"I told you I'd be here." He grinned, shook the umbrella, and propped it up by the door, then wiped his feet on the mat.

"Well, get in here. You look like a drowned cat." She giggled and pulled him inside, shutting the door behind him.

"I don't know, Cici. Maybe I should stay on the porch. Your mother might not be too happy with my dripping all over the place." He grinned. "Besides, I need to speak to you privately."

"Oh, all right." She smiled then called out, "Mother, I'm sitting on the porch with Jimmy."

Mrs. Willow stepped from the parlor. "Oh my. Perhaps Jimmy should come in the kitchen and get dried off."

"I'm fine, ma'am. I'll just get soaked again in a few minutes when I leave."

"Well, my goodness, young man. Why did you come out in this weather if you're only staying a few minutes?"

"Mama. . ." Cici threw her mother a pleading look.

"I'd best return to my knitting. I'm making socks for the children in the tenements."

"That's nice, Mrs. Willow. I'm sure they'll be appreciated."

When they were finally seated on the porch swing, Jimmy leaned back and took her hand. She smiled up at him.

"Cici, honey, you must know that I love you." He laid his hand on her cheek. "And I pray you have feelings for me as well."

A pink blush kissed her cheeks. She ducked her head then looked straight up at him. "I love you, too, Jimmy."

Joy filled his heart and he slipped out of the swing and onto one knee. He ran his tongue over his suddenly dry lips and took a deep breath. "Will you marry me?"

Cici gasped. With her eyes wide and bright with tears, she flung her arms around his neck. "Oh yes, Jimmy. I want to be your wife more than anything in the world."

His hands trembled as he put the ring on her finger. Then he sat beside her and took her into his arms.

"It's beautiful. The most beautiful ring I've ever seen." Cici held her hand out and admired the ring. "Jimmy, it's a diamond."

He grinned. "Diamonds are all the style for engagement rings now. Are you sure you like it? I can exchange it for one with a different stone if you'd rather."

She covered the ring with her other hand as if to protect it. "I'll never part with this ring as long as I live." Her upturned lips were too much to resist.

"You are precious." Jimmy kissed softly at first, then deepened the kiss until she drew back, trembling.

Jimmy barely noticed his damp clothing as the hours passed and they declared their love for each other over and over again. It was nearly midnight when he arrived home. He climbed the stairs, reliving the evening, examining every word, every kiss. Yes, he'd done the right thing. He had the most precious fiancée who ever lived, and no one had ever loved the way they did.

But as he got ready for bed, the thought he'd kept at bay finally forced its way into his mind. What would she say if she knew he hadn't yet made arrangements to return to school?

⍥

Silver tinkled against twinkling crystal. Soft candlelight bathed the white tablecloth and red napkins with a romantic ambience, perfect for this night.

Cici blushed and bit her lip as Jimmy sent her an adoring smile across the table. "Jimmy, don't look at me like that. People will notice." Her whispered words didn't reflect the delight that coursed through her being.

"Well, I guess I don't care if you don't." He grinned and reached across the table, taking her hand. He ran his thumb across the diamond, which appeared enormous to Cici as it winked in the candlelight.

"Behave yourself." She slipped her hand from his and darted a glance around the room.

"There, you see? No one is paying the least bit of attention."

He was right. They could have been on an island for all the attention they were getting. Even the waiter seemed to know they wanted solitude and only appeared when it was time for another course of the excellent meal or to refill their water glasses.

When the last delicious bite was eaten, they lingered over their tea until finally Jimmy rose. "We'd better be getting to the theater. We don't want to miss the opening act."

Cici's heart thumped hard against her rib cage. When she'd suggested to Jimmy that they go to see the new musical comedy, it had seemed like a great adventure. After all, she'd never been to the theater. But as they walked into the luxurious, sparkling lobby, she swallowed past a lump and darted a glance around. What if some of her parents' friends should see her? Of course they wouldn't have any right to talk if they were here. But what if someone mentioned seeing her here to her parents, just in passing? Her father and mother never judged others for theatergoing, but her father often said a minister and his family must be above reproach.

"Honey, what are you so nervous about?" Jimmy squeezed her elbow and she drew closer to him and smiled.

"I'm not nervous. Just looking around. This is my first time at a play."

"Really? If I'd known that, we could have come sooner."

How was she going to get it across to him not to mention this to her parents? What would he think of her when he found out she was going against her father's wishes? But she was an adult. Soon to be an attorney's wife. She needed to learn how to conduct herself in society.

"Perhaps we should have invited your parents to join us."

Cici drew her breath in sharply then calmed herself. "Yes, that would have been very nice. Perhaps another time." She sank into the luxurious seat. How could anything be so superbly comfortable? Red velvet curtains hung from some secret place near the vast ceiling. Golden cords hung down on each side. Surely this must be dreamland.

The theater filled up to capacity and the lights went off.

Cici sat mesmerized as the curtains rose on a bright, colorful kingdom where not only birds sang their songs to one another, but people did, too.

During intermission, Jimmy excused himself for a moment, but Cici sat glued to her chair, afraid of missing even one magical moment.

A young woman in a frilly blue dress stepped out on the stage and sang a song while waiting for the crowd to return.

When Jimmy returned to his seat, Cici clutched his arm and smiled.

"Enjoying your first show, sweetheart?" He squeezed her hand.

"Oh yes. It's wonderful and amazing. I can't imagine why. . ." She stopped herself before giving her secret away. But why did her parents think the theater was inappropriate?

When the curtain came down after the final act, Cici applauded with everyone else and then followed Jimmy down the aisle, almost in a daze. She blinked in the bright electric lights of the chandelier in the lobby.

Jimmy guided her through the crowd toward the door then suddenly stopped, almost jerking Cici to a halt.

She gasped as she saw Sutton facing them.

He swept an amused glance in her direction then turned his attention to Jimmy. "Well, Jimmy, my boy, it's been a long time." He pressed his lips together and nodded. "Much too long. It's always good to see one of my children."

Cici gazed at Jimmy in wonder. A muscle by his mouth jumped as he stared at Sutton in stony silence.

"Tell me, Jimmy"—Sutton's eyes burned and Cici could see fury in their depths—"how is the lovely Danielle? Please give her my love and tell her I'll be seeing you both very soon."

Jimmy clutched Cici's arm and pushed past him. His breath came in ragged bursts, his face tense with anger. Silently, he hailed a carriage and held the door for Cici.

She climbed in, not speaking until he was seated beside her. "Jimmy, what's wrong? Did you know that man?" Of course Jimmy knew him. Sutton had called him and Danielle by name.

Jimmy inhaled deeply and turned to her. He smiled. "Don't worry about him. He's a very unpleasant person whom I hope you never have to see again."

Unpleasant? She wouldn't call Sutton unpleasant. He'd always been very gracious to her. But of course, Jimmy mustn't know she was acquainted with a man he was obviously at enmity with. She waited, hoping he would reveal how he knew Sutton. Why had the man called Jimmy one of his children?

"I hope you enjoyed the evening, sweetheart. I'm sorry if the last incident hindered your enjoyment in any way."

"No, no. Not at all." She hesitated, not sure how to broach the subject of her parents. "Jimmy, I wonder if you would mind not mentioning that we went to the theater. To Mama and Papa, I mean."

Astonishment crossed his face. "What? Why ever not?"

Heat filled her face. "It's just that, you see, they wouldn't approve of my going." A sick look crossed his face.

Cici felt tears surfacing. Oh no. He would hate her now.

"Cici—" His voice broke. "Why didn't you tell me? Or for that matter, why. . . ." He stopped, but disappointment clouded his eyes.

"I'm sorry, Jimmy. But I wanted to see a show so badly. I know it was wrong to go against my parents' wishes."

He slipped his arm around her and kissed the top of her head. "Well, what's done is done. I love you, sweetheart."

"I love you, too." The words came out in a sob. "I love you so much."

CB

Jimmy sent the carriage away and took the streetcar home. The clacking sound of the wooden seats and *rickety-racketing* of the wheels grated on his nerves. The jerking of the car, which he usually didn't notice, caused his head to pound.

He had frozen at the sight of Sutton. And when the evil rascal dared to mention Danielle's name, all Jimmy wanted to do was put his hands around the evil man's neck and squeeze the life out of him. Had he ever been angry enough to willingly consider violence? He didn't think so.

It was obvious Sutton had a plan that involved Jimmy and his sister. Jimmy knew the man well enough to know the plan wasn't a benevolent one. He was set on revenge, and there was no telling what measure he would take to achieve his goal. Jimmy also hadn't liked the way the man's eyes had wandered over Cici.

And that was another thing. Why would Cici have asked Jimmy to take her to the theater when she knew her parents would not approve? What did that say about her character? Guilt bit at him at the thought. There was nothing wrong with Cici's character. She was still very young. It was simply a girlish whim.

When he entered the house, his eyes wandered up the stairs. Should he wake Blake? Warn him about Sutton? But what good would it do to rob him of a night's sleep? There was nothing Danni's and his former captor could do here in their own home. He'd make sure he spoke to Blake in the morning and leave it up to him what to say to Danni.

He practically dragged himself up the stairs. He changed into his pajamas and robe then threw himself into a chair.

God, I don't know what to do.

But his words seemed to fall like stones on the carpeted floor, muffled and going nowhere. How could he come to God when his conscience was stabbing him so? When the eyes of the tenement children haunted him? Their voices called to him when he slept.

He groaned and stepped to the window. Moonlight streamed in, enveloping the room in a ghostly aura. He jerked the curtains shut and climbed into bed. This should have been a day of delirious happiness for him and Cici. Instead, his whole world seemed to be caving in.

Chapter 14

"Jimmy, when you complete your studies, you'll need to begin studying for the bar right away. You'll find everything you need here in my library and the one at the office." Mr. Nelson sank into a leather armchair and motioned for Blake and Jimmy to do likewise.

"Thank you, sir." His stomach sank, as it always did lately, at the mention of his career in law.

"What's on your mind, son?" Mr. Nelson had an observant eye and little got by him.

Jimmy opened his mouth to deny anything was wrong, but the words wouldn't come. He sighed. "I can't stop thinking of the conditions in the slums by the river, especially around the Clark Street docks. I feel that I've deserted those people."

Blake leaned forward. "But you're still feeding the children from your own lunch pail every day as well as taking food to pass out on Saturdays."

"I know, but it doesn't seem near enough."

"Are you reconsidering your decision to return to law school? I notice you've not made the arrangements yet." Mr. Nelson stretched his feet and legs onto the leather ottoman.

"Jimmy?" Blake raised his eyebrows in question.

"I'm not sure. But I can't get the poor tenement people off my mind."

They spent an hour discussing the law firm and various pending cases, then talked about a recent fishing trip on which Blake and his father caught several large bass.

Finally, Mr. Nelson rose. "Katie will kill me if I keep you to myself any longer. We'd best join the women in the parlor. Tea sounds good anyway."

Blake and Jimmy followed the older man from the room.

"Oh good. You're here." Mrs. Nelson crinkled her eyes and smiled at her husband, who bent and kissed her brow.

Jimmy glanced at Cici, who smiled and patted the cushion next to her on the sofa.

"Jimmy, I'm so glad you came today and brought Cecilia." Mrs. Nelson smiled and turned to Cici. "He used to join us for Sunday dinner every week. But now"— she sent a teasing smile Cici's way—"he seems to have other things to do."

Jimmy grinned. "I'm sure we'll be here more often now that we're engaged. Cici will want to get to know you better."

"And we certainly want to know this lovely young lady better. The girl who caught Jimmy's heart." Mr. Nelson grinned and winked at his wife. "Her hair is the exact same lovely color yours is."

"Was, dear, was." Mrs. Nelson smiled and, reaching up, patted his hand.

"Still every bit as lovely as ever." He bent down to kiss her cheek, and as they gazed into each other's eyes, it seemed to Jimmy as if they shared some secret.

He shook his head in wonder. After all these years, it was obvious that Blake's parents were still very much in love.

After the men had seated themselves and received cups of tea, Mr. Nelson turned to his wife. "Katie, you know Jimmy has been feeding children down by the docks. Why don't you tell him about your charitable work before the great fire?"

"All right." Her clear blue eyes shone and she smiled at Jimmy. "Let me see, now where shall I begin?"

"How about the soup kitchen?" her husband coached her.

"Soup kitchen?" Surprise rose in Jimmy. "You worked in a soup kitchen?"

She nodded and her face became serious. "You see, there were many Irish immigrants in Chicago back then. Some, like my father, were accepted and respected. But a lot of people resented the poor folk who'd come over to escape the potato famine."

"But why? Why in the world would anyone begrudge a safe harbor to people who were starving?"

She nodded. "Why indeed? You see, they came in droves, looking for employment. Many folks thought they were stealing jobs, and perhaps they were in a way, for they'd work for a pittance simply to put food on the table." She sighed. "Shantytowns popped up all over the city. Tents and shacks. The largest and most notorious was Conley's Patch. Have you ever heard of it?"

Jimmy shook his head. "Where was it?"

She looked pointedly into his eyes. "Just across the south branch of the river, by the Clark Street docks."

Jimmy inhaled sharply. "Where the tenement section is?"

She nodded. "That's right. Some of the people there are descendants of the poor Irish in Conley's Patch."

"And you did charitable work there?" Jimmy looked at the dainty matron in awe.

"Not at first. I started out working in a soup kitchen near Harrigan's. I'd go volunteer when I was off duty from the theater. I met a girl named Bridget Thornton. A very proud but desperate young woman trying to keep her family from starving." She took a sip of tea. "We became dear friends. She taught me the plight of the proud but poor people of the Patch who wanted nothing but to make a living for their families. I'll never forget my first sight of the Patch." Mrs. Nelson pressed her lips together and moisture filled her eyes. "The shanties, the tiny yards. Dirt settled everywhere. The women worked constantly keeping it out of their homes. But worse than the dirt were the ditches that ran down the center of the streets. Raw sewage, garbage, even dead animals floated down the open sewers. Sometimes a child would fall into the ditch."

"Oh yes." Mr. Nelson seemed to be reliving a memory. He shook his head and took a sip of tea.

Mrs. Nelson reached over and patted her husband on the arm, smiling into his eyes. "Sam, dear, remember when you rescued Bridget's little sister from the ditch?"

"You mean the time those little hooligans shoved her in? Oh, I remember, all right. We were both a mess. And the smell. . ." Mr. Nelson quirked his eyebrows and wrinkled his nose at the memory.

Mrs. Nelson grinned. "So I heard. But to continue, Bridget and I helped start a daycare so some of the single mothers could earn a living and married women could get jobs to supplement their husbands' incomes. Some of the women ran the daycare while others got jobs in the city."

Jimmy heard Cici give a soft sigh. He glanced her way. The smile she gave him was pinched. Unease knotted his stomach as he turned his attention back to Mrs. Nelson's story.

"Bridget and I did what we could to raise funds for the child-care center. The troupe at Harrigan's pitched in." A cloud crossed Mrs. Nelson's face. "Then the fire came."

Mr. Nelson shared a long glance with his wife. "The Patch was completely destroyed."

Jimmy could hardly imagine the devastation the poverty-stricken people must have felt. "What a tragedy. It must have been terrible for them."

"Yes," Mrs. Nelson whispered, "it was horrible. Not just for the Patch. Most of the city was destroyed or severely damaged. But my husband's father pulled the people of the city together. There was plenty of work for whoever wanted it. The people worked hard. And the city was rebuilt, including housing for the lower-income people. Instead of shanties, tenement houses were built. There were paychecks for anyone who was willing to work."

"But the people of the tenements are still poor."

Danielle sighed. "Jesus said the poor would always be with us."

"That's right." Mrs. Nelson nodded. "And just as it was before the fire, evil men often exploited the poor, paying them unfairly low wages. And then people moved from other areas and brought their problems with them. It is true. The poor will always be with us."

"You have a heart to help people, Jimmy." Mr. Nelson smiled. "Just as my wife did and still does."

"What happened to your friend Bridget?" He wished he could take back the question as pain crossed her face.

"Bridget died a number of years ago. I kept in touch with her sister for a while. When she married and moved away, we lost contact."

Jimmy glanced at Cici. Was that impatience in her eyes? Then she smiled. Jimmy breathed with relief. She'd been disturbed by the sad story. That was all.

"Thank you for telling me about the Patch, Mrs. Nelson. And I'm very sorry you lost your friend."

He leaned back and took Cici's hand. It lay in his, cold and rigid.

⁓

Cici stood facing Jimmy outside the parsonage door.

"What's wrong, sweetheart?" Jimmy's concerned gaze cut through her. "You've been awfully quiet."

"Nothing. I'm fine." Tension, like a wound-up spring, threatened to burst any moment. Why did Mrs. Nelson have to tell her story? It was heartbreaking in one sense, but it also showed what a few people could do if they cared enough. Cici hated the feelings the stories had created in her. And she was pretty sure they'd had a strong effect on Jimmy.

"Are you sure?" His brow furrowed and he tucked a loose curl behind her ear.

"No! No, Jimmy, I'm not sure. In fact, I'm quite sure I'm not fine." She jerked away from him.

A startled look crossed his face. "Honey, what is it? Why are you so upset?"

"I need to know, Jimmy. Have you made a decision about law school? I assumed you had, but you never really said for sure."

He looked away then faced her again. "Let's sit on the swing for a little while."

With dread pounding at her, she sat beside him.

He took her hand and gazed into her eyes. "Cici, if I should decide not to, will you still marry me? Do you care for me enough to be the wife of a missionary?"

Her mouth quivered, and before she could stop them, tears began to roll from her eyes and down her cheeks. "So you've made your decision?"

"I didn't say that, Cici." He ran his thumb across her cheeks, wiping the tears away. "But I need to know if you'll marry me either way."

"I don't know."

Resignation crossed his face.

She felt as though a knife had pierced her heart. "I love you. I promise I do. But I don't know if I can be a missionary's wife, Jimmy."

"But honey, it's not like we'd be going far away. We'd be right here near those we love and. . .this is about doing what Jesus would want us to do."

"And you believe He wants you to be a missionary to the poor."

He took a deep breath and ran his hand through his hair. "I thought so. I'm not sure anymore. I'm confused, Cici. And I don't like it."

"It's because of me, isn't it? It's my fault you don't know what you're supposed to do."

"No, of course not."

"I think it is. I'll try not to influence you, Jimmy. I have to think now. I love you." Jumping up, she ran to the door, pushed her way through, and slammed it behind her.

☙

God, help me. Help me to at least give it a try.

Cici's lips trembled and she pressed them together and forced a smile as Danielle opened the door of her home. "Hello. I hope I'm not late for the meeting."

"Not at all. You are just in time. We're about to begin." With a big smile, Danielle motioned for her to come in. "I'm glad you decided to come."

About twenty women crowded the parlor. Blake's mother waved from across the room, and a woman sitting on a sofa moved over and made room for Cici. "Aren't you Reverend Willow's daughter?"

"Yes, ma'am." Cici sat by the woman and smiled.

"Everyone, I'd like for you to meet Cici Willow." Danielle looked around the room. "I believe her mother has agreed to be a part of our group as well but had other duties to fulfill today. Now if we could call the meeting to order. I believe Mary Baker has some news about a building."

"Yes indeed." A younger woman stood. "An empty church building, as a matter of fact. It has been abandoned for so long the owners were quite willing to let us use it free of charge. We will, of course, be responsible for the upkeep. There is no gaslight or electricity, so we'll need to gather up lamps and kerosene to take over."

Several women offered lamps. Danielle counted and wrote down the names.

"Are there any tables?" another woman asked.

"Yes, that's the good thing. All their Sunday school tables are still there." She grinned. "And even better, there's a stove, so we won't have to cook the soup elsewhere and transport it there."

"We'll need to find someone to bring wood," Danielle said.

"I think my father-in-law might be willing to do that. I'll ask," Mrs. Baker said.

Plans were made about who would bring what ingredients.

"Now about the food baskets. . ." Danielle tapped a pencil against her chair.

"A man who owns a box company goes to our church." Cici was happy to be able to make a contribution to the conversation. "He always gives away the imperfect ones that he can't sell. They would work very well as containers for the groceries. Would you like me to check with him?"

"That would be wonderful, Cici." Danielle smiled and made a notation.

"Oh, and one more thing." Cici leaned forward. "My mother wanted me to extend an offer on behalf of her sewing circle to make socks and hats for you to include with the baskets."

Murmurs and nods went around the room.

"That would be grand." Mrs. Nelson smiled. "Winter will be here before we know it. Please extend our thanks to your mother and the ladies of her sewing circle."

Warmth enveloped Cici as she returned the smile and nodded.

For an hour they planned; then they agreed to get together again on Tuesday.

Cici felt more peace as she rode home on the streetcar than she had since the dinner on Sunday. Maybe if Jimmy really did become a missionary, she could handle it. At least by getting involved with this project to help the people in the tenements, she'd find out.

Chapter 15

An icy chill ran up Jimmy's spine as he spotted Cobb and Sutton through the dusty window. He took a step back into the darkness then cautiously peered in once more.

They sat at a table in the far corner, laughing. Cobb turned up his mug and took a long swig of coffee.

Nausea hit Jimmy and he closed his eyes. Cobb, his friend, he'd thought. Could he have just run into Sutton? Maybe he was getting information for Jimmy. But reason told him otherwise.

Sutton stood and threw some coins on the table, said something, and headed for the door.

Jimmy ducked around the corner of the building until he heard the man's footsteps walking off down the sidewalk. Anger rose in him. More at himself than at Cobb. He should have known better. Cobb had been Sutton's main boy for years before Jimmy and Danni had fallen into their lives. He peered into the window once more.

Cobb stood and sauntered across the café. The door swung open. Cobb stood there, a look of shock on his face. "Hey, Jimbo."

"Hi, Cobb, old friend." He made no attempt to keep the anger from resonating from his voice. Cobb would know right away he'd seen them.

"You were right, Jimbo. I just ran into Sutton. Matter of fact, you just missed him."

"Yeah, I know." Jimmy narrowed his eyes. "What's the big idea, Cobb?"

"What do you mean? I told you. . ." He stopped and shook his head. "Oh, what's the use? All right, I knew Sutton was out."

"Why'd you lie to me? We're supposed to be friends."

Cobb huffed out a loud breath of air. "I didn't figure you'd believe me that Sutton's changed, that's why."

Jimmy laughed. "Changed? Sutton? Okay, Cobb, how's he changed? Does he have a new type of crime ring going this time?"

"No, Jimmy, listen. He really has changed. You should hear him talk." Cobb's eyes were bright as he grabbed Jimmy's shoulders. "He wants to help the people around here. Just like you do. He was happy when I told him what you were up to."

Jimmy jerked away. "You really believe that, don't you? Wake up. Sutton is the same rotten crook he's always been."

"Well, that's a fine Christian way to talk." Cobb's face twisted and he

311

narrowed his eyes. "Don't give the man a chance. Just take it for granted he can't change. And to think I'd almost decided maybe you were right about the God stuff. I was even thinking about going to church with you."

Uncertainty wormed its way into Jimmy's mind; then immediately he pushed it away. "Cici and I ran into Sutton at the theater. He hasn't changed. He practically threatened Danni."

"Why? What did he say?"

"He said. . . Well, it wasn't so much what he said as the way he said it and the look he gave me when he said it." He narrowed his eyes. "Believe me. He's up to no good. At least where Danni and I are concerned."

"Aw, come on, Jimbo. Can't you admit you might be wrong? Give Sutton a chance. He wants to talk to you."

"Sorry. Let him fool you if you want to, but I'm not having anything to do with him."

"Okay, have it your way." Cobb swung around and started down the sidewalk then turned and faced Jimmy. "But Sutton's a changed man, Jimbo. You're gonna see." Cobb stalked off down the street.

Jimmy sighed. Could Cobb be right? He turned and headed toward Clark Street and the streetcar line. No, Sutton was the same. He only hoped Cobb would see that before he got himself into trouble.

When Jimmy got home, he found Danni and Blake in the parlor. He dropped into a chair.

"Is something wrong?" Danni threw him a worried look. "It's not Cici, is it?"

He inhaled and let the air out with a *whoosh*. "No, I went to the tenements to take some medicine to Mike. He's been sick."

"Oh, how is he?"

"He'll be okay. But I saw Cobb with Sutton." He relayed the conversation they'd had.

Danielle frowned. "Is it possible? Anyone can change, you know. Maybe Sutton found Jesus while he was in prison."

"I don't think so, Danni." He hadn't had a chance to tell Blake about his encounter with Sutton, as he'd intended. But Danielle had begun to go about alone again. They both needed to know. "I ran into Sutton while I was leaving the theater the other night."

Danni's hand trembled as she laid it on Blake's.

He put an arm around her and drew her close. "What happened?"

"Well, he seemed threatening to me. But I may have been mistaken." He went ahead and relayed the conversation word for word, describing Sutton's attitude and expressions as well as possible.

Blake's lips were tight. "Danielle, you need to stay near the house again."

She jumped up and stomped her foot as her face crumpled. "I won't let that man run my life. I'm not afraid of him."

"Sweetheart, please." Blake drew her down beside him again.

Jimmy's heart felt like it would tear in two at his sister's anguish. "Danni, please, just for a little while. Let me watch him for a while."

"We'll do better than that." Anger tightened Blake's face. "I'll put a private detective on his tail. If he goes near her, the police will be there before he can make a move."

"Well then, I won't need to stay inside." The hope in her eyes clutched at Jimmy and he glanced at Blake.

"No, sweetheart." Blake brought her hand up to his lips and kissed it. "You don't want to take chances. Please stay inside until we know what he's up to."

"But what about the soup kitchen and food baskets?" Despair filled her voice.

"There are twenty or more women involved with it, Danni." Jimmy's reminder only brought a frown his way. "They can get by without you for a while."

She sighed. "Very well. But this can't go on forever. I won't remain a prisoner in my own home."

Jimmy thought of her words as he went up to his room. He intended to do everything in his power to make sure she wouldn't be.

CB

The smell of cabbage and tomatoes assaulted Cici's nostrils as she dipped soup from the large pot and filled another bowl. She handed it to an old woman who flashed a toothless grin and walked away. Cici stretched her back and looked toward the door. The line ran down the street as far as she could see. How could there be so many hungry people in this one neighborhood alone?

"Cici, dear," Mrs. Baker called from the end of the food line, "could you get some bread out of the other room, please?"

"Yes, ma'am." She gladly turned the soup ladle over to a woman walking by and headed for the back room. The smell of yeast wafted up from the stacks of long loaves of bread that stood on the table by the open window. She grabbed four loaves and carried them back to where Mrs. Baker stood with a sharp knife. "Would you like me to help slice?" She swiped the back of her arm across her damp forehead.

"No. Why don't you relieve Dottie? She's been standing over that cauldron for an hour now."

"Yes, ma'am." She headed back to the kitchen and took over for the hefty woman who stood moving a big wooden spoon around the enormous pot.

"Be sure to keep stirring so it doesn't stick." The woman handed her the big wooden spoon and stepped over to the water barrel.

She did as she was told for another hour, dizzy from the overwhelming smell of cabbage, onions, and tomatoes swimming in beef broth until the last pot had been removed to the serving line. Cici grabbed a tin cup and filled it with water. She drank it all then went to relieve someone on the food line.

With so many of the women taking care of the food boxes, a handful of them were kept busy dishing up the food.

"Here, Martha, let me take over here. Go get yourself a cool drink."

With a grateful look, the young girl relinquished her place by one of the soup pots.

Cici picked up the ladle. She scooped soup into a bowl and looked up.

A small boy, not more than six or seven, stood staring at her with rounded blue eyes. The hunger in those eyes nearly made her heart stop. She handed him the bowl, and when his hands wrapped around it, he grinned. "You sure are purty, miss."

She smiled as warmth enveloped her heart. "Why, thank you. You're pretty handsome yourself."

Red washed over his face and he grinned again. A tiny girl who followed with her mother giggled. The boy moved on down the line and the little girl peered up at her.

Cici smiled. "Yes, you're mighty pretty, too." She filled two bowls of soup and smiled at the mother. "Do you need help carrying these?"

"Oh no, Patsy can carry hers." She turned to the child. "Be careful now, honey."

Cici watched them as she filled another bowl. She breathed a sigh of relief when the little girl set her bowl safely on the table then ran back to where the bread was being handed out.

The door opened and a boy hobbled in on one crutch. He glanced around as though looking for someone then came to the line. He eyed the soup as though he hadn't eaten in days. Mrs. Nelson filled a bowl for him and he started toward a table.

Suddenly the door flew open. A red-faced man stomped in. He looked around and with thunder in his eyes headed for the lame boy. He jerked the bowl from his hand and set it on the nearest table. With his jaw clenched, he spoke quietly.

The boy nodded and followed him out of the room.

"Why did he do that?" Pain pierced Cici's heart, and she wiped at the tears that gushed from her eyes. "The boy was hungry."

The woman who stood in front of her shook her head. "Hiram Jones is a proud man. Won't take no handouts."

"But. . ." Cici could find no words. Nausea clutched her stomach.

The woman reached over and took the bowl from her hand. She smiled at Cici. "Don't worry, honey. Hiram makes sure that boy has his supper ever' day. He may be a little hollow, but he ain't starvin'."

Cici stared as the woman took her bowl and went down the line to get her bread. How could she be so uncaring? The boy was lame. And he was hungry. And how could a father be so cruel? A shiver ran over Cici. She couldn't stand this. She started to untie her apron.

A young girl, maybe thirteen or fourteen, faced her with lowered eyes.

Cici sighed and dropped her arms. She filled a bowl and held it out. "Here you go."

The girl raised her brown eyes and reached for the bowl. "Thank you, miss," she whispered.

Well, okay, she'd stay until everyone had soup. And she'd help clean up. But she wouldn't come back. Ever.

♋

The coolness of the foyer greeted Cici as she walked into the parsonage. She stood for a moment just inside the door and inhaled the smell of the furniture oil that made the hall tables shine. She breathed a sigh of relief. She'd thought the smell of cabbage and unwashed bodies would remain in her nostrils forever, but as she stood there, the familiar home smells took over.

"Cici, dear, why are you standing there?" Her mother stood in the doorway, a concerned smile on her face.

Should she tell her? No, Mama was so strong. What would she think of her daughter being so weak that she would give up her charitable work after one day? "I'm just tired, Mama. I think I'll go up and change. Do you need my help with anything?"

"No, not for an hour or so. Is Jimmy coming over tonight?"

"No, ma'am. Not tonight." She started up the stairs. "Oh, Jimmy, I tried. I truly did."

Chapter 16

Jimmy took a bite of ham and one of cheese then followed with a hunk of rye bread. He glanced sideways at Cobb who was peering up and down the street. Jimmy grinned. "What are you looking for?" As if he didn't know.

"Where are all the kids?" Confusion crossed his face. Lately, to Jimmy's satisfaction, Cobb had been sharing his lunch with the hungry children, too.

"The soup kitchen. Haven't you heard about it?"

"Yeah, of course I've heard of it. Everyone's heard of it. But I thought. . ."

"What?"

"I thought the kids would still come."

Jimmy smiled at the look of disappointment on Cobb's face. "They'll be here later. I always tell them a story after work."

"Yeah? I guess I missed out on what's been going on while I was out with the *Eastland*."

"Guess so."

Cobb cleared his throat. "Hey, Jimbo, I got something to tell you."

"Yeah? What is it?" Probably one of his corny jokes.

"It's about Sutton." He picked nervously at the paper around his sandwich.

Jimmy stiffened. "Cobb, I don't want to hear anything about how Sutton has changed."

"No." He took a deep breath. "You were right, Jimbo."

Alert to the tension in Cobb's voice, Jimmy put his food back in the bucket. "What is it? What do you know?"

"I'm not sure. But Sutton's been making remarks lately. Nothing I can really put my finger on." His brow furrowed. "Jimbo, I think he's planning some kind of revenge on you and Danni."

Jimmy's voice rose as he stared at Cobb. "What kind of revenge?"

"I don't know. I promise I don't. It's more a feeling than anything else. The way he looks when he mentions Danni. And you, too." He took a swig of water from his canteen. "Be careful, and tell that husband of Danni's to watch out. Sutton hates him."

Jimmy took a deep breath. "Thanks, Cobb. I know it isn't easy for you to go against Sutton."

"It isn't. He's been like a father to me."

Jimmy shook his head. "Cobb, a father doesn't teach his kids to steal for him. He was using you the same as he was using the rest of us."

Cobb sighed. "Yeah, I guess I know that now. He's been hinting around for me to do a job for him. I've dodged the idea though."

Jimmy nodded. He hoped Cobb would continue to hold out. Sutton was ruthless and wouldn't bat an eye if Cobb went back to prison.

"I'm sorry for the way I acted, Jimbo. I should have believed you. Guess I did, really, but didn't want to admit it."

"It's okay. I understand." It was hard to face the fact someone you cared about wasn't what you thought. Jimmy's stomach clenched. He only hoped that wasn't the way it was with him and Cici. But she was helping out at the food kitchen. So that proved she had a heart for the people. . .didn't it?

"I've been thinking." Cobb scratched his head. "Maybe I'll go to that church with you next Sunday."

Jimmy laughed and clapped Cobb on the shoulder. "That's great. I've been praying you would. You won't be sorry, Cobb."

Cobb grinned. "I hope God don't faint when I walk in."

Jimmy winced then grinned. Cobb didn't mean any disrespect. "You don't need to worry about that, buddy. God's a lot stronger than that." Jimmy wrote down the directions to the church and promised to be waiting on the steps for Cobb.

They finished their lunch and went back to work unloading a cargo ship. They seldom had the chance to work together since the *Eastland* was so busy.

Jimmy was surprised when Cobb followed him to where the children were waiting.

They were both surrounded the moment they seated themselves.

Little Mike peered up into Cobb's face. "You going ta tell us stories, too?"

"Naw. We better all listen to Jimmy." Cobb grinned at the boy and rubbed his shock of greasy hair.

After everyone was settled, Jimmy looked around. "Okay. How many of you went to church last week?"

One little hand went up. Maria Consuela. "I did, Jimmy. I like church."

"That's good, Maria." He glanced around. "Anyone else?"

Looking everywhere but at Jimmy, the children managed to avoid answering.

Jimmy sighed. "Okay, but you know I told you my stories don't take the place of the house of God. Remember?"

"I'll go next week, Jimmy," Bridget piped up. "I promise. And I'll take Patrick and Mike, too."

"Good girl, Bridget. You can tell me all about it next Monday, okay?"

She nodded and gave a nervous laugh.

Jimmy hoped she wouldn't back out. Maybe he should offer to take some of the children with him on Sunday. Something to think about. Silence fell as he told them the story of a boy named Samuel who lived in the temple and heard the voice of God.

"Hows come I can't hear the voice of God, Jimmy?" Little Sally, always wanting to know and never afraid to ask, peered up at him.

How could he answer in a way she'd understand? "You can hear Him, Sally." He placed his hand on the front of her torn dress. "Right here, in your heart."

She looked down. "How?"

Jimmy groaned. *Help me, Lord.* He smiled into the little girl's innocent blue eyes. "Hmm. Well, let's see now. Do you ever think about doing something naughty and then something tells you not to?"

She nodded. "Mama says it's my konchunch."

"Yes, your mama is right. God talks to us sometimes through our consciences." Okay, but that wasn't enough. He could see in her eyes that it wasn't. "And He also talks to us through the Bible. Did you know that?"

"Mama has a Bible. Sometimes she reads it to me." She scrunched up her face. "But I can't unnerstan' it."

"You will, Sally, when you get a little older." What now? *Help me, Lord.* He took a deep breath and smiled. "But that's not the only way God talks to us, Sally. Do you ever want to tell your mama thank you when she's worked hard to do something nice for you?"

"Like when she makes sweet johnnycakes?" Her mouth puckered into a little pink bow. "Is it God that tells me to give her a hug?"

"That's exactly right, Bridget."

She rubbed her dress in the spot over her heart and her eyes lit up. "Oh, I know now. God talks to me lots of times. You know what, Jimmy?"

"What, sweetheart?"

She smiled and held out her arms. "I think God's telling me to give you a hug, too."

ଓ

"Mama." Cici bit her lip as she folded the turnover dough over the apple filling.

"Yes, dear?" She straightened with the pan of cookies she'd removed from the oven. Smiling, she set them on a towel on the counter.

"How do you keep it up? I mean, all your responsibilities as a minister's wife must be overwhelming."

Mama stared. "Whatever do you mean? Of course I'm busy. But most wives and mothers are."

"But it's different with you, Mama. Everyone depends on you for everything." Cici frowned and threw both hands up, inadvertently slinging flour in the air. "Oh, I'm sorry. I'll clean it up."

"Wait, Cecilia. Let's sit a minute." She pulled out a chair at the table and Cici followed suit. "Now, why don't you tell me what this is all about?"

Cici sighed. "I'm pretty sure Jimmy will decide to give up law to be a missionary."

"I see. And you don't like the idea?" She picked a piece of lint from her apron and stuffed it in the pocket.

"Well, of course I want him to follow his heart." She sighed again. "I'm not sure, though, if I should marry him."

"But you're in love with him, aren't you?"

"Yes, but I don't know if I can be a minister's wife, Mama." She ducked her head, avoiding her mother's eyes.

"But darling, if you love him, does it matter which direction he chooses to go?" Her brows furrowed. "Isn't it a woman's place to conform to her husband's choices?"

"Yes, which is why I'm not sure if I should marry him."

"I'm not sure I understand, Cecilia. Does my life seem so bad to you?"

Cici groaned inwardly. Why couldn't she be more like this wonderful woman? "Mama"—she reached over and placed her hand on her mother's work-worn one—"I've watched you stay home night after night while Papa took care of other people. And I know it was his duty, but I saw how lonely you were. And you've dropped everything at a moment's notice to go cook and clean for someone who was ill."

"But any Christian would have done the same." She slipped her hand from beneath Cici's and lifted it to Cici's cheek. "You would have done the same."

"Once in a while, perhaps, but it's constant. Every time people have needs, they run to you and Papa." Perhaps she shouldn't have begun this conversation. She was only making herself sound selfish and uncaring.

"This is what God has called us to, daughter. Surely you know that. When I married your father, I answered his call as well."

"Maybe that's the answer." Cici frowned. "Maybe God isn't calling me to the same thing he's calling Jimmy to."

"Perhaps not. That's something you need to find out for sure before you marry him."

"How do you stand all the sacrifices you have to make?" The words shot out like a cannonball from a cannon. Cici covered her mouth with her fingers. "Oh, Mama, I'm sorry. I didn't mean to shout."

"Cecilia, I have never considered anything I've done for God and His people to be a sacrifice. To me, it has always been a work of love."

Cici stared at her mother's serene face for a moment. She meant it. This was true love. Her mother's love for her God and her husband. Oh, how she wished she could be like that. Why wasn't she? She'd been raised by God-fearing, wonderful parents who had taught her all about the love of Christ. And they hadn't just taught her with words. They'd taught her with their own lives. What was wrong with her that she wasn't like them?

"Cecilia, is there something else you're not telling me?" Worry sounded in her voice.

"Oh, Mama, I don't know how you stand to see people hurting all the time. And some people are so mean. How do you deal with them?"

"Did something happen at the soup kitchen?" Mama took her hand and looked into her eyes. "Something did happen. Tell me."

Starting at the beginning, Cici let it pour out. The hungry children, the mothers trying to keep starvation from the door, the lame boy and his angry father. Finally, she burst into tears. "I know I can't stand it, Mama. How can I help people when I'm so weak?"

"Oh, honey, of course it's difficult when you come face-to-face with the hard side of life." She pulled Cici's head over against her shoulder and smoothed her hair. "Perhaps I was wrong to shelter you so."

"No, Mama, you weren't wrong." She took a deep breath and forced a smile. "We'd best finish the baking so we can get started on supper."

Her mother smiled, but worry shadowed her eyes. "You're right. We wouldn't want your papa's supper to be late." She faced Cici. "You need to take all these concerns to God. He's the only One who can give you the answers."

Cici nodded and went to get the broom to clean the flour off the floor. Maybe if she tried harder, she could change. That was it. She hadn't planned to go help out at the soup kitchen anymore, but she'd force herself to go. After all, if God saw she was trying, He'd help her. Wouldn't He? And who knew? Maybe Jimmy would decide to go back to law school after all.

⍥

Blake stood and paced the study. "And Cobb said it was an impression he got? He couldn't give you anything specific to go on?"

"No." Jimmy shook his head. "But Cobb's not one to imagine things. And Sutton's been like an idol to him. If he thinks Sutton's up to something, I believe him."

Blake nodded and leaned against his desk. "I've got a man following him. He hasn't reported anything suspicious yet. We'll have to keep our eyes open, too. I'm thinking about working at home until this is settled."

"Good idea. I'd feel a lot better knowing you were here. What about your appointments?"

"I'm sure Dad won't mind taking them. Or we can assign them to someone else. If anyone insists on seeing me personally, he or she will have to wait." He sat behind his desk and leaned back. "I'm thinking of paying a personal visit to Sutton."

Startled, Jimmy stood and leaned over the desk. "Don't do that, Blake. First of all, we're not sure where he's staying. And second, you know what he's capable of. You need to stay here and take care of Danni."

Blake tossed him a side grin. "Okay. I won't do anything stupid. But I suggest you don't either."

"It's a deal. Let's wait for Cobb or the detective to get more information then go from there. In the meantime, we'll keep Danni safe."

Blake sighed and stood. "I'd better tell her."

Jimmy gave him a look of sympathy, glad he wasn't the one who had to impart the disturbing news to his sister.

Lord, protect Danni. Don't let that man get his hands on her.

As worried as Jimmy was about Danni, he could only imagine how hard it must be on Blake to know the man had evil plans against his wife.

Chapter 17

The fishy smell permeating the building wasn't bad at all. Cici chuckled as she stirred the pot of chowder. Amazing how quickly one could get accustomed to things. And to think, just a couple of weeks ago, she was ready to run away in hopeless tears.

A tap on the back window drew her attention and she grabbed a tin bowl from the shelf and filled it to the brim with the soup. She headed toward the window, snatching up a slab of bread she'd cut ahead of time.

Larry grinned and propped his crutch against the building so he could take the food she passed through the window. "Thanks, Miss Cici."

"You are very welcome, Larry. Just leave the bowl and spoon on the window ledge when you're finished." She tousled his head and headed back to the stove.

"Cici, we need a refill." Mrs. Baker's granddaughter, Nancy, set an empty pot on the table beside the stove.

"All right. This is ready. I'll help you carry." She tossed the girl a thick rag and, with another, grabbed the handle on one side of the pot. Together they managed to carry it to the food line.

"Thank you, girls." Mrs. Nelson smiled and motioned to the short line that scarcely reached the door. "Don't bother to make another pot. This should be plenty."

"Do you want me to start kitchen cleanup?"

"If you'll take over here, I'll do that. I need a change." Blake's mother wiped her sleeve across her face and stepped back from the long counter.

"That's fine with me." Cici took her place, noticing that a mother with four children stood waiting.

Cici smiled at her. "Why don't you find a table for you and your family? We'll bring your food over."

"Thank you kindly." With a smile of relief, the woman guided her children to a corner table.

Cici started filling bowls then turned her head at a tap on her shoulder.

Nancy stood behind her. "I can carry two at a time while you fill the rest."

"Oh good." She handed two filled bowls to the girl, then grabbed two more bowls and spooned the chowder into them. Nancy was back by the time they were filled.

"Here, if you'll take these, I'll take the last bowl and some bread."

A tiny girl with wild blond curls grinned at her as she set a bowl in front of her. "You have hair just like mine."

"Well, so I do." Cici wrinkled her nose and grinned back at the child.

"My name's Sally. What's yours?"

"Cecilia. But my friends call me Cici."

"Am I your friend?" The little girl's round blue eyes waited.

"I would like very much for you to be my friend." Cici held out her hand and Sally grasped it with her tiny one and gave a hearty shake.

"Whew. You have a strong handshake." Cici shook her hand, pretending to be in pain.

Sally giggled.

A boy across from her snorted. "Aw, that ain't strong. Here, feel mine." He stuck his dirty hand across the table.

Cici forced herself not to cringe, took a deep breath, and reached for his hand. "Now don't hurt me. I'm not too strong."

"Okay, I'll try not to." He gave her a firm shake.

"I think he's right, Sally. His handshake is stronger than yours or mine." She rubbed her hands together.

"Yeah, but he's not as strong as my friend Jimmy." She frowned at her brother.

"Aw, Jimmy's a grown-up. And besides, he ain't just *your* friend."

"Is, too."

"Is not."

Maybe she'd better try to break this up. She smiled at the mother who was spooning soup into her toddler's mouth. The mother shook her head and smiled back. "You kids get to eating and stop bothering Miss Cici."

Cici laughed. "They aren't bothering me. But I do need to get back to work." She waved at the children and went back to the food line.

"The children seem to like you, Cici." Mrs. Baker placed bread on a plate and handed it across to an old man whose trembling hand tried to steady a bowl of soup.

"Here, let me help." Cici took the bowl and plate and walked beside him to a chair at one of the tables. He seated himself and began to eat, ignoring her. But after all, she wasn't doing this for thanks.

Warmth flooded over her as she continued serving the nourishing soup. She wasn't sure what had changed her, but there was no doubt she was changing. She was able to have contact with the people without falling apart. And she was learning to do what she could and leave the rest in God's hands. Could it be that He had answered her prayer to help her change? It must be.

But what was she to do about Gail? She was supposed to meet her at the café tomorrow. But she didn't want to meet her. She sighed. She'd have to see her one more time and let her know. That would be the polite thing to do.

ᙦ

The early summer foliage brightened the park with greens, yellows, and pinks, with an occasional blue or red scattered about. Jimmy smiled as Cici stepped around a patch of wildflowers so she wouldn't crush them. Her face was radiant today and a burst of hope penetrated the doubt that Jimmy had carried around lately. Maybe the work she'd been doing at the soup kitchen had helped her to see ministering to the people in a different light.

"Oh, here's a good spot, Jimmy." She turned toward a wrought-iron bench that stood beneath a silver maple. "I love to hear the leaves rustle, don't you?"

Jimmy would have loved to hear a steamroller today as long as Cici was smiling and happy. "Yes, my favorite tree." He sat beside her and took her hand.

"Now, Jimmy. Don't do that. Someone will see." But her hand remained in his, and she smiled up at him. She leaned back and sighed. "I'm so glad we had this Sunday afternoon free. I love our families and friends, but this is better."

Jimmy inhaled sharply. This was good. All right—this was very, very good. "I feel the same way." Maybe he should wait until another time to tell her. No, that would be cowardly and unfair. She had a right to know. She had a right to decide what she wanted to do. "Cici." He rubbed his thumb across her ring, praying she wouldn't fling it at him. "Honey, I've made my decision."

Only a slight tightening of her hand revealed that she'd heard him. She bit her lip. "All right, Jimmy. It's good that you know what you're supposed to do. I know the indecision has been difficult for you."

"And for you as well." An almost imperceptible nod of her head answered her agreement.

"There's something I need to tell you, Cici. Something that might help you to understand. I should have told you before." But how he hated to speak of the subject.

"All right, Jimmy. I'm listening." She squeezed his hand.

"When I was four years old, my father died at sea. Mother, having no means of support, went to work cooking and cleaning in a boardinghouse. At least I think that's what it was. A few months later, she died in childbirth."

At her gasp, he paused for a moment.

"Danni was ten. The next morning, the woman who owned the place turned us out on the street with nothing but our few articles of clothing."

"Oh, Jimmy, how awful." Cici eyes filled and she blinked rapidly and squeezed Jimmy's arm. "But what did you do?"

"We wandered the streets all morning, in the cold October wind, hungry, as we'd had only a bite or two of bread since the day before." A shiver ran over his skin at the memory. "We walked to the docks and hid behind a large crate to get out of the wind for a while. We didn't know what to do, because we'd always had our mother to take care of us. Anyway, due to a series of events, we wound up at the home of a man who ran a child crime ring."

"No. How terrible." Her voice trembled.

Jimmy squeezed her hand. "Of course, we didn't know he was a criminal at the time. All we knew was that the house was warm and he gave us hot soup and bread. And a cot to sleep on."

He ran his hand over his eyes and took a deep breath. "For some reason, he took a liking to us and didn't send us out to steal the way the other children did. At that time, my leg was lame. That's probably why he didn't send me out. And later, we found he had other things in mind for my sister. Thank God, we were rescued before his plans were fulfilled."

Cici nodded. "I think I understand now why you have a heart for the poor. Especially the children."

"Yes, that was it in the beginning. But God has shown me His plan, sweetheart. With my compassion for the people and my connection with people of means, there is much I can do to help." He tilted her chin up and looked into her eyes. "Cici, I intend to enter seminary in September. I've already spoken to your father, and he is making arrangements for me to meet with the dean of his old school."

She nodded. "How will we live?"

Jimmy inhaled sharply. Had she said *we*? He gazed at her questioningly.

A smile started in the blue depths of her eyes and then tipped her pink lips. "We do have to live, you know."

He pulled her close and she gave a contented sigh. "I was so afraid of losing you."

"I was afraid, too, Jimmy. I didn't know what was wrong with me. I had a dread and a terrible fear. And not only that—I wanted excitement." Suddenly she grew very still. "Jimmy, where is that terrible man?"

"He was sent to prison, but he's out now. In fact, you saw him that night we were leaving the theater." He sighed. "And I'm afraid he's up to no good again. He may even have plans to harm Danni."

She took a deep breath. "What happened to the children?"

"Some of the older boys were sentenced to jail. The younger ones were placed in a children's home. "But what's wrong? You're so pale."

She shook her head. "Was Danni the only girl?"

"No, there were two others. Both about my age."

Her face crumpled. "Jimmy, there's something I need to tell you. I don't want to, but you have a right to know. After you hear, you may not want to marry me." She pulled away, and once more her eyes filled with tears.

Startled, Jimmy tried to draw her close again but she resisted. "Cici, what is it? There's nothing you could tell me that would change my mind about marrying you."

"Not now. There's one more thing I must do. Then I'll tell you. If you still want to marry me afterward, I will joyfully become your wife and share your ministry."

☙

That swine. That monster. Sutton. Cici nearly gagged at the thought of him. And to think she had thought he was a gentleman. Cici shoved through the door at Tony's Place. After the bright sunlight, it was dark and almost frightening. Strange, she'd never noticed that before. She stood inside the door for a moment, letting her eyes adjust.

Gail, at her usual table, waved when she saw Cici walking toward her.

Cici seated herself across from Gail and looked at her silently. Her heart thumped so hard her chest hurt.

A startled look crossed Gail's face. "What's wrong?"

"You tell me, Gail. What is wrong?" She clenched her fist and narrowed her eyes at the girl she'd thought was her friend.

Gail gave a nervous laugh. "I don't know what you're talking about."

"Tell me again how you know Sutton. A friend of your family, you say?"

"That's right." A guarded shadow filled her eyes.

"Your family being. . . ?"

"What?"

"Tell me about your family, Gail. And tell me exactly what part Sutton plays in it."

"Cici, listen—"

"No, you listen. I know all about your little family of criminals. Sutton being the father criminal of them all."

Gail's eyes darted around the café. "Keep your voice down. All right. I don't know how you found out, but yeah, it's true. I was part of his gang from the time I was six. I would have starved to death otherwise. But I couldn't expect you to understand that. You with your oh-so-prissy upbringing. And look at you now. I didn't know any better and couldn't do any better. But you've turned your back on a family who loves you. Why do you think you're any better than me?"

"That's right. I did turn my back on everything I knew to be right. But as for your not knowing any better, what about now, Gail? You pretended to be my friend to set me up for Sutton. And what was that all about, I'd like to know?"

Gail's face had tightened. "I don't know what you're talking about."

"I want to talk to him." She would find out what he was plotting against Danni and Jimmy. Whatever it was, she'd find out and tell Jimmy so he could stop him.

"But why? I don't understand what has you so riled up. Sutton's not breaking the law anymore."

"Just tell me how to get in touch with him."

"He's out of town."

"Send him a message."

"I don't know where he is, Cici. Honest." A light appeared in her eye. "But I know where he'll be on Saturday morning."

"All right, tell me."

"I'm supposed to meet him on board the *Eastland* around seven Saturday morning." A look of cunning crossed her face. "In fact, he asked me to bring you, too. Some big shot invited him to this big company picnic. They're going to

Michigan City, Indiana. There's supposed to be a talent scout on board."

"I don't care anything about a talent scout. But I am going to talk to Sutton one way or the other. Where should I meet you?"

"On board, I guess."

"So you can talk to Sutton before I get there? No, I'll meet you first."

"All right. Meet me on the dock." She smiled. "I won't tell him anything, Cici. I promise."

Without saying good-bye, Cici jumped up and left. Gail was up to something. But what could happen on a ship with a crowd of people around?

Chapter 18

Jimmy tapped on the chapel door and waited, the hot July sun boring into the top of his head. Slow footsteps approached the door. That didn't sound like Paul's quick step.

The door swung open. The pastor's wife, Anne, faced him, her eyes weary. "Mr. Grayson, please come in."

"I don't wish to intrude. Would it be possible for me to see the pastor?" Something didn't feel right. She wasn't her usual friendly self.

"My husband has been ill. He's still not well. But I'm sure he will see you. If you'll be seated, I'll go ask."

"Perhaps I should come back when he's fully recovered. I don't want to intrude if he's not feeling well."

"No, no. He is feeling some better today and will probably be happy to have someone besides me to talk to." She smiled weakly and turned to go.

A twinge of worry bit at Jimmy. If Paul was better, why was his usually cheerful wife so downcast?

In a moment, she was back. "He's eager to see you, Mr. Grayson. Please come on up."

Jimmy followed her up the narrow stairs to the small but clean and cozy apartment.

She led him down a short hallway and held a door, motioning him in, then turned and left.

Paul sat beside an open window, his Bible on his lap. "Jimmy, I'm so glad to see you. Please come in and visit awhile."

Jimmy shook the pastor's hand and sat in a small overstuffed chair facing him. "I'm sorry to hear you've been ill." Jimmy peered at Paul's face.

The pastor's normally tanned skin had faded to a sickly yellow. "But I'm better now." He smiled. "I'm glad you came over, Jimmy. I wasn't sure I'd get to see you again before we leave."

"You're going away?" He hoped not for long. Jimmy had come to depend on the man's friendship.

"I'm afraid so." He took a sip from a glass of water on the table. "You see, I seem to have some sort of lung condition. Nothing fatal or contagious, but it appears to sap my strength. The doctor insists that we take an extended vacation in a dry area." He sighed.

"For how long?" Surely he'd be back.

Paul shrugged. "He doesn't seem to think I should return to this area. I've informed my headquarters that I'll be requesting a church in a drier climate when I'm able to perform my duties."

"I'm so sorry, Paul. I'll miss you."

"We'll keep in touch. After all, there's always the post." He smiled. "Now, what's on your mind, my friend? You must have had a reason for coming out in this heat."

Jimmy shook his head. "I wanted you to know I've decided to enroll in seminary in the fall. Reverend Willow put me in contact with his old administrator there."

"That is wonderful news. Jimmy, I'm so happy to hear that. And especially glad you'll be attending the school I graduated from. I've been praying for guidance for you since you told me what was in your heart."

"Yes. If I can be half the spiritual leader you are, I'll be content."

"Jimmy, have you ever thought of pastoring a church?"

"The thought has crossed my mind. But of course, you are the—" He stopped and realization dawned as Paul grinned. "Oh no, I could never take your place."

"Then don't try. Take your own place. I'm sure with recommendations from Reverend Willow and myself, you could fill the position here."

"But I haven't even been to seminary yet."

Paul laughed. "You wouldn't be licensed at first, of course. And you would be closely monitored. But you could hold Sunday services for the members of my little church while doing what you do best—charitable work with the people."

Could it be possible? Was this God's plan all along?

"Perhaps the Lord has raised you up for just this time, Jimmy. It's hard to get a pastor willing to take over a ministry such as this. The thought of leaving these dear folks with no one to lead them nearly broke my heart. If I knew you were here, it would be a great weight off my mind." He smiled. "Of course, you realize there's not much monetary compensation. A small stipend. And you probably wouldn't get that at first."

"That wouldn't matter. I can work on the docks part-time."

Paul nodded then sighed. "If you marry, it won't be easy. A wife has to have the same calling in order for it to work."

Jimmy jumped up, laughing. "I haven't told you, but I'm engaged to be married. To the sweetest girl—Cecilia Willow."

"That is exciting news. Congratulations. Would Miss Willow, by any chance, be Reverend Willow's daughter?" He rubbed his hands together, grinning. "That's just like God, isn't it? He's brought you the perfect mate."

☙

Jimmy headed toward the cargo ship where he was working today and reflected on Paul's remark. The perfect mate. It was true. His heart said so. He hadn't seen Cici since her strange declaration. She had asked him not to press her just now, promising to tell him everything on Saturday.

He sighed. Two more days. Well, she was worth waiting for, and whatever

329

this mysterious upset in their relationship was, he was determined it could and would be overcome. Now that he knew in his heart that Cici loved him and loved the ministry he was called to, nothing would tear them apart.

"Jimmy." He turned and saw Patrick and several other boys trailing down the street carrying what looked to be wet cats.

"Hey, what are you boys up to?" Satisfaction swept over him. Most of the children looked better these days. Still dirty and ragged, but their cheeks had color and their ribs weren't showing. Between the soup kitchen and the food boxes, they'd lost the defiant, angry look a lot of them had carried. It was hard to be happy when you were hungry. Now if they could get enough spiritual food, everything would be fine.

"Aw, we just found these cats in a sack in the river. Must have just been throwed in 'cause they were all alive. They sure were scared though."

Jimmy winced. "Yeah, I'll bet. They were lucky you found them. But don't make a practice of going into the river."

"Aw, whatcha think we are, nuts?" Tony, an older boy scowled. "Who'd wanta swim in that dirty old sewer?"

Jimmy laughed. "I guess you're right. I won't worry then."

They waved and walked away.

What could he do about getting them to church? He'd like to take them with him, but it was too far for them to walk. Well, if he did get the church here, as Paul thought was very possible, he'd do everything he could to persuade them to come on Sunday mornings.

The *Eastland* was just pulling into harbor when Jimmy's shift ended. He shaded his eyes and tried to catch a glimpse of Cobb. True to his word, he had shown up at church the last two Sundays. He'd also bought a Bible, and when the *Eastland* was in, the two of them had studied together during their midday break. Now that Cobb had a taste of God's Word, he seemed hungry for more.

Jimmy was thankful to God for that and for his love for Cici and the ministry. If only Sutton hadn't shown up again, life would be a beautiful thing.

"Waaahooo!" Jimmy grinned at the sound of Cobb's familiar yell. He ran down the *Eastland*'s gangplank and took a wide jump onto the dock.

Jimmy grinned and waved. "Hey. How long are you in for?"

"Just tonight. We're one of the boats the Western Electric bunch chartered for their picnic in Indiana." He whistled. "Company must be loaded. Five charters for a picnic."

"Five? Must be quite a crowd." Jimmy leaned against a post.

"Must be. The *Eastland* alone holds around twenty-six hundred." Cobb shook his head. "Sure glad I won't be cooking lunch for all those folks."

Jimmy wrinkled his brow. "Why do you need to go, then?"

"Some of them will be wanting breakfast. And probably sandwiches and stuff on the way back." He nodded. "Don't worry. They'll keep me busy."

Jimmy laughed and clapped him on the back. "I gotta get home. Maybe

I'll see you later."

"Not if I see you first." Cobb laughed and waved. "Hey, Jimbo, wait a minute."
Jimmy turned.

"Just wanted you to know. . .had a serious talk with Jesus the other day." A grin
split Cobb's glowing face. "He's my Savior now."

 C3

"Are you serious?" Danni's squeal of joy shot through Jimmy's head and he
flinched back against the parlor sofa, even while he grinned and nodded.

"I never expected that. I didn't." She shook her head and her face shone. "God,
forgive me, I didn't expect that."

"Yeah, but you haven't been around Cobb lately. He's a changed man."

"I am awed at God's might and goodness." She leaned back in her chair,
pressing her hand to her back, then propped her feet back up on the little footstool. She poked her needle into the pillowcase she was embroidering. "Hmm.
Maybe he'll be a good influence on Sutton."

"Don't count on it." Jimmy narrowed his eyes. He had forgiven Sutton—at
least he was almost sure he had—and maybe he could even forget if not for the
new threat against Danni.

"Jimmy"—Danni's voice was low and soft—"no one is beyond God's grace
and mercy. All he would need to do is surrender, and God could change him in
a second." She sat there quietly, so sweet and sincere.

Jimmy's heart stirred. Would things change between him and Danni when
he got married? He took a deep breath. Of course they would. There was a lot
of change when she married Blake. But it wasn't a bad thing at all. Simply different. Now she was going to be a mother. They were grown up. They didn't
need each other the same way they had when they were children. "Danni." He
paused.

"Yes, little brother?" She grinned.

He grinned back. "Nothing. Just thinking." *Let's stay close, Danni. Let's always
stay close.*

"I'm praying for Cici." Her tone grew serious. "I don't know what's wrong.
But I know she loves you. And she's a sweet girl. You should see her at the soup
kitchen. Everyone loves her, especially the children."

He nodded. "She promised to explain Saturday. I hope I'm busy tomorrow so
I can keep my mind off it."

"You'll be fine. You're a strong man." She started. "Oh."

"What?" Jimmy jumped up. "Are you all right, sis?"

She waved her hand and flinched. "I'm fine. Junior is making his presence
known. Sit down, for heaven's sake, Jimmy. You should be used to it by now."

He flopped down on his chair. "Don't scare me like that."

She threw him a tender smile. "Thanks for caring about me."

"Junior is going to be a lucky little boy to have a mother like you."

"Oh really?" She tilted her head to one side. "And what if Junior should turn out to be a little girl, Uncle Jimmy?"

He grinned. "Then she'll be the luckiest young lady who ever lived."

"Let's stay close, Jimmy. Promise me. No matter what, we'll always love each other just like we always have."

"Always."

ೲ

Cici paced her bedroom floor. Was she making a mistake? Confronting Sutton had seemed like a good idea, but now she wasn't so sure. After the things Jimmy had told her, it was obvious the man was dangerous. But he was older now. How dangerous could he be?

A laugh turned into a hiccup. She cleared her throat. She had made up her mind. She wouldn't back out now. And the deck would be teeming with people. What could he do? She tossed her curls and sat on the chair by her lace-curtained window.

Should she tell someone? But that person would only try to stop her from going through with it. She straightened her neck and lifted her chin. She wouldn't be a coward and back out now. She would do this for Jimmy and Danni. When Sutton realized he was exposed, he'd give up his evil plan, whatever it might be. The night was half gone before Cici finally dropped off to sleep.

She woke with a start. Jumping out of bed, she switched on the light and peered at the clock by her bed. Six o'clock. She'd need to hurry. When she got to the kitchen, she was met by the aroma of apples and cinnamon wafting up from a bubbling pot of oatmeal.

"I know you're in a hurry, Cecilia, but you need to eat a bite before you go to the docks."

She complied, happy that her mother assumed she was headed for the soup kitchen. And she did plan to go there as soon as she'd talked to Sutton.

"Good morning, daughter." Papa laid his paper down and turned up his cheek for her kiss.

"Good morning, Papa." She grabbed his coffee mug. "Here, let me fill this for you."

Everything seemed surreal as she hurried through breakfast, washed her dishes in the kitchen sink, and kissed her folks good-bye.

The Clark Street Bridge was crowded with carriages and automobiles, probably filled with the picnic-going employees and their families headed to the boats. The streetcar clacked past them on the center rails.

Cici got off and adjusted her hat to protect against the light mist that had begun. Five chartered boats were lined up and there must have been thousands of people boarding. She frowned. Was the *Eastland* leaning? It appeared lopsided. She shook her head. Her imagination, of course.

She glanced around trying to catch a glimpse of Gail in the crowd but didn't see her. She slipped between two quarreling children and was shoved aside by a large woman carrying a birdcage. Her glance slid up the side of the *Eastland* to the crowded deck. It would be just like Gail to be on board already even though she'd promised to meet her on the dock.

Her gaze brushed across the mob and she inhaled a sharp breath. Sutton stood by the rail looking down. His eyes met hers and he smiled and motioned upward. A dark-haired girl stood just behind him. Was that Gail? She couldn't see her clearly, but it must be.

She glanced toward the gangplank. The crowd had thinned and a short line was all that remained to board. Should she? It wasn't too late to change her mind.

She reached into her jacket pocket for the handwritten ticket Gail had given her. Lifting her chin, she took a deep breath and stepped toward the *Eastland*'s crowded gangplank.

Chapter 19

Cici!" Jimmy let the door of the employee shack bang shut behind him and rushed across the dock toward the *Eastland*. Cici was halfway up the gangplank. He'd know those curls and that walk anywhere.

"Cici!" His shout went unheard.

An orchestra played on the promenade deck and some of the passengers were dancing. Voices clamored and deckhands tried to shout to each other above the music. The noise drowned out Jimmy's call. He stopped and exhaled a huff of air. The gangplank was being pulled into the *Eastland*. The *Theodore Roosevelt* and one other boat were still loading passengers, and they called out to one another, adding to the clamor.

Jimmy scanned the *Eastland*'s deck, hoping to catch Cici's eye. Why would she have boarded? Did someone invite her on the excursion? She hadn't mentioned it. Jimmy frowned as the *Eastland* listed to portside. Soon it righted and he breathed a sigh of relief.

A man stood at the edge of the wharf, frowning toward the listing boat. Several people stood at the rail, laughing and shouting for him to come on aboard. Suddenly he jumped across the water and his friends helped him over the rail. Crazy people.

Jimmy's gaze swept the crowd on deck again. There she was, and there. . . Jimmy's heart froze. Sutton. What was she doing with Sutton? They faced each other, seeming not to notice the people who crowded around them at the rail. Why hadn't she told him she knew Sutton? Was she involved with him in some way? Surely not. They hadn't acknowledged each other at the theater that night. But maybe. No. He wouldn't believe for a moment that Cici would be involved in a plot against Danni.

A couple of women crowded in front of them, and when they moved, there was no sign of Cici or Sutton. Jimmy shaded his eyes to see if he could spot Cobb aboard, but he was probably in the galley.

Fear clutched his chest. If Cici wasn't involved with Sutton, and he was certain she wasn't, then she must be in some sort of trouble. Should he inform the harbor authorities? But what would he say to them? His fiancée was on the ship with another man? They'd laugh, more than likely. He turned and headed for the *Theodore Roosevelt* to help set the gangplank in place. There was nothing he could do.

But he could pray and trust God.

ભ

Cici shoved her way across the crowded deck. There he was, and Gail stood beside him. She'd give her an earful as soon as—

Fear stabbed her at the glint of satisfaction in Sutton's eyes. Why had she thought this was a good idea? She darted a hopeful glance at Gail, but the girl gave her an apologetic shrug and rushed toward the gangplank.

Cici started to turn and felt herself jerked backward. Before she could scream, Sutton yanked her to his side so tightly she gasped. She struggled to no avail against his deathlike grip. Pain stabbed her as something hard was pressed against her ribs.

"Be a nice girl and you might get off this boat alive, my dear." Sutton's hot breath blew against her neck as he whispered into her ear, "I would be devastated if I had to shoot you."

She opened her mouth to scream, but a jab from the gun caused her breath to catch in her throat. Who would hear her over the orchestra anyway?

He maneuvered her to a short flight of steps and guided her down to the deserted deck below.

She struggled as he half carried, half shoved her down a narrow hall. Suddenly she lost her balance as the boat rocked from side to side.

Sutton grabbed her and pushed her into a tiny alcove. He was quiet for a moment then shrugged.

"Nothing to be afraid of. The boat is merely listing. Now, Cici, dear, listen closely, for I'll only say it once. If you wish to get off this ship alive and see dear Jimmy again, you had best go quietly the rest of the way."

"But where are you taking me?" Her voice trembled. This was not the way she'd planned things. "And why are you doing this?"

He gave a short laugh and drew her closer to his side. "Because, my dear, I want young Jimmy and the abominable Blake Nelson to know what it's like to lose something they hold dear."

"But. . ."

"Enough." He gave her a slight shove, and they started down the hall once more. He stopped at a door, unlocked it, and threw it open, revealing a medium-sized stateroom.

Cici gasped. Fear pierced through her. The room was dark except for a small lamp. She had hoped there might be someone there who would help her, but there was not a soul in the cabin. "No. I'm not going in there."

Laughing, Sutton gave her a shove.

Cici stumbled through the door and watched in horror as he closed it behind him.

"Don't look so frightened, my dear. I'm not a monster." He laid the gun on a small table and removed his coat. His dark eyes devoured her for a moment. Then he went to a small sideboard and poured wine into two glasses. He held one out to her.

"No." She shoved it away. "You know I don't drink."

He shrugged and tipped the glass up, downing the liquid, then placed it on the counter. "Sit down, my dear. You may as well relax. You're not going anywhere."

"I don't understand why you would do this." A shuddering motion told her the boat was pulling away from the dock. Hot tears rushed to her eyes and she blinked them back. "The ship is leaving. Please let me go, Sutton."

Sutton shook his head. "No. You're not going anywhere. For then my plan would be spoiled, you see. But you still don't understand. They must not have told you the story of how I was robbed of the lovely Danielle. Sit down." He motioned to a small sofa.

"I'd rather stand." Cici pressed her lips together and threw him what she hoped was a determined glare.

He sighed. "I said sit." He shoved her onto the sofa and sat beside her. "So you wish to know why I must have my revenge." He leaned back and narrowed his eyes. "Danielle Grayson was the most beautiful woman I ever knew. She was ten years old the first time I laid eyes on her. Even then I knew she was special, with red curls wild around her tiny head and green eyes that flashed and sparkled. As she grew up, her beauty overwhelmed me. And not only her physical beauty. She was graceful and gentle, always caring about those around her. Especially her little lame brother. I kept her close, not sending her out on the streets with the other children. She did chores around the house and I even brought a tutor in for her and Jimmy."

He took a long drink then sighed. "I knew if I was ever to have a chance with her, I must be kind to Jimmy. She adored him and was always very protective." Sutton's words slurred and his eyes were wild.

Cici squirmed and moved farther away from him.

He reached out and grabbed her wrist. "Don't try it." Pain filled his voice as he continued. "Then she spurned me." The man was either drunk or mad, and he hadn't had that much to drink. "To teach her a lesson, I sent her out with some of the boys to do a job."

His breath came in rapid gasps and he leaned back and ran his hand over his eyes. "Something went wrong. The boys got away, but she was caught. Somehow she managed to talk her way out of it. She always was a good little actress." Bitterness filled his voice. "As she showed me well. Lying to me. Making me think she was still part of our little family while all the time she plotted to betray me. She was in love with someone else. She came home to try to talk me into letting Jimmy go. The police raided, and thanks to Danielle Grayson, the one love of my life, the one intended for me, I was sent to prison and my little family was scattered."

"You were a criminal, Sutton." Cici almost shouted the words. "What did you expect? You taught innocent children to steal and made them think it was all right. Family? You only used them."

His eyes darkened in anger and he raised his hand then lowered it. "No, I took care of them. They were my children."

She jumped up. "Let me go, Sutton. You're insane. You're never going to have Danielle. She loves her husband and they're going to have a child."

He jumped up, eyes filled with rage. "No. . .Jimmy Grayson will know what it feels like for the woman he loves to be claimed by another. And his pain will be hers. She will see what she has driven me to. And through her, that seducing husband of hers will suffer."

Fear gripped Cici as he lunged for her. Then the floor fell away and she began to slide. She screamed.

The ship had turned onto its side. It must be sinking.

A table flew through the air and hit Sutton's head. Blood gushed. His lifeless body tumbled head over heels toward the door, where water had begun to seep in.

Cici screamed again, continuing to slide toward the wall. Suddenly the boat listed more and she fell, grasping for something to stop her plunge. She hit the wall hard and something exploded in her elbow.

God, help me.

Ↄ

She was innocent. She must be. There was no way Jimmy would believe Cici was mixed up with Sutton and his plots. But then, why was she with him? Was this what she had to tell him? Something about Sutton?

Shouts broke into his thoughts as he swabbed down the dock. Probably some of the dockhands roughhousing. He straightened his back and glanced around. He drew his breath in sharply. No. No. He stood still, too stunned to move, not believing what he saw. Not more than forty feet from the wharf, the *Eastland* lay halfway on her side and continued to roll as she sank into the river.

Dear God, Cici.

He dropped the heavy mop and ran. At the edge of the wharf, he stood transfixed. The *Eastland* groaned and then came to rest on its side. The water was thick with passengers and crew swimming toward land. Jimmy looked over the mob frantically, trying to locate Cici.

Yanking off his boots, he jumped in, barely missing a man and a woman who clung together as they made their way to the dock. He swam toward the ship, shoving people aside as he went. The one thought that went through his mind was Cici, trapped in the boat.

A man with two children clinging to his shoulders bumped against him, his eyes pleading for help. Jimmy pulled one of the children from the man's back and swam back to the dock, where someone took the child. Then he turned and headed back toward the ship. How much time had passed? He swam on through bodies, some coughing, some screaming and kicking. But where was Cici?

Oh God, please don't let her be below deck.

The steamer had sunk so fast, there wouldn't have been time for her to get up the stairs. She could be trapped beneath the water. She could be dead by now.

A loose lifeboat bobbed on top of the water. A young boy scrambled over the side and fell into it.

Almost to the boat, Jimmy jerked as someone, gasping, grabbed him from behind. He struggled but couldn't get loose from the arms entwined around his neck. He felt himself sinking and drew in a deep breath. He tried to kick his way back up to the surface, but the arms tightened in a near stranglehold. His mind and body cried out for air.

Suddenly the choking arms fell away. Kicking, Jimmy fought his way upward toward the precious air. Blackness threatened, and he knew he couldn't make it.

Lord Jesus, receive my spirit and please save Cici.

Something grabbed him and he felt himself floating upward. Blackness overcame him.

೧

Cici struggled to shove Sutton's body away from the door. Pain stabbed her elbow, but it was lessening. She must have hit a nerve. Thank the Lord it wasn't broken. Tugging and pushing at Sutton's body, she finally moved him away from the door. After working at it for a few minutes, she managed to pull it open and fell through, landing against the wall beyond. She glanced around, trying to think what to do.

Water was coming in at one end of the corridor. She was alone but could hear screams from above and below. A sob caught in her throat. What should she do? The stairs were farther down, but that was where the water was coming in. She needed to get to a higher place.

Turning, she saw the side rails, which were now going upward toward the side that was above the water. Her heart pounded and dizziness overcame her. She had to keep focused. Grabbing the rail, she pulled herself onto an overturned table then forced herself to climb onto anything she could get a foothold on.

The sound of pounding came from above her.

She cried out, "Help! I'm down here!"

At another noise behind her, she turned. Water was filling the corridor. Objects bobbed up and down in it.

Cici gasped. She must get higher.

What had she been thinking to confront Sutton alone? She scrambled frantically upward, grabbing at swinging doors and rails to haul herself up. Her progress was slow and the water rose steadily.

Would Jimmy be among the rescuers? *Lord, please save me. But if I'm to die, please don't let Jimmy find my body. And please comfort him and Mama and Papa.*

She heard drilling above her. Oh, if only they could get through before it was too late.

Something touched her foot. She jerked it up then glanced behind her. Sutton's body floated on top of the water, which was now just below her. Fear and nausea washed over her. Once more she started to climb. Toward safety. Toward people who were attempting to get through to her. She must reach the top.

Chapter 20

Jimbo, Jimbo, wake up. Come on, Jimmy."

Something slapped Jimmy's face, hard, and he heard Cobb's voice as if from a distance. He blinked and opened his eyes.

Cobb was bombarding his face with one slap after another.

Jimmy grabbed his wrist. "Okay, I'm awake." But why was he lying on the dock, soaking wet? He sat up and shook his head, water flying from his hair. He blinked. Cici. The boat had gone down. He struggled to get up.

Cobb grabbed his arm and yanked him to his feet. "I saw the guy pull you under." Cobb's eyes were wide. "Didn't think I'd ever find you."

Jimmy grabbed him by his shoulders. "Have you seen Cici?" The torment in his mind sounded in his voice.

"Cici? No. Why?" He threw a puzzled glance at Jimmy. "Maybe you better sit down."

"No. Cici was on the *Eastland*. We've got to find her." He pulled his arm loose and ran barefoot to the edge of the wharf, where he stood in horror.

Bodies floated in the water, bumping against each other. Cries came from the living trying to make their way to shore. Divers avoided the still forms, focusing their efforts on pulling the living from the river.

A grating, screaming sound jerked Jimmy's attention to the above-water portion of the steamer. Rescue workers with drills knelt on the exposed side, trying to remove the side plates. He took a deep breath to prepare for the cold water.

Cobb grabbed him. "Wait, I'll go with you." He squeezed Jimmy's arm. "We'll find her, pal. I promise."

Slowly they made their way through the water, checking each female body that floated by.

Jimmy had a strong feeling that Cici was trapped inside the steamer. "I'm going to dive below and see if I can see inside the portholes."

"No, wait. You're still weak from lack of oxygen. I'll go. Keep looking around through the bodies."

Jimmy knew if Cici was trapped inside the submerged side, it would be no use. There was no chance anyone could be alive underwater that long.

A shout went up. Jimmy looked up and saw a rescue worker pulling someone, alive, through an opening. His heart lurched, and he swam toward the outer rails. He grabbed the bottom one and started up.

"I'm right behind you, Jimbo." Cobb's welcome voice was like velvet to his ears. "You didn't see her?"

"Couldn't see anything down there. I'm sorry."

Jimmy hauled himself up and peered around. Two women and several crying, frightened children were being loaded onto stretchers.

Jimmy walked over and looked down at one of the women. "Do you know Cici Willow? Blond curls, very young and pretty. Did you see her?"

She groaned and shook her head. The other woman couldn't offer any help either. Two of the rescuers were pulling someone from another hole in the ship. This time a young girl, followed by a middle-aged man.

Something pounded beneath Jimmy's feet. "Hey, over here. Someone's down there."

In a short time, the flap was cut away. Jimmy peered around the workers and his heart jumped at the sight of blond curls. He groaned when the woman turned her face upward. Not Cici.

Dear God, please let her be alive. And help us to find her.

"Over here! Someone help me get this woman out of here. She's stuck or something."

ఇ

Pain seared through Cici's leg as she tugged to try to get free. Somewhere in the dark water that now reached her waist, her foot was caught. A heavy chest had slammed against the wall, pinning her foot and lower leg. Tears of frustration stained her cheeks as she stared up at the rescue worker. She shook her head. "I can't move it."

"Cici!" Jimmy shoved the man away and reached for her.

She reached her arms up to him. "Oh, Jimmy." She gazed into his wonderful face. The face she'd feared she'd never see again. "My foot is wedged tight. I can't get out." Panic clutched tight at her chest and throat. Was she going to die when she was so close to being with him once more? Water rushed around her waist, lapping at the walls and everything it touched.

"Sweetheart, I'll get you out. I promise. Try not to panic." He turned. "Cobb, grab a rope, okay?"

In less than a minute, Jimmy handed the end of a rope down to her. "Cici, I want you to tie this around your waist. Make sure you get it tight enough that it won't come loose. Can you do that?"

She nodded and wrapped the rope around her waist twice, then tied it in a knot. She gave it a tug to be sure then nodded to Jimmy.

"Now, honey, you're going to have to trust us, okay?"

"I trust you, Jimmy." And she did. More than she'd ever trusted anyone. Even though her heart pounded against her chest and her throat was constricted with fear, she trusted him.

He turned and spoke to the men behind him, then turned back to her. "Honey, I want you to try to lower yourself into the water so I can get through to help you."

Panic pierced her heart and her breathing came in short gasps. She hung on to Jimmy's hands and shook her head. "I can't."

The choked whisper must have reached him, because pain clouded his eyes. "Yes, you can. Three strong men are holding on to the rope. They won't let you go. I promise, sweetheart. Please. We have to get you out of there. The water will continue to rise. Don't you see?"

She glanced down. The water was still at her waist, but it did seem a little higher. She bit her lip and nodded. "All right, Jimmy."

She swallowed past the sudden lump in her throat, slid one hand out of his, and grabbed the rope just above her waist. Taking a deep breath she let go with the other. She sank to her chin and water whipped around her shoulders and neck. "Jimmy!" Angry waves of water swirled around her and she held on to the rope with both hands, making sure the knot at her waist wasn't coming loose. The light from outside disappeared and terror beat at her as she fought the watery darkness.

Then light streamed in once more and Jimmy's arms were around her, holding her close. "It's all right, sweetheart. I'm with you. I'll get you out of here." He pulled back and looked into her eyes. "I have to go under the water to get you loose. Don't be afraid. I won't be long." Then he was gone, beneath the dark evil that waited to devour them both.

No, I won't think like that. God is taking care of us. He sent Jimmy and the other men, and He'll save us from this.

Pain shot through her ankle and up her leg as the chest shifted. Where was Jimmy? It was taking too long. Another shift and suddenly her foot was free.

Jimmy bobbed up beside her, coughing and gasping. He looked into her eyes and grinned. "Let's get out of here."

With Jimmy lifting and Cobb pulling, Cici crawled out through the hole in the side of the ship, ignoring the throbbing pain in her leg and foot. Cobb lifted her up and put his arm around her shoulders, supporting her until Jimmy stood beside them.

They fell into each other's arms. Cici basked in Jimmy's kisses and the sweet words he whispered in her ears.

"Uh, excuse me, miss. We need to get you to the hospital." The emergency worker stood grinning, with a stretcher at his feet and another grinning man at the other end of it.

"Jimmy, I want to go home."

"Now, sweetheart, we need to get that ankle taken care of and make sure you're okay after being in the water for so long."

"Will you come with me?" She was acting like a baby, but she didn't care.

He picked her up and laid her on the stretcher. "Just let anyone try to keep me from it." His lips brushed against hers.

She closed her eyes and dizziness engulfed her. She needed to tell him something. But what? Oh. Sutton. Then darkness came.

ॐ

Jimmy stumbled into the house, exhaustion in every muscle of his body.

He'd stayed at the hospital for nearly two hours waiting for Cici to awake. The doctor had assured them there was nothing wrong with her except exhaustion and a bruised ankle. The minute her eyes had opened, she'd motioned him close.

"Sutton. . ." She took a deep breath. "He's dead, Jimmy."

A surge of relief shot through Jimmy. The lifting of the burden he'd carried so long swept over him in a lightness very near dizziness. But almost immediately remorse stabbed through him. How could he be happy with the news of someone's death when the man didn't know Jesus?

"Cici, are you sure?" But she had fallen back asleep. He brushed his lips across her forehead and whispered good-bye to her parents.

Jimmy had made a quick trip to the house to tell Blake and Danni the news, and after making sure Danni was all right, he and Blake had gone to help with the rescue attempts.

He'd stayed until darkness was so thick there was no possibility of saving even one more person. He shuddered at the memory of row after row of sheet-wrapped bodies lying on the floor of the makeshift morgue at the Reid Murdoch plant. He didn't think he'd ever forget the feel of those waterlogged bodies as he helped load them onto trucks later for transport to the armory.

"Jimmy"—Danni stood in the parlor doorway—"come in and put your feet up. You look like you're about to pass out."

"I'm too dirty, so I'd better not. I'll ruin the furniture." But the sight of the overstuffed chair by the window drew him and he took a step forward.

"Nonsense. Get in here." She peered into his eyes, then gave a little gasp and wrapped her arms around him.

"Oh, Jimmy, I'm so sorry. It must have been horrible out there." She released him then guided him to the chair.

"It was terrible. Danni, you wouldn't believe it." He dropped onto the soft cushion and buried his face in his hands. Sobs wracked his body. Sobs that had a life of their own and would not be stopped.

Her comforting hands patted his shoulder then brushed his hair from his eyes.

Finally, he sat up straight. "Thanks, Danni. I haven't cried like that since I was a kid."

"It's all right. There's nothing wrong with a man crying, and you have plenty to cry about."

"I need to get cleaned up and back to the hospital."

"Mrs. Willow sent a message a little while ago. She said to tell you Cici is at home and sleeping like a baby. Cici asked her to tell you to please get some rest and come see her in the morning."

"But you're sure she's all right?" She'd been so pale when he kissed her good-bye.

"I'm sure. Mrs. Willow said all Cici could talk about was how brave you were and how proud she was that you went back to do your part to help." She brushed his hair back, a motion he'd resent any other time. "How about something to eat?"

He shook his head. "There were volunteers handing out food and drinks all day. I'm not hungry. Is Blake asleep?" He probably was. Blake wasn't used to long hours of physical labor but had worked tirelessly alongside Jimmy and the other volunteers most of the day and into the early hours of the night. He'd only left because he didn't want to leave Danni alone in the house.

"Yes, he was so tired he took a short bath and fell across the bed. I don't think he's moved since."

He reached up and touched her cheek. "Danni, are you okay?"

Her face paled, but she smiled then reached over and placed her hand on his arm. "I'm fine. Go on upstairs and get some rest."

Jimmy nodded and headed up the stairs. He'd take a long hot bath and go to bed. He only hoped his dreams would be sweet ones of Cici and not nightmares of the scenes he'd witnessed today.

❧

Jimmy tapped on the parsonage door, the sound blending in with the pelting of the rain against the roof and sidewalk. In a moment, the door flew open and Mrs. Willow beamed at him from the foyer.

"Come in, my boy, before you get soaked." She took his umbrella and placed it in the stand.

"I hope you don't mind my early intrusion." Jimmy loosened the knot in his tie, which seemed about to choke him. "I wanted to look in on Cici before church."

"No, it's not too early. She's in the parlor. Go right in. I have to finish making salad and put the roast in the oven before church." She smiled and stepped into the dining room.

Jimmy walked into the parlor and stopped.

Cici sat on the sofa, her foot and ankle wrapped and resting on a footstool, her head bent over the Bible in her lap. Golden curls fell forward and rested on each side of her face. No girl was ever this beautiful. She glanced up, and when she saw him, her face lit up and she smiled. "Jimmy, come sit by me. Are you rested? It must have been awful."

"I'm quite rested." He sat beside her and ran his thumb down her cheek, concerned that she was still wan. "How is your ankle?"

"Oh, there's some swelling and it's tender, but I'm fine. Mother put ice on it. And the doctor said I was fine. Not a thing wrong." She sighed. "He said to stay off it for a few days, so Mama won't let me go to church."

He took her hand in his. "I was so afraid when the boat went down."

Confusion slid across her face. "How did you know I was on it?"

"I saw you boarding. I called, but there was such a din of noise, you couldn't hear." He had so many questions to ask. Why was she on the *Eastland*? How did she know Sutton? What was it she wanted to tell him? But all he could do was gaze at her and thank God she was safe.

She bit her lip, and her hand, resting in his, trembled. "Jimmy, there's something I have to tell you."

"What is it, dearest? You can tell me anything." And almost anything would be better than this doubt and worry.

"Jimmy, it's time to go." Mrs. Willow stood in the doorway pinning her hat. She sent a beaming smile their way.

Jimmy sighed. Whatever she had to tell him would have to wait until after church.

Chapter 21

O ver eight hundred known dead so far?" Jimmy shook his head in disbelief and groaned. "They were so close to the harbor. It seems unbelievable."

"I know, son. A horrible tragedy." Rev. Willow leaned forward in the wingback chair in the parlor. "And they still have no idea what caused it."

They'd all come into the parlor after dinner. The horrors the city had faced seemed to be the only topic on their minds. The church congregation had been in a state of shock. It seemed everyone knew someone who knew someone who had died on the *Eastland*.

"According to the newspapers, they're still pulling bodies from the ship." Cici's voice caught in a sob and she jumped up.

"Cecilia, dear, I think you should lie down for a while. You're very pale." Mrs. Willow leaned over and touched Cici's forehead.

"I'm all right, Mama." She smiled and pressed her mother's hand. The next moment she swayed. Jimmy caught her before she hit the floor.

Mr. Willow took his daughter from Jimmy's arms. "I'll take her upstairs. Apparently she should have stayed in bed today."

"But should we call the doctor?" Jimmy glanced frantically from Cici to her father.

Mrs. Willow placed her hand on his arm. "She'll be fine, son. She just overdid it. Go home and get some rest. I promise we'll take good care of her. See, she's coming around already."

Sure enough, Cici's eyes had opened. "I'm sorry, Jimmy. We'll talk tomorrow. I promise."

"It's all right, sweetheart." He glanced at her father, took a deep breath, and leaned over and kissed her cheek. "Are you sure you'll be okay?"

"I'm sure. I just need to rest."

Jimmy headed home, disappointment in missing their talk all mixed up with concern for her health and joy in her changed demeanor today. She'd seemed humble, with a seriousness in her smile that hadn't been there before.

When Jimmy arrived at home, he said a quick hello to Danni and Blake and went upstairs to change. They probably needed volunteers at the dock, so he'd decided on the way home to see what he could do to help. He came back down and leaned against the parlor door. "I'm heading down to the dock to see if I can help for a few hours."

"Wait a minute, Jimmy. I'll go with you." Blake set his coffee cup down and gave Danni a hug. "Just give me a minute to change."

When they got to the docks, it was almost a repeat of the day before. Except that now everyone who was being pulled out of the water was dead.

Cobb stood next to a body, his hand over his face. It had to be Sutton for Cobb to be grieving so.

Jimmy hurried over to Cobb and squeezed his shoulder.

Cobb stared at Sutton's body. "They found him in one of the hallways. It looked like he died from a blow to the head."

"I'm sorry, Cobb. At least it was sudden. He didn't suffer." And he was sorry. Sorry for Cobb's grief.

೧೫

Jimmy sat once more in Blake and Danni's parlor. The senior Nelsons and Pops were there, and the Kramers had also joined them. It was good to have family at a time like this. They'd all been worried about what Sutton might do.

"So now the blighter's gone. He won't be bringin' grief to this family." Pops voiced what they were all secretly feeling.

"But Pops"—Danni wiped her eyes—"Sutton wasn't a Christian."

"Now how would you be knowing that, lass?" Pops turned a stern eye on her. "Were you a wee fly on the wall before he went to his watery grave? Maybe he had a chance to call on the Lord and ask forgiveness."

Danni's tear-filled eyes lit with a gleam of hope. "Do you think so, Pops?"

"Now, now, I know you're worrying in that tender heart of yours. But you just have to leave the man in God's hands." Pops reached over and patted her shoulder.

"Mr. O'Shannon is absolutely right, Danielle." Mrs. Kramer, who had taken Danni under her wing eight years ago, smiled at her now. "God's business is God's business. Our business is with the living. And there will be plenty of those who need our help, especially now."

Danni nodded. "You're right, I know that."

Once more a pang of remorse shot through Jimmy. *God, forgive me. I'm not sorry that Sutton is dead. He can't hurt Danni now. Or anyone else. Change my heart, Lord.*

Mr. Nelson turned to Jimmy. "How are your little friends in the tenements, my boy?"

Jimmy's heart lurched. He had been so focused on the disaster and Cici that he hadn't seen the children in a couple of days, except to send them away from the docks after the *Eastland* went down. He'd waved them away several times during the day and early evening. "They were pretty shook up yesterday. I intended to check on them all today to find out how they were handling things. Then when I saw Sutton, I forgot." He shook his head.

"Well, that's understandable. Don't beat yourself up over it."

"Thank you, sir. I won't. I guess now that everyone is here, it would be a good time for me to tell you my plans." He glanced around.

Mrs. Kramer sat on a dainty chair with her husband standing behind her, his hand resting on her shoulder. Mrs. Nelson, seated next to her husband, sent Jimmy an encouraging smile. Pops leaned forward. Blake and Danni waited, their eyes expectant.

"I'm definitely entering seminary next month. Pastor Paul and Reverend Willow have both agreed to sponsor me, and they feel sure I'll be allowed to minister in a layperson's position at the chapel Paul is leaving. I'll have to work part-time at the docks because I'll only be receiving a small stipend, but I'm sure I can earn enough to support us."

"You know very well you can count on us for help, Jimmy." Danni's eyes held concern, but she'd finally accepted his choice.

"I know, sis, but I believe if I do my best and trust in the Lord, He'll take care of me. His Word promises that." He smiled. "I know you have big faith. Can't you trust Him with me, too?"

She brushed tears away and hugged him. "Okay, little brother. I guess I can stop trying to be your mother now." She sniffled. "But I'll still cook for you until you get married."

Jimmy grinned and stood. "That's a relief. I thought I might be overdoing the independence thing. And now, I hate to leave good company, but my fiancée is waiting."

෬

Pain and dread hit Cici's heart as Jimmy walked into the parlor. If only he still loved her after she told him everything. She managed a smile. "Jimmy, would you mind helping me out to the porch swing? I've been inside too long, and I need fresh air."

"I'd be happy to." He helped her to stand on one foot, and she managed to walk and hop out to the porch. The rain had stopped, but the air was still damp, so Cici drew her shawl around her shoulders.

How she wished she could snuggle close to Jimmy and feel his arms around her. But that wouldn't be fair. He had a right to know first. He had a right to choose whether to love her or not.

All right. *Help me, Father, please. I know You have forgiven me. Please let Jimmy forgive me, too.*

"Cici"—he brushed his hand across her cheek—"don't be afraid to tell me. Whatever it is, it won't change the way I feel for you."

"Oh, Jimmy, I pray that's true. But I won't hold you to it. You see, I've been living a double life." She could barely choke out the words. How could she bear to say more?

"In what way, sweetheart?" Why was he so calm? He didn't even sound surprised.

"You see, a few months ago I met a girl named Gail. She was exciting and full of adventure. I'd never met anyone like her." She cleared her throat. "I'm not saying she persuaded me. I've always had a little bit of a rebellious spirit. Even when I was a little girl, I was naughty."

347

"All children are naughty sometimes, Cici."

"I know that. But as I grew older, I was very restless. I didn't want to go to church and my friends began to bore me. Even Helen. And we've been best friends all our lives." She lifted her eyes to him. But he only nodded.

"I began spending time with Gail. I met her at Tony's Place and she introduced me to her friends. One of them was James Sutton." She gave Jimmy a quick glance. Surprised that his expression hadn't changed, she cleared her throat. "He seemed very charming. He invited all of us to an evening of dining at the home of one of his wealthy friends. That's where I was going the night you saw me boarding the boat. I lied when I said I was going to see a friend downriver." Heat seared her face as she confessed the lie. But still, he didn't appear shocked at all.

"By then, I was starting to lose some of my awe of my new friends. Most of them drank, and even though I didn't, it bothered me. That night I stayed over at Gail's apartment. She was drunk and I could hardly stand it." She took a deep breath. "After I knew you loved me and I met your family, I began to pull away from them."

Shame washed over her. "I never should have gotten mixed up with them in the first place. I know that and I'm so terribly sorry. I've repented and I know God has forgiven me."

Jimmy peered into her eyes. "Cici—"

But she stopped him before he could say more. "The night you told me what Sutton had done to you and Danni and so many other children, I decided to face him and convince him to leave you alone. I was so foolish. I thought Gail would be on the boat that night, but it was all a trick to get me on there alone with Sutton. She was one of the children you knew."

"Gail. . . I had hoped she would have gone on to a better life." Jimmy sighed. "But she was very close to Sutton. Like so many of the children. He was their only parent figure."

"A terrible parent figure."

He spoke gently. "Yes, but to children who had never known parents, he was all they had."

Was it possible that he didn't hate her? "Jimmy, I'm so sorry. I love you. That's all I can say." She bowed her head and fought against the desire to throw herself into his arms and beg.

The touch of his hand beneath her chin brought a sigh to her lips, and she closed her eyes. He lifted her chin and she opened her eyes and looked into his. She could hardly breathe. Was that love she saw in his eyes?

He rubbed his thumb across her cheeks and wiped away the tears. "Cici, sweetheart? Did you mean it when you said you loved me?" He gazed into her eyes.

"Of course I did. I love you with all my heart."

"And you want to be my wife, even though you know it will likely be a struggle to do God's work among the poor?"

"Oh yes, I do want that, Jimmy. More than anything. I love you and I've come to love those poor people. Especially the children. They have good hearts, Jimmy. And they have the right to better lives. And even if you don't want me as your wife, I still intend to work among them in any way I can, because God has called me, too."

Jimmy closed his eyes, and when he opened them they were filled with sheer joy. "My darling Cici, my precious wife to be, with all my heart I want you by my side for the rest of my life."

"And you forgive me?" Wonder filled her heart.

"Sweetheart, the main thing you were guilty of was selfishness, and most of us have been guilty of that. Yes, you were rebellious and made some very bad choices that could have led to terrible things for you, but God has forgiven you. I hold nothing against you. You are my wonderful love. And in my eyes, you've always been wonderful." He brushed his lips across hers. "So—when will you marry me?"

"What?" She laughed. "You want to set a date now?"

"The sooner the better." He grinned. "After all, I'll be moving into Paul's apartment soon and I've never lived alone before."

"Oh, you." She giggled. "How about next summer?"

He frowned. "That's too long. How about Christmas?"

"A Christmas wedding? Really?" Butterflies danced in her stomach. What a wonderful idea.

"Really. What do you think?"

"I think it's a wonderful idea. I'd love a Christmas wedding. But don't think you'll get out of giving me an anniversary gift each year."

"I promise. So it's Christmas, then?" His eyes sparkled with excitement.

"All right. We'd better go tell Mama and Papa."

"Yes, but not just now."

Once more his lips touched hers. Softly at first. Then his kiss deepened and they held each other as if they'd never let go.

A Letter to Our Readers

Dear Readers:

In order that we might better contribute to your reading enjoyment, we would appreciate you taking a few minutes to respond to the following questions. When completed, please return to the following: Fiction Editor, Barbour Publishing, Inc., P.O. Box 719, Uhrichsville, OH 44683.

1. Did you enjoy reading *Windy City Brides* by Frances Devine?
   ❑ Very much. I would like to see more books like this.
   ❑ Moderately—I would have enjoyed it more if _____
   _____
   _____

2. What influenced your decision to purchase this book?
   (Check those that apply.)
   ❑ Cover   ❑ Back cover copy   ❑ Title   ❑ Price
   ❑ Friends   ❑ Publicity   ❑ Other

3. Which story was your favorite?
   ❑ *A Girl Like That*   ❑ *Sugar and Spice*
   ❑ *Once a Thief*

4. Please check your age range:
   ❑ Under 18   ❑ 18–24   ❑ 25–34
   ❑ 35–45   ❑ 46–55   ❑ Over 55

5. How many hours per week do you read? _____

Name _____

Occupation _____

Address _____

City_____ State_____ Zip_____

E-mail _____

♡

HEARTSONG
PRESENTS

If you love Christian romance...

$12.⁹⁹

You'll love Heartsong Presents' inspiring and faith-filled romances by today's very best Christian authors. . .Wanda E. Brunstetter, Mary Connealy, Susan Page Davis, Cathy Marie Hake, and Joyce Livingston, to mention a few!

When you join Heartsong Presents, you'll enjoy four brand-new, mass-market, 176-page books—two contemporary and two historical—that will build you up in your faith when you discover God's role in every relationship you read about!

Imagine. . .four new romances every four weeks—with men and women like you who long to meet the one God has chosen as the love of their lives—all for the low price of $12.99 postpaid.

To join, simply visit www.heartsongpresents.com or complete the coupon below and mail it to the address provided.

Mass Market, 176 Pages

✂ -

YES! Sign me up for Heart♥ng!

NEW MEMBERSHIPS WILL BE SHIPPED IMMEDIATELY!
Send no money now. We'll bill you only $12.99 postpaid with your first shipment of four books. Or for faster action, call 1-740-922-7280.

NAME _____

ADDRESS_____

CITY_____ STATE _____ ZIP _____

**MAIL TO: HEARTSONG PRESENTS, P.O. Box 721, Uhrichsville, Ohio 44683
or sign up at WWW.HEARTSONGPRESENTS.COM**